THE DROWNING
SEA

Also by David Hair

THE DROWNING
SEA

TALMONT BOOK 2

DAVID HAIR

Jo Fletcher
BOOKS

First published in Great Britain in 2025 by

Jo Fletcher
BOOKS

Jo Fletcher Books
an imprint of
Quercus Editions Ltd
Carmelite House
50 Victoria Embankment
London EC4Y 0DZ

An Hachette UK company

The authorised representative in the EEA is Hachette Ireland,
8 Castlecourt Centre, Castleknock Road, Castleknock,
Dublin 15, D15 YF6A, Ireland

A CIP catalogue record for this book is available
from the British Library

HB ISBN 978-1-52943-314-2
TPB ISBN 978-1-52942-290-0
EBOOK ISBN 978-1-52942-292-4

1

Typeset by CC Book Production
Printed and bound in Great Britain by Clays Ltd, Elcograf S.p.A

Papers used by Jo Fletcher Books are from well-managed forests and other responsible sources.

This book is dedicated to *family*.

My parents, Cliff and Biddy Hair, have been a constant of love and support through my life. As I write this, it's June 2024, early winter in New Zealand, and my wife and I have just moved to Hawkes Bay, to be closer to Mum and Dad and my sister Robyn, a nurse at the local hospital. It's a kind of homecoming; the first time I've lived here since I set out on the Kiwi 'OE' in 1984, forty years ago. Kerry's never lived here, but she's visited many times and it's closer to her East Coast roots too.

It's good to be back.

TABLE OF CONTENTS

Part Three:
THE DEVOURER'S MAW

H·Y·T·A·L
Fyna
Shyll
Mir Avas
Gaudien
Beradin
VANDARATH
Vanburg
TORAS NARROWS
ELIDOR
GULF of ELIDOR
Tyr
Nexus Isle
PETRAXUS
Secordium
TALMONT
MIRAVIA
Fregamund
Cape Foulair
SARAS OCEAN
GULF of FOYLAND
Hyastor
QOR-MASSIF
Denium
KHARAGH
Folkstein
Casimund
Viramund
Slaver's Bay
Camaris
FOYLAND
BRAVANTIA
SOLADAS
Baluarte
Ferasto
Vantium
Tar-Nareth
Qorium (ruins)
QOR-ESPINA
Eravandar
Bespar
AQUINIUM
THE BLOOD SEA (MAR-ORTAS)
NEPARIA
Mardium
Lenzia
BEDUMASSA
SEA of ERATH (MAR-ERAS)
Moratab
SEA of PELAS (mar-pelas)
Marez
BEDUM-MUTAZA
Sharif
LOST PELAS
THE JAWS of LEOS
ZYNOCHIAN CALIPHATES
Hamuztab
Vintab
PELASIAN ARCHIPELAGO
KHETIA
ABUTHA
DAGOZ
NORTHWEST CONTINENT of COROS

What Has Gone Before

The world of Coros is being devastated by an ecological crisis, with endless droughts, rising seas and failing harvests. The Hierophant, the God-Emperor Eindil Pandramion III, ruler of the Triple Empire, claims on the advice of his mage-scholars that this is nothing more than an entirely natural super-cycle, and he reassures his people that it won't last.

But at least one scholar disagrees. Nilis Evandriel has been declared renegade for declaring that the crisis is caused by elobyne shards, crystal pillars sited throughout the empire, which he claims are leeching life from the ground, the foliage and all living things. That energy is used to wield glyma, a magic power used by the mighty Vestal knights to defend the Triple Empire. It is also used by the shape-changing vyr to wage guerrilla warfare against the empire. Neither will relinquish that power, and all the while, Coros spirals deeper into chaos.

Mastering glyma requires immense mental and physical control, which the Vestal knights deal with by demanding rigorous discipline of their knights and mages – and they are ruthless with those who fail. Most Vestals have an active career of only a dozen years, retiring when their control of the glyma begins to slip. In contrast, the vorloks (mages) and draegar (knights) of the vyr surrender to the maelstrom of the glyma, gaining stronger powers, like the abilities to incite berserk battle-fury and shape-changing among their followers – but their lack of control turns most into raging monsters who perish quickly.

1

Nevertheless, the Vyr Rebellion is growing, year by year, their campaign based on destroying the elobyne shards in devastating fires that are ravaging the countryside and speeding the ecological crisis. The future of Coros is at stake, and the battle lines drawn.

Romara Challys leads the Falcon Century, one hundred men-at-arms of the Vestal Order, alongside the glyma-users of her 'pentacle': Jadyn Kaen (whom Romara loves); Ghaneen Suul; the veteran Abuthan Obanji Vost; and the mage, Elindhu Morspeth. The Falcons are currently stationed on Avas Island, helping to evacuate the islanders, whose homeland has been ravaged by vyr.

Amid the chaos, three fateful events occur. First, during a life-or-death mêlée, Romara loses control of her glyma. Her comrades cover for her, but she knows she must retire as soon as they get to safety.

Then Ghaneen is slain by the vyr – but a young refugee, Soren var'Dael, accidently sparks the dead knight's elobyne blade to life, revealing himself to be capable of wielding glyma. Soren is taken from his family and inducted into the Order as an initiate.

Finally, the Falcons capture one of the attackers, Gram Larch. As the man showed no signs of shape-changing, Jadyn and Romara decide to interrogate him – despite a rule that only the imperial lictors, the Justiciary arm of the Order, are permitted to question vyr. They are desperate to understand why the vyr are destroying the land.

Under questioning, Gram echoes the words of the renegade scholar Nilis Evandriel: that elobyne shards are destroying the world. But he also reveals a new thing: a spell, Oculus Tempus, which will, he says, prove Evandriel's claims. It's a spell on the 'forbidden list', one which even Elindhu doesn't know how to cast.

The Falcons are evacuated to Gaudien, a port on the mainland. There they are debriefed by the lictor Yoryn Borghart, who has been tipped off about the illegal interrogation and threatens Romara and Jadyn with severe penalties. Romara expects her Order's commander, Corbus Ritter, to stand by them, but he refuses, as he's entangled with House Sandreth, enemies of Romara's family. Elan Sandreth wants to force Romara into marriage to gain her family's wealth, then have her locked up. He uses Jadyn's arrest as leverage, threatening execution if Romara doesn't comply.

Romara breaks into the dungeons and frees Jadyn, along with Gram and another prisoner, Auranuschka ('Aura') Perafi, a Nepari thief. Aura proves invaluable, using her underworld contacts to help the fugitive knights, along with Romara's loyal comrades Obanji and Elindhu and the new initiate, Soren, escape by ship.

Now outlaws, Romara and Jadyn decide to investigate Nilis Evandriel's claims as a means of redemption. They sail to Solabas, and then head for Neparia, where Gram says Nilis Evandriel can be found. They're pursued by Yoryn Borghart, Elan Sandreth and Romara's former mentor, Tevas Nicolini. Borghart uses portali gates to enter the 'Shadowland' where time and distance are distorted, enabling rapid pursuit.

During the chase, Romara is increasingly drawn to Gram, but her relationship with Jadyn becomes strained. Their love grew in the regulated world of the Order, where passions are forbidden. Outside that environment, it begins to fray.

This is partly because Romara's loss of control is mitigated by Gram; as a potential vorlok, he has the innate ability to leech glyma-energy from her, preventing her from having a complete breakdown, but creating a co-dependency. Meanwhile, Aura is revealed to share an unnamed precognitive talent with Jadyn.

Closely pursued by Borghart and the Order, the Falcons cross Semmanath-Tuhr, a mountain valley peopled by erlings, the oldest inhabitants of Coros. They once dominated the north, but were driven out in ancient times; those who remain retreated to the wild, just a remnant of the once-dominant civilisation.

When the Falcons are assailed by a wild erling, Jadyn kills it – and is accused of murder by the erlings. To prevent erling retribution, Elindhu is forced to reveal her deepest secret: she is in fact an erling herself – a 'Rann', or princess – and has been masquerading as human, using her people's shapeshifting skills, to learn the truth about Nilis Evandriel's claims. This severely strains the pentacle's unity, but friendship prevails, mostly thanks to Obanji, who is quietly in love with Elindhu and doesn't care what race she is.

The Falcons reach the village of Sancta Cara in Neparia, only to discover from the local vyr coven leader that Evandriel has retreated into the mountains, researching the Sanctor Wardens, an ancient order of knights who preceded the Vestal Order. Agynea tells them the Wardens used a type of magic known as the aegis, which doesn't require elobyne, but they were massacred by the Vestal Order, centuries ago. She also speaks of *ninneva*, a state of grace that some vyr attain, that holds the glyma-madness at bay.

Disillusioned by increasing evidence that their beloved Order is the iron fist of a tyranny, Romara's pentacle press on, hoping to overtake Evandriel and learn the whole truth, but Borghart and his allies are gaining on them. The lictor kills Agynea and her people, after forcing her to reveal where Romara's group are going.

The Falcons find a mountain-top stone circle of eight thrones etched with ancient runes. The sun goes down as Borghart's men are closing in – but somehow, they manage to open a mysterious portal, which transports them to the ruins of an ancient Sanctor Warden base. Jadyn and Aura discover they alone have been marked with runes on their palms – which further tests Romara's bond with Jadyn. The universe appears to be driving them apart.

The Falcons follow the trail further and find the lost monastery of Vanashta Baanholt, where legend says the Sanctor Wardens learned the aegis. But as they arrive, they are surrounded by soldiers of the Vestal Order, led by Vazi Virago, the Exemplar (champion knight) of the Vestal Order. She is there with her century to study, then destroy, the monastery.

Romara persuades Vazi that her Falcons are there for the same reason. Vazi is excited to learn of Jadyn's palm-marks, which match sigils found in the caverns beneath the monastery. But Romara's deception is revealed when Borghart and his men arrive. The Falcons flee into underground tunnels below the monastery, seeking a way out. Jadyn and Aura manage to open the huge locked doors trapping them – but they lead only to a ledge and a broken bridge over a vast void. Facing capture or death, the Falcons fight heroically, buying time for Jadyn and Aura to trigger a vestige of the aegis: the destroyed bridge reforms, but it bears only those with the aegis marks. Jadyn and Aura escape over the mystic bridge, but Vazi kills Obanji, Soren and Elindhu fall into the void, and Romara and Gram are captured.

Jadyn and Aura land on a tiny island off Neparia, where they find a note from Nilis Evandriel, urging 'Those who Follow' to journey on 'to the centre of the world'.

The void beneath the ledge was an illusion concealing an underwater river – Soren would have drowned, but Elindhu keeps him alive. Exhausted, still perilously close to their enemies, they are rescued by an erling, Fynarhea of Semmanath-Tuhr, who has been shadowing Elindhu to protect her.

Gram and Romara wake to captivity. Wounded and bereft, they take comfort in each other's presence. Their captors, Vazi Virago and Yoryn Borghart, must confront the alarming fact that during that final confrontation, the aegis-bridge momentarily bore their weight, hinting that they too might be capable of learning the forbidden aegis. To pursue Jadyn and Aura, they will need that power, but that risks falling into heresy themselves.

The End is Nigh

Salvation

Akka the Righteous is a just God, who offers eternal salvation. Elysia the Merciful, his Handmaiden, intercedes for us before His sacred throne, so that we the faithful may be raised up at the End of Days, and dwell in His light for ever. Unbelievers shall be cast into the Devourer's Maw for all eternity.

PATRIARCH VYNE, AT THE CORONATION OF EINDIL III, 1454

On one level, it astounds me that people will give up their hard-earned money for priests to squander on monuments and gluttony. But then again, I'm not surprised at all, because those who dare question the orthodoxy are derided, ostracised, beaten and murdered; all the while being threatened with eternal damnation. What chance do the rational have against these fanatics?

NILIS EVANDRIEL, RENEGADE SCHOLAR, 1469

Petraxus, Talmont
Autumn 1472

Eindil Pandramion III, the Hierophant, God-Emperor of Talmont, Zynochia and Abutha, shifted uncomfortably on the Throne of Pearl, his thoughts trapped in a spiral of despondency, despite the circling priests with their swinging censers sending plumes of holy incense to the gilded ceiling, their sonorous voices begging Akka to cleanse His humble servant – Eindil himself – of all sin.

It was vaguely amusing, given it was theologically impossible for Eindil to sin. Scripture proclaimed him faultless, his every deed

7

sanctioned by Heaven: a Living God, with dominion over Earth and Sky. Paradise awaited him, no matter what he did.

'In Paradise, we are cleansed of desire, cleansed of all hunger,' the priests chanted.

But I don't wish to be cleansed of desire and hunger, Eindil thought. *I wish to be desirous and hungry, so long as my desires and hungers can be sated. As they are, right here.*

His life contained everything he wanted – or *almost* everything. He had gigantic palaces filled with every luxury imaginable, and thirty beautiful wives to choose from. He had myriad children and grandchildren to dote upon. Every man alive was subservient to him. These were things all wished for. But it was that which he didn't have that consumed him.

Where is she? My Vazi Virago – where is she?

According to reports, the Exemplar was hunting heretics in the south. Her perfect face swam before his eyes, a divine visage wrought in burnished copper, framed by glorious ebony hair and the most lustrous golden-brown eyes. A child of the Zynochian caliphates, so young and delicate-looking, and yet she was the greatest sorcerer-knight alive.

I am sixty years old, but when she is in my presence I feel like a stammering boy.

The day he finally possessed her would be the day he truly attained Akka's Paradise.

A gong roused him from reverie, signalling the end of the morning's blessing, and he gazed blinking upon this many-pillared hall in his Holy Palace in mighty Petraxus. Hierophants had ruled Coros from here for two centuries now, ever since Jovan Lux revealed the sacred elobyne and united the three great powers, Talmont, Zynochia and Abutha, into the Triple Empire. Jovan's holy blood ran in Eindil's veins, but still he was afraid.

Will I be the last? Have we come to the End of All Things?

As the priests shuffled away, Eindil signed to Robias, his stentor, both herald and major-domo, to approach. Robias was a typical Aquini, a race prone to baldness. His pate gleamed in the lamplight as he knelt to kiss the footprint of Jovan on the lowest step, then sat back on his heels and unfurled a scroll.

'Good morning, Great One,' he said. 'Greetings on this Holy Day. May Heaven shine its light upon you. Let Elysia wash away all your pain and discomfort and Akka bless you with insight and wisdom.'

It might be a Holy Day, Eindil's weekly break from court duties and advisors, but with his empire afflicted by disasters and rebellion, he had to stay abreast of current events.

'Ar-byan, Robias,' Eindil replied. *May it be.* 'What tidings?'

Robias consulted his scroll. 'Seven coursers arrived overnight, Great One. One came from the Caliph of Bedum-Mutaza, with greetings and love, extending his formal invitation for his city to be your quadrennial residence. He assures you that all is prepared.'

One of the traditions established by Jovan Lux was for the reigning Hierophant to spend every second year in Petraxus, while the alternate years he would alternate between Dagoz, the capital of Abutha, and Bedum-Mutaza, the centre of the old Zynochian Empire. The palaces there were magnificent, but Eindil was a child of the north; he loathed the heat and simmering resentment in the south.

Tradition was tradition, however. 'That is well,' he responded, for the court scribes to record. 'I eagerly await my return to my beloved Bedum-Mutaza, and the joy of seeing his Highness, my cousin, again.'

The next six missives were all bad. The island of Shyll, last of the empire's possessions in the northwestern archipelago, had fallen to vyr rebels, with twelve elobyne shards destroyed. Grain riots in Mardium, Lerzia and Bespar, on the coast of the Inner Seas. An earthquake in Viromund, with hundreds dead and thousands displaced. And vyr attacks in southern Bravantia had burned out swathes of grain fields. The armies were already overstretched and the Vestal Order couldn't be everywhere.

It was a struggle not to let his head hang.

'Any word from Dagoz and Bedum-Mutaza of rebellions there?' Eindil asked.

'Nothing official, Great One.' Which told him, unofficially, that the news was bad and he'd learn more in a less public setting.

The foundation of the Triple Empire had ended open war on Coros. Talmont had elobyne, the sorcerous crystal that empowered the Vestal Order to rule any battlefield, but the north lacked manpower, unlike their heavily populated southern rivals, Abutha and Zynochia. Jovan Lux's genius had been not to overthrow but to unite the powerful southern rulers under his ambit. As well as taking ten northern brides, he'd married ten Zynochi and ten Abuthan women, creating a multi-racial elite who owned *everything*. Inside two generations, every throne on Coros was ruled by one of his descendants, and Abutha and Zynochia were as invested in the success of the Triple Empire as Talmont – and they were all yoked together by their dependence upon elobyne.

Open warfare might have ceased, but internecine vendettas, rivalries and resentment remained as toxic as ever, however. Empire politics were a perennial bloodbath, even for hierophants, whose reigns seldom exceeded ten years. Four had been murdered in the south by kin, hushed up as untimely illnesses so as not to alarm the populace. His reluctance to travel there wasn't just based on comfort.

'Is there no good news, Robias?' Eindil asked tiredly.

'Happiness comes from bird song, Great One, not coursers,' the herald quipped.

No, then.

Eindil tried to appreciate the vivid morning sunlight streaming through the massive stained-glass windows, creating shifting shafts of glorious red and green and blue light that penetrated the smoke of the censers, a magical display of Heaven's Light.

All is not lost, that Light proclaimed. He wasn't convinced.

But the day awaited. He rose and went to his Mentus Sanctorum to await this morning's Confessor. It might be yet another pointless piece of ritual, but at least this one came with coffee. He trailed Robias through the maze of corridors behind the throne hall, barely noticing the grovelling servants, their faces pressed to the floors, out of the shadowy halls into the light.

The gardens were awash with roses, the scents dispersed by the playing fountains. Statues of nymeths and huirnes cavorted lasciviously along the path to the meditation chamber, a wonder of marble lattice-work. A coffee pot steamed on a stool beside the low but ornate throne and Robias was already pouring as Eindil sat.

He had just taken a first sip when a white-robed and hooded figure emerged from the garden – and Eindil realised it wasn't a Confessor.

Assassin, was his first thought – and Robias began to signal the nearby guards. But the hooded man raised his head, showing just enough of his face for Eindil to recognise him. His fears of untimely death vanished – but not his fears of worse.

'Leave us,' he told Robias. 'Take the guards out of earshot. All is well.'

If Robias heard the fear in his voice, he didn't react, signalling the soldiers to withdraw, then sitting on a stone seat within calling range.

Eindil took a shaky breath. 'Father,' he said hoarsely. 'How do you fare?'

The newcomer sat opposite him and lowered his hood, revealing a man in his prime – no, *beyond* his prime, for Genadius Pandra-mion II had never been so flawlessly perfect. His skin was smooth and unblemished, without even a hint of stubble; his thick hair was perfectly styled, blond again, as it had been in his youth. His frame was muscular, lithe. Only his eyes, grey and unwavering, gave any hint of his true age.

He'd died thirty years ago, aged seventy.

'I am well, my son,' he replied, his voice free of the rheumy tones Eindil remembered. 'And you?' Their conversations had always been stilted and formal.

'I grow old,' Eindil said wistfully. 'The Sunburst Crown is heavy.'

Genadius nodded. 'I remember it well, the weight of the world crushing my skull. I was grateful to pass it on.'

The Church taught that hierophants did not die as mortals did. So beloved of Akka were they, that they were taken bodily to Paradise. There were no tombs of past hierophants, only memorials. Eindil's father had been dying in his bed one night, his body gone by morning.

And now this.

Eindil had thought it religious nonsense before he ascended the throne and met such 'Alephi' – the Undying – on previous visits to

Nexus Isle, where it was said all the dead hierophants now dwelt in harmony, serving Jovan Lux.

But he'd never been visited by an Alephi – or Serrafim, as the Church named them – here in the palace in daylight. 'Why are you here, Father?'

Dear Akka, does he know it was I who poisoned him?

'I come to tell you that the time is nigh,' Genadius replied. 'The End of All Things approaches.'

His words confirmed all his suspicions. Coros was destroying itself. An Age of Fire was upon them, bringing death, plague, war, fire and flood. The soil was drying, the snows melting and the seas rising, while the pitiless sun burned the land black.

Nothing can be done, the priests said. *This is fated.*

'What must I do?' Eindil asked fearfully.

'To quote Scripture: "The Serrafim shall mark the Faithful for Elysium, the sanctuary of the faithful,"' Genadius replied. 'One man in a thousand shall live, and the rest shall burn. The end cannot be stopped: all you can do is decide whom you wish to save."'

Eindil reeled. *Is it so far advanced?* 'How shall I know who to save?'

Genadius smiled coldly. 'That's up to you. My advice: if you like them, trust them or desire them, preserve them. If you like their singing or their art, or their cooking, save them. But remember: *One man in a thousand.* And though I say "man", I include women, for what is forever without them?'

It was a crushing responsibility – and who knew that Paradise would be so venal? But Scripture also said, *In Paradise as it is on Coros.*

'Where is Elysium?' he asked. 'Will we be taken up into the skies?'

'No, my son. Paradise will be revealed to you. We are building it right now, a holy place the unwashed and blighted can't reach. Within it, we will dwell in eternal bliss, while outside the walls, the wretched sinners will wail and gnash their teeth. That is how life is: the deserving are rewarded, while the undeserving perish.'

Eindil shuddered. 'One man in a thousand?'

'Aye.' Genadius rose. 'Be strong, my son. Protect the elobyne at all costs, for on it our salvation rests. Even if the whole of the world rises against us, hold firm. It is sad, but not all can be saved. Harvests will fail and disasters multiply, but hold the course and know that all is according to Akka's will.'

'His will be done,' Eindil echoed, his mind churning. 'Father, what's it like—?'

Genadius smiled his reptilian smile. 'I have no discomfort, no pain. No illness nor imperfection. Food and drink are optional – glyma-energy provides me with all I need. I am perfected, as you will be.'

'Was Mother also saved? I would love to see her!' Memories of her kindly face, her long, soft grey hair scented with camellias, washed over Eindil. She had been a giver of life and love when his father was distant and cold. All these years later, he still felt her absence – none of the grasping whore-brides he'd wed could fill her place in his heart.

Genadius shook his head. 'She was not worthy.'

'But you said, "choose who you will",' Eindil blurted. 'You could've saved her.'

'But I didn't,' Genadius said dismissively. 'She is gone forever, my son. Even I cannot restore her. But mourn her not. Think only of the Paradise of Elysium that awaits us.'

With that, he rose and swiftly vanished into the depths of the lush garden.

He could have saved Mother . . . Why wasn't she 'worthy? Eindil wondered.

Scripture might say she was with Elysia, but clearly she was just dirt now, and the Elysium the Alephi were creating would never welcome her. He would never sink into her arms and find true peace again.

But he could make his father pay.

Eindil bade Robias bring him a blank scroll, ink and a quill. On the parchment he wrote the first name of those he would save: Vaziella al'Nuqheel, known to the world as Vazi Virago, Exemplar of the Vestal Knights, the greatest knight alive, and his only dream. She would be his avenging angel.

Let the world burn, so long as in the end there is just her and I . . . standing over my father's corpse. Ar-byan.

Part One
TO THE HEART

1

Scattered and Lost

Akka's Blessing

The Rich say, 'Look, Akka has blessed me with wealth.' The Beautiful say, 'Look, Akka has blessed me with beauty.' The Happy say, 'Akka has blessed me with happiness.' By extension, one might be tempted to see the poor and ugly and miserable as cursed. But Akka is a loving God, and at the End of All Things, the Righteous shall be given all that they lacked in life. Do not envy your betters, but live in Righteousness. Rejoice in your lowliness, for nature has made you lesser only in this life, not for eternity.

THE TEACHINGS OF JOVAN LUX, 1282

Cap San Yarido, Neparia
Autumn 1472

It was morning, bright and blue, but all Sier Jadyn Kaen saw was grey. He sat on a boulder beside the sea, beneath an abandoned half-ruined lighthouse on a tiny islet, gazing across the waters at a shabby little port at the southeastern tip of Neparia.

Auranuschka Perafi, his travelling companion, was asleep in the tower. Not long after their arrival via the Shadowland, she'd collapsed on the bed and winked out like a snuffed candle. But Jadyn was too overwhelmed by revelations, impossibilities and loss to sleep.

Their opposite reactions were typical – Aura often felt like another species to him – but now they were bound together by the *aegis*, the power the ancient Sanctor Wardens had once wielded, even though neither knew what it was or how to use it.

He looked again at the note they'd found in the tower above.

To those who follow. If you are a fellow seeker of truth and enlightenment, marked by destiny, as I have been, then you are my soul-kindred, a pilgrim on the road towards revelation.

Journey on, my friend, knowing that I have gone before. We are treading a path laid down long ago by wiser men than me. Perchance, we shall meet along the way.

Seek the Shield of Heaven, where earth kisses sky at the centre of the world.

It was signed by Nilis Evandriel, a man Jadyn had crossed half the known world to find. This was the closest he'd come to the elusive scholar, while he'd lost everyone he loved.

I saw Obanji die; Elindhu and Soren fell into the void, and Romara and Gram are surely prisoners, slated for torture and death.

Going on without them felt impossible, but he was marked for the aegis – by scars burned onto his palms – and so was Aura. There was no going back in any case: the path that had led them here was closed. There was only onwards, and he was increasingly certain that the fate of Coros was at stake.

There's no doubt any more – elobyne shards are destroying our world, and millions will perish, but our rulers care only about their grip on power and wealth and their own safety.

It was enough to make him weep.

He didn't, though – Vestal knights were made stoic – so he just stared glassy-eyed at the glistening water, too tired to think. He'd been awake for almost three days, after all.

With a groan, he rose and walked back into the lighthouse.

It was only a short climb, but it felt like ascending the Qor-Espina. At the top he found Aura still dead to the world, sprawled across the only bed. He glanced in the mirror through which they had arrived, which reflected a hollow-eyed man with unruly brown hair, his boyish face too lined for someone yet to turn thirty. His cloak was ripped and bloodstained, his green erling tunic little better.

He unbuckled his shoulder scabbard and propped his two-handed flamberge against the wall, feeling too fragile to deal with any kind of glyma use just now, even to veil himself. *It'd break me, the way it broke Romara.*

Thinking about her and Gram in captivity was too painful to bear.

He replaced Evandriel's note on the desk where they'd found it, then looked at the sleeping woman. Aura was Nepari, with thick black hair and coppery-olive skin blemished by old nicks and cuts, though she was only about twenty. Awake, she was lively, full of cheek and curiosity, but she'd lived the sort of life that 'good folk' deplored, stealing and duping the unwary, even earning money with her body when all else failed. Her morality was not his. Yet fate had thrown them together and her smile sparked something inside him that made him feel like a moth circling her flame. He hoped she might put aside her worst traits and become the person he some-times glimpsed behind her cloak of deviousness.

As if sensing his regard, Aura's eyes flickered open. For a moment she flinched at waking to find someone looming over her, then her face cleared. 'Oh, just be Jadyn Knight. Buenos dios. You have slept? No?' She rolled against the wall, leaving room on the narrow bed, and patted it. 'Come, lie.'

His ingrained decorum and prudery flared up. 'I can't.'

She *tsked* at him. 'Why? No glyma inside you now, so no danger. Come, lie.'

She was right that he was drained entirely of glyma-energy – and he wasn't a Knight of the Order of the Vestments of Elysia Divina any more, in any case. But his need to control body and mind remained. Glyma use required total control, and that always failed during sex, with fatal results for the partner. For that reason Vestal knights took vows of chastity. He couldn't tell if Aura really wanted to bed him or was just teasing, but the loss of Romara and the others was like a stone in his belly. All he wanted was to grieve. Alone.

'You go back to sleep,' he told her. 'I'll be downstairs. It's cooler there.'

With that he turned and tramped down the stairs, found a spot against the wall, rolled his cloak into a pillow and closed his eyes. Even though he was drowning in grief, he floated away into the dark.

Poor Jadyn Knight. Aura strove to return to sleep, but his stricken face kept dragging her back to wakefulness. She'd wanted to comfort him, just to hold him, nothing else, but his Order's ingrained strictures, even though they no longer applied to him, were a barrier she couldn't overcome. It was as if misery was his only joy.

Stupid man, why do I care?

But she did: he'd saved her life, and she'd saved his. They'd laughed and cried together, shared wondrous things, and she knew in her bones that if she had to throw herself between him and danger, she would. He was honest, caring and dependable, all words she'd once despised – but no longer. And in tantalising moments, she'd seen strength and passion too. If she could just free him from all the chains wrapped round his soul, she knew they could make each other happy, if only for a time.

Before the Order finds and kills us . . .

All her lovers – and there had been a number, though not so many as everyone thought – had been his opposite: wild and exciting, but unreliable and self-serving, men who stirred her blood and loins, but lacked a heart. Even Sergio Landanez, her greatest love, had been a faithless scoundrel, yet she'd been infatuated, utterly in love – right up to the minute he'd sailed away, stranding her in Port Gaudien. It still felt inexplicable.

So much had happened since then: she'd been the prisoner of a mad lictor who played cruel games with her; then she'd travelled with Vestal knights, and even discovered the potential to use a lost magic. Looking back, she wouldn't have changed anything.

Except maybe that Jadyn Knight cares for me . . .

At first, she'd amused herself playing with his affections, because he was so naïve and sheltered that she couldn't resist some mischief. But she now realised he was a rare true soul in a harsh world – and the aegis had knotted their paths together. *He and I are fated to be,* she mused. *I just have to be patient. I can do that.*

With that, she rose, tiptoed to the ground floor, past the snoring Jadyn, his boyish face finally at peace, and clambered down to the rocks to seek shellfish. She pulled out her knife – one of six secreted up her sleeves, down her boot-tops, in her bodice and between her shoulder-blades – and found a few promising-looking clams. As she foraged, boats came and went from the little fishing village across the waves, but none came near.

The tide was receding, she realised, and as she studied the water between the islet and the beach, she grinned. There was a sandbar below the surface.

In hour or two, we can walk to the shore.

She gathered the clams in her skirt and headed back to the tower. Jadyn was still so deeply asleep she was able to start a fire using driftwood and a flint she found beside the hearth without him even stirring. She boiled the clams in a billy she'd found in the tower's tiny kitchen. When they popped open, she shook him awake. 'Jadyn Knight, be lunching time.'

He came to blearily, smiled at her dreamily, then she saw the memories hit as his face fell and his eyes welled up. He looked away, brushing at them. 'What is it?'

'Food,' she said brightly. 'Che marisco – seafood, si?'

'Si, I see the seafood, see-nora,' he quipped tiredly.

'Idiot. Come, eat.'

She drained the clams and took the billy outside, where they sat with their backs to the lighthouse shaft and gazed at the distant coast. 'Oh, look,' Jadyn said. 'There's a sandbank running all the way into the beach.'

'Am knowing. Soon be low tide. We . . . what is word – "wade"? – si, we wade for shore.'

'For sure, we'll wade for the foreshore,' Jadyn replied, winking.

'Stopping now, not funny. When you be speaking seven languages like Aura, Jadyn can make word jokes.'

'Sorry.' He flashed his heart-melting grin and indicated the shell-fish. 'Are they safe?'

'Not knowing. You go first.'

He snorted wryly, but took a clam, shucked and ate it. She waited for him to turn green and vomit, but instead he reached for another. 'They're tasty.'

'So Jadyn liking Aura's clam,' she giggled, making him blush. 'What, joke not funny?'

'Not proper,' he mumbled, looking away.

All too soon the meal was over, but their bellies still felt empty. Aura sighed in disappointment, then faced him, feeling a touch mischievous. 'So, Aura be learning Talmoni language. Have question. Jadyn help?'

'Of course.'

'There be Nepari word, *generamoro*, which is love for parents,' she told him. 'What is word in Talmoni?'

Jadyn frowned. 'Um, we just say "love".'

'Ah, si. So, word in Nepari, *filiamoro*, is love for brother. In Talmoni?'

'Um, we just say love again.'

'And *sotreyamora*, love for sister?'

He wrinkled his nose. 'Aye, that's "love", too.'

'And *divinamoro*, love of God?'

'Love.'

'And *amaratomori*, the love of passion, wild and uncontrolled sexing?'

He coloured again. 'Love.'

'And the *mascomora*, the love for pet dog?'

'Uh, "love".'

She gave him a look. 'Is big word for small word, this "love". Neya precisamento! No wondering Talmoni cannot express true feeling.'

He shrugged. 'I guess not. But that makes it a safer word. If love can mean anything from care to respect to, er, passion, then no one has to define it precisely, so we can imagine the best and carry on.'

'Or imaginate worst,' Aura pointed out.

'True.' He looked away. 'Aura, I don't want to talk about love, or anything else. Thanks for the meal.'

Then he stood and drew his sword, and she felt a frisson of fear – not *of* him, but *for* him.

'Jadyn? What you doing?' she asked anxiously.

*

What am I doing? Jadyn examined his flamberge thoughtfully. It was beautifully made, the grip long-handled, for two hands, the wavy-edged blade flat-planed with ripples in the steel-like water. It was hugely valuable – and deadly, especially the milky crystal orb set in the pommel. If he drew on that orb now, energy would course into his system, filling his muscles and tendons with glyma-energy and vitality, and his nerves with jittery, edgy anger. And just like that, he'd be back to where he started this journey, fighting himself, battling the demons of fury, always on the edge of being consumed by blood-fury, like the vyr they fought.

He'd wielded a flamberge for ten harrowing years. He'd killed those the Order told him to, and helped preserve an empire he'd now decided to bring down. Owning it somehow felt perilous, marking him out as something he no longer wanted to be. And there was clear evidence that the glyma and the aegis were at least partially inimical; to pursue one, he increasingly suspected, was to undermine the other.

Moreover, he felt he needed to make a gesture of commitment to the aegis. So he drew back his arm – and threw. The flamberge caught the sunlight as it arced out over the waves and plunged in with a splash, vanishing in a wash of ripples.

Aura came to her feet, wide-eyed. 'What?' she spluttered. 'What is doing?'

'I didn't need it any more,' he told her. 'I will only use the aegis now.'

'E Cara! You not even know what aegis is!' She stared at him, utterly aghast, then sagged. 'Stupido,' she muttered. '*Stupido.*'

'Why? I don't want it, and it'll draw unwanted attention. So it's better we don't have it.'

She patted her empty belt-purse. 'You have money? No. You sell sword, make money. Then we have horses, sleep in tavern, buy new clothings? But no, stupido hombre throws sword into sea! *E Cara mia!*'

Watching her work herself into a rage was often diverting, but he wasn't in the mood. 'There's no one in that village over there who can give us what it's worth, and it would mark us out. We're better off without.'

'Si, that village be scum-puddle! But big port next bay, half-day travel. Sell easy!' She gave him an exasperated look. '*Imbecilio!* How now we pay for travel, eh?'

'We'll work our passage.'

'Work?' She stamped her foot. 'Si, man can work, sail ship. But woman like Aura – beauteous, wondrous woman – men want for whoring only! Maybe you want too, eh? Make whore do whoring!'

'No,' he said firmly. 'You're overdramatising. I'll do the work, and I'll protect you.'

'With what?' she shrilled. 'Your big sword?' She flung up her hands. 'Am not *dramaticoso!* Am resonating and calming, you stupido knight-wit!' She pointed out to sea. 'Dive in, find! Or Aura do!'

'Go ahead. But I'm not going after it.' He gestured dismissively.

Aura hissed, then tossed up her hands. 'Fino. Then we go, si? Break mirror, burn note so no one can follow, then go?'

Jadyn thought about that, then shook his head. 'I'm not so sure. If Nilis Evandriel hadn't left that note – or if he'd sabotaged the mirror-gate – we'd have been stranded and probably died. In good conscience, I can't do that to someone else.'

Aura gave him a pitying look. 'You saw Exemplar Woman and Bad Lictor? They stand on bridge – only Aura making bridge break stops them follow us. We must close pathing.'

'No, remember what we were told about the aegis? It's a *state of grace*. I believe that in finding the aegis, we will also find enlightenment – which means that Vazi Virago and Yoryn Borghart will too. So I'm prepared to take the risk.'

She gave him a raw look. 'This be Exemplar Woman and Bad Lictor: woman who kill friend Obanji, capture others. Man who torture Aura. They not en-lighted. They be evil.'

She might be right about that, he admitted to himself. *But she might also be wrong.*

'I've decided.'

'Why you decide?' she flared. 'Why not Aura decide? Because she be *only* a woman?'

'No! Because ... well, I'm more experienced—'

24

'Experienced?' Her eyebrows shot up. 'You be naïve halfwit.' Then she threw her hands up. 'Whatever, eh. Man decide, woman obey, same as always.' She spun, stomped her way down to the water and began wading towards the other shore.

He cursed and hurried after her.

The receding tide was strong and Aura with her slighter build was soon struggling. Jadyn offered his hand – which she refused with an exasperated hiss – as a rogue wave hit them and took them both under. Soaking wet, they stumbled ashore.

'What use be magic that not keep Aura dry?' Aura fumed.

'To be fair, the glyma would've been little help either,' Jadyn started, but Aura was off.

'Huh – we have no food. Magic provide? No, cannot. Have no blanket, no money. Magic provide? No. Have no horse, not even other clothings. Magic provide? No, magic useless—'

'I wish there were a spell to conjure such things,' Jadyn told her. He gazed along the beach in the direction of the fishing village. His belly was rumbling and his throat dry, but the chances of walking into a foreign place in their current state and not being assailed were remote. 'How far to that big port you spoke of?'

'Am not knowing – have only sailed, not walked,' Aura grumbled. 'Only peasant walks.'

'Fair enough. East or west?'

She looked at him, her face resigned. 'East.'

'Come on, then. We'll wash and refill the water bottles at the first freshwater stream, work our way around the village and find that port.'

Neparia's coast was rugged and unforgiving, the soil thin and arid. Powerful storms could blow in at any time from the vast expanse of ocean to the west, claiming ships and crews. But to survive, let alone prosper, people had to gamble on the whims of the sea, so settlements clung on tenaciously.

Jadyn and Aura saw many abandoned farm buildings but few people as they passed inland of the fishing village. The stony paths were punishing to walk on, the heat was sapping and their salt-encrusted clothing chafed their skin. When they finally found a freshwater stream, they took turns to stand watch while the other bathed and rinsed clothing, then put them back on wet; they would have to dry on their bodies as they walked.

Just before dusk, they found a track leading down to a ramshackle port, where a mass of houses clung to the rocky bay like limpets around a rock pool. Jadyn paused on the ridge above, worrying that Aura was right: without something to barter, how could they secure a room or passage? His goal now was Bedum-Mutaza – surely the 'centre of the world' in Evandriel's note – but it was a thousand kylos east of here.

Neparia was Aura's homeland, though, and her strut returned at the prospect of interacting with her own people. She combed her fingers through her drying hair, preening. 'Church give food for poor,' she told him. 'Preach at us, boring, but we eat.'

With that she led the way down the slope towards the town, where they found people snoozing in the shade, no one paying any attention to them. They slaked their thirst gratefully at a well in a plaza, then trudged into an Akkanite Church, where there was indeed a small refectory serving what turned out to be a stew of seafood and unleavened bread. A preacher was droning; Jadyn didn't need Aura to translate to know the man was speaking about Akka's love. The lay people serving had kindly faces, but he kept his head down and let Aura do the talking.

The food was plain but filling, and there was a public dormitory for the homeless. Aura warned they were dangerous places at night, but he saw little other option.

'We do better,' she replied. 'Come.'

She led him to the docklands, where sailors of all races and colours were drinking and carousing, and went swaggering through the crowds, flashing her perky smile at anyone glancing her way. The prostitutes manning curtained booths had long queues outside, and impatient men called out to Aura as she swayed past. When one tried to grab her, Jadyn seized the man's collar and lifted him off his feet.

'Neyen,' he growled.

'No problemo, no problemo,' the sailor squeaked.

Jadyn dropped him, the man went for a knife, so Jadyn kicked him in the jaw – *thwack!* – and he was down and unmoving. Those watching took a step back, but Aura bent over the stricken sailor and shamelessly removed his purse.

'You can't just take his money,' Jadyn protested, regretting his violent response.

She slipped her arm through his. 'He want to spend on me – now he do. Come.'

Muttering a pointless apology to the unconscious sailor, Jadyn allowed her to lead him into the nearest tavern, where Aura stopped at the door, her eyes went wide.

'*E Cara mia!*' she squeaked.

'What is it?'

'*Neyessa – non se posso!*'

The large, dim taproom was noisy, thanks to a raucous band in one corner. The air stank of burned food, spilled beer and effluent from the alley outside, which clearly doubled as a pissing chamber. Jadyn couldn't work out what Aura had seen, until she jerked from his grasp and stalked towards a booth where five men and a woman were drinking.

'Do you know them?' he called after her, but she ignored him.

The six strangers looked up and the only woman, a blonde Vorska with startling blue eyes and perfect skin, went white as snow. The rest, a mix of races, all looked stunned – one of them, a young Abuthan, made a warding gesture as if dispelling a ghost.

Then the man at the far end of the table rose. The rakishly handsome Nepari with curling black pigtails and sculpted whiskers, his silk shirt open to the waist, went from shock to gimlet-eyed calculation in an eye-blink.

Then he ululated, shouting, '*Aura! Mia bella! Mia angelica! Se tei? Se vero tei?*'

With that, he launched himself over the table, knocking over cups and spilling wine, landed at her feet and lifted her to the ceiling, roaring triumphantly.

'*Sergio!*' she shrieked, bouncing in his arms. '*Mia Sergio – e vero, seti mai—*'

She seized his face and kissed him with utter abandon, while the men with him pounded the table. The rest of the room began cheering, despite having no idea what was going on.

Jadyn finally realised, though. This was *Sergio* – her lost love.

He wasn't sure why he was so shocked, or why seeing her kissing another man made his gut twist, when his feelings for her were entirely fraternal. He glanced at the others at the table. The Abuthan boy was watching the reunion mockingly, his disdainful expression odd until Jadyn noticed that his legs were entwined under the table with the older man beside him, a silver fox with hard eyes. Silverhair had the look of the Order about him.

The other two men were ruffians, a giant young Pelasian and a Nepari who looked like kin to Sergio, although his features were coarser. Neither seemed pleased, and the blonde woman was clearly aghast: Sergio's new lover, or someone who wished she was, Jadyn guessed.

Their eyes met, hers narrowed, then she called in a cold, clear voice, 'Auranuschka, won't you introduce your *handsome* companion?'

Jadyn had never felt less handsome, but her words were no compliment, just a means of gaining Sergio's attention – and they worked. The tall sea captain peeled his mouth from Aura's and looked at Jadyn warily.

'What's this, amora?' he asked in Talmoni, presumably for Jadyn's benefit. 'You have a new man?'

Aura tore her eyes from Sergio's face, her chest heaving and face red. For a moment she appeared to have forgotten Jadyn's name, then she said, 'Be nobody, whatever, just servant.'

Her words hit Jadyn like a gut-punch, and Sergio took in his sickly reaction with a dark smile. 'It's good to meet you, Nobody Whatever,' he drawled. 'Want a drink? You look like you need one.'

'Aye,' Jadyn managed. *I surely do.*

Aura waved a semi-apologetic hand, but she couldn't tear her eyes from Sergio.

The group made room for them and Sergio placed Aura at his side, opposite the Vorska woman, who was hurling eye-daggers at them both. Drinks were ordered, along with bread and oil and Zynochian dukkha, and despite the churning in his stomach that *definitely* wasn't jealousy, Jadyn ate ravenously.

What was I thinking? he thought. *I knew she never gave a damn about me. The times she kissed me – that was just a cruel game.* Despite this, he found himself glancing at her constantly, as if seeking reassurance that she was just toying with this rake. But none came: she was hanging on every word her beloved Sergio said, her face adoring.

Aura knew she was behaving terribly, but she couldn't help it. Seeing Sergio again hit her so hard that all rationality vanished. She'd been rehearsing this reunion in her mind for months, but now it was actually happening, nothing felt real. If someone had shaken her awake and she'd found herself back aboard his ship, she wouldn't have been at all surprised. Sergio, the most handsome, audacious, clever man alive, her soulmate and lover, her conspirator and collaborator, was back in her life as if he'd never left.

But the truth was, three months had passed, and nothing was the same.

That fateful day in Gaudien, Sergio had sent her with Gostan, one of the crew, to pick up some contraband. But watchmen had burst in on them, Gostan had been killed and she'd had to use all her ingenuity to escape. When she returned to the rented apartment she shared with Sergio, he'd cleared out – along with every coin they had, all her jewellery and possessions – even her clothes. By the time she reached the port, the ship had already weighed anchor.

Worse, her name was now on the Justiciary proscriptions: the list of those who had a bounty on their head. She'd gone into hiding, doing whatever it took to survive, but she'd been caught eventually. That's when she'd come to the attention of Lictor Borghart, who'd had no compunction about abusing her – until Jadyn Knight's friends had broken in to rescue him, and she'd managed to tag along.

Now I'm Magic Girl on a Quest, she reminded herself. *Sergio is my past, not my future.*

But why Sergio had abandoned her remained a mystery, one she had to solve.

Jadyn was looking utterly wretched, which was foolish: he was supposed to be her servant – had he forgotten that?

'It's amazing to see you all,' she said in Nepari, beaming at young Ossaman, the Abuthan amatoruno – a lover of the same gender – and his hard-faced partner, Largan Rameleau, an ex-knight. She patted the shoulder of Tonio, Sergio's muscular brother, fully aware he disliked her, and winked at Grigio, the Aquini sailing master.

Was it one of you who sold me out to the Watch? she wondered.

But she doubted that. They'd all been reliable. But Marika was another matter. It was her man, Gostan, who'd been slain that day, but they'd had a violent relationship. Marika was a useless sailor, too, so for her to be here at all meant she was screwing one of them – and it wasn't hard to work out who.

She must have latched onto Sergio the moment she lost Gostan, Aura realised. *Perhaps even persuaded him to abandon me.* But that implied she'd been preying on Sergio even before Gostan died, and for all his roving eye, she'd never felt Sergio was being unfaithful. Impossible, surely?

Though she'd been wrong about men before . . .

'What happened in Gaudien?' she asked him. 'Why did you sail away without me?'

The narrowing of Sergio's pupils told her he was about to lie. 'I only found out afterwards – I had to think of the crew and the ship,' he said, not quite managing to meet her eye. 'Gostan was dead, the Watch were storming the port and you were missing. So we had to run. They pursued us down the coast, so I couldn't return to northern waters, though I wanted to, but . . .' He spread his hands. 'You were already dead. Everyone said so.'

Liar, she thought, but somehow she managed to stay silent. Her eyes went to Marika. Meeting that cold gaze was like crossing blades.

I bet you sold out Gostan and me to clear your path to Sergio.

But accusing the Vorska woman without proof would get her nowhere.

'Aura, what happened to you?' Tonio asked.

She gave a storyteller's version: daring escapades replacing the bad times, skimming through her strange incarceration by Borghart, somehow forgetting to mention that Jadyn and his people were Vestals.

'It's good to see you again,' Ossaman said half-heartedly, when she was done.

'But things have changed,' Marika put in sharply.

'It's true,' Grigio agreed. 'Everyone's moved on from those days, Aura. We exchanged our ocean-going cog for a coastal trader. We're honest merchants now, running the route from here to Bedum-Mutaza.'

'And Sergio and I are together now,' Marika said possessively.

'It's so,' Sergio confirmed. 'We've put our, um, shady past behind us.' He shuffled uncomfortably. 'I can't take those risks any more. Marika is carrying our baby.'

'*Una bebe?*' Aura blurted, truly shocked now. 'How?'

'Oh, the usual way,' Marika snickered. 'Or maybe one of the unusual ways? We do get up to all sorts, don't we, Sergio darling?'

Sergio gave her his 'shut up, woman' look, which Aura noticed without pleasure. He'd always told her to protect her womb whilst fertile, rather than risk pregnancy. 'Our life has no room in it for children,' he'd told her.

But he's knocked Marika up instantly, she thought resentfully. *Why her?*

'The old life was growing too risky,' Grigio was saying. 'Losing Gostan and you in Gaudien was the shock we needed to turn respectable, before our luck ran out.'

All of a sudden, she felt as wretched as Jadyn looked. This dreamed-of reunion tasted like ash shovelled down her throat.

It also roused her two inner voices: Akka the Skyfather and Urghul the Devourer. *If Sergio plies the coastal route, then he's about to head east, the direction Aura must go*, the Devourer noted, her scratchy voice redolent with malice. *And he owes her.*

He does, Akka added, for once in agreement with the Queen of Evil. *But can Aura trust these rogues?*

Probably not, Urghul sniffed. *But who else can she buy passage from?*

True, Akka answered.

Go on, girl, ask – no, demand it!

Demanding anything from Sergio usually achieved the opposite – but Aura knew well how to twist him round her finger – or she used to. 'Dear Sergio, I'm happy for you. And as it happens, I'm seeking a ship to sail east. If you transport me to Bedum-Mutaza, then all is forgiven and our debt repaid.'

'What debt?' Marika demanded.

Sergio hesitated, his eyes flickering to Marika. 'There's no, uh . . .'

'You owe me,' Aura stated. 'You sold a ship I helped buy.'

'We're not smugglers now, girl—' Grigio began.

'She's not coming aboard our ship—' Marika snapped.

But Sergio was still captain. He raised a hand for silence. 'It's a stain on my honour to have left you behind, Aura. Though it wasn't my fault,' he added quickly. 'Of course we'll take you east.' His eyes flickered to Jadyn, who was listening to the torrent of Nepari uncomprehendingly. 'Just you, or does this one come too?'

Aura smiled inwardly. 'He comes – he has skills I require.'

'What skills?' Marika asked archly, sensing a weakness. 'Fanny riding?'

'No, he's an ex-Vestal,' Largan said shrewdly. He switched to Talmoni. 'Hey, "Nobody Whatever". You're ex-Order, aren't you?'

It took a moment for Jadyn to realise he was being spoken to, in words he could understand. 'Aye, retired. But the land I was allotted was shit, so I hit the road.'

It was an old tale, the poor knight discarded by the powers that be; though Jadyn wasn't a good liar, Largan appeared to believe him.

'Do you have a flamberge?' he asked.

'I surrendered my sword,' Jadyn replied. 'Too risky.'

'Then how do you protect her ladyship?'

'With whatever's to hand.'

Jadyn glanced down and they all followed his eyes: he had a dagger tip against Largan's ribs. The Talmoni's eyes went glacial, then he smiled, as if at a good joke.

'I'm Largan Rameleau, once of the Wildeboar century.'

'Sier Jerome Baen, of the Styrbeest century,' Jadyn replied, sheathing the dagger calmly.

Aura smiled to herself, because Jadyn had managed a fluent lie. *I'm such a good influence.*

'Nice to meet you,' Largan said. 'But don't ever draw steel on me again.'

There was a tense moment, then Jadyn said, 'Of course.'

Everyone exhaled.

'More drink,' Sergio shouted. 'We sail at dawn – and no one's going to sleep before then!'

He was good as his word, and evidently his new respectability had come with some sterling profits, because he bought the best wine and co-opted the tavern's band into mutilating all his favourite songs, insisting Aura dance with him, under the pretext that Marika couldn't, though she was only a couple of months pregnant.

The hours slipped away in false conviviality.

Around the third bell after midnight, the Night Watch arrived, clearing out the taverns and robbing anyone too drunk to resist. Sergio paid them off with beer, then took the surly Marika's arm and led them along the docks to a two-masted trader, which was being readied for the tide. Some of the crew recognised Aura, but many were new faces to her. She wasn't surprised; sailors came and went all the time. The wind was rising: by dawn they would be underway, part of a convoy for mutual protection.

Aura and Jadyn were told to bunk down in the crew's mess. Aura made a point of greeting those men she knew, hoping she could rely on old ties to keep them safe, but she could already name those who would cause trouble.

It's like I can see inside their heads, she realised. *It must be the aegis.*

That gave her hope that if things went wrong, she might have some warning. Not that it was likely to matter, if trouble came when the ship was twenty kylos offshore, leaving them surrounded by would-be killers.

*

Jadyn stood with Aura at the prow, watching the sun rise over the sea, as the grandly named *Duce di Mundi* sailed out of port and swung eastwards. The wind was favourable, but Aura was too full of misery to appreciate it.

'He want bebe, why no with Aura?' she whined.

Jadyn looked surprised. 'Is that something you wanted?'

'He say world too cruel for bebe,' she muttered, glaring along the deck to where her inconstant lover stood directing his crew. 'But he knock up Bitchface Marika. Me not understanding – we had love.'

'Let it go,' Jadyn advised. 'We're on a journey to something better.'

'Better than love? Not thinking so. Love is . . . *love*. Can Jadyn give love?'

Startled, he blurted, 'Maybe I can give you the aegis?'

That shut her up. With a torn expression, she mumbled about seeing to their bedding and hurried away.

Did I just win that bout? he wondered numbly. Not that it mattered. He hated seeing her miserable, and travelling with her former lover felt like a big, big mistake.

And about mistakes, I hope I'm right about leaving that mirror and letter behind us. It still felt unfair on others the aegis might call, to cut the thread of clues behind him. *But please, Akka and Elysia, let those who follow us have good, not evil, in their hearts . . .*

Qor-Espina Mountains, Neparia

Yoryn Borghart woke before dawn and went to his balcony overlooking the unnamed lake above which Vanashta Baanholt, the last refuge of the Sanctor Wardens, was built. It was cold, the snow-clad peaks hemming them in, despite it being summer.

The chill in the air matched his mood. As a lictor, an investigator into heresy, he craved black and white situations, but all too often life came in inconvenient shades of grey. Making those uncertainties vanish was part of his art.

But now, I am part of the doubt.

34

Two nights ago, in the lowest chamber of the mines beneath this ancient structure, he'd cornered a group of renegades. They were seeking the heretical power called aegis, which appeared to involve some kind of precognition – although the Sanctor Wardens who had first wielded it evidently hadn't seen their own end coming.

Somehow, cornered and about to be captured or killed, the renegade knight Jadyn Kaen and the thief Auranuschka Perafi had conjured a bridge across a void and escaped. He could just about come to terms with that, although failure was never acceptable, least of all for him. But what troubled him more was that for a few seconds, that mystic bridge had borne his own weight – and that of the Exemplar, Vazi Virago. That surely implied that he and she also had the potential to wield the aegis.

I know my own soul. I have never *deviated from the Path of Righteousness.*

So how could this be? And more to the point, what should he do about it? He had no desire at all to be marked by some other form of magic. Indeed, his enemies in the Justiciary – which was practically everyone he knew – would beat a path to his door to accuse him of heresy. No doubt Vazi Virago had the same issue: as the youngest Exemplar and only the second female to win that honour, she was already the target of a welter of jealousy and hate. Indeed, had he not been in the same position, he'd have been the first to turn on her. Her doll-like beauty offended him, as did her incredible martial skill. The glyma was a great leveller, enabling smaller but skilled practitioners to defeat bigger, bulkier fighters, but Exemplars were supposed to be men, not women, and certainly not women who looked like her.

Despite her beauty, he wasn't moved by her. She had all the charm of a spitting cobra, and in any case, his sexuality was something he kept in a tightly locked box, as any lictor should. Sexual release, like hate and love, the strongest emotions, could trigger uncontrolled flares of glyma-energy, with disastrous results. As a consequence, the Order was a cauldron of seething emotions and desires – you had to know when to leave, before it broke you. But it was different in the Justiciary: rape was a legitimate torture technique, written into the statutes. No one cared if prisoners survived – and the moment of climax, as fatal glyma-energy surged from him into the woman, was such an exquisite pleasure that it had become addictive. It gave him the best of both worlds.

It had been his intention to end Auranuschka Perafi that way, until he'd discovered her precognitive spark. The ensuing voyage of self-discovery had given him the means to explore his own potential; he now knew for certain that the instincts that had so often led him to resolve an investigation were indeed more than guesswork and luck.

I have a form of precognition, and now I finally know why: I have the potential to wield the magic of the old Sanctor Wardens.

But then he'd dreamed that Aura was a danger to him, so he'd signed her death warrant – only for her to escape that same night, with the similarly Gifted Jadyn Kaen. It was surely no coincidence.

The sound of boots on the steps heralded the advent of Vaziella al'Nuqheel, known to the empire as Vazi Virago. She was clad in silver-plated, beautifully embossed armour, fitted perfectly to her slender frame. Her classical Zynochi face, copper complexion framed with crisply curled black hair, was eye-catching, and she moved effortlessly, with grace and poise. He'd seen her fight and was in awe of her fusion of the glyma and the blade. To see her as a woman was folly; she was a lethal killing machine disguised as one of the Serrafim: glorious, but chilling.

And she's got this aegis Gift too . . . That's surely why she's so good.

'Exemplar,' he greeted her warily, putting his right fist to his heart. 'Did you sleep?'

'A little,' she said, stifling a yawn.

'Have you decided on our next step?' It rankled having to defer to her, but she was one of the few people within the Order who outranked him.

'I have,' Vazi replied. 'Those renegades killed four of my five knights and almost killed my magus. I'm pulling everyone out and sending them to the nearest portali gate, while you and I pursue Kaen and Perafi. I'll leave Arghyl Goraghan in charge, with Centurion Prade and my squire, Bern Myko, to support him.'

It was as he expected. 'But what of us?' he said quietly. 'How will we proceed?'

In other words, did she still hold to their earlier decision to pursue the aegis, even if it resulted in being branded a heretic and cost them all they had?

How will we proceed?

Vazi Virago – her name had been Talmonised to suit the north – had seldom felt doubt: she *knew* what was best, and did it. But this moment felt pivotal.

A few days ago, she'd have said her future was assured: whilst in the Order, she would accrue glory and status, then before her perfect glyma-control slipped, she'd retire and make a powerful marriage. There were caliphs of immense wealth queuing up for her, and indeed, the Hierophant himself desired her. He might be old and withered, but he gushed over her like a love-struck boy when she was at court. Repulsive, but she didn't need to be in love.

I could be First Wife before I'm forty, and my children could rule the Triple Empire. But unless I fully possess the aegis and can use its precognition accurately, I'll be nothing but a dynastic broodmare. I need to be more than that. I must rule, through him.

Of course, a lot could go wrong: she could lose control of the glyma; or be crippled or slain while on duty. Disease could take her, or an accident at sea; such things happened to anyone. But she'd always had a nose for danger and how to avoid it. Even in the deadliest melees, she'd found an instinctive path to survival and victory.

And now I know why. I have this aegis in some form.

Nevertheless, she feared the tag of heretic. She'd helped hunt down knights who'd been tarred by that brush, running them to ground like old boars, and she dreaded her own life ending the same way. *So what to do?*

She faced Yoryn Borghart – a chilling man, shaven-skulled, with a cruel face, a bristling goatee and teeth like a carnivore. By reputation, he was a ruthless seeker of truth, someone who took pleasure in torture and pain – but she felt a kinship with him. They were both implacable and self-serving.

Him, I can understand, she thought. *But can we talk frankly?*

The risks were huge: if he turned on her once they returned to civilisation, he had the rank to bring accusations that could destroy her. To bring down a heretical Exemplar would surely be the pinnacle of his career. But he was hell-bent on capturing the fugitives, especially the Nepari woman. *He's fixated on her,* Vazi thought. *Maybe I can exploit that.*

'I hold by my decision,' she told him. 'I hate all heresy, and anything that undermines our glorious Triple Empire. You believe Kaen and Perafi are a threat to our empire, and I concur. If they escape, how many more such snakes will arise? They must be stopped.'

She watched his face carefully, but could glean no clue to his thoughts. 'But how can we follow them, when only a heretic can walk that bridge?' he asked eventually.

'Heresy is an evil of the heart,' she replied, quoting Jovan Lux himself. 'It exists in our weaknesses and doubts. But power is a tool, for good or evil. I know *my* heart to be pure.'

He put his fist to his heart. 'And I know mine to be likewise.'

He's with me, she decided. 'Then it's simple: we will do whatever it takes to pursue them. One must know evil to recognise and defeat it.'

'I agree, Exemplar. And I believe I know how to retrace their steps and unlock whatever gates they have passed through. It all started at a stone circle three days' ride from here.'

'Are you sure?'

He smiled coldly. 'I visited our prisoners earlier and administered a dose of an opiate to Romara Challys, then used a mind-melding technique on her during her delirium. It can be unreliable, and confessions obtained this way are inadmissible, but what I learned confirms my guess: this stone circle is the start of the path to the aegis. It will lead us back here, but with the crucial difference that we'll be able to open that bridge ourselves.'

'Well done, Lictor,' she praised, thinking, *So easily, we dip our toes into this heresy, because we both want it so badly.*

She'd been born with a sense of destiny and an unquenchable thirst for advancement. She *knew* that she was destined for greatness, so anything she did to attain that goal must be justified. To possess and perfect the aegis, which appeared to be concerned with precognition and foresight, would be priceless in her ascent.

To see my enemies' moves, whether moments or years ahead, would give me an advantage over all-comers. There'd be no limits to my rise – and it will all be on my own terms.

'One thing,' she said. 'What about your friend Sandreth and his new bondsman?'

'Elan Sandreth and Tevas Nicolini aren't my friends,' Borghart sniffed. 'Sandreth wants to go back north and claim his "wife's" estate. They can go, for all I care.'

Sandreth claimed to be married to Romara Challys, but Vazi was certain that was a fiction. He was a born liar, if ever she'd met one – and not someone she wanted to set loose, lest he started bragging about finding Vanashta Baanholt. But eliminating a highborn was complicated. 'That's fine, provided they swear silence regarding this place.' *Fear of me should still their tongues.*

'I'll trust your judgement on the matter,' Borghart said, bowing his head.

She faced him squarely. 'Regarding the matter of trust: we'll be travelling together, so there will be some ground rules. I command, and you obey. Do not mistake my gender or youth for weakness. Do not think of me as a woman at all. I will not develop feelings for you, so do not waste any you have on me. My destiny is to save the Triple Empire by destroying the Vyr Rebellion, and Akka and Elysia will raise me to immortality. My fame will last a thousand years. Be loyal to me, and so might yours. Am I understood?'

He probably thought her pompous and egotistical, but he smote his chest and declared, 'I am yours to command, Exemplar.'

She didn't trust his display, but she approved of him feeling the need to make it.

'Good. Then let us begin.'

*

Tevas Nicolini was an ex-knight, an Order veteran with decades of service, but these days he preferred to blend in with the troops – which was why he was saddling two horses, his own and Elan Sandreth's, amid eighty-odd Vestal men-at-arms. Forty years old, balding and hard-faced, he felt old among them. But he had a flamberge over his shoulder, wielded legally now, thanks to his bondsman contract with Sandreth, so everyone gave him a wide berth.

An hour ago, the Exemplar had summoned her magus, Arghyl Goraghan, the last survivor of her pentacle, and told him to muster the remaining men of her Golden Dragon century and leave Vanashta Baanholt. They were forming up now.

Lictor Borghart had sought them out and told them in no uncertain terms that if they ever returned to Vanashta Baanholt – or even spoke of it – they'd regret ever drawing breath. He'd demanded they swear an oath of silence, and Elan agreed instantly.

Tevas had echoed the nobleman with alacrity, but couldn't help wondering, *Why is it necessary, when the Exemplar's supposed to be destroying it?*

But he'd been there when the mystic bridge in the mines below took Virago and Borghart's weight – and then vanished again, almost sending both into the void. When he'd heard Jadyn Kaen challenge the Exemplar to take up the aegis herself, he'd realised, *She's got the same heretical streak as Jadyn.*

It was a fascinating thought, but not one he was prepared to voice. Borghart – who likely had the same trait himself – would murder him in an eye-blink.

So yes, we'll leave. But what will you be doing, Exemplar – and you, Lictor?

It was probably better not to know. Borghart was a power-mad slaughter-whore, and for all her beauty, Tevas doubted Vazi Virago was any different.

Elan Sandreth, thirty-something, with his blond hair thinning and his youth faded into premature middle-age, came sauntering through the crowd, accompanied by Arghyl Goraghan. The obese mage had long, unkempt grey hair, dun robes and a torc, a bronze ceremonial necklet from his native Foyland. He'd been left in charge of the century, an unusual circumstance, but Jadyn and Romara's people had gone through the Exemplar's pentacle like a reaper's scythe and all the knights were dead.

He couldn't help a moment of pride. *I taught Jadyn and Romara well.*

'So, Tevas, are we ready?' Elan called jovially. He and Goraghan looked like they were getting on well.

Tevas turned to the last six surviving Pelasian pirates, weighing them up. Scum, but his scum. They all looked like they just wanted to go home, a feeling he shared. 'Sure, we're ready,' he answered for them. 'What's the plan?'

'Arghyl knows a portali gate near here. We'll follow the river downstream to get out of the mountains, then head north towards Foyland.'

'Foyland? With due respect to your homeland, Magister Goraghan, Foyland's a mess.'

'Oh, I know dat,' Goraghan drawled. 'But I've got kin dere, an' dey'll help us out.' He looked up at the monastery. 'I'll take dese heretics to Folkstein, while the Exemplar destroys dis place.' His voice had a faint edge of sarcasm. 'After all, what makes more sense than t' put a magus in charge of soldiers, and a knight in charge of dealin' wit' sorcery, eh?'

He disapproves, Tevas realised. *The scholar in him wants to know more.* 'Ours is not to question,' he said, a little sternly.

'Good advice, t'be sure.' Goraghan gave him a lugubrious look, then proffered a flask that reeked of whisky. 'Take a good swallow, fella. Plenty more where dat came from.'

He took a grateful slurp and returned the flask. 'Happy to lighten your load.'

'Excellent,' Goraghan grinned, before turning to the waiting soldiers. 'Mount up, ye rabble. Let's be riding, northwest to da river an' on downstream. We're goin' home!'

Tevas fell in beside Goraghan and Elan in the middle of the column, saluting the Exemplar and Borghart as they passed under the arch, then out onto an old, overgrown road. It ran south, but they turned off, instead following the game trails the scouts had found.

He glanced back at the brooding bulk of the monastery as it was swallowed up by the forest. 'Well, I'm not sad to leave that damned place behind.'

Goraghan scowled unhappily. 'I don' understand, I confess. Dismantlin' t'spells woven into dat place needs my skills as a magus. I told Vazi so, but she's adamant it's her task.'

The Foylish magus had been unconscious when the fugitives escaped and had missed the crucial events. Tevas considered voicing his suspicion that neither Virago or Borghart intended destroying Vanashta Baanholt, but thought better of it. *None of my business.*

Elan Sandreth joined them as the horses bearing the prisoners were led past. Romara Challys and Gram Larch were heavily roped to keep them in the saddle. Neither looked up, both barely conscious.

'Arghyl, I've a question for you,' Elan said. 'What would it take for you to turn a blind eye so I can have a little time with my good wife tonight?'

Tevas felt his stomach curdle. Despite what Romara had become, he couldn't hate her, or forget the years of friendship. But nor could he afford to jeopardise his Sandreth's goodwill.

The Foylish magus licked his lips. 'Well, m'lor'ship, I'm afraid dat's nae poss—'

'I can pay well,' Elan interrupted.

'Money don' interest me,' Goraghan rumbled. 'She's a glyma-user, too dangerous to ride.'

'But isn't her power chained up?' Elan asked, 'So she can't hurt me.'

Tevas shook his head. 'Sorry, Milord. They say vorlok women can grow teeth inside their fannies and bite your cock off. Not even those ensorcelled manacles could prevent that.'

'Akka on high,' Elan breathed, and nudged his horse ahead, leaving them behind.

'Were you protecting 'im, or your former student, fella?' Goraghan asked Tevas, with subtle menace.

'My only loyalty is to Milord Sandreth,' Tevas replied, then he forced a sly wink and added, 'If it weren't so, I'd be wanting to do her myself, for old time's sake.'

The Foylish magus chuckled darkly, while Tevas told himself, *Just survive. Romara's as good as dead now, so none of this matters. Just survive.*

2

An Awakening

Ninneva

The vyr say their way of mastering glyma is better than the Order's rigid code. Indeed, they believe it can lead to 'ninneva', a mystic state of peace and harmony. But there's no evidence of truth in this claim. In truth, the vyr are just slavering berserkers, barely more human than the animals they resemble when they change shape.

THE ANNALS OF TALMONT, 1402

Qor-Espina Mountains, Neparia

Romara Challys woke, roused by the rhythmic motion of her horse. Her eyes went instantly to Gram Larch on the horse in front, his back straight, his head upright. He glanced back at her, giving her a fraught look, but didn't try to speak.

She'd been dreaming of him; those visions of love and tenderness sustained her through the pain of returning to this cruel world and recalling their plight.

Sunlight dappled through the pines, sprinkling glitter on the lake to their right, probably the same one below Vanashta Baanholt, though the monastery was out of sight. They'd been riding all day and her stomach was growling, her lips parched.

But the column was stopping to make camp and she was soon untied from the saddle and lowered to the ground by the stony-faced soldiers. They let her rise, though, and limp to the water's edge, where she drank deeply. Only then did she look at the face reflected in the still water: pale and haggard, framed by a curtain of matted scarlet hair, the colour offset by the torn remnants of grey-green erling cloth over her chainmail.

Then she sat back and gazed skywards as memories hit her.

Vazi Virago striking down Obanji.

Soren and Elindhu falling over the edge of the blank drop into nothingness.

Jadyn and Aura together – as always – on the bridge of light.

Her Falcons were lost to her.

She'd disliked Aura intensely, seeing only a man-hungry amoral leech who'd clamped herself onto naïve Jadyn, but now it felt like they'd always been fated for each other: the only ones marked for the aegis.

Perhaps they're right for each other? It was a vaguely comforting thought, though a little self-serving, she knew, because it excused her for falling in love with Gram. *Let Jadyn find joy in Aura*, she wished. *Let one of us be happy.*

Then Gram stumbled up, also still bound, and dropped to his knees beside her. After drinking loudly, he plunged his head into the icy water before shaking his shaggy head, spraying water everywhere. 'Romara,' he breathed, 'stay strong.'

Her name on his tongue thrilled through her.

He was a big man, one of the tallest and broadest she'd met, a gentle giant with thick brown hair and beard, soft eyes and a quietly spoken solidity she'd come to lean on. She'd been having a breakdown, having lost control of her glyma, but by drawing the wild energy into himself, he'd saved her. He'd been able to do that because he was a potential vorlok – a vyr-sorcerer . . . now, so was she.

Why doesn't that horrify me any more? she wondered, but it didn't, even though she knew they both had the capacity to morph into monstrous beings.

From Gram, she'd learned that to be a vyr wasn't all evil – it was more about wildness, an inner maelstrom that one could learn to ride. She'd never be able to master it on her own, but with Gram, anything seemed possible.

What is that state of grace the vyr seek? Ninneva . . . Is that what I'm feeling now?

If it wasn't, she had no other name for it, except *love*. She felt lit from within, despite their plight. Her every sense trembled at his presence; she wanted to drown in the calm lake of his soul. She longed for a future with him.

But no such future was on offer right now. They were both weak, unsteady as colts, and there were soldiers all around them. He'd been badly wounded, taking a sword in the side; she'd almost died keeping him alive as he bled out, sharing energy she didn't have. They'd been helpless when the Exemplar's men seized them.

Now they had halters round their necks and the soldiers holding the ropes were gazing at them with utter loathing. To these men, she and Gram were vyr, worse than beasts. Three months ago – was it really so short a time? – she'd have agreed with them, but now she knew the truth: the vyr were much more, and much better, than that.

On impulse, she shuffled on her knees to Gram and lifted her face. Their lips met fleetingly, the taste of him warm and bitter – until the soldiers yanked their ropes, jerking them apart. The nooses closed round her throat, leaving her thrashing desperately, her windpipe closing – until a knee rammed into the small of her back, slamming her face-first into the gravel.

Rough hands loosened the rope. 'None of that,' the soldier growled. 'Jaggin' animals.'

'Bitch,' the man holding Gram's tether muttered. 'I hate knights what go bad. Hope they burn you with wet wood.'

She tried to draw on the glyma from nature, as the vyr did, but the manacles on her wrist sizzled, burning her skin. Then a boot slammed into her side, leaving her writhing in agony.

'Don't do that again, bitch.'

Despite the fear and abuse, her control didn't waver. Gram was alive and, irrationally, she found she couldn't despair with him here, even when the men dragged them to separate trees, where they were roughly tethered again.

She wondered where they were going – and if there would be vyr along the way who might see them . . .

*

There was a supernatural creature of Elidorian myth, whose legend Tevas Nicolini had always felt contained a valuable lesson. The Kerech looked like a majestic stag, so impressive that hunters seeing it would lose all judgement, pursuing it beyond reason, unable or unwilling to stop the chase – until the Kerech led the hunters over a precipice, or into a bottomless bog, or turned into a ravening beast and devoured its pursuers.

The lesson he took from the tale was never to let his guard down, because all too easily the hunted could become the hunter.

Perhaps it was Romara's tawny-red hair that made him think of that old tale as he pitched his tent in sight of where she lay. He kept an eye on her and Gram Larch as they were given water and fed, although the manacles made eating awkward for them.

If I were a better man, he thought ruefully, *I'd kill them as they slept, to spare them what's to come.*

But he wasn't that man any more.

Then he saw Elan Sandreth approaching Romara and somehow found the guts to intercept him. The young nobleman was gazing sullenly down at his bound 'wife'; he didn't look at all pleased to see Tevas.

'What?' he asked.

Tevas dropped his voice and asked, 'Milord, what do you want with her?'

'I just want to see my beloved wife,' Elan snarked. Then he added, in a low murmur, 'We need to kill her before we arrive wherever we're going. I don't want her dragging my name through the mud, telling the blasted Order that there was no wedding.'

Not my problem, Tevas thought stonily. Except it was, because he was now Elan's bondsman, his personal protector. 'Goraghan's been charged by the Exemplar to get her home. He'll not let you do any such thing, and if you did, he'd drag you in front of the Justiciary instead.'

Elan pouted. 'Thought as much. But what if she convinces everyone—?'

'Milord, you're worrying about nothing,' Tevas interrupted. 'The

Hierophant himself has ratified your marriage to Romara, at your mother's behest. Romara can say what she likes, but you're legally in the right.'

Morally, you're a shit-smear, mind.

'I suppose so,' Elan conceded. 'Who'd've thought I'd ever be grateful for my mother cuckolding my father, eh? She must like living dangerously, to bed a glyma-knight.'

'I doubt Corbus has used the glyma in years,' Tevas replied. 'I'm sure she's safe.'

'What a relief,' Elan said sarcastically. 'I've been so worried.'

Romara was looking back at them with a calmness that almost made a mockery of her predicament. The Avas man was also watching; having seen him in battle, Tevas could well imagine him uprooting the tree he was bound to.

'Damn it, let's just get this over with,' Elan exclaimed, turning and stalking away.

Tevas was left standing in the full glare of Romara's accusatory eyes, a weird sensation, when she was the vyr, not him.

Jagat, girl, he thought, *why'd you have to crash back into my life like this?*

The lands surrounding Vanashta Baanholt were a jagged, fractured maze of sheer cliffs covered in dense but summer-dry forest, with snow-melt lakes and rivers filling every valley. There were no settlements, no roads and few signs of humanity. The birds and beasts ruled unchallenged here, and in the two days Soren var'Dael had sheltered here, none of the searching enemies had come near.

He and Elindhu had plummeted into an apparent void in the chamber beneath Vanashta Baanholt, only to plunge into water. They'd been rescued by the erling Fynarhea, but Elindhu Morspeth was still unconscious, so they'd not been able to move on, despite their dangerous proximity to the ancient monastery. But finally, after two days, Elindhu was waking. She'd eaten nothing, but he'd been able to dribble a little water between her thick dark lips.

She'd been asleep in her erling form: tall and angular, with an outsized nose, bronze skin and slanted eyes. Her long, wavy silver hair had a weird capacity to move as if it were alive, which he found curiously fascinating.

Now her amber eyes flickered open and she exclaimed. '*Obanji?*'

Then she burst into tears.

Soren tried to comfort her, weeping with her, although she must feel the loss far more deeply – her relationship with Obanji had been as close to love as the Order permitted.

His own grief was raw, too. Obanji had been his mentor when he'd been forced to join the Order. Having just lost his mother, father and sister, he had fulfilled Soren's unspoken need for parental guidance and affection. They'd become close in the few weeks they'd travelled together; losing him felt like an open wound.

'I'm sorry, child,' Elindhu whispered. 'My addled brain saw him in you.'

Obanji had been pure Abuthan, his skin so dark it was black, while Soren was of mixed blood, but they had similar facial structure and curly black hair. To be mistaken for the older man didn't hurt his feelings at all. 'May I always remind you of him,' he replied shyly.

Elindhu sat up and her body smoothly flowed into the human shape Soren knew best, a diminutive, portly woman with a rosy-cheeked white face, a rudder nose and big hazel eyes. Her mass of grey hair braided itself and knotted into a tower. Losing more than a foot in height had to go somewhere; her buttocks, breasts and belly swelled alarmingly.

The contrast between the lithe erling and this homely dumpling couldn't have been greater, yet somehow, he could see she was the same person in both guises.

Elindhu stood, sniffed her armpits and winced, then peeled off her dress as Soren averted his eyes, waddled naked to the lake and plunged into the icy water. The ripples she made had time to entirely fade before she rose with a large trout flapping frantically in her hands. There was another snared in her braids.

'Dinner,' she proclaimed cheerily, wading ashore with water cascading from her hair and body. 'It must be my turn to cook, if you've been looking after me.'

Soren blushed, but he felt a weird burst of pride in having such a strange friend: comical, yet wise, like a spooky aunty. 'It was Fynarhea looked after us both. She's off scouting.'

Elindhu's eyebrows shot up, then she smiled. 'Ah, so she found us. Excellent.'

Fynarhea was also an erling, one of the elder folk of Hytal. Though most believed them all but extinct, Soren had learned that there were many erlings hiding in the wilderness. Most were family groups or clans, but there were bigger havens too, where hundreds lived. Fynarhea came from one of these erlhaafens, Semmanath-Tuhr, on the Solabas-Neparia border. He had seen erlings with greenish or bluish skin there, and others with webbed feet and fingers who could breathe underwater through gills. Some were less than three feet tall, some thrice that, giants with terrifying strength; there were so many variants it boggled him.

There were deeper mysteries, too, especially concerning erlings and gender. Erlings *chose* their final gender, he'd been told – Elindhu was fully adult and had chosen to be female, but Fynarhea was young and could still become either male or female at will. In either form, Fynarhea had a hard face, framed by midnight hair, but when a woman, *she* was shapely; while as a man, *he* was lean and muscular. And the wolfskin cloak knotted around her neck was more than an affectation: Fynarhea was also a morphian, able to take animal form.

And she keeps looking at me like I'm a piece of meat, he thought uncomfortably.

As if summoned by the thought, Fynarhea appeared from the trees, a spirit warrior of the forest, intimidatingly alluring in either gender. *He* was in male form now, wearing a thigh-length tunic and leather leggings; his bow and tuelawar, the erling curved sword, slung over his shoulders.

Fynarhea had been following the Falcons at Elindhu's behest, an extra protector, and had found Soren and Elindhu by an underground river, half-drowned and exhausted. It was he who'd dragged them ashore and kept them safe.

Soren was grateful, but he found the young erling highly disturbing.

'Good to see you again, Fyn,' Elindhu greeted the newcomer casually. Gesturing at the two fishes, she added, 'Are we far enough from danger to risk a small fire?'

'As long as we avoid green wood,' Fynarhea said, putting an arm round Soren's shoulder. 'We'll look after it, Rann Elindhu. You need to rest.'

Fynarhea's touch was disconcerting; every time their eyes met, Soren remembered their first encounter in Semmanath-Tuhr, where Fynarhea had tried to lure him into a tryst – because she was bored, she'd said later, claiming she'd meant no harm.

Soren still felt ensorcelled by her.

It wasn't that he was totally averse: Fynarhea was attractive and exotic and Soren hadn't yet come to terms with the Order's strictures about sex and love. And to be openly desired by someone so striking was hard to deny.

But I'm not sure I even like her . . . or him, or whatever . . .

'Sure, Fynarhea can handle the meal,' he managed to say.

'It's "Fyn" when I'm in male form.' *Fyn* leaned in, a teasing light in his gaze. 'Start with the head and work your way down the belly to the tail,' he snickered.

It felt like an uncomfortably direct invitation.

When Soren winced and went red, Fyn added, 'That's how you fillet a trout.'

'That's enough,' Elindhu put in sharply.

Soren flinched. *Gods, what must she think?* He wasn't sure he knew his own mind. *Fyn is still Fynarhea; the same person, just a different body. I'm not an amatoruno, I know that . . .* But he still blushed.

Fyn backed away, smiling teasingly. 'I'll go for firewood,' he said, and sashayed away.

Soren pulled his eyes away and asked Elindhu, 'Why did you have him follow us?'

'Because he asked to, and because it's good for him,' the magia replied. 'One day Fynarhea will rule Semmanath-Tuhr, and will rule more wisely if he's seen something of the world outside.'

'Oh,' Soren mumbled, his cheeks still burning. 'Can you tell him I don't want him to, uh, flirt with me? Whether woman or, um, man.'

'You should tell him yourself, dear.'

'I can't. Every time she . . . or he . . . looks at me, my brain freezes.'

'I understand.' She squatted beside him and gave him a sympathetic look. 'Fyn's nowhere near as confident as he seems. This is his first time out of the erlhaafen.'

'But surely he knows we can't . . . um . . .'

'Can't make love?' Elindhu said frankly. She tapped her head. 'He knows in here.' Then she patted her heart and groin. 'But not here.' She gave him a sly grin. 'Young erlings are notoriously promiscuous. Imagine having two genders to choose from, two sets of genitals to play with and all the lust in the world.' She snickered softly. 'When I was his age . . . oh my!' Then she too went pink. 'But you don't want to hear about that.'

'No, I don't!' Soren agreed, with some fervour.

'Then I'll spare you the torrid details.' She fanned herself ostentatiously, then cast about, looking annoyed. 'On a more practical level, I've lost my staff, which is a damnable nuisance. But I carry an elobyne sliver for emergencies, so I can veil us for a while. Later on, I'll try and scry our comrades.'

But surely they're all dead, Soren thought miserably. He distracted himself with the tasks at hand, and once Fyn returned, they got the fire going. After they'd eaten, Elindhu called them both to attention.

'We need to know what happened to the others,' she said, 'so I will try and scry them – I've some of their personal items I collected for such an occasion, to anchor the spell. If I can locate anyone, we'll decide what to do. It'll be difficult with so little elobyne to empower the spell, so I'll be busy most of the evening. Set a watch, please – I'll be too tired to take my turn later, I'm afraid.' She met Fyn's eyes. 'Don't do anything foolish.'

The erling looked vexed, but Elindhu was not just older, but of higher rank. 'Of course, Rann Elindhu.'

'Just call me Elindhu,' she told him. 'Out here, titles mean nothing.' Then she flapped her hands. 'Off you go. I need to concentrate.'

While the magia prepared her spells, Fyn and Soren cleaned up, banked the fire to ensure it wasn't visible at a distance, then climbed up the rise behind their camp to a small ledge they'd found; it offered a view inland and across the lake, an ideal place for a guard post.

'First or second watch?' Fyn offered.

'I'll take second, if you don't mind,' Soren replied. It might be hard to breathe around him, but he didn't want to be anywhere else. 'How long can you choose to be male or female?' he asked awkwardly.

'Mostly we choose a final gender in our early twenties,' Fyn replied. 'If we bear a child, we will always remain female, so we must be a bit careful. Otherwise, it's just a matter of your body settling on one or other, whatever feels most natural. By about thirty, you can't change gender any more, so you do have to choose.'

Soren shuddered. 'That's *really* weird.'

'But fun.' Fyn put a hand on Soren's knee, which made his skin prickle and his pulse quicken. 'What about the glyma?' Soren heard fascination and envy, but also respect. 'Why can you do this? Is it in your blood?'

'Until a few months ago, I didn't know I could,' Soren replied. 'I and my family, we were waiting to be evacuated from Avas Isle, when vyr attacked. A draegar – that's a vyr-knight – killed my parents and was going to kill me. I picked a sword off the ground – its owner had just been cut in half – and the orb on the hilt lit up. I don't know why, and I'm still learning to deal with it – if I don't get proper training, I'm scared it'll kill me, so maybe it's a good thing I lost my flamberge at the monastery.'

He hadn't meant to voice his fears; they all just came tumbling out, to his shame. His father would have punished him for speaking so openly – but Fyn put an arm round his shoulder, which felt comforting . . . and then somewhat alarming.

'I, uh, better get back and get some rest,' he stammered, hastily disentangling himself and hurrying away in case the erling tried to kiss him.

He found Elindhu bent over a pool of water in a natural bowl beside the river, soft light streaming from the water, lighting her homely human face. She looked up and smiled anxiously when she became aware of him.

'Romara's alive, and I think I glimpsed Gram with her. They're about twenty kylos northwest of us, but they're surrounded by Order soldiers. I used a lock of her hair to reach her, but the mage who was trying to conceal her will have sensed my presence, so I reckon they'll pick up their speed.'

Soren swallowed. 'And the others?'

'Nothing. But they could be blocked by veil spells, or distance, or stone or water . . .'

Or death.

He shook off the thought and asked, 'So what do we do?'

'We go after Romara and Gram,' she said, 'In the morning, when I've regained my strength. Get some rest, lad. We're in for some hard work if we're to catch them up.'

Sometime after midnight, Soren was shaken awake by Fyn, who was holding a smouldering branch as a makeshift torch. The erling guided him to the lookout perch, talking about the animals he'd seen – deer and rabbits, and unexpectedly, a sow with a litter of piglets. It was clearly just a pretext, and sure enough, Fyn perched beside Soren as he sat, their thighs touching.

'I'm not sleepy,' he said. 'I'll stay a while.'

Uh-oh, Soren thought, sensing another test of his emotional fortitude, but for a time they just sat, sharing warmth.

He watched the moonlight shining on the flat planes of Fyn's handsome face, gleaming on his long dark hair, and wondered, *Why am I finding him attractive? I'm not inclined like that.*

But *Fyn* was also the bewitching *Fynarhea,* whose allure he couldn't deny.

'Do you like me more as a woman or a man?' the erling asked.

Soren swallowed. 'I don't know. We've only just met.' *And you're a creature of magic and dark forests.* 'I'm only sixteen – and I've just joined the Vestals. I don't know about anything, but Obanji told me that glyma can kill people who . . . um . . . get too close.'

'That is so,' Fyn answered. 'We have glyma-users too, you know. I've always been drawn to them. Don't you think love is worth any danger?'

'No!'

'But I do,' the erling said, his luminous eyes filling Soren's gaze. 'Imagine what it must be like, to be caught up in such rapture as you die—'

Soren pulled away. 'I don't want to hurt anyone . . . You'd better go now. We're no use as watchers if we talk all night, and you need to get some sleep.'

Fyn pulled a sour face, then shrugged as if what *little boys* wanted didn't matter to him at all. He leapt down to the path below. 'I like you, Soren var'Dael,' he declared. 'And you like me. We'll find a way, one day.'

Then he vanished into the dark, leaving Soren confused and disturbed.

Well, I'm wide awake now, he thought ruefully. *There'll be no falling asleep after that.*

Fyn churned with a multitude of thoughts and emotions as he slunk back into camp, not at all pleased. *Too impatient, too aggressive*, he berated himself. *Stupid, stupid, stupid!*

He was heir to a kingdom, even if it was just one tiny upland valley containing fewer than a hundred erlings, most of whom had the intellect of children. Only two dozen or so were worth talking to, and only a handful were the same age. He'd befriended, slept with, then fallen out with them all, over and again, until he was bored witless. Most of them had now chosen their final genders and were starting families; they felt lost to him.

So when Soren had appeared in his woods, with his exotic colouring, urgently kissable lips and tangled black curls, it felt like a prayer had been answered – and he couldn't stop himself from going after the young human like a wolf with blood in its nostrils.

Erlings did marry humans at times; it was frowned on, but not forbidden. *But I'm messing it all up*, he worried. *I'm too aggressive when I'm female and too needy when I'm male.*

It was an old dilemma. Some days he felt male, other female. He made his best decisions when neither, but he hated being neuter. *But maybe that's what I must be, to think this through.*

So he checked that Elindhu was sleeping and the woods were quiet, then closed his eyes and willed the changes, drawing another self from within. *'Jagatai,'* he groaned through the pain, then his voice went half an octave higher, wordless and agonised.

But it was soon over: he was still young enough for it to be relatively easy. He opened his eyes again, neither male nor female but a *tuhana* – and a little more at peace with himself.

This is better, he thought. *If I can't be Soren's lover, I'll be his friend.*

Elindhu woke to the sound of the burbling river. It was morning, someone had re-lit the fire and fish was sizzling gently on the cooking stone. She rubbed grit from her eyes and sat up, blinking in surprise when she realised that Fyn had changed to neuter during the night. Her eyes went to Soren, who was looking bewildered – as he often did around Fyn – but trying to pretend everything was normal.

Young people and their tedious romantic dramas. Elindhu sighed. She'd been through it all when she was that age, done stupid things with other foolish younglings. But she'd had to cast it all aside when the glyma manifested in her. There was no point sharing what she'd learned with these children, though: they'd just tell her she was old and knew nothing.

After breakfast she went to the shore to clean up, and Soren joined her. 'Are you all right?' she asked him, thinking he looked strained and edgy.

'I guess.' He flinched and glanced over his shoulder, at Fyn.

Elindhu took that as permission to give some advice. 'When an erling reaches what you humans call "puberty", they develop the capacity to be male, female or neuter – "tuhana" – at their own will,' she told him. 'It's a difficult period, as they're trying to work out who they are, while being bombarded with competing urges caused by these changes to their body's chemistry. You're going through the same thing, but far more mildly. I will send Fyn away at the first opportunity. It's not fair on either of you to go through this.'

Soren looked both relieved and upset. 'That's probably wise,' he murmured.

'You're mature for your age, Soren,' she said encouragingly. 'I know you're drawn to Fyn, but you're too responsible to get entangled. I'm impressed by that restraint.'

He coloured and mumbled, 'Thank you, Aunty.'

'*Aunty?*' She snorted, a little offended, then she decided it was amusing. 'I suppose I am old enough to be your aunty.' She ruffled his hair and chuckled. 'Come on, Nephew, let's get moving. Romara and Gram need us.'

3

Under Sail

Race and the Order

The Vestal knights are the most powerful military force in the Triple Empire. Originally, they were exclusively Talmoni. Integrating magically gifted Abuthan and Zynochi into the Order – as well as those of subordinate kingdoms like Neparia – was controversial, as most feared that once these nations had their own knights, they would set up rival orders. But that was to ignore the collegiality of the military. Vestal knights invest themselves, body and soul, in the Order. They have no other loyalty.

ROSSLYN MUIRNE, ARCHON, HYASTAR, 1398

Mar-Pelas (Sea of Pelas)
Autumn 1472

Accepting passage on Sergio Landanez's ship meant that Jadyn had to help the crew. The first few days were painful and exhausting as he learned new skills: the ropes blistered his hands, the work exercised muscles he never knew he had and sleep was impossible in the hold, which was crowded and stinking. In the end, he dragged his bedroll to the prow of the ship, hoping he'd be out of the way of the night watch.

Aura promptly joined him, which was disconcerting, but perhaps she didn't trust their shipmates either. For once, she didn't tease him, just rolled herself up in her own blanket and slept. His own mind was too restless, though; he found himself wide awake at midnight, thinking through the events of the past weeks.

Nilis Evandriel wanted them to go to the centre of the world – that was Bedum-Mutaza, surely. But everything else was a mystery, especially the nature of the aegis.

How can I master it if I don't even know what it's supposed to be?

Agynea had said the aegis was a 'state of grace'. Whatever that meant, it did seem to involve short-term precognition, like reading the direction of blows in combat, or the flight of an arrow, or warnings of danger. But the erlings said the breathable lake at Semmanath-Tuhr had been created by the aegis, and that was nothing to do with foresight.

So what exactly is it? Try as he might, he couldn't work it out.

He turned his thoughts to Aura's tale of her time in the Gaudien bastion, and Lictor Borghart's strange interrogations. The lictor had forced her to guess at things like the flip of a coin – when she chose incorrectly, he'd cut her. He'd even blindfolded her and made her walk across a room strewn with broken glass.

He was forcing her to use precognition – so how did he know to do that? Is it because he has the Gift himself?

It was a cold night, and except for a watchman in the stern, no one else was on deck but Aura and him, and she was deep in sleep. He turned to see her tough but pretty face, softened by the moonlight; against his will, he took in the spread of her black hair and the curves of her breasts beneath her blouse as her chest rose and fell. Then he looked away guiltily.

He'd been in love with Romara, of that he felt sure – yet she'd never drawn his gaze as Aura did.

He remembered her turning cartwheels beneath the lake at Semmanath-Tuhr, the joy on her face as she kissed him, setting her hooks in his unwilling flesh. Everything had felt possible in that moment and he'd fallen a little in love. He still was.

But nothing can come of it, he scolded himself. *Think about the aegis, not her.*

Thinking was easier without the glyma-energy inside him, that was one benefit. His mind felt clearer since his body had been purged of that restless power. He re-focused on Borghart's methods and an idea struck him. He drew a dagger, set it on its side and spun it, guessing with his eyes closed the direction it would come to rest in.

To the left of me . . . He called it wrong.

Again . . . Wrong.

Right this time . . .

Wrong again.

He called nine of the first ten wrong, feeling worse than useless – until he saw that getting it *that* wrong wasn't natural. There was a pattern, but he couldn't identify the signs he was basing his guesses on. *It can only be the way the dagger hilt feels coming out of my hand, and the force I've imparted* – but concentrating on those elements increased the randomness; his success rate was now fifty-fifty. He cursed, realising he was confusing himself.

'Jadyn Knight?' Aura yawned, looking up at him and stretching. 'What be doing?'

After he'd explained, she sat up and drew a big Abuthan copper coin from somewhere within her clothes. 'Lion or Fish?' she said, sitting cross-legged and facing him. 'Call.'

In the three hours until the sun came up, they made little progress. Eventually she lost her temper and hurled the coin at his stomach.

His hand flashed out blindly – and he caught it.

'E Cara,' she exclaimed. 'Now you.'

He threw, gingerly . . . and she caught the copper, smirked and hurled it back, hard. Her throw was erratic, but it still smacked into his blistered right palm as he flung it out.

They both gasped, she in excitement and he in pain. But it felt like progress. There was no way he could've anticipated that throw and caught it normally. Perhaps it was tiredness, but he was certain he'd glimpsed pre-images of where the coin was going, and after-images too. He threw the coin back, focusing on how Aura's catching hand seemed to leap from one place to the other in a single blinding instant.

When he pointed that out, she claimed that his hand moved in the same way. 'Faster than the coin,' she mused, her perky face alive with interest. 'Not be offending, but Jadyn Knight is not fast with hands. Not more than other mans, si?'

'I'm not as fast as the top swordsmen,' he admitted.

'But when Jadyn catch coin now, is moving *flash-flash*. Faster than eye can see. Not normal, neya. This be Jadyn dancing with body and soul. Comprendo, neya?'

This was the Aura he most admired, the girl who hurled herself into everything, full of determination and self-belief, uninhibited by doubt. Just as he'd felt during this exercise.

It was a sensation he'd experienced before. 'Listen, at times with Romara, we'd be in battle together and suddenly reach this kind of harmony where I'd know exactly what she intended and match my movements to hers, so that when she opened up someone's guard, I could take advantage, or I could cover her when she attacked. We fought well together.'

'Ah, buena,' Aura exclaimed, 'this come from you, not she, si? She move, you add needful . . . the thrust, the block, si? She act, you . . . what is word? Re-act, si?'

He reflected on that. He'd attributed that special synchronisation to love – but perhaps it was the first vestiges of the aegis awakening in him? Romara had always led, while he'd fitted around her, augmenting her attacks or protecting her . . .

'You're right,' he admitted, trying to ignore the pain thinking of Romara brought. 'And the more I believed in it, the better and more instinctive it became,' he mused.

'Believe in aegis, aegis reward.'

'The aegis isn't aware,' he said flatly.

'Maybe, maybe not? But we are aware, si? Believe, Jadyn Knight,' she said, tapping his chest. '*Believe.*'

By now, the sun was rising and the ship was coming alive, the crew emptying night-waste buckets over the side or standing at the rails and pissing. Those who did notice Jadyn and Aura together in the prow leered at them, but knowing their status – ex-Order and ex-lover of the captain – said nothing.

Jadyn didn't care. This morning, he felt like he'd got back the

Aura he wanted. Her smile warmed him, right through another day of hard sailing, ploughing along the coast towards the rising sun.

One thousand kylos was a long, long way – though it was only one fortieth of the circumference of Coros, or so Elindhu had told Jadyn, one evening. 'We talk about the Triple Empire as if it were the whole world, but Hytal, Zynochia and north Abutha is all we have properly mapped,' she'd said. 'That's about six million square kylos, but the scholars tell us that the surface of Coros is some 160 million square kylos. More than half of that is water, another 30 to 40 million square kylos is ice ... so really, we know about only a quarter of the land. There may be whole nations out there we've never heard of – different civilisations, gods, religions – whole new types of knowledge and history ...'

'Why haven't we found them?' he'd asked, and she'd laughed.

'Because we're terrible sailors.'

Her reasoning was that any ship that sailed more than a few hundred kylos from shore inevitably struck storms and sank, or shambled broken-backed back into port, lesson learned. Land-based exploration had fared a little better, but eastward explorers met Kharagh nomads and were slaughtered, while southbound travellers either ran out of supplies, contracted deadly diseases or vanished into Abutha and never returned.

That was hardly encouraging, Jadyn mused as he hauled on ropes with inexplicable seafaring names under the hawkish eye of Arno Grigio, the sailing master. But it gave him something to think about in between bouts of furious work.

We're averaging a speed of about six knots – that's about ten kylos an hour – during daylight hours ... I guess we can't sail at night off these rocky shores. So we're making roughly one hundred kylos a day ... so ten days to Bedum-Mutaza, if all goes well.

It was the 'if' that troubled him. So much could go wrong – storms, reefs and shoals, lack of wind, too much wind, and worst of all, piracy. The Sea of Pelas was vast, and contained thousands of islands, many too small to be marked on a map, but large enough to harbour the seaborne brigands whose galleys ravaged the shipping lanes.

For the hundredth time that day, he missed his flamberge. But done was done. And the experiments with the aegis had lifted his spirits immensely, despite the lack of sleep. Last night they'd had all kinds of good intentions of making more progress, but had fallen asleep around midnight ... and woken wrapped chastely in each other's arms.

It was four days since they'd left Cap San Yarido, and Sergio's *Duce di Mundi*, which Aura said meant *Duke of the World*, was trundling eastwards at what felt like a crawl. The crew were mostly indifferent to him, and Sergio was treating Aura like a long-lost sister, but the pregnant Marika muttered about 'that Nepari whore' to anyone who would listen. To Jadyn, a veteran of barracks feuds, a flashpoint was inevitable, and with his aegis slowly awakening, he could sense that moment fast approaching.

Today, he realised. *There'll be a crisis, today.*

'Oi, Jerome!' Arno Grigio shouted. 'Oi! *Jerome Baen!* Wake up!'

It took Jadyn a moment to remember that 'Jerome Baen' was him. 'Aye, sir!'

'Three pulls tighter – we're coming about! Pay attention, man!'

He took his place in the rigging, working to keep the mainsail taut as they jibbed to starboard, rounding a little fleet of fishing boats busy hauling in their nets. The other trading vessels accompanying the *Duce* were following their lead.

Everyone was working except Sergio, Aura and the sullen Marika, who were standing together on the bridge. Jadyn glanced their way, troubled by increasingly strong premonitions of danger. Tying off his rope, he headed for the water barrel, dipped a cup and gulped it down.

'Jerome,' Largan Rameleau greeted him. 'A cursed hot day.'

As seneschal of the Falcons, Jadyn had been responsible for morale and discipline, leaving Romara free to strategise. Unlike the Falcons, this thrown-together crew was dysfunctional, split into different cliques. Most were just hirelings who just wanted to get paid and move on, but the core group had been with Sergio a long time. Largan was one of those, the strongest warrior aboard, thanks to the glyma, but his sexuality made him an outsider. Ossamon, his young lover, was the target of the subtle contempt of many.

These things made Largan dangerous to befriend – and dangerous not to.

'Aye, it's a scorcher,' Jadyn replied, handing him the mug. 'These days it's either burning hot or tipping it down.'

Grigio was stalking the main deck, dispensing orders. He glared at Jadyn and would have ordered him back to work, but for Largan's presence. He contented himself with warning, 'Two minutes to the next jib, Baen. Be ready.'

Largan gestured rudely at Grigio's back, then clapped Jadyn on the shoulder. 'It's good to have another ex-knight aboard. Just a shame you didn't keep your flamberge.'

Jadyn pretended regret. 'I do miss that glyma-*jang*.'

'Ah, the *jang*,' Largan purred. 'Better than sex.' Then he guffawed. 'On a bad day.' His eyes strayed to Ossamon. 'Ever had an Abuthan? Men or women, they're like opium, I tell you.'

One of the stranger results of the unification of the Triple Empire was that the three very different cultures had fused – not just coinage, languages and the like, but mores too. In Zynochia and parts of Abutha, homosexuality was acknowledged and accepted, but in the north it wasn't. To break down barriers, successive hierophants brought known homosexuals to court, and even, some whispered, enjoyed their company. Gradually, it became acceptable, at least among the elites in wider society.

Jadyn's own upbringing had been deeply traditional, but he'd known those in the Order who'd faced the same strictures on love and sex as anyone else. 'I joined the Order young, still a virgin,' he replied honestly. 'I took my vows seriously.' His eyes flicked to Ossamon. 'I take it you keep things safe with him?'

Largan's face took on a none-of-your-business expression, then he shrugged. 'I rarely need the glyma these days. I mostly live without it. And you?'

Jadyn shook his head. 'I'm Aura's protector, nothing more. There was someone I was waiting for in the Order, but she died before getting out.'

Largan sighed sympathetically. 'No one escapes the Order unscathed, eh?' He glanced towards the stern. 'What does Aura mean to you, then?'

'She needs a guard, and I need money.'

'What does she want in Bedum-Mutaza?'

Jadyn feigned ignorance. 'She's got some scheme to get rich. She's promised me a cut.'

'That'd make Sergio prick up his ears, for sure.' Largan jerked a thumb at the captain and the two women. 'Some women will put up with three in a bed, but three-way power struggles get bloody, even if things start amicable. Marika fights dirty, and some of the lads will back her. It could get messy.'

'That's what worries me.' Jadyn leaned in. 'What happened in Gaudien?'

Largan gave him an assessing look. 'I don't know for sure, but here's the thing: Aura was fun but toxic. Sergio wanted to go legit, but she was stuck on their old ways. And Gostan – well, he was scum. I don't know who dobbed them in, but they weren't missed. No one's happy to have her back aboard.'

Sadly, that gelled with what Jadyn had guessed – but Aura was different now, or so he hoped. The promise of the aegis and their quest was forcing her to grow up.

'Thanks for that,' he said. 'I'll bear it in mind.'

'I know you say you're just a hireling, but the way you watch her says different,' Largan observed. 'You're besotted – don't deny it. But you need to watch your back.' He clapped Jadyn's shoulder. 'Better yet, watch mine and I'll keep an eye on yours.'

Can I trust that? Maybe. 'Deal,' Jadyn answered.

They nodded to each other in understanding and returned to their respective stations. But Jadyn found himself breathing a little lighter, even if Largan's promise was a ruse to make him lower his guard. The antipathy between Marika and Aura was palpable, and it was going to break out into something bloody, very soon.

*

Never look back. Aura had lived by those three words since before she was old enough to understand them. Nothing good lasted, and when it died, it couldn't be revived. The lessons had been hard-won, in some horrible places.

Yet here she was, back on Sergio's ship, laughing at his jests and marvelling at his plans, even pretending she and Marika were the best of pals, when the bitch had stolen her man. She regretted joining them now, even though Sergio represented their one chance to reach Bedum-Mutaza quickly.

Jadyn and I should just walk away.

There was one good thing, though: she *loved* sailing. She'd never been to sea until she and Sergio purchased their cog two years ago, but she'd fallen in love with the life. So she'd made a pest of herself with Grigio and the others, trying to learn all she could. It'd been her ship as much as Sergio's – that was another thing that rankled about her abandonment. But for now, they were all pretending that didn't matter, either.

'So, there's this fellow in Maratab,' Sergio was enthusing. 'Rich as an Abuthan plutassa. I know his son – we can distribute for him and make a fortune.'

'I want our babies to grow up in a mansion,' Marika purred, stroking his arm. 'With their own nannies and tutors. I want them to have *everything*.'

Aura stifled a yawn, exhausted from the nights exploring the aegis. She knew she was falling a little bit into *corazamora* – love of the heart – with Jadyn. It was a nice feeling. But the betrayal in Gaudien gnawed at her, especially when Sergio prattled on about boring things he'd never used to care about.

Where did my rakish rogue go? she wondered. *When did he change?* And worse: *Was it he who betrayed me in Gaudien?* The more she thought on that, the sicker she felt.

At the last port, Marika had told her, 'Get out of our lives while you still can.'

She'd declined the offer; this part of the coast wasn't safe, so they'd stayed aboard – and were staying alert. She'd identified the most likely threats: Marika often spoke to Uelo, a sly-looking Pelasian with sun-blackened skin, and Leman, a burly Bravanti. She'd pointed them out to Jadyn.

'What are your plans, Aura?' Marika asked. She spoke Talmoni, as her Nepari was poor.

She just wants me to admit that I have none, Aura knew. She couldn't speak of the aegis – but she couldn't remain silent. 'Me? Oh, big plans, si, tresa mucha. But secret, si, too secret for you.'

Marika snorted. 'What? Are you going to rob poorhouses in Mutaza or something?'

Aura bristled, aching to demonstrate that she wasn't just a thieving whore any more, but someone special who Sergio should have *treasured*, not cast aside. 'Neya, te scamaga—'

'Aura, cálmate!' Sergio interrupted. *Calm down.*

Marika smirked and patted her barely swollen belly, secure in her position as Queen of the Captain's Bed. Aura longed to slap the *peradita*, but a tumble of premonitions showed her the consequences: a chain of events that started with a brawl and ended with Jadyn and her hitting the water, wrapped in chains.

She was learning to trust these flashes of insight, so she raised both hands, stepping away. 'You be right. Am fool. Apologetica, si?'

Sergio smiled in relief, while Marika simpered.

It occurred to Aura that maybe she'd pursued a berth on the *Duce di Mundi* not to rekindle her old love affair, but to give it closure. So maybe she should just let the Gaudien affair go, too. *Don't look back.*

Acting on that impulse, she faced Marika. 'I be wishing well with Sergio and bebes. Mucha felicite.' She curtseyed and headed for the stairs, needing to be alone.

But before she reached the deck, the lookout shouted, '*BLACK SAILS! LANDWARD!*'

Every head turned to the north, to see a pair of black-sailed galleys, banks of oars flashing, emerging from a rocky inlet just half a kylo away.

Two ships against our one . . . This is not good.

It was late afternoon and the loose flotilla they'd been sailing with, edging along the barren shore, had become strung out. The nearest ships were now too far away to aid them, if they even wanted to.

A visible shiver of fear ran through the crew. In seconds everyone was on deck, even those who'd been off-duty and slumbering below. Sergio and Grigio were shouting orders, trying to get up speed, while Largan was taking charge of the defences.

Aura's eyes flashed to Jadyn, who'd joined the line of men queuing for the weapons Tonio was distributing. Uelo and Leman, Marika's tame thugs, were lurking nearby.

A skirmish with pirates would be the perfect time to knife someone in the back.

But in the press she couldn't get to Jadyn. Men were collecting weapons, bows and quivers of arrows. Tonio tossed Jadyn a bow, as well as a pathetic hatchet, but gave Uelo and Leman savage-looking cutlasses. Others who could shoot were given bows too, and Largan mustered them all to the stern and forecastle. The *Duce di Mundi* tried to run south, using the tailwind, but the galleys had the same wind, and oars as well, and they were sleeker, built for speed. They bore down on Sergio's ship relentlessly.

'Get below,' Sergio told Marika and Aura.

He'd always tried to protect Aura in such situations, but she'd never been helpless. 'I stay—' Aura began.

Sergio shook his head. 'No – Tonio, get the women below – my cabin.' He grabbed Marika's forearm. 'I don't want to have to worry about you during the fight.' Then he bit his lip. 'If I fall—'

'You won't,' Marika shrilled, seizing and kissing him. 'You fight for our child!'

Sergio's hulking brother appeared, Marika released Sergio and headed belowdecks, while Aura protested again, 'I can fight—'

'No,' Sergio snapped. 'Go with Tonio.'

Seizing her arm, the younger brother growled, 'Come.' He hauled her down the steps, manhandling her with ease, shoving her past the tiny officers' quarters to Sergio's cabin, which was barely big enough to contain the bed that dominated the space. Marika was sitting on it, pale and clearly not wanting Aura here.

She tried to leave again, but Tonio thrust a hand into her chest and shoved her backwards. 'Stay,' he rasped, before slamming the door in her face, locking it and thumping away.

'We'll never escape,' Marika wailed in Talmoni. 'Those galleys are too fast.'

Aura had a sick feeling she was right. She looked about the room for weapons, finding none, but she always had her knives on her. She opened the shuttered window, allowing fresh air in, and giving her a view of the galleys behind them, just a couple of hundred paces away now and closing fast.

Whilst travelling with the Falcons, she'd felt somewhat safe, even at the worst moments, because the Vestal knights were the greatest warriors alive. But Sergio's sailors were an untrained rabble, and the pirates along this coast had a bloody reputation. A brief and ghastly future billowed before her; she didn't need the aegis to see it coming.

'Elysia have mercy,' Marika wailed. 'Better to die than be taken.'

She was probably right.

Aura wavered, then pulled a knife from her sleeve-sheathe, reversed it and offered it to Marika. 'For to protect,' she said. 'Kill self before taking, si?'

The blonde woman gave her a hollow-eyed stare, then took the handle . . .

. . . and the next moment unfolded to Aura in vivid clarity as Marika shoved the gifted blade into Aura's left breast with a savage, vindictive snarl . . .

. . . but she saw it all *before* the blonde woman moved . . .

Jadyn wanted to follow when Aura was dragged to the hatch by the giant Tonio, but Largan was already bellowing orders. He knew as well as Largan that even the glyma might not get them out of this, but a few fire-arrows could make the difference, he thought, as the cook brought up a tripod filled with coals and lit it, while another man started dousing small strips of cloth in cooking oil, then passing them around.

Jadyn took one, knotted it to the shaft of his first arrow, just behind the head. As he tested the pull of the bow he'd just been given, he noticed Uelo and Leman were right behind him.

So, it's to be like that . . .

'Fire-arrows, lads,' Largan shouted. 'Light 'em up and be ready!'

It was infuriating, knowing what was coming but having to wait for the blow, because if he got his retaliation in first, he'd be the one condemned. For now he could see no other way out.

I really shouldn't have thrown away that flamberge . . .

But done was done, and all he could do was hope the trap failed to close. So he nodded thanks to the man who lit his arrow, then drew back his bowstring, knowing that in such close quarters, he mightn't be able to react to any treacherous blows in time . . .

To conceal their attack, they'll stab me as the enemy overwhelm us . . .

They all knew the pirates wouldn't deploy fire-arrows themselves: they wanted the *Duce di Mundi* intact, at least until they got the cargo off. But they'd be well prepared to deal with such a tactic, with water barrels and dousing blankets at the ready. As the enemy ships loomed closer, Jadyn saw the rowing decks were lined with men of every nation, the fighting decks thronged with archers. They too were readying their initial volley; he could hear the voices of their officers carrying across the waves.

'Nock your arrows!' Largan raised his flamberge, which he'd recharged in the last port, and counted, '*Una, dua, treya . . .*' Blazing a bolt of energy upwards, he screamed, '*Fire!*'

Jadyn loosed with the rest, the arrows a hissing flock, arcing and sleeting towards the enemy vessels. The pirates also fired, the flights crossing, as Jadyn sought the Eye of Silence, the mote of calm inside from which one manipulated the glyma. That power was no longer in there, but something else was . . .

It gave him a flood of imagery in one drawn-out moment: the enemy arrows turned to comets, with tails of after-images flowing out behind, and he saw the trajectory of every shaft, where each would strike, and who would go down . . .

One arrow would strike him – he could already see it, jutting from his chest . . .

And behind him, he sensed Uelo's dagger thrust towards his back.

Throwing himself into the dance, his right hand, now free, flashed back, grasped the Pelasian's shirt-front and wrenched. The knife scoured his ribs instead of plunging through, as he jerked Uelo into the path of the approaching arrow, which thudded into the sailor's left arm instead of Jadyn's chest, piercing the bicep and pinning it to Uelo's chest. He howled as the pain and shock hit him, and fell.

Jadyn allowed momentum to carry them both to the deck, dropping beneath the gunwale as the man beside him took an arrow in the eye socket and collapsed. But he kept his gaze on Leman as the dying man fell against him. The ship wallowed as Leman met his gaze, eyes wide and panicked, and staggered backwards.

'Archers,' Largan shouted. 'loose—'

Most weren't listening, still reeling in the aftermath of the pirates' punishing volley. The smell of shit and piss filled the air, and not just from the dead and dying. Jadyn lost sight of Leman in the press and threw his gaze outwards: one galley now had burning sails, but its rowers were still working the oars. The other, unscathed, was closing in. A second volley of arrows flew from it, but they broke upon Largan's glyma-shield.

'Fire again!' the ex-knight roared once more, his voice filled with desperation.

Jadyn got another arrow nocked, picked out a pirate archer and let precognition guide the shot. His shaft pierced the man's throat. His next shot slew another, while Largan fended off another volley.

Then the first galley shipped oars and a dozen grappling hooks were hurled over the sides of the *Duce di Mundi*. Some fell short, but three flew over the top and crunched into bodies or timber. Largan shrieked at his men to cut the ropes, but more hooks flew and this time, four more stuck.

Jadyn grabbed his hatchet and hacked at one, then, sensing danger, sent the back of his axe-head into Leman's jaw and broke it – even as the Bravanti tried to drive his cutlass into Jadyn's back. The would-be assassin collapsed, his blow unstruck.

'*Jagat, sorry!*' Jadyn exclaimed, pretending it was all an accident, then he finished chopping through the grappling rope and the line fell away. But the others remained, and moments later the sides of the two ships slammed together and a screaming wave of pirates tried to swarm aboard.

Aura had no time to avoid Marika's vicious blow, even forewarned. In horrified denial she shrieked *No!* inside her mind – and it was as if everything stopped but her. She knew that wasn't what actually happened; instead, like the way the coins she and Jadyn had been throwing at each other with increasing speed had flown in slow motion to their sight, she had pulled free from the bounds of normal time and space.

She used that freedom to twist violently from Marika's stabbing blade, still barely evading the blow, then the bigger woman's shoulder slammed into her. The impact threw Aura back, her head cracked against the bed knob, then a flailing hand gripped her throat. Through dazed eyes she saw Marika's face red with fury, and the knife flashing down again.

Her hand blurred and caught Marika's wrist, but her windpipe was now clamped shut and another vision hit her, of dying right here, right now.

But she also saw the way the ship was about to pitch as men above howled and roared and arrows thudded into timbers and bodies, and how it would cause Marika's weight to lift. As it happened, Aura got her pinned left leg free and drove her knee into the other woman's groin. Marika howled, her grip slipped and Aura wrenched free, twisting the Vorska's wrist as she snaked on top and slammed her forearm into Marika's throat.

The dagger spilled to the floor and Aura, fuelled by rage and fear, threw herself howling into keeping her attacker pinned down, crushing her throat. Marika's face went purple, her eyes bulging in panic. She thrashed desperately, but swiftly weakened . . .

Jagat, she's pregnant, Aura suddenly remembered.

She seized Marika's hair, pulled the stiletto from her chest sheath and sank the tip into the Vorska's breast, drawing blood and yelling, 'Stop, *now!*'

Marika went rigid.

'For bebe, you live,' Aura told her. 'Comprenda? Is *only* for bebe.'

Marika whimpered, then choked out, 'Yes, understood.'

Aura pushed her face into the other woman's. 'Be listen! *Aura not want Sergio now*. He be yours, si? Not rivalling! Don't care! Comprenda?'

Marika blinked in surprise, then nodded meekly. 'I'm sorry. I just love him so much.'

No she doesn't, she's just leech, Aura thought. *But she's scared.*

Then they both froze, hearing and feeling another ship scrape alongside. There was a ragged cry, then dozens of bodies hit the port side of the ship . . .

Jadyn felt like he'd stepped into another reality in which images blurred, past and present in a shifting dance where every foe's attempted blow was slow and obvious. The grappling hook he'd pulled free he used to crush the skull of the first man up, then his hatchet took the next hand to grip the ledge, while he fished blindly but precisely behind him, snatched up Leman's cutlass and blocked a blow he'd barely seen coming, his riposte opening the attacker's throat in a spray of blood. On either side, screaming men spat hatred and terror, but moments later the attack fell apart as Largan blasted energy through the pirates' commander – and suddenly it was the invaders themselves hacking at the grappling ropes. The ships heaved apart, the rowers trying to get them moving – until a great wave crashed the ships together again and the sturdy hull of the *Duce di Mundi* shattered the long oars into splinters, causing havoc.

'Archers!' Largan shouted again, blasting fire into the sails of the wallowing galley. The *Duce di Mundi*'s crew retrieved arrows and bows and slaughtered more rowers, then their sails caught the breeze again and the ships pulled apart.

The second galley was already shipping oars and turning away, while Sergio's crew roared in triumph. Four wounded pirates were dragged to the edge, had their throats slashed and were hurled overboard, along with nine of their dead shipmates, while wounded defenders pleaded for aid. The cook apparently knew some healing, though that wasn't a lot. Those dying died, still begging. Jadyn managed to staunch one man's chest wound, though his eyes remained on Leman and Uelo in case they remained a threat. But the former was still unconscious and the latter was lying with his arm pinned by the arrow in his side, bleeding, but not fatally wounded.

Jadyn made his way over and knelt, made sure Uelo knew it was him, then said cheerily, 'Let's see what we can do for you, eh?'

Ignoring the terror in the man's face, Jadyn snapped the head off the arrow, then pulled the shaft back through the man's arm, while looking him in the eye. 'Shouldn't be fatal,' he murmured. 'But who knows?' he added, almost as an afterthought.

The Pelasian knew exactly what he was saying. His eyes trawled to Leman. 'Is—?'

'He'll live. Won't be eating solids for a while, though. Shall I tell Largan what you and he tried to do?'

'He ... won't ... believe ...' Uelo gasped.

'Yes, he will. He doesn't like you, and he and I are Order.' He grabbed the man's arm and began wrapping it with a scarf he'd pulled from a dead man's neck. 'This will stop the blood, but you need to wash it in boiling water or it'll be blood-poisoning will take you, not me.'

The man broke, sobbing, 'I'm sorry—'

'Don't draw attention to yourself,' Jadyn muttered, rising.

He headed to the lower middle deck, joining Largan, who was watching the two galleys. The first was now ablaze and most of the crew were swimming after the other vessel, which, to someone's credit, had actually heaved to and was waiting for them. Those pirates who couldn't swim were clinging to the burning wreckage as it broke apart, screaming for help.

Just villagers, Jadyn guessed, *probably forced to join the crew at swordpoint.* Then he saw a big fin carving through the water at speed – and a swimmer vanished. The remaining men started thrashing about in panic as more sharks closed in. It was a mercy that the *Duce di Mundi*'s sails were filling and the ensuing horror soon faded into the distance.

'Happens nearly every journey now,' Largan growled. 'It didn't use to, but the vyr rebellion is making the pirates bolder.'

Explaining that the rebels were in the right wouldn't end well, so Jadyn just muttered, 'Most of them didn't know what they were doing,' and turned away – to see Aura emerging from the cabins below. Her face was flushed, her throat bruised and she looked furious. He closed the distance and hugged her before any other thought crossed his mind, and for a moment they just clung together. 'Are you all right?' he breathed in her ear.

She whispered, 'Marika try kill.'

He stiffened. 'Is she dead . . . ?'

'Bitch deserve, but neya. Aura be merciful. No slip throat.'

'Slit,' he corrected.

'Si, that.' She looked up at him. 'Eya tu?'

'I saw all the dangers coming – the aegis showed me how to survive.'

Her eyes lit up. 'For me also. Am Magic Girl.' She stroked his arm and winked at him. 'With Magic Knight guardian. How lucky Aura be.'

For a moment, he felt like he was alone with her in Paradise. All round them, their fellow sailors were slapping backs and embracing in the relief of aftermath, some already boasting of their deeds. He let it all wash over him. There was only her.

Then a sweating Sergio bustled in. 'Mia bella, com es ta?' he asked her, arms spread as if to pull her from Jadyn to himself. In several future flashes, Jadyn punched him, *hard* – but he didn't need to.

Aura remained in his arms, saying, 'Essa buena, grafia. Marika altra, c'en dormito. Ir'a ella, Sergio. Tengo a mia cabellero.'

Sergio's face fell and for a moment he looked like a lost boy, then he glanced at Jadyn before hurrying away, visibly cowed.

'What did you say?' Jadyn asked.

'Aura say: "Your woman below, go to her. Aura has her knight."'

The prick thinks he can have both of them, Jadyn thought disgustedly. He couldn't imagine the ego required to think oneself so irresistible. But Aura was here, with him. 'I thought you still loved him?' he asked tentatively.

She shook her head sadly. 'No. Not love. Just be sadding.'

'You told me once you'd either reclaim him as your own, or cut his throat.'

She smiled at the recollection. 'Si. Have dagger sharp. But mercy also be cruel.'

Ah, I see . . . 'Jadyn be liking this,' he murmured. 'Be better way.'

Why he chose to mimic her speech patterns he had no idea. Pure stupidity, as it turned out, because her eyes lit up dangerously. 'Is Jadyn Knight *teasing* Aura?' she asked. 'Careful, Jadyn Knight. Men who tease be teased. Not be war you win, am thinking.'

He went to reply when she put her hand over his genitals and squeezed. His whole body and brain froze while his face suffused with crimson.

'See?' she said airily. 'Jadyn never win tease battle. Aura is mistress of tease.'

Then she giggled and sashayed away, leaving him in speechless mortification.

Largan clapped him on the shoulder. 'Well, I wouldn't want to take you on with a blade, Jerome. But she can disarm you pretty damned easily.' He laughed broadly, then dropped his voice, and said, 'Problem solved?'

Jadyn met his gaze. 'For now.'

But maybe the next try won't be so obvious?

Qor-Espina, Neparia

Yoryn Borghart growled in triumph as the low cloud and murk clinging to the mountain peaks gave way, revealing the ridgeline ahead, with the stone circle he sought silhouetted against the sky. 'This is it,' he told Vazi Virago, nudging his horse into motion again. 'It's the place Romara Challys mentioned in her confession.'

The Exemplar's flawless copper face turned his way. 'Tell me of it again.'

'About a week ago, we had the Falcons trapped here. We

charged – there was a flash of light, and they vanished, leaving just a few pieces of baggage.'

'They just vanished?' Vazi wrinkled her shapely nose. 'In a burst of light?'

'I know: impossible. I suspect it's actually a portali gate. We weren't close enough to see how they opened it, but Romara told me under the opiate-questioning that it has to happen at sunset, when light strikes it.'

Vazi fiddled with her headdress – she'd removed her helmet and wrapped a scarf over her head and hair in an elegant Zynochi style – and contemplated the scene. 'Are you sure this is where they first triggered the aegis in themselves?'

'It could have been earlier,' Borghart admitted, 'but the only other possibility I'm aware of is Semmanath-Tuhr, the erling valley. We'll try that next, if this doesn't work out.'

'An erlhaafen? We'll not achieve anything there without an army.'

'I'm confident this is the place we need.' Borghart took the lead again. They were close enough to make out the eight stone thrones set at the primary compass points. 'As the sun sets, light should pass through the lens at the top of the seats – that's when the gate opens.'

'Did it occur the next day?'

'We didn't know about it, so we didn't stay to find out. The Solabi century-commander escorting us wanted to leave, nothing made sense and we were low on supplies. It was days before I finally scryed them again and tracked them to Vanashta Baanholt.'

She swung from her saddle. 'Negligent, Lictor. I'd thought better of you.'

The criticism was just. 'Not my finest moment. I let disappointment cloud my thinking.'

'Then let us hurry.' She glanced west. 'We have only half an hour or so before sunset. Let's use it well.'

She was half Borghart's age, but had a manner that subordinated others effortlessly. He caught himself resolving to impress her as they entered the stone circle, going from throne to throne, noting the Leafman-faces and the glass-filled holes on the backrests.

It was Vazi who made the vital discovery. 'These symbols!' she exclaimed, pointing at the runes carved into the armrests, where the hands would lie. 'Jadyn Kaen had them etched into his palms – I would swear the Nepari woman did too, though I saw her only at a distance.'

Just then, the sun broke through the cloud to the west and instantly a beam of light flowed from the western throne through the glass hole on the backrest and struck the foot of the opposite throne.

It wasn't logic but intuition that guided them. Without needing to speak, they somehow *knew* what to do. Borghart strode to the western throne and sat, while she took the eastern one opposite him, a dozen paces away, seated like some ancient Goddess of Wisdom as the beam crawled upwards. *It's a lens*, he realised, as the circle of light moved up her body, then lit her face so that it shone.

It struck the opposite lens, shooting beams of light around the circle, then the whole world *flashed*, a livid white blaze – and agony *shrieked* through him, his whole body jolting rigid as energy gripped him, harder than the glyma ever had.

He pitched forward and fell into darkness.

4

Prisoner

Lictors and Justice

When the judicial arm of the Vestal knights was formed, using former mages and knights to investigate heresy, the hierarchy feared giving them unlimited power. No one wanted the lictors overstepping their authority. One way to control them was to institute mandatory trials for anyone accused of heresy. That is why the rewards for bringing a Fallen knight, draegar or vorlok to trial are so great. Despite this, many lictors prefer to kill rather than capture. Presumably those are the flimsiest cases.

JUSTICE AND THE ORDER, YARMON GALBRAYTHE, IMPERIAL
SCHOLAR, 1428

*Qor-Espina, Neparia,
Autumn 1472*

Romara drifted out of a bad dream to find herself still tied on the horse. By the angle of the sun, only a few minutes had passed since her last flirtation with awareness. She wished she'd stayed unconscious longer.

They'd been riding all day, her wounds were leaking and her head was pounding. Her buttocks and back were shrieking due to her enforced bad posture and her stomach was a ravenous void. Gram, just a few yards away, looked little better.

She must have groaned, because the nearby men-at-arms, soldiers of the Golden Dragon century, turned to peer at her with pitiless curiosity, but offered no aid.

Someone ahead ordered a halt as they emerged from the trees into a glade beside a stream. Despite the pain racking her body, she noticed that neither the Exemplar nor Lictor Borghart appeared to be with them. For some reason an obese grey-haired magus, presumably Arghyl Goraghan, was leading the column.

Tevas Nicolini appeared, untied her and helped her dismount, before carrying her into the undergrowth, wrenching down her trousers and gruffly telling her to purge.

Humiliated, but grateful it was him, she did as commanded, dropping to her haunches while he averted his gaze just enough to remain alert to anything she might try. She still had the magic-deadening manacles on, the rune *Ruqaz* carved on the iron cuffs, presumably empowered by Goraghan. He'd be bleeding energy because of it, though that was of no consolation, because she was powerless.

'You're as much a piece of shit as what I just passed,' she growled at Tevas as he redressed her.

'Good to see you, too,' Tevas replied sadly. 'What happened to you, Rom?'

'Regulation 17: don't question a vyr,' she snarled back.

'Jag off.' Tevas faced her squarely, his face bleak. 'I never thought you'd fall.'

She tried to see if looks really could kill. It didn't work.

'What happens next?' she asked. 'Surely Elan doesn't want me to testify?'

'He doesn't care; nothing you can say will stop him taking your family's estates.'

Painfully, that was probably true. 'They're going to torture me, you know – for the crime of falling.'

'For the crime of being a draegar,' Tevas rasped back.

'That wasn't my choice,' she told him. 'Once I lost control of the glyma, it just happened – as it could happen to you.' She dropped her voice. 'Kill me – Gram too. Please, Tevas! For the sake of friendship.'

He looked at her pityingly, shaking his head. 'Sorry, Rom, but if I did that, I'd be putting my own head on the block. I can't do that.'

Predictable, but it'd been worth a try. Only the inner serenity that Gram had placed inside her soul kept her from breaking down completely.

'Here's the plan,' Arghyl Goraghan said. 'We'll head for my kin in Foyland – we've got a portali gate local, see, an ol' erling place. Damn useful it's been, I tell thee.'

I bet it has, Tevas thought. *A secret way into the Shadowlands would be priceless.*

The Order tried to claim control of every gate, but many – perhaps most – remained outside their control, particularly in Foyland, a former powerbase of the Sanctor Wardens and, before them, the erlings.

'That way, we'll elude our pursuers,' the magus went on.

Elan gave him a startled look. 'Someone's chasing us?'

Goraghan made a casually dismissive gesture. 'Some little mouse has been tickling my veil spells,' he chuckled. 'A mouse I think I can name: Elindhu Morspeth.'

So the Moorhen survived, Tevas mused. He remembered what he'd seen at Vanashta Baanholt, and what he'd heard later: that Elindhu had changed shape in the fray – that she was an erling. It sounded incredible, but the witnesses had been adamant. A woman he'd known on and off for years, one he'd regarded as a pleasant, if bumbling, creature, had been a cuckoo in the Order's nest all along.

I'm told she all but killed this fat fool, he thought, gazing at Goraghan. 'Is it just her?' he asked. 'Why not let her catch up and set a trap for her?'

The obese Foyle shook his head. 'In my land, we don' give de old folk offence. Dey haunt de wilds, ye know – an' dey can put your eye out with an arrow from two hundred paces. We'll just get out, quick-smart.'

It sounded farfetched – everyone knew the erlings were a dying race who always gave ground and never fought. But Tevas also remembered the air of sullen menace as they'd passed through Semmanath-Tuhr.

'Fair enough. Let's get home safe.'

*

The pursuit of Romara's captors became a race. Fynarhea ran in wolf form, forging ahead, seeking scents. The magia reverted to her lithe erling form, growing more than a foot and running smoothly, leaving Soren to dig into his glyma reserves to keep up.

That evening, they found a clearing full of trampled pasture gnawed to its roots, abandoned cooking fires and discarded rubbish. The Vestals hadn't even bothered covering over their shitting holes.

'They're in a hurry,' Elindhu observed. 'They know we're coming.'

'Surely they aren't afraid of us, Aunty?' Soren asked, not quite looking at her; in erling form her clothing, which was fitted to her plump human body, left her legs bare to the thigh, not to mention a disconcerting amount of shoulder, back and chest. She might be fifty or so, but she was a dauntingly fine sight.

She gave him a knowing look, then flowed into her 'Aunty' shape, her silvery hair knotting itself with bewildering precision into its normal tower of braids as she shrank and widened into the woman he was more familiar with – and more comfortable around.

'I'd like to think that I gave Arghyl Goraghan a fright, back at Vanashta Baanholt,' she chuckled. 'They're probably running away from us.'

'Don't forget I wounded the Exemplar's arm,' Soren boasted. 'They're running scared.'

They shared a laugh as a wolf appeared on the opposite side of the clearing, rearing onto hind legs while pulling its own hide off in a smooth gesture that revealed a gory display of muscles, veins and organs, until human skin flowed over, covering it. Fynarhea's face reformed last, her skull going from lupine to human. She'd chosen to be female again.

She stalked up to Soren. 'You have my clothing?' she asked, looking him in the eye.

He kept his gaze on those amber orbs to avoid seeing her body, although that meant letting her eyes bewitch him, instead. 'Uh, yeah,' he gulped, flipping the pack from his sweaty back and offering it. Half-turned away, he asked, 'Are the enemy far ahead?'

'A day, at most,' she replied. 'We're catching them.'

'Their horses are of little advantage in this hilly terrain,' Elindhu observed, eying the two young people with a kind of disapproving amusement. 'Clothing, Fynarhea. We mustn't catch a chill.'

She stuck her chest out and said, 'No danger. I'm all sweaty from running.' She took the pack and sashayed away.

Soren felt his cheeks sear.

'I see you're in no danger of getting cold, either,' Elindhu noted drily. 'Do we need to have a talk?'

'Uh, no, Aunty.'

She patted his arm. 'Stay away from her, Soren.'

His eyes refused to leave Fynarhea's enticing backside. She was heading for the stream that ran through the dell and it occurred to him that cold water might feel wonderful on his over-heated skin.

'You're not going to stay away, are you?' Elindhu observed drily.

'I . . . uh . . .' *I don't know that I can.*

She sighed and indicated a fallen tree, pulling him along and making him sit beside her. Her big-nosed face filled his sight, her amber eyes disturbingly like Fynarhea's.

'Lad, most young erlings blow hot and cold, capricious as spring gales. They aren't ruled by thought, just urges. You saw Fyn a couple of days ago, swearing off being male *or* female, resolving to let you be. She's already forgotten that. She's ovulating and all she wants is to be ploughed. But if you couple with her, in the moment of your release, glyma-energy will boil out of you as if you'd cast a battle-spell upon her. You will ruin her womb for life, and possibly kill her. You don't want that and neither does she, but right now she can't think straight. That's why you must think for her.'

He bowed his head. 'Of course, Aunty.'

Elindhu smiled with sad kindness. 'You're a good lad, Soren. Obanji would be proud.'

Soren gulped; his sight blurred. 'I miss him . . .'

'I'll miss him all my life,' Elindhu replied, in a cracked whisper.

He put his arm around her and for a time they weren't knight-initiate and magia, human and erling, or even young man and mature woman; they were just two people sharing the same grief. Elindhu in human form was small, but she had a gentle warmth that reminded him of his Abuthan mother, for all they were utterly unalike.

I've missed having someone to hold me when I'm sad. Perhaps Elindhu feels the same.

Eventually, he looked up to see Fynarhea, fully clothed now, her wolf-pelt tied round her neck, pouting at them. 'Oh, so you cuddle up with her, but won't look at me,' she growled.

'Don't be silly, dear,' Elindhu said tiredly. 'We were thinking about those we've lost.' She eyed the erling with narrowed eyes. 'Are you here to help us, or must I send you home?'

Fynarhea flared and then faltered. 'No, you *can't* send me away—'

'Then don't give me reason to.'

She bowed her head, and muttered, 'Sorry. I'm just . . .'

'We know.' Elindhu patted her shoulder. 'I remember what it was like, darling, I really do. Come, let's just take a deep breath and cool down, mmm? Then we'll make camp.'

'Dey're still follerin' us,' Arghyl Goraghan said, 'but dey're nay closer.'

Elan Sandreth glanced behind him anyway, unsettled to know that anyone with the glyma was pursuing them. Such a threat couldn't be measured by numbers: glyma-knights and mages were capable of stealth and deadly attacks that only those like them could counter, meaning he still needed Goraghan and Tevas Nicolini's protection. But he didn't entirely trust either of them.

He was also profoundly nervous of Romara and the hulking brute beside her. Even though they were wounded and manacled, he'd seen them at Vanashta Baanholt: deformed freaks who could break a man in two. *I hate that these damned animals have such power. It's not fair.* It was galling to need a bondsman to protect him from such beasts, but he was glad Nicolini was there; even if he did have a troubling past with Romara Challys.

'How do you know they're following us?' he asked Goraghan.

'Scryin' an' spyin', she are,' the Foylish magus grunted. 'It's de erling witch, Elindhu.'

She almost killed him, Elan remembered. *He's genuinely afraid.* 'We need to get home without being overtaken,' he reminded the magus. 'Getting Romara and that damned vorlok to Folkstein is all that matters.'

I'll get my share of the bounty, make sure they kill her, then claim her estates.

'I've nay forgotten,' Goraghan growled, checking the column of mounted men-at-arms, strung out under low, misty clouds that swallowed the heights above and the depths below. They'd reached the borderlands of Foyland now, and everyone was wary.

'What's the plan?' Elan pressed him.

'Simple enough,' Goraghan replied. 'Dere's a portali gate near where I grew up, in a sacred wood. We go dere an' walk de shadow paths to Folkstein.' He looked at Elan. 'Have ye used a portali afore?'

Elan remembered Yoryn Borghart leading him through an ominous landscape of mist and rocky peaks, utterly lifeless but for ghostly voices in the fog. It has been a chilling place, but they'd traversed hundreds of kylos in a few hours. If that put them beyond pursuit, he was willing to chance it again. 'Once, a month or so ago. Borghart took me through.'

'Den ye ken dem. Good. Me lads have walked de Shadowlands afore too. We'll be fine.'

'When will we reach this gate?' Elan asked.

'Three days,' Goraghan replied. 'Den I'll 'ave to persuade me kin to let us in de gate.'

'Will they?'

'I don't care. If dey get in me way, I'll beat da shit outta dem.'

Elan grinned. 'Sounds like my family.'

'Oh, much worse, Milord. Much worse.'

The Golden Dragon century crossed into Foyland without incident or fanfare. There were no border markings, no milestones and no one in sight as they topped a ridge and descended through forest, over rocky outcroppings and across torrential rivers. Dew and mist clung to every blade of grass, and moss grew everywhere in the permanent damp. Ruins dotted the landscape, but they saw no living people. Foyland was a place of decay and collapse, and had been for centuries.

The Sanctor Wardens arose here, Tevas mused. *Vestals haven't ever been welcome.*

He'd been left in charge of running the century, more or less, because Goraghan knew little about actually soldiering, Elan Sandreth knew nothing at all, and the only glyma-knight was the initiate, Bern Myko, a wet-behind-the-ears boy. Tevas worked diligently with Centurion Prade, knowing the Order was hated here, like all outsiders. The Foylish were insular, warlike and xenophobic. He feared ambush, despite Goraghan's assurances.

What's his standing here, anyway? Tevas wondered. *Hero or turncoat?*

Then his eyes went to Romara as she passed by, still manacled and slumped painfully in the saddle. Gram Larch, behind her, was unconscious, his shoulder wound turning septic – but he needed to survive a day or two longer, that was all, so he could be delivered to the bastion in Folkstein and the bounty could be collected.

If we make it.

On a whim he drew his mount in beside the man leading Romara's horse, told the man to take a break and took the reins. 'Rom,' he murmured, 'can you hear me?'

She looked up, her eyes glazed. 'Tevas?' she mumbled. With an effort she roused herself, taking in sodden landscape and blustery skies. 'Where are we?'

'The borders of Foyland,' He nodded towards Gram Larch. 'Who's he to you?'

She followed his gaze and emitted a distressed gasp at the state of the big man. 'Gram?'

'Did that bastard turn you into a vyr?' Tevas asked. Rumour had that if one bit you – or screwed you – then you'd become like them. 'How did it happen?'

'I'm alive because of him,' she answered dazedly. 'Please, let me help him.'

'No chance.'

'You've got to clean those wounds,' she told him fearfully. 'Please, Tevas.'

That told him everything about her and Larch. She loved him, which was somewhat earth-shaking. Romara had been in love with Jadyn Kaen most of her adult life.

'He's better off dying,' he told her frankly. 'It'll spare him the torture table.'

'If he dies, so do I,' she said in a low voice. 'Gram and I now share a heart.'

'With that animal?' She sounded delusional to Tevas. 'You chose him over Jadyn?'

She flinched, her face filled with what looked like real pain and remorse. 'Jadyn and I had to let it go. There's only Gram for me now. It's called ninneva: we have perfect glyma control because of that bond.' She met his eyes. 'It's deeper than love.'

She means it, he sensed. Her soul was bared, as was her hopeless love for this vorlok man. Oddly, his contempt evaporated. 'Jagat,' he breathed. 'I'm sorry. I thought you and Jadyn would make it through, if anyone did.'

Tears welled up and ran down her cheeks. 'So did I.'

He swallowed, a little overcome by all they'd once meant to each other – he, Romara and Jadyn. *But now he's a renegade and she's a vyr*, he thought bleakly. *Nothing good lasts.*

'You're better off if he dies and it drags you down with him, then,' he said brusquely, disengaging his emotions. 'Just don't die 'til we get paid.'

She gave him a pitying look, as if he were the one who had fallen.

Just then, a mounted scout came hammering into the clearing and Tevas, fearing a sudden attack, flung Romara's reins to her guard and went to hear his report.

'At ease, lad,' Goraghan was saying. 'What's ahead?'

'There's a ford across a big river, and a warband guarding the far bank,' the scout panted. 'Foylish warriors – at least two hundred. Their banner's got a red badger on it.'

Tevas looked at Goraghan. 'An enemy clan?'

'Worse,' Goraghan guffawed. 'Dat's me family, waitin' to give us a big hug.'

An hour later, the Golden Dragons were lined up facing the river, a hundred paces or more wide, but shallow and easily forded, according to the mage. On the far side was the horde of Foylish warriors, clad in furs or bare-chested, their bodies painted with crude green whorls, hair teased up with what looked suspiciously like dried blood. They were all waving spears and axes, and many had bows too, enough to cause some serious damage. Some – the leaders – wore bronze torcs and brandished longswords.

'What now?' Tevas asked. 'Do we go around them or through?'

Elan shrugged and looked at Goraghan, who was chuckling darkly. 'Let's 'ave a parley, first, eh. Dis'll either be a whoppin' party or a bloodbath. Or maybe both.'

He nudged his mount ahead to the edge of the river, raised his elobyne-tipped staff, making the crystal glow, and raised his voice. 'Oi, Grenfel Goraghan, ye fat slug! Ye want me to pull your heart out through yer arsehole? Or ye gonna lay out the beer and beef an' make yer brother welcome, as ye should?'

In response, a big man lumbered out, shouting, 'Dat ye, Arghyl? Avast an' abide, ye stinkin' pile o' shite! Ye've gotta a jaggin' nerve comin' back 'ere!'

5

The Heart of the World

The Cradle of Civilisation

Talmont is the supreme power of the modern age; but that is a recent thing.
Civilisation spread north from Zynochia and Abutha, and the first great northern
power was Aquinium, from whom the north took its concept of culture. Talmoni
is an Aquini dialect, and architecture in Petraxus is adapted from southern
designs. New empires are built on the debris of older ones.

INCHALUS SEKUM, SCRIBE TO THE CALIPH OF MUTAZA, 1469

Bedum-Mutaza
Autumn 1472

The *Duce di Mundi* had suffered minor damage and lost a few crew
members, but fighting off the pirates changed the atmosphere on
board for the better. The camaraderie of survival and triumph, not
to mention the prowess Jadyn had displayed, earned respect. And
Marika, clearly cowed by Aura, kept away. Days slipped by in peace
and Jadyn began to take more notice of the journey itself.

The southern Bedumassa coast was legendary, the scene of ancient
wars, love stories and heroic tales, with a castle on virtually every
headland and a port in every cove. But most of the keeps were ruined
and the ports abandoned: history might have been made here, but
power and prosperity had moved on.

What stood out now were the beached ships littering the har-
bours and the miasma of smoke from the dung-fires of refugee
camps. 'They're Pelasians, fleeing the islands,' Sergio announced,

after quizzing some passing fishermen. 'There's been earthquakes and tidal waves in the isles, and now people are afraid the volcanoes will blow.'

All of humanity is on the move, Jadyn thought. He wondered how these uprooted people could possibly survive on Bedumassa's desolate coast. It felt like an unfolding disaster . . . or the End of All Things.

What would hopefully be their final night at sea began with a blood-red sky, auguring fine weather the next day, as they anchored off Cap Haluud, where a Bedumi fortress and naval base protected the approach to the fabled Jaws of Leos, the straits to the Sea of Erath. The sea was discoloured by the red dust of the Inner Seas, but the skies were clear and the already risen moon shimmered. Villagers rowed out to them and the other anchored ships, selling Bedumi yellow rice, spiced rum and arak.

'Well, Sier Jerome, we'll reach Bedum-Mutaza tomorrow,' Largan commented, settling beside Jadyn. 'Have you been there before?'

'Never,' he said truthfully. 'What's it like?'

The former Vestal knight had been seeking him out regularly since the pirate attack, apparently in friendship, but he'd asked plenty of probing questions about his service in the Order, places he'd served, and names of past comrades he might know, as if scratching away at his story. Lying required a good memory, Jadyn was finding.

'What's Bedum-Mutaza like?' Largan grinned. 'It's a vice-laden cesspit – every sin you could imagine is for sale, along with all the gold and grain of the Caliphates – and opium, of course. Lots of that. It's my favourite place in all of Coros.'

Jadyn was somewhat shocked. 'Surely the hierophant's had it cleaned up?'

Largan snorted. 'Hardly. The rich and powerful are above all laws, and the opium and vice trade are the foundation of their wealth anyway, so they'll never give those up. And every four years the hierophant's court rolls in, and all his courtiers want is to go wild. This city is insane – the western side, Bedum, anyway. Mutaza is more traditional.'

Jadyn's eyes strayed to Aura, perched on a bulwark listening to

Sergio reminisce. It sounded like she'd be well at home in this city, but he was filled with trepidation. 'Where I grew up, having a third ale was riotous behaviour.'

Largan chuckled darkly. 'You need to live more, Jerome. I'll show you around. It's the oldest capital of the Three Empires – some even call it the Heart of the World.'

For a second, Jadyn wondered if Largan had guessed his quest, but he schooled his features and replied as a devout Akkanite should, 'Petraxus is the Heart of the World.'

Largan grunted dismissively. 'Before the rise of Talmont, there were three empires: the Aquini, the Bedumi and the Mutazi. Fearing the Aquini navy, the Bedumi and the Mutazi united and made Bedum-Mutaza their capital. They defeated the Aquini at sea and on land, and dominated the next two centuries. They built the great domes in honour of their gods, forged trading links with the northern Abuthi and claimed dominion over the known world.'

That wasn't the history Jadyn had been taught. 'The *Book of Lux* says they were decadent and weak?'

'By the time Jovan Lux founded the Order, the Bedumi and Mutazi were in decline,' Largan agreed. 'He could have invaded, sure, but Jovan was a genius: instead of pursuing an unending, unwinnable war, he sought peace and alliances with the southern elites. Now his descendants rule three empires. War isn't the only way to conquer, you know.'

'I suppose,' Jadyn replied, playing the blinkered Talmoni. 'But is it safe for a northerner?'

'Is anywhere truly safe?'

'Fair point,' Jadyn acknowledged. 'So, what's there to see?'

'Well, if your taste doesn't run to opium dens and belly-dancers – and I can't believe that of any man – there's the Grand Bazaar, where you can buy every kind of food, drink, entertainment or vice known to man. If you want grand buildings, there are seventeen domus religio here, including the Hejiffa Dhouma on the Mutazi side, which is stunning if you like heathen art and architecture. The inside has a mosaic that maps the known world.' He grinned wryly. 'With Bedum-Mutaza at the centre, of course.'

The centre of the world ... Jadyn's heart thumped. *That's where we need to go.*

'What about the Order?' he asked. 'Is there a strong presence?'

'Keen to see our former brothers and sisters?' Largan asked wryly. 'Or to avoid them?' He raised a placating hand. 'You don't have to say. There's a bastion in the new imperial quarter on the Bedumi shore.' He thought for a moment. 'Come to mention it, the hierophant's due shortly, so the city will be in ferment. There's always a massive influx of folk seeking to profit from direct access to the court. You'll be lucky to find a bed.'

Jadyn glanced at Aura, still chatting to Sergio in the bow. 'We'll manage.'

Largan frowned, then pulled out a handful of coin. 'Here, take these. They'll purchase your first meal – no, it's the least I can do. There's a hostel called *Dera's Hope* in Bedum, north of the port, where it's clean and safe.'

Jadyn hated accepting charity, but he took the coins gratefully and shook Largan's hand. 'Thank you – and best wishes go with you, too,' he said. 'Akka be with you.'

'Come on, amoretta mia, tell me,' Sergio was saying, speaking their native Nepari, fixing Aura with his most beguiling look. 'What are you really doing in Bedum-Mutaza, eh? Do you need help? Anything you need, I can give.'

While it was good to speak her own language regularly, and even to be called *my little love* again, Aura felt Sergio wasn't really interested in helping her. Quite clearly, he liked the idea of being a father and leading a law-abiding life.

He wants me gone, and I want to go. It was sad, but it was time to part ways.

'It's nothing,' she told Sergio. 'Nothing of value to you.'

'I don't believe you!' He rubbed fingers and thumb together. 'You love gold – you always have a scheme.'

'There is a prize,' she admitted, 'but it's not riches.' Her eyes turned towards Jadyn, who was talking intently to Largan. 'No one can gain from it, but me.' *And my knight.*

Sergio sighed. 'One day you'll tell me the truth.' He followed her gaze. 'What are they plotting, I wonder?'

'Jerome couldn't plot his way out of a soap bubble.'

'Former knights are useful, but not to be trusted. They never truly leave the Order.'

'Our arrangement is temporary,' she lied. 'After this place, we'll go our separate ways.'

Of course, that wasn't true: in all the futures that came to her in nightly visions, Jadyn was bound to her, and she to him. But it still hurt to leave Sergio, whose ardour and laughter had been scratched into her soul. They'd set hooks in each other, and pulling them out hurt.

'What really happened in Gaudien?' she asked, as much to remind herself that he *abandoned* her as real curiosity.

'I've told you: they were waiting for us. You were taken and we had to run.'

'I was told you sold me in a card game,' she told him. 'Gambled me away, then ran.'

'Not true!' he flared. 'That's a lie! Who told you such a thing?'

'Butamo – who looked after me without demanding anything from me.'

'Butamo Gulhambu,' Sergio sneered. 'That Khetian liar.'

'He tried to smuggle me out, but we were searched,' she fired back. 'I had to jump overboard and swim away. I was left with no protector – I had to beg and grovel and whore.' She thumped her breast. 'Si, I had to *whore*. Your *amoretta*, reduced to such things! And where were you? Running like a craven!'

'I believed you dead – I was bereft—'

'So bereft you knocked up Marika the minute I was gone from your bed?'

He flung his hands into the air. 'I needed someone. I was distraught, and it made me weak,' he blurted. 'It just happened – but I *never* betrayed you to the Watch.'

Then he realised he was raising his voice and stormed off, heading for the cabin and Marika. Aura was left with the crew glaring at her, still none the wiser. But *someone* had sold her to the authorities in Gaudien . . .

Largan had promised that sailing into Bedum-Mutaza at dusk was one of the greatest sights a man could see; and Jadyn willingly conceded he was right.

The twin capital of the Zynochi empire was situated at the narrowest point of the Leotian Straits, which was just a kylo or so wide. The currents flowing in and out of the Inner Seas were strong, so the approach had to be made at just the right moment. By the time they arrived, there were hundreds of ships waiting south of the heads for the tide to turn. The silhouettes of the great domes and towers against the golden evening skies were breath-taking, as was the play of light on the massive imperial quarter built of white marble on the western Bedum side. It was a picturesque contrast to the giant Hejiffa Dhouma dominating the skyline of the antiquated sprawl of the eastern Mutazi shore.

Jadyn stood with Aura in the prow, trying to etch it into his memory. 'Magnificent,' he breathed. 'What a sight. The Heart of the World.'

'This be many-splendoured,' she agreed. 'Bellisima, si?'

He could tell that she was hurting at leaving Sergio behind, but she'd voiced no doubts or remorse, which heartened him. 'Largan's told me where to seek accommodation,' he said. 'Apparently the hierophant is arriving soon and the city is filling up.'

Aura frowned. 'Hierophant be hunting us? Did Exemplar Virago make him come?'

'No, he's here every four years. I hope the Exemplar is still in Neparia,' Jadyn replied. 'But we must keep our presence secret, regardless. We need to find whatever clue Evandriel told us to seek, and I think I know where to look: the Hejiffa Dhouma.'

She closed her eyes. 'Si, feeling this be right.'

He stared. 'What did you just do?'

'Remember we play predictating game on toss of coin? Am thinking, what else can Aura predicate—'

'Predict.'

'Si, that. Am asking self, "Is Hejiffa Dhouma right place?" Answer I feel is, "Si, that is right".' She looked at him smugly. 'Maybe Aura be prophetess, hmm?'

'It makes sense, given what we know of the aegis,' he breathed. 'You're amazing.'

'All men say so, but is true! Aura be amazamenta in all things. Breaking hearts, everywhere. But not heart of Sergio,' Aura concluded sadly. 'We had love, lost love. Is sad, but must go on, with Jadyn Knight.'

'You won't regret it, I promise.'

'Hmm,' she grunted. 'Cannot prophecy that.'

Sergio took the *Duce di Mundi* west to Bedum's port in the shadow of Tar-Luxium. The imposing Order bastion loomed over the imperial precinct, its white banners fluttering in the evening breeze, as a long twilight settled over the twin cities.

'Well, good luck,' Largan Rameleau told Jadyn as he and Aura prepared to disembark. 'Dera's Hope, remember. It's a decent inn, and they let ex-Order folk in cheap.'

Jadyn thanked him again, and turned to Aura, who was saying something to Sergio, while her ex-lover shook his head. Several of the crew wished Jadyn well, but no one spoke to her. Then the gangplank slid into place, they shouldered their meagre belongings and with a wave to Largan, Jadyn led the way. In moments they were engulfed by a swarm of labourers and sailors flooding the docks. The tantalising smells of spicy food mingled with the reek of salt water and dead fish, bilge-water and sewerage. Traders shouted offers, a discordant racket blending with the distant calls to prayer from across the water in Mutaza, where the worship of Akka blended with older traditions.

Here we go, Jadyn thought, *into the biggest city in the world, with nowhere to sleep and no friends.*

'What were you saying to Sergio?' he asked Aura as they walked.

'Warn him, say danger waits. Sail on, or sell ship, run and hide. He no listen.'

Jadyn glanced sideways at her in concern. 'You foresaw something?'

'Si, mucho! Danger be here, Jadyn Knight. Danger follows. All is peril.' She threw up her hands. 'Sergio no listen.'

'What kind of danger?'

'Not knowing, cannot say,' she worried. 'Behind, before. Am frightened for all.'

Chilled, all Jadyn could do was pick up the pace and pray she was wrong.

Largan Rameleau had a side-line, sporadic but lucrative. Many retired knights couldn't be trusted to put aside the glyma, and such men made difficult and dangerous prey. So, in return for turning a blind eye to the sins of their sources, the lictors cultivated informants among the retired, knowing that birds of a feather were drawn together. Largan had been working with one such lictor for four years now. Jerome Baen – or whatever his real name was – would be the seventh ex-knight he'd turned in for bounty. Whether Baen was guilty was irrelevant; Largan's word would be enough to earn the bounty and have Baen executed.

He waited until his prey had vanished into the crowd, then gave Sergio the nod. The captain would receive his share; his only stipulation in this case was that Baen alone would be taken, while his precious Aura was left unharmed.

That won't be happening.

Largan grabbed Tonio and set out, but they soon split up. He left Tonio to follow their prey while he went to find his patron. Ignoring the entreaties of the dock prostitutes, including the boys dressed as women on the balcony of his favourite tavern, he pushed through the packed streets to the rear of Tar-Luxium bastion and entered via the postern gate. He knew the passwords and the guards let him in without fuss.

Within minutes his old friend Lictor Adu Duenvost appeared. Despite his northern surname Duenvost was Abuthan, with a cheery face, skin like midnight, rosy lips and an affable air that belied his grim reputation. 'Rameleau,' he drawled, 'Good to see you. What have you got for me?'

Largan went to answer when a cacophonous chiming of bells rent the air from above.

Duenvost sighed. 'Timing, eh? Someone's just come through our portali gate.' He gave Largan a speculative look. 'Come along, my friend. Let's go find out who.'

Vanashta Baanholt, Qor-Espina, Neparia

After their awareness collapsed inside the mountain-top stone circle in the Qor-Espina, Yoryn Borghart and Vazi Virago woke in an underground chamber with runes burned into the palms of their hands, just as they'd hoped. They'd taken the first steps on the path leading to the aegis.

They quickly found their way out, seeing clear signs that the Falcons had been there before them, to emerge into a mountainous wilderness on a cliff overlooking a torrential river, with no boats to hand. Hoping that the river would lead them to Vanashta Baanholt, they followed it, clambering up exhausting, precipitous paths and down teeth-grindingly frustrating descents, but their agonisingly slow progress was unavoidable. Finally, they came upon the road that Borghart had discovered just a week or so ago. This time, though, they had to walk, and Borghart felt his irritability grow as he contemplated Kaen and Perafi escaping them.

Controlling his anger was made easier by the loss of their glyma-energy, stripped out by whatever had happened to them in the stone circle. They'd made a pact to not draw on their elobyne to replace it, at least for now, presuming it had been done for a purpose. Whatever the reason, it was calming. Borghart had always been driven by anger, albeit tempered by a veneer of cold-hearted distance that had kept him from losing control. That hadn't changed, but it had somehow rebalanced the ice and fire inside him.

Without the glyma, they had merely human endurance, though, and were subject to exhaustion like any ordinary person. Both suffered from blisters and neither had washed for days, a discomfort they were unused to.

Despite that, travelling with the Exemplar became a perilous temptation. Borghart still didn't like her, despite her peculiarly Zynochi beauty and athletic body. But knowing they were both without glyma right now made him hanker for fruits that were normally forbidden. He'd dropped hints to that effect, but she was having none of it. It only made him want it more.

But he'd seen her fight – she could behead him in a heartbeat – so he knew better than to force the issue. *Damn, it's hard to watch those swaying hips and not reach out . . .*

'Lictor,' Vazi Virago said sharply, as if sensing the drift of his thoughts, 'how far to the lake and the monastery from here, do you think?'

He got a grip on himself, forcing himself see her as a warrior again, not a succulent piece of eastern meat. 'It can't be far, Exemplar,' he growled, 'but last time I was here, I was mounted and we were riding through the night, so I don't know the landmarks.'

'Our food is low,' she noted. 'We must arrive soon.'

His stomach growled in response. 'I'm well aware of that.' He indicated the river gorge gushing through the canyon, below their path. 'If this river doesn't lead back to the monastery, we're in entirely the wrong place.'

'We'd better not be. I'd be forced to eat you to survive.'

In her head, it might have sounded like a jest, but it didn't come out like one.

Fortune smiled, though – or more accurately, their persistence was rewarded: a few kylos on they saw a headland overlooking a mountain lake, topped by the broken outline of Vanashta Baanholt. 'There,' he breathed. 'I'm spared being turned to steak.'

'So long as my men left supplies behind,' she muttered.

'If they left us nothing, I'll disembowel the lot of them,' Borghart added. 'As a ghost, obviously.'

They walked on with renewed energy, despite the burning aches, weeping blisters and parched throats, almost jogging as they rounded the final bend and approached the partly ruined complex. They drew their flamberges but didn't kindle energy, holding to their no-glyma pact despite the threat of ambush.

'We search top to bottom,' Vazi ordered. 'I want to ensure we're alone.'

It took them an hour, going room to room and down into the mines, amid the echoing silence of the Sanctor Wardens' monastery. They found the promised supplies behind a closed door on the second floor, safe from scavengers.

They then set to work like common soldiers, lugging up water and firewood. She might look like an eastern princess, but Vazi was no shrinking violet, even without the glyma to bolster her strength. But they lacked a hatchet for the wood and swords were a poor substitute, so they had to make do with uncut deadwood. The cooking took *for ever*, but when the boiled hardtack and roots were finally ready, they bolted the meal like starving refugees.

'We should wash tonight, and rest,' Vazi said, when they'd emptied the pot. 'The mines can wait.'

She looked edgy, and he felt the same. The arduous journey, the knowledge that their quarry could be anywhere, the impotence of not having the glyma at their fingertips and the fear that they were putting their heads in a noose by pursuing the aegis were all taking their toll. Seeing her filthy and unkempt humanised her, though. It made him feel better to know first-hand that her shit stank like anyone else's.

He dragged his eyes from her body. 'I'll go first.'

He went down to the jetty, stripped and dived in, surrendering himself to the cold water until it brought him clarity. Jadyn Kaen's people had eluded him for more than two months. Summer had slid into autumn. He wasn't used to failure, or privation. It felt corrosive, as if it were tarnishing his soul.

Recognising that helped him deal with it. His breathing slowed and the rage ebbed away far more easily without the glyma fizzing inside him. Then he waded ashore, dried himself on his cloak and rinsed his filthy clothes, then took them back up the stairs, hung them on a rail and went to the room he'd selected.

Tomorrow, he told himself, *we'll solve these riddles and work out what this damnable aegis actually is.*

Vazi Virago stared into the embers of the cooking fire, feeling more tested and less capable than ever before. Her whole career – indeed, her whole life – had been built on dispassionate, ruthless rigour, augmented by unemotional rationality. Glyma was a tool, a means to an end, and she had swiftly mastered the narrow set of spells the knights used in combat. Defeating more physically powerful knights than herself had been no fluke: she could read their minds and bodies, anticipate their every move, countering even as they unleashed their stroke, as well as meeting them head-on, at least as strong in the glyma and using that energy to overpower bigger and more muscular foes.

She was more than just a knight, though. She'd always known that. All her life she'd had dreams of a great destiny: of thrones and crowns and cheering masses, of endless victories – and not unspecific visions, but detailed and clear. Many had already come true. Her rise was truly fated.

But right now, with no glyma to give her lean body the power it craved, she felt vulnerable. It didn't help that Borghart could barely suppress his lust. Putting up with his coal-dark eyes mentally stripping her was deeply uncomfortable – and he'd be just as happy to have her on his torture table as Kaen and Perafi, she had no doubt of that.

By the time the lictor returned, it was deep twilight. The Skull moon above was illuminating the water, the reddish Dragon's Egg was rising, and up here the stars were like a blanket across the sky. She didn't need any other light as she descended to the lake.

Not quite ready to relax, she sat and fished out a coin from her belt pouch, an imperial auroch. She closed her eyes and mentally called 'crown'. It came down bull. She tossed again and again, getting roughly half right. *Just random odds*, she realised gloomily. *This isn't working.*

She'd had glimpses of the immediate future sporadically all her life, mostly in battle or at a moment of crisis, but never at will. She'd hoped it would become controllable after the stone circle imprinted the rune-marks on her palms, but nothing had changed.

Tsking in annoyance, she rose, stripped off and dived into the lake, the dark water closing round her and the chill shocking her flesh. She rubbed at her face and body, desperate to be rid of the sweat and grime of travel, letting herself sink, her hair billowing around her as she enjoyed the silver ceiling of the surface from below.

Then danger *flared* – she felt the shock of anticipated pain that almost paralysed her, sensed a change in the water pressure and *felt* jaws snapping shut on her right leg. She spun, lashing out and glancing a fist off the head of a crocodile longer than her body, its jaws snapping together where her thigh had just been, then she was kicking away, thrashing to the surface as it came round again. She turned and battered it under the lower jaw, the impact forcing its body up and over hers, trapping her beneath, almost out of breath. Its stumpy claws and tail-spines brushed her thighs as it flashed by, coiling to strike again . . . but she speared her left-hand fingers into its saucer-like eye, plunging them into the socket and *ripping*.

Black fluid flowed and the creature thrashed away into the depths.

She broke the surface, kicked urgently for the jetty, scrambled up and collapsed on the wooden deck, shaking with delayed shock. She was horrified at how close the thing had come . . . but also excited, because she was still in the moment and the whole of creation felt clear to her. She fumbled in her belt-pouch for more coins, tossed them all and saw exactly where each would land, which way up.

Eight out of eight.

She fell back again. She understood now.

You didn't force the aegis, you opened a door and let it rush in.

'Good morning, Lictor.'

It was dawn, and Yoryn Borghart felt immensely better for the sleep. He attributed that to being shut away from Vazi Virago. *Why couldn't she have been ugly?*

This morning she looked radiant, damn her: newly clean and much revived. He could smell the coffee she'd brewed, and Nepari sausage, gently sizzling in a pan on the embers of the previous night's fire, along with scrambled eggs; she must have raided birds' nests for them.

'You look ready for whatever the world might throw at you,' he grunted, filling a mug of coffee and inhaling its rich aroma. 'Ah, thank Elysia.'

'I am ready for anything, and I'll see it coming,' she said smugly.

He threw her a resentful glance. 'Cracked the aegis, have you?'

He didn't expect her to share, but she responded, with irritating smugness, 'Stop reaching for it. Let it happen.'

He'd rarely felt more like slapping someone. 'That's it? Are you making fun of me?'

She looked surprised at his ire. 'No, I'm being helpful.'

'The jagat you are. "Let it happen"? Who do you think you're talking to? A child?'

She sat up, her face hardening. 'Perhaps I am? All this way we've been trying to force this thing to obey us. Last night I stopped forcing it – and it came.' She rose, glaring down at him. 'You're welcome.'

'That's of no use to me!' he shouted at her.

'Neither's getting snotty about it,' she retorted. 'You've been angry ever since we met – angry that I'm the better fighter and magician, angry that you can't stick your cock inside me, angry that I'm not subservient – and angry that I'm smarter, too.' She jabbed a finger at him. 'You need to let that anger go.'

He glared, feeling his face going red. 'You don't know anything about me—'

'Oh, I do,' she interrupted. 'I have this same conversation with every man I encounter. They all want to prove that they're better than me in some way, whether it's by beating me or screwing me: to be the lord and prove me their inferior. You're no different, Lictor. No different at all.'

He was halfway to inhaling the glyma and drawing steel when

decades of self-control reasserted itself. A blaze of heat welled up inside him, but instead of using it, he spun and mentally flung his hate – for that's what it was, right then – away.

She is right, on every count.

It was so deflating that for a moment even his iron spine bent – then he turned his anger on himself. *Analyse this, you fool. Contribute. Show her what* you're *made of.*

'We've both been given glimpses of the future, all our lives,' he started, working through it logically, rationally. 'And we've both lived with the glyma since puberty – so aegis and glyma can't be *completely* inimical. They *can* exist side by side. But that stone circle purged us of glyma for a reason: presumably, to make us concentrate on the aegis. The path we're on must have been created by the surviving Wardens after Jovan Lux turned against them – hence the secrecy, the cryptic clues, the hidden monasteries.'

'I doubt the stone circle is the first step,' Vazi replied thoughtfully, matching his tone. 'I suspect there was an earlier one, somewhere in the civilised world, which guided those with the talent to these mountains. So yes, I think we're supposed to arrive here cleansed of the glyma and open to the aegis.'

'Aye, but what is the aegis? Just precognition? Or something more?'

'You say "just precognition", but that alone is immense,' she replied. 'It's an advantage over every single enemy – I am who I am, thanks to that edge.' She made an offhand gesture. 'And all my other advantages.'

'An incredible capacity to channel elobyne, precognition, wealth, beauty and lineage,' Borghart listed drily, unsure why he was play-ing with fire by provoking her. 'Your tale is a real triumph against all odds.'

'You've have no idea what I've been through to become me, so spare the sarcasm.'

It was fair. He exhaled. 'You're right, I'm sorry.'

She grunted wryly. 'When was the last time you apologised to someone?'

'Just now.' He bowed his head.

A gold auroch pinged painfully off his shaven skull a moment later, spun away and clanged on the stones. 'Ow!' he exclaimed.

'Edge,' she replied.

He glanced down at the coin as it rolled, hit a crevice and settled on its edge.

Somehow, he kept his temper. 'Did you have to bounce it off my head?'

'You should have seen it coming,' Vazi sniffed. 'So, ready to work together, or not?'

'Aye,' he said stiffly, 'I'm ready.'

Vazi wasn't overly concerned about Borghart's surliness. He'd bear watching, but she was confident she'd see him coming and best him if she had to. It was far from the first time she'd dealt with his like. Dozens of men had either tried to woo her, seduce her or force her – several women too, mistaking her indifference to men for something it wasn't. The truth was, she was utterly uninterested in either.

I don't need other people, their bodies or their minds. I don't need to belong.

A bitter drunk had once told her, 'Other people only exist to torture us.' But he'd been a loser. Other people existed to be *used*. She also fervently believed that she was the only truly awake person alive; her mastery of both glyma and aegis would prove that to the world.

They spent the rest of the day preparing for the next part of the journey: cleaning gear, packing the food and whatever else of use they could find among the supplies her men had left behind. She wondered how they were faring, but wasn't overly concerned. Only what *she* did mattered. After some discussion, they decided it best to rest another night – neither felt fully recovered, and they had no idea what they would face next.

Her dreams were troubled by Kaen and Perafi flitting around a stone maze, never quite within her reach. There was another presence, too, a winged being made of light, and dangerous, though she barely glimpsed it. She woke several hours before dawn. Her dreams were always significant, so she spent a lot of that time pondering this one.

After they'd broken their fast, they entered the mines again, this time laden down with packs. They found a pair of pitch torches on the wall and lit them with flints – a tedious task without glyma – then descended to the lowest chamber, where they found the eerie ledge facing the stump of a bridge and a void with stars glittering far above. The silence was absolute. The air didn't move.

The stone pillars of the broken bridge had runes carved into the stonework – which matched those now etched onto her palms and Borghart's.

'Are you ready for this?' she asked the lictor. She had no doubts for herself.

'We'll find out the hard way, I guess,' he muttered, unable to hide his nervousness.

'I'll not wait for you,' she warned, striding towards the bridge. 'If it won't take your weight, you're on your own.'

Without waiting for a response, she placed her hands on the runes. They flared – and she watched in fascination as dust motes appeared, merging into a span that stretched out across the void, growing more tangible by the moment.

She prodded the bridge with her fingers and found it solid as stone. 'Our prayers are answered, ar-byan,' she said. 'Let's see how far ahead of us the renegades have got.'

She stepped onto the bridge, utterly certain it would support her, and it did. Then she turned to watch Borghart, who was placing a wary toe on it. For a moment, she thought his foot would go right through, but instead of backing away, he closed his eyes, took a deep breath – and stepped wholly onto the span.

She wasn't sure whether that was an act of faith or stupidity.

It held.

'Even old dogs can learn,' he noted. 'Lead on, Exemplar.'

Oddly, for all her self-reliance and confidence, she was glad of the company. And as to running down their prey, she had no doubt they'd catch them. There was nowhere they could run she couldn't follow.

The next few hours were as eerie as any she'd known, even though she'd used portali gates many times. This was less frightening, and more beautiful, treading a bridge of light under brilliant constellations.

It spoke to her inner core of loneliness in ways she'd not felt before. The Shadowlands were full of whispering menace, but up here all was serene.

The end came suddenly: an arch made of light appeared before them, signifying the end of the glowing path. They stepped through – and found themselves in the top room of what turned out to be a tiny lighthouse on an offshore island. The air temperature and humidity instantly made them both sweat, which suggested they were closer to the equator.

They searched the tower, finding evidence of Jadyn Kaen and Auranuschka Perafi having been here. There was a note on a desk against one wall, signed by Nilis Evandriel, exhorting 'Those who follow' to seek him at 'the centre of the world'.

'I've heard Bedum-Mutaza referred to as that,' she noted.

The lictor was nodding his agreement. 'Aye – probably the Hejiffa Dhouma. The Mutazi Caliph's old orologists set their clocks by the passage of the sun over the dome's spire – "where earth kisses sky". The Wardens helped them devise the mechanisms.'

'How soon can we get there?' she wondered.

'There's bound to be a bastion near here, and most have a portali gate. We can be there by sunset, I'm sure.'

6

Seeking Gates

The First Portali Gate

There is a tale from Miravia, of a young man who vanished near some standing stones and returned a decade later, having aged not a day. It's said that those stones – which are no more – were the first portali gate. The Vestal Order now use dozens of them to traverse the entirety of Hytal in hours, unifying the kingdom. But although the Order use them, they don't claim to have created them.

VARANOR GRENHYTHE, IMPERIAL SCHOLAR, 1402

Foyland-Neparia borderlands
Autumn 1472

Soren watched, disappointed, as the column in the valley below crossed the river unmolested and entered Foyland. They'd arrived at dusk after running all day – Fynarhea as a wolf and Elindhu in her erling form – only to find they were too late. The Golden Dragon century, having been welcomed by the Foylish warband blocking the ford, had passed on. The warband still guarded the river, though.

'Damn. I really hoped they'd fight,' Elindhu panted. 'But Goraghan likely knows them.'

She was still in erling form, her silver hair a mane of filigree. Her face reminded Soren of a parrot's, so pronounced was her beak-like nose, but her lean shapeliness was disconcertingly at odds with her human persona.

Fyn was sitting, panting breathlessly, having just resumed his male erling shape. He'd knotted the wolf-pelt over his shoulders but made no other effort to dress.

'What now?' Soren asked, averting his gaze from the erling's naked body.

Elindhu was studying the valley. 'Clearly Goraghan came straight here, so there's probably a portali gate nearby – they aren't uncommon here. If we don't retrieve our friends quickly, we may lose them for ever.' She rose and gestured down the slope. 'Let's try and cross upstream, out of sight of the crossing guards. Fyn, get dressed, dear.'

Soren went to follow her, but Fyn rose and put a hand on his shoulder. 'She's not bad-looking in that shape, eh? Your "Aunty Eli".'

Soren coloured. 'I haven't noticed.'

'She's thrice your age and can't have children any more,' Fyn added. 'If you want to look at an erling woman, look at me.' He stepped in front of him, licking his lips. 'If you like me better as male, though, just say. I don't mind.'

Male or female, the young erling had the same hungry, intense gaze, and the body wasn't much different, lean and well-made. In either shape, he could freeze Soren like a rabbit before a fox.

'I want to like you,' he blurted, 'but the glyma—'

Fyn gave him a sad look, the mad fervour in his face dissipating. 'I know – I do know. I just can't help myself.'

Then he kissed Soren on the mouth and though Soren recoiled, it was in surprise. Fyn smiled slyly. 'I'm getting to you though, aren't I?' He grabbed the pack with his clothing and swaggered off to change, leaving Soren once again in a swirl of confusion.

Feeling more at home in her true form out here in the wild and cloaked by darkness, Elindhu ghosted through the dank countryside, over mossy boulders and fallen trees festooned in ivy, around still pools ... There was less need for haste now, and more for stealth. Warriors had been left at the ford a kylo to the north, but it was possible there were watchers elsewhere.

The tension between Soren and Fyn was growing, too. Fyn was still simmering with aggression, but in a few days he'd pay the price;

menstruation would start – even in male form – and he'd be unwell, but at least he'd become sensible again. Relatively.

Her greater concern was her own depleted glyma. She was capable of little more than a dim light-spell just now, her sliver of elobyne was almost dead and she knew of no shards in Foyland, so she couldn't replenish. Soren had no flamberge – he'd lost it when they fell in Vanashta Baanholt – so they'd be in a perilous state if they met any resistance.

She was particularly cautious as she led them down the slope to the river, wending a path through the deepest thickets until finally reaching the water's edge, opposite what looked like marshland on the far bank. The sun was falling, twilight setting in.

'We have to cross, regardless,' she said. 'We could lose them otherwise.'

The river was up to her hips at the deepest point, but worse, the far side did indeed prove to be swamp. The light faded, ground mist rose and still they were stumbling through reed banks and oozing mud.

'You're beautiful in your true form, Elindhu,' Fyn said, when Soren was out of earshot.

'And twice your age,' she snapped. 'Deep breaths, Fyn.'

'I don't mind older women,' he dared to reply. 'I've had several.'

'I thought it was Soren you liked.'

'I do, but he won't play. But he said you're almost out of glyma-energy,' Fyn added hopefully. 'It'd be safe.'

'I have more than enough glyma-fire inside me to leave you a eunuch,' she replied tartly.

A few dozen paces on and their boots, soaked through and mud-caked, finally struck firm ground at the edge of a tangle of ivy-clad trees. Fyn stepped before her, his bow drawn and ready, and a few seconds later, Soren appeared from the fog behind them, trudging forlornly.

He overheard our conversation, Elindhu realised. I need to remind him yet again that young erlings are half-mad when they're ovulating, so he doesn't end up hating Fyn.

But even as she opened her mouth to speak, the woods boiled

with dark silhouettes and rustling and an arrow thudded into the nearest tree trunk.

'Hold there!' a harsh voice snapped in Talmoni. 'Hold or die.'

The command from the half-glimpsed archers was still ringing in Soren's ears when the pile of bracken next to him uncoiled and stood up. The silhouette of a vaguely human form was wrapped inside it, with slitted amber eyes that gleamed as the creature swayed over him with eerie grace.

Soren groped for his missing sword, but Fyn caught his wrist.

Elindhu faced the dark shape and asked, 'Sheaf'a rek erla?'

The woods went silent again.

Then the trees on all sides swayed, branches cracked and sinuous shapes appeared, moving with startling speed. Birds shot skywards, shrieking fearfully – Soren saw one snatched from the air by a coil of vines that lashed out and pulled it into an alarmingly wide mouth, which crunched wetly. All round them, heads and shoulders appeared from the pools and mud, eyes glinting in the twilit mist.

'Steady,' Elindhu hissed. 'Keep your hands away from your weapons.'

Dozens of erlings had emerged from the undergrowth, most clad just in loincloths and the odd tunic, all bearing bronze spears and short knives that glinted in the fading light. Saucer-like eyes of pale amber and deep green stared at them; sharp teeth clicked and snapped.

Elindhu took a step forward, silver hair swirling about her head as if underwater. Her eyes were as amber as those facing them.

'Kia nai Crysophalae Elindhu Aramanach, Rann dri Tyr,' she called out. 'Keh aro passa.' Then she murmured to Soren, 'I've given my name and assured them we're here in peace.'

The erlings confronting them muttered to each other, and Soren had a few moments in which to marvel at their diverse nature: those from the water were mostly under four foot tall, with fish-like skin and gills, webbed fingers and feet and no hair except on their scalps. Most were ugly, at least to Soren's human eyes, though some had graceful forms and delicate faces with an unsettling allure.

Fyn laid a hand on his arm possessively.

On the forest side, sylph-like archers, male and female, mingled with heavy-set trulkas. They appeared to be waiting for some signal. Then two figures strode through their midst to confront them.

The male was what Soren considered classically erling: tall and angular, with a long narrow skull, flowing hair and slanted eyes, clad in silk and living leaves. He held an elegant curved tuelawar. But his feet were hooves and his legs backwards-jointed, giving him an awkward gait.

The woman with him was much earthier. Her heavily pregnant form was clothed in rough cloth and furs; antlers protruded from her tangled ginger hair. She wore a tarnished crown looped over the right horn. Her ears were tufted like a doe, and she had hazel eyes.

She doesn't look erling, Soren thought. Then he realised, *She's a vyr . . . maybe even a vorlok!*

'Humans and erlings in our lands,' the crowned woman exclaimed, speaking Talmoni with a Foylish accent. 'Including the Princess of Tyr. Miracles never cease, I'm thinkin'.'

'It's a long tale, and we're passing through on a matter of urgency,' Elindhu replied. 'I don't suppose you could just let us be on our way?'

The woman chortled. 'Sweet leaf, we en't decided if ye be dinner or breakfast.'

There was a snicker from the archers, cold laughter through jagged teeth. An erling girl fixed Soren with her stare and drew a finger across her throat expressively, licking her lips with a snaky blue tongue.

Fyn was holding his breath, but Elindhu remained composed, with her head held high, and Soren was struck by a nobility she seldom showed, a light she kept hidden.

'You see but half our party,' the magia said, in a stately voice. 'We are seeking kindred, a vorlok and a draegar who are captives of the Order – they're just a few kylos away.'

The woman frowned and exchanged whispers with her erling consort, while her people strained to listen. Soren, studying them surreptitiously, realised that not all the warriors were erlings. Some were human men and women, with the animal traces of the vyr – and some of the erlings shared those traits.

People said the vyr and the erlings are working together, but Elindhu always says they aren't, he thought, wondering if she'd been ignorant or had wilfully misled them.

The pregnant vyr-woman turned ponderously and faced Elindhu again. 'We clearly have much to discuss. Will you join us for the evening meal?' She smiled slyly. 'You won't be the main course . . . this time.'

Elindhu looked happy enough, for all they had little choice, falling into step with the woman and conversing in a low voice. Soren and Fyn followed them through the marshes, flanked by uncanny half-seen figures. It wasn't far, just ten minutes until they reached a rustic village ringed by a fence of sharpened stakes bound together by cord, enough to keep wolves out, though not human predators. A dog barked and more erlings appeared to open the gates. Cattle were lowing in the pens and cooking smoke rising, making Soren's mouth water.

His nerves jangled as they were herded inside, but nothing unto-ward happened as the villagers, human, erling and vyr, crowded around. Then drums banged, fiddles shrieked to the rising moon and the villagers started dancing reels around them, in some kind of welcome dance.

The four travellers were made to sit with the erling lord and ant-lered Foyle woman, who was clearly the more senior. She clapped her hands and food was brought by older children with skinny bodies and inquisitive eyes. Everyone ate with their fingers, the plain fare well-cooked and full of flavour.

The musicians were playing so loudly that conversation was near-impossible, but once the food was mostly gone, the crowned woman raised a hand and shouted at the players, 'Give us some quiet, fellas! We wanna talk to these folks, see!'

The noise subsided and she tapped her immense breast. 'I'm Kef-frana, an' this is me fella, Raeldaran' – she indicated the erling lord with the deer-legs. She patted the children at her feet, both horned – 'an' these be our childer. Together, we rule this wee enclave.'

'Vyr and erlings in alliance,' Elindhu noted. 'Just like the Order alleges.'

'I tink we're fairly unique, 'ere,' Keffrana answered. 'Meself, I'm a bit of all sorts, an' that was a . . . what's the fancy word? *Catalyst,* that's it. A half-erling lass what went vyr, ran away from home an' blundered into Raeldaran's territory. Thought he'd do me in, but instead we got jaggy an' fell in love. Risky business, but we's careful, an' eight years on, 'ere we are. The local lord hates us – despite bein' me brother—'

'You're a lord's sister?' Elindhu interrupted.

'Aye, me brother Grenfel rules 'round 'ere.'

'Grenfel *Goraghan?*'

Oh, jagat, Soren thought, *she's Goraghan's sister! Now they'll definitely eat us.*

'Aye, I'm Grenfel's sister. How'd ye know that?!' Keffrana exclaimed.

'We're hunting your brother Arghyl,' Elindhu replied, her gaze intensifying. 'He's captured our friends . . . who are both vyr. We're on the same side, Rann Keffrana.'

But are we? Soren wondered anxiously. *Isn't blood thicker than water?*

Keffrana's eyes bulged and her erling husband Raeldaran spoke, his expression forbidding. 'We are few, and our survival relies on secrecy and not attracting Grenfel's wrath. We kill strangers, or adopt them into the tribe and keep them with us for ever.'

When he ceased, everyone looked at Keffrana, who stroked her chin thoughtfully. 'Well den,' she drawled. 'En't dis a pickle? Mebbe you should tell us yer tale, Rann Crysophalae?'

Elindhu pondered, her face taut with concentration, then she began to speak. She chose her words carefully, making no mention of the aegis, and her story didn't feature Jadyn and Aura at all. But she spoke of Agynea, the vorlok they'd met, and Gram and Romara's transformations, the visit to Semmanath-Tuhr, and Fynarhea joining them, and their hope to meet Nilis Evandriel. And she kept reiterating that it was Keffrana's brother Grenfel holding Romara and Gram.

She's hoping the Goraghans hate each other, Soren thought. *She'd better be right.*

The hall was quiet until she was done, when an excited murmur rose – until Keffrana raised a hand for silence.

'If you're hoping we've got Nilis Evandriel tucked up in an 'ut 'ere, we'll 'ave to disappoint,' she remarked. Then she put her head together with her husband Raeldaran, before asking her people, 'Well, what do we think? Give us yer thoughts, my people.'

There was a quick babble of voices, then an erling boy called out, 'Can we eat them now?'

There was a dark titter, and a few hungry growls in the erling tongue, but a woman shushed him and said, 'It was a fine tale. I'm satisfied these folk are friends, Keffy. Let's give 'em the blessing and have done.'

There was a loud clamour of agreement, at which Keffrana grinned and turned to Raeldaran. 'Here, you do it, lovie, I'm too fat an' lazy to get up again.'

The lordly erling-vyr rose, picking up a bowl that had sat beside him untouched, and approached the travellers. He dipped his thumb into the bowl and daubed red paste on Elindhu's cheeks, three lines each, then did the same to Fyn and Soren. After that, the drums and fiddles rose again, and everyone went back to singing and dancing.

Elindhu turned to Soren and Fyn. 'Stay alert, and stay out of trouble. There'll be ale and dram now – it's heady stuff. Drink it slowly and sparingly. I will talk things through with Keffrana and Raeldaran, and see if they'll help us.'

Soren turned to Fyn as they were immediately swarmed by younger villagers, tugging at their sleeves and saying, 'Come, come with us.'

A tall erling girl with spindly body and pointed ears thrust mugs of something sweet and potent into Fyn's hands, speaking in a teasing voice and swaying to the music. Soren felt a spark of annoyance, especially as Fyn said something that made her laugh, and allowed himself to be pulled away.

Then two girls looped arms through his and he felt a flash of alarm.

'On second thoughts, Soren, you stay with me,' Elindhu called. Then she snapped something in erling and the two girls dropped Soren's arms and shrank away.

The erling leaders chuckled as a relieved Soren joined them. 'Don' worry 'bout yer friend, lad,' Keffrana chortled, as Fyn vanished into the dancers. 'We love outsiders 'ere: fresh seed for the harvest does us all good. Our lasses and lads will give him a good seeing-to.'

Soren felt a pang of jealousy, despite all the tangled emotions that lay between them.

'That's as may be,' Elindhu said curtly, 'but Soren's got the glyma.' The magia made a gesture of finality and changed the subject. 'You've heard our situation. Will you aid us?'

Tevas Nicolini twitched back to semi-consciousness, slapped awake by the cold. Dew soaked his cloak and a chill had seeped into his bones, his joints cracking as he blearily looked around.

I'm too old for this shit.

It'd been a strange night, by turns hostile and raucous, drunken and wild. At times, when distant drums had rumbled in the surrounding hills, the Foylish warriors made gestures to ward off evil. But all was silent now, even the dawn chorus sounded muted and far away.

Like the calm before a storm.

Fully awake now, he cast off his blanket, left his tent and pissed behind a tree. Then he poked his head in the next tent, where Romara Challys was slumbering, with the man-mountain that was Gram Larch snoring and shuddering nearby. His shoulder was badly discoloured where blood poisoning was setting in.

Sleep while you can, he thought bleakly. *And may Elysia have mercy on you.*

Their Vestal century had made camp outside Grenfel Goraghan's hill-fort, Dun Ebrocc, about a kylo from the ford. Tevas had expected blood, but the Goraghan brothers had embraced midstream and Arghyl had been permitted to bring his men cross. Tevas made damn sure that these wild Foylish men didn't get a look at Romara and Gram, otherwise there'd have been a burning. He'd even spoken to all the officers in the Vestal century, ensuring *everyone* knew that their prize wasn't to be spoken of. That seemed to have held.

As it turned out, Grenfel Goraghan had been lavishly hospitable. They'd been ushered into the fort, beasts had been spit-roasted, kegs of malt beer rolled out and the soldiers and warriors had mingled freely. There'd been the usual drunken brawling and fisticuffs, but nothing had got out of hand. Fiddlers had been summoned and village women had joined the dancing under clear, starry skies, teasing the sex-starved Vestal soldiers before draping themselves over their own men, taunting the northerners and their frustrated urges. But somehow the drinking to excess and mountains of food kept the men from each other's throats long enough for most to pass out. The fort looked like the aftermath of a battle, littered with motionless bodies.

The Goraghan brothers had set about drinking each other under the table in the chieftain's throne hall. Grenfel had apparently fallen out with his younger siblings and wanted Arghyl's support in what sounded like a brewing clan war. Arghyl probably didn't give a stinking turd for the dispute, but he'd been loudly supportive.

Tevas watched the eastern skies lighten, trying to think his way through the day to come.

There's a portali gate we can use, provided Grenfel and Arghyl stay friendly. That's all fine, so long as I get my share of the bounty for Romara.

What worried him was that he had no written contract over his status as a bondsman. Elan said it'd be sorted out in Folkstein, but until then, he was reliant on Elan's word.

Just how much is that worth? he wondered darkly.

The sun was well up by the time Elan Sandreth woke, gave Grenfel Goraghan's youngest daughter another hard tupping and sent her on her way, then washed in the bucket someone had provided and, finally, dressed. He'd been given a room in the chieftain's squalid half-ruined keep. Dogs slept in the rushes, gnawing on fresh bones and shitting everywhere, and there was an unconscious Foylish warrior slumped against the bedroom wall who he was sure hadn't been there last night. But all he truly remembered was music, shouting, food and drink, and the plump princess with red pigtails and shockingly bad teeth he'd just seen to. *A good lay, with a juicy clam – Elysia, I pray I've not accidently married the chit*, he thought. The girl had been thrust through the door minutes after he'd turned in, but she'd been willing enough.

He downed some water and poured the rest of the copper jug over his throbbing head. But he'd had many worse nights. Grenfel was a braggart, but generosity to guests was obviously a matter of honour here. They'd even talked trade a bit: Elan had promised him Talmoni steel for Foylish venison, but nothing he couldn't back out of if it didn't stack up under the light of day, so all in all, a satisfying night.

Now, let's get the jag out of here and cash in my dear Romara and her animal lover.

He emerged to find half the men shambling around aimlessly; the rest were still comatose. Big tattooed Foylish warriors kept coming up and hugging him, clapping him on the back and calling him *brathair*, which hopefully meant what it sounded like. Those awake were helping themselves to the remnants of food on the tables and swilling the dregs of the ale and wine kegs. A fiddler began to play, but someone knocked him out again, mercifully.

Elan found some food himself, then lurched out into the sunlight – it was a clear, cold day, with a brisk chilling wind rippling through the surrounding pines. Villagers were already going about their daily tasks in the fort and the stubbled cornfields surrounding; only the warriors and their women had been at the feasting last night, the privilege of rank.

He spotted the gross Arghyl Goraghan waddling from one of the latrine buildings, hobbling on his staff. The magister looked decidedly green about the gills. 'Good morning, Magister,' he called.

'What's jaggin' good about it?' Goraghan growled, spitting phlegm.

'Oh, c'mon,' Elan chuckled. 'We thought we were going to have to fight and instead we got lavished with roast deer, given enough alcohol to float a warship, and I got to screw one of your nieces. Life is good!'

Goraghan gave him a foul look. 'Nae women'll come near me, an' Grenfel don't have slaves. Ye might've got good ale, but he kept feedin' me a wine that'd gone sour, an' me bed had rocks in it. Feckin' place.'

'You grew up here, then?'

'Aye. Once a shithole, always a jaggin' shithole.' The magus glowered about. 'But at least Gren and I sorted some things out. I'm leaving most of me century here and I'll return once we've got those two vyr monsters to Folkstein an' my share o' de bounty. I'll help 'im deal wi' our younger siblings.'

'Are you actually going to?' Elan asked.

'Well, mebbe,' Arghyl grunted. 'I'd rather get back to Vanashta Baanholt before Her Ladyship wrecks the place. Most valuable find this century and she wants it in ruins. Madness.' He looked around. 'Elysia's Clam, what a feckin' dump, eh? Let's get our men briefed, then you, me an' those vyr scum can take the portali gate out of here . . . Provided it still works.'

Elan shot him a look. 'It'd better. It's a long ride home if it doesn't.'

'I've got me fingers crossed, an' I'll even tie a knot in me cock if dat brings luck.' Then his eyebrows raised as they heard a sudden rumble of distant drums. 'Ach, let's hurry. Summit's got the forest folk roused.'

Elan shot him a glance. 'Forest folk?'

The Foylish magus gave him a tense look. 'Erlings . . . or vyr . . . or both. Best we move.'

The Garran Effa, or Sacred Wood, was only half a kylo from Dun Ebrocc, upstream along a tributary to the river they'd crossed yesterday. Tevas checked the elobyne on the hilt of his flamberge before hooking the sword over his saddlebow before him. The orb was worryingly depleted, but there was nothing he could do about that here. He swung up, nudged his horse alongside Romara's and took her reins. Her face was concealed by her cowl, but he caught a glimpse of her pale face. Gram Larch swayed on the horse behind, barely conscious.

Foylish warriors hovered near, watching the Order men construct a proper camp, where they would await the return of their commanders. *The magus will be back in two to three days*, the officers were telling their men. Tevas doubted that was true.

Grenfel was asking Arghyl about the prisoners, but the magus was curtly fobbing off his questions. Elan was occupying himself kissing the hand of a girl who looked barely fifteen, a rotund little gingaretta who giggled a lot.

'Right den, let's be off,' Arghyl shouted, before embracing his brother. 'We'll be back afore ye know we're gone.' He mounted up, making the poor animal's back bow from his weight, gestured at the cohort of thirty men-at-arms selected to protect them, and everyone nudged their mounts into motion.

The column moved at a trot up a gentle rise to the edge of the woods, where they found a hewn-out clearing flanked by old trees with huirnes carved into them, different faces of the forest god. A Foylish drui emerged to greet them. Tevas knew the sort; these old pagan shamen were Gifted but not trained, and as they lacked elobyne, they were capable of little in the way of real glyma. But in the land of the blind, the one-eyed were king, and this man was as imperious as any high priest, though sullenly respectful of Arghyl.

'Huirne be with ye, Milord,' the drui said grandly. 'May he light yer way.'

'May Akka grant you enlightenment,' Arghyl responded, with heavy irony. In places where the empire ruled, the Church executed such heretics. 'May Elysia grant you mercy.'

The drui lowered his eyes. 'Let me show you the way—' he offered.

'No need,' Arghyl interrupted. 'Wait here – and don't come looking.' He kicked his beleaguered horse into motion, Elan followed. Tevas was next, leading Romara's horse, with Gram behind, followed by the men-at-arms.

The woods were too quiet for his liking, and he loosened his sword in the scabbard.

The morning forest soon closed in around them, misty and dewladen. Distant birds warbled and shrieked intermittently, and the horses' breath plumed in the cold air. Romara tossed her head, the cowl slipping back to reveal her drawn face. She was sniffing the air like a predator who's scented their prey, making the soldiers around her flinch.

'Ah, 'ere we are, den,' Goraghan remarked, as they entered a clearing.

Before them stood a giant boulder some sixty paces high, dark and grey with moss in every crevice, rising from the ground like an iceberg on the northern seas. A huge head had been carved into it, a single visage, but halved, one side male, the other female. Its open mouth was large enough for a man to walk in without bending – the eyes peered downwards as if assessing whoever approached.

Elan whistled appreciatively, but the soldiers all made the fist of Akka to ward off evil. Tevas, still uneasy, scanned the clearing, seeking hidden foes.

'Lughasheel,' Goraghan named the face. 'In winter a male, the hunter and protector; in summer a woman, the nurturer. Load'a pagan tosh, o' course, but instructive: the Foylish gods were erling gods, t'is said, an' Lughasheel is one of the twelve erling gods.'

Tevas saw Romara's eyes narrow at his words. Behind her, Gram Larch was still unconscious, swaying with every step his horse took. Around them, the surrounding trees oozed silent menace.

Unconsciously, they all edged together.

Then a strident woman's voice rang out, shouting, '*MARAI!*' – the Foylish command to attack – and the air immediately filled with the malevolent hiss of arrows thudding into men and horses or carving the air between. Four of the men-at-arms reeled and crashed to the ground, several horses staggered and began to drop; a shaft slammed into Tevas' mount too, even as he was kicking free of his stirrups. He managed to leap clear as his horse went down.

Romara and Gram were untouched.

'Jagga!' Goraghan snarled as the woods exploded with shrieking warriors, men and women wearing nothing but green war-paint. Some were weeping blood and sporting hideous deformities; horns and tusks and claws – but worse, many of their attackers had the amber eyes and weird shapes of erlings.

They're here for Romara and Gram, Tevas guessed, shouting, 'Form up! Keep 'em back!'

He steadied himself, levelled his flamberge and blasted a bolt of energy into the foremost vyr, a man with a horned, lupine skull, punching a hole in his chest, then he grabbed Romara's reins as she tossed back her head and keened, as if calling to the attackers.

In answer, *something* howled, and he saw a large silhouette among the trees, antlered and roaring. '*ARGHYL, YE BASTARD*,' a woman shrieked, '*I'M COMIN' FER YA!*'

'There's a vorlok out there!' Tevas shouted, as the remaining soldiers – more than a score, and every one of them battle-hardened – formed a cordon around Elan and Arghyl. 'Goraghan, get that gate open!'

Soren went to bed miserable, lying in a hut under a blanket on his own, hearing the drummers and fiddlers, raucous laughter and squeals of pleasure, the sound of other people getting drunk and having fun. Fyn was somewhere out there, but he had no idea where.

With his own people, doing all the things I can't.

He didn't blame the erling, although he was a bit surprised to find he felt like that. When his younger self fantasised of being a Vestal knight, he had no idea the price of the Gift would be hard to bear. Young boys had no idea why older people seemed so obsessed with love. But now with an aching hollow in his chest, he felt like all the best things in life were to be denied him. A career of abstinence felt intolerable, just now.

He was so caught up in misery that he didn't notice that someone had come in until a body settled against his back and an arm slid round his waist. His skin prickled in surprise.

It wasn't a remorseful Fyn, seeking forgiveness, but Elindhu. She'd reverted to her human form, a little bundle of heat that nuzzled the back of his neck, and murmured, 'Go back to sleep, lad. It's only me.'

'Aunty?' he asked tentatively, alarmed at the liberty she was taking.

'Shh,' she murmured. 'Indulge me.'

In minutes she was breathing softly and rhythmically against his back, already asleep.

He was initially rigid with confusion, though admitting to himself that it was comforting to be held. But gradually her steady breathing soothed him, the tension ebbed away and he drifted away into quiet dreams.

*

Elindhu woke Soren what felt like moments later, nudging his shoulder and whispering, 'Wake up, dear. It's morning and we need to move.'

Soren rolled over and found himself facing her, his snub nose almost touching her enormous one, her amber eyes luminous in the faint light. 'What are you doing here?' he blurted, feeling a rush of embarrassment.

'Sorry,' she replied, her voice strained. 'I just needed to be close to someone. A moment of weakness, that's all. I'm fine now.' Then she choked and sobbed.

Obanji, he realised. *She's missing him still.*

Tentatively he wriggled closer and hugged her, petrified he was doing wrong. She let him, though, and in moments his collar was wet with tears.

After a time, she pulled away, sat up and dried her face on her sleeve, then gave him an apologetic look as her braids piled themselves on her head. 'Thank you, Soren. You've got a good heart and a wise head.'

He coloured at the praise. 'What time is it?' he asked, rubbing his eyes.

'It's almost dawn and the scouts are out, seeking our enemies. Keffrana has agreed to help us. Romara and Gram are vorlok and draegar, so they're more or less obliged to – and Keffrana hates her brothers.'

'What's the plan?' he asked, sitting up eagerly.

'We think it's likely they'll make for a portali gate in a sacred grove nearby. Last night we sent out scouts to watch the likely routes. And Keffrana's loaned me an elobyne orb – and this.' She produced a flamberge, in a shoulder harness. 'For you, if you want it?'

His mind went back to his despairing thoughts during the night, about the dark side of the glyma. But this beautifully crafted weapon called to him.

'It's a prize of war, taken from a knight they slew,' Elindhu went on. 'Vyr don't like elobyne – it's too much for most of them. So it's yours, until we can get you another.'

He hesitated, but their need was for a glyma-knight now. With a sigh, he took the weapon. 'I'll wield it only as long as it's necessary, Aunty,' he promised.

And not a moment longer.

She looked at him with understanding. 'Be careful, dear. I'd hate to lose you too.'

Her gaze drew his, reaffirming to him that just as Fyn was also Fynarhea, Elindhu was both an alluring silver-haired erling princess and his birdlike 'Aunty'. Body wasn't identity.

She's a wonderful person, in either form, he mused. *I'm lucky to know her.*

As if sensing his thoughts, she smiled uneasily. 'Soren—' she began.

Then Fyn ducked through the door, and smirked. 'Am I interrupting something?'

'Grow up,' Elindhu said, her voice tart. 'I trust you had a fulfilling night?'

'Uh, yes . . . I mean, no . . .' the young erling mumbled. 'I just, er . . .'

'I don't want to know. We leave within the hour,' Elindhu said curtly, rising and forcing Fyn to stand aside so she could leave.

The younger erling gestured rudely behind her back, then swaggered in and faced Soren. He reeked of sex and beer. 'Did you two *sleep* together?' he asked slyly.

'Nothing happened,' Soren replied stiffly. 'She just wanted to make sure I was fine.'

Fyn glanced over his shoulder to ensure Elindhu was really gone, then smiled broadly, not quite meeting Soren's eyes. 'What a night,' he purred. 'They actually *want* outsiders to impregnate them! Something about refreshing the harvest, whatever that means. I must've had a dozen girls. No sooner I was done and another little cutie would sidle up and—'

'I don't care,' Soren told him. 'Shut up and get ready.' With that he grabbed boots and blade, crawled out and headed for the washing troughs.

The sun was rising over the woods, burning away the mists and setting the dew in the grass and spider-webs aglow. Then an erling with rabbit ears and a bounding gait arrived with news of movement around the Clan Goraghan keep.

Soren joined the rest, pressing around the leaders to hear.

'Most of the soldiers are staying put, but one cohort rode out,' the man was telling Keffrana, Raeldaran and Elindhu. 'Grenfyl's not with 'em; just a couple of what look like knights, and they've got two pris'ners tied to mounts. One's a woman – an' here's the best of it: the man in charge is your lard-arsed brother, Arghyl.'

Keffrana's face lit up. 'Jus' thirty men t'protect 'im? Just two knights? Ye sure?'

'I ken numbers, Lady. Thirty and two is all.'

'Perfect,' Raeldaran purred. 'Let's hit 'em hard.'

An hour later, they were charging from the forest wall, a shrieking horde of blood-crazed erlings and vyr, Soren and Fyn with them. They went storming through knee-deep grass towards a shieldwall of men-at-arms of the Order, arrows flashing over their heads.

Elindhu was somewhere behind them. She wasn't suited to the front line, but Soren knew she'd appear at need. He focused on what lay before him, watching shafts slamming into the Order soldiers, then the volleys stopping as they got too close. All around them were wild-eyed mutated beast-men and erlings that looked every bit as savage. They carried him forward as he lit his borrowed flamberge.

The men and women in front slammed into the shield-wall and the crouching soldiers rose with a roar, bellowing 'Dragons!' and thrusting swords or spears over their shields in unison, at the same time slamming the shield bosses into the faces of their foes. To the left and right, vyr and erlings were thrown backwards, many going down.

'*Dragons!*' The soldiers roared their century's name, locking shields again, the wall bristling with spears. '*Dragons!*'

Fyn hit the line, dashing his sharp but lightweight tuelawar ineffectually against the shields, unable to find a gap, reeling back from a spear jab. In fright, Soren unleashed a blast of fire and force that splintered one shield, but the gap closed instantly.

'Glyma!' the cry went up from the Vestal soldiers. 'There's a feckin' knight here!'

124

All eyes seemed to turn his way, but Soren's concern was protecting Fyn, whose composure was fraying as he was driven back, the soldiers fighting as a team against the wall of vyr and erlings.

Soren summoned glyma and crashed back into the shield-wall, stabbing over the nearest shield and punching a gap as his victim fell. Flailing left and right, he forced the men-at-arms away from Fyn, shouting, 'Get behind me!' He unleashed a blast of force, shouting, '*Pulso!*' at the men closing in on him, realising that he was about to be engulfed and cut down—

—until an immense massively antlered figure loomed up on his right. Keffrana in her vorlok form was swinging a huge battle-axe that crunched effortlessly through shields, hurling men away, and Raeldaran was behind her, his tuelawar flashing. Their people quickly flooded into the gap she'd smashed and the line reeled and broke.

Fyn was lost somewhere behind as Soren was swept forward. This time he was calm, remembering all his father and Obanji had taught him. His wavy-bladed flamberge cleaved a shield in two, sending the arm holding it spinning away in a spray of blood. He cut down the shocked soldier gaping at the stump and strode on. A bald man with a flamberge stepped before him, coolly composed; their elobyne-empowered swords crashed together, and in moments the entirety of existence was focused on their blades.

Tevas despatched a skinny half-naked erling with blue-green skin, only to face a young man holding a flamberge. He looked initiate-aged, but the kid fought like a demon. They traded lightning parries, each riposte unerring, and Tevas found himself giving ground. He tried to slow the young man's momentum, but the line broke and the enemy flooded past him, led by the antlered female vorlok with a ginger mane, brandishing a battle-axe.

Jaggin' redheads will be the death of me, he thought despairingly. *Or this boy will!*

He tried another feint-and-flurry, but the damned prick – Soren

var'Dael, he realised, finally recognising his mixed-race features –
kept parrying him, and driving him back. Off to his right, Elindhu
Morspeth and Arghyl Goraghan were shouting spell-words and fire
and light erupted round them, so Tevas went the other way, backing
up towards the portali gate.

If I can get through, I can close it behind me, he thought furiously, trying
to keep Soren var'Dael at bay. *Who taught you to fight, boy? You've got
moves I've never seen . . .*

Then another deadly combination unravelled his defence, he flung
himself backwards, tripped, and slammed into the wet turf, tried to
roll aside as Soren loomed over him—

—but two men-at-arms, seeing his peril, hurtled in, forcing the
young man to turn aside. Soren recovered easily, though, his parries
sure, and drove at them, his steel a blur.

He'll have them down in seconds, Tevas realised. He rose and ran.

Elan Sandreth was hauling Romara's horse towards the mouth-cave
in the giant stone head. 'Tevas!' he shouted. 'Here!'

Tevas' eyes went to Gram Larch, who'd roused and was staring
about. It would have been a few seconds' work to turn aside and
butcher him – but he didn't have time. Instead, he dashed past
Elan, shouting, 'Bring her!' while cutting down a vyr bounding in
on his flank.

The last of Goraghan's men were being overwhelmed, carved into
knots and surrounded. Goraghan was somehow managing to keep
Elindhu at bay, though. The little erling woman was lit up like a
murderous hen, but unable to advance. Then Arghyl hurled her
backwards with a blast of force, scorched the horned giantess and
lit a wall of fire that tore along the turf left and right, creating a
barrier taller than man-height for a dozen yards in either direction.
It cut off half their men, but gave the magus time.

Elan cut down a vyr-woman Tevas hadn't even seen while Arghyl
roared aloud, filling the mouth of the giant carved stone head with
phosphorescent green light.

'Get into the cave!' the magus shouted. '*Get in!*'

Romara tried to throw herself from her horse, so Tevas punched her in the jaw, knocking her sideways, then cut her limp body from the saddle and slung her over his shoulder. The glyma pulsing through him made light of her weight. He darted past Elan while Goraghan faced the cave and howled, *'Open! Apperio!'*

Something responded, a flare of radiant emerald emanating from the back wall, which was smooth and carved with runes lighting up at the magus' invocation. Tevas staggered towards it, Elan beside him, as the back wall split into two doors which swung away, revealing a patch of stony ground, dimly lit and surrounded by darkness. Tevas glanced back at Goraghan, who'd been assailed by the immense female vorlok, a red-headed horned woman twice his height, with a belly like a boulder.

Dear Akka, is she pregnant?

With child or not, her axe crunched down, splitting Goraghan's staff in two, and his orb went flying. *'No, Keffrana!'* the magus howled, his voice cracking. *'Sister, no—!'*

Sister? Tevas thought. *Elysia's tits!*

Her axe crunched down, lodging in Arghyl's chest. He collapsed in a wet spray and she howled in glee. Elan grabbed Tevas' shoulder, shouting again, *'Come on!'*

They stumbled through the light-limned doorway, where Tevas dropped Romara and turned, gripped one door as Elan put his shoulder behind the other and threw everything into slamming it shut.

It crashed closed.

The task wasn't yet done, though. Tevas cast about, saw the glowing rune he needed and rammed his elobyne-empowered blade into the symbol. Energy crackled, the green light went out and he was jolted backwards, tripped and fell. But the gate was closed, now – more than that, it was wrecked.

They heard a shriek that might have been female, and thudding blows against the barrier, but nothing could get through.

Tevas looked round in the dim light of his flamberge orb and saw Romara's face, empty and slack. He knotted his fingers in her hair and tried to get his breath back and slow his thudding heart.

Elan stared at him, at first in horror and then rocking with laughter. 'We're a great team, Nicolini,' he roared. 'And it'll just be us collecting that bounty now – how good is that?'

He threw back his head and cackled hysterically.

7

The Domus

The Akkanite Unification

Men do not lightly put aside centuries of religious beliefs. It's inculcated into them, part of their core being. So elevating Akka above the pagan gods of Zynochia and Abutha was a delicate matter, achieved over many decades. Even now, two centuries later, ancient practices colour the worship of Akka in those regions. Most visible among those are the Domus Religio, the shrines of old eastern gods now converted to the worship of Akka. Peel back a layer of paint and you'll find those Old Gods.

BENTIUS JODINE, SCHOLAR, PETRAXUS 1458

Bedum-Mutaza
Autumn 1472

Largan Rameleau was surprised that Lictor Duenvost took him to see the portali gate open, but he wasn't about to question the invitation. Having left behind his illegal elobyne orb, if this turned messy he'd be running for shelter, but being back inside a bastion was a rare privilege for a retired knight.

Tar-Luxium was a maze, but he trailed the black-clad Abuthan lictor briskly as white-clad knights and soldiers converged on the portali chamber. There was little welcome given Duenvost – lictors were never popular – but plenty of grudging respect. They all crowded into a large underground hall facing a portcullis and an open-sided hexagonal chamber. In it, two people in travelling clothes were holding onto the wall, trying to recover from the debilitating travel through the Shadowlands: a woman knight and a male lictor.

Largan heard an awed murmur: *'It's the Exemplar!'*

He'd retired long enough ago to have never seen the new Exemplar, the Zynochi girl everyone seemed to revere. He watched her emerge from the portali gate dazed, but in remarkable shape for someone who'd just endured a portali journey. Her perfectly formed face was unblemished by scars or bruises and her build was more dancer than fencer, but among knights, glyma-prowess mattered more.

With her was a bald lictor with a goatee and accusatory eyes. Together they approached the portcullis, apparently unconcerned by the ranks facing them. The Exemplar saluted the grandmaster respectfully, and called, 'Milord, may we confer? In private, please?'

The lictor with her pointed at Adu Duenvost. 'Bring him, too.'

Few people could arrive at a bastion and throw their weight around, but the grandmaster – a silver-haired man called Rolf Rendreth – complied with the Exemplar's wishes immediately, snapping orders to lift the portcullis and waving Duenvost in.

'Stay close,' Duenvost told Largan. 'I may need you.'

The newcomers were ushered through to a dining hall and Largan settled in a chair outside, under the doubtful eyes of the guards. But he didn't have to wait long. The door opened and an aide emerged. 'Sier Largan Rameleau? You're needed.'

It was almost unheard-of for a former knight to be included in high-level matters, but Largan had met Grandmaster Rendreth before and was greeted respectfully, given a seat and a goblet of wine. The Exemplar and her lictor friend were devouring stew and roasted potatoes; the succulent smells filled the room.

'This is Largan Rameleau,' Adu Duenvost told the newcomers. 'He and I have a special relationship: he watches the sea lanes for retired knights using elobyne illegally. Largan, this is Exemplar Vazi Virago, and Lictor Yoryn Borghart of Gaudien.'

Gaudien, Largan thought. *That's where we left Aura Perafi.*

'So he's a bounty hunter, then?' Borghart frowned.

'I don't like seeing retired knights abuse their vows,' Largan replied.

'We've arrested several oath-breakers with Sier Largan's aid,' Duen-vost added. 'He's a valued member of the Tar-Luxium bastion, despite his unofficial capacity. Renegade knights often frequent the shipping lanes and he is ideally placed to identify them and direct our efforts in apprehending them.'

Borghart frowned, but asked, 'Are you aware of the latest renegade pentacle, the Falcons, Sier Largan?'

Largan dredged his memory: news travelled swiftly inside the Order, thanks to the coursers and the portali gates, but slowly outside it. 'The Falcons? Aren't they stationed in the Isles? They're Romara Challys' century, aren't they?'

'They were disgraced and disbanded after losing Avas,' Borghart said coldly. 'At least two of them went over to the vyr. I've been pursuing them since.'

Largan sat up. Fallen knights rampaging about were bad enough; those who went vyr were worse, and had massive bounties on their heads. 'Who are you are hunting?'

'Romara Challys. Jadyn Kaen. Elindhu Morspeth. An initiate, Soren var'Dael. And two vyr travelling with them: Gram Larch and Aura-nuschka Perafi.'

Largan's eyebrows hit the top of his forehead. *'Aura Perafi?'*

Borghart's eyes bored into him. 'You know her?'

Clearly they wanted her badly, but if he let too much slip, he risked missing out on his cut. So Largan took a moment to choose his words. 'A few months ago I was in Gaudien – your base, Lictor Borghart. There was word on the street of a Nepari woman who'd been arrested.'

Borghart glanced at the Exemplar. 'Is that all you have?'

Largan looked at Duenvost and rubbed his nose, to signal that yes, he had more, but he expected to be paid properly for whatever he disclosed. The Order had rules against paying bounty hunters, so he needed his patron to back him now, to guarantee his share.

Duenvost didn't let him down. 'Sier Largan risks his life every day, mixing with people who often have a strong hatred of the Order. He must pose as a renegade himself, with all the attendant risks. If his relationship with us was discovered, his life would be forfeit. His knowledge is hard-won, and must be used with discretion.'

'My bastion will cover his reward,' Borghart promised. 'Triple the rate, for anything leading to an arrest.'

Triple? Akka be praised! Largan was only going to ask for double. But he made a point of arguing anyway. 'Arrest? But what if they elude you? Do I then get nothing?'

The Exemplar stepped in. 'A confirmed sighting is all we'll need to guarantee your payment,' she said crisply. 'Do I take it you can help us?'

'I think so,' Largan replied, keeping his expression neutral. 'But I'll need to see my contacts at the docks. It may take a little time.' He faced Borghart. 'Do you think she's here?'

'We believe they're coming here, and may even have arrived,' Borghart answered. 'We have strong evidence that Perafi is travelling with Jadyn Kaen – a blond Vandari, of about thirty years.'

Jadyn Kaen . . . Jerome Baen. Largan smiled to himself, because even now Tonio was shadowing them. The pieces were already in place for him. *We make our own luck. I could lead the Exemplar right to them.*

But for now, he needed permission to 'investigate'. 'I know the right people to seek out,' he told them. 'You're lucky I'm here. No one else could get you answers so quickly.'

'Yes, yes.' Borghart glared at him. 'I've already promised you a fat purse. Earn it.'

Vazi Virago turned to the grandmaster. 'For obvious reasons, we need to be discreet. Rogue knights going over to the vyr hurts morale. And I'm guessing the local people notice when you put troops in the streets?'

'They do indeed,' Rendreth replied. 'The Bedumi resent our presence, and officially, I should warn the caliph's vizier in advance, but I wouldn't trust him as far as I can spit.' He glanced up. 'With respect, Exemplar.'

She shrugged. 'I am Order first, Zynochi second and Bedumi not at all. I wouldn't trust them either.'

That brought a wry smile to everyone's lips. Adu Duenvost clapped

Largan on the shoulder. 'Then we're in your hands, my friend. Let me see you out.'

They rose, bowed to the grandmaster and the Exemplar, then headed for the rear doors. Once alone, Largan told Duenvost to assemble a squad promptly, as he 'had a hunch' he knew where to look for the fugitives.

'I thought you knew more than you were letting on,' Duenvost noted.

'Thanks for backing me in there. I'll deliver on this, I promise.'

The Abuthan lictor grinned. 'Which runner do you want?' He had a coterie of boys who ran messages and errands for him, and he knew Largan's favourites. 'Nali?'

Nali was a pretty Bedumi youth with a clever tongue. 'Perfect.'

Ten minutes later, he was hurrying back to the docklands, Nali scampering alongside him, gossiping breathlessly. Largan took it all in, but his mind was focused on netting Jadyn Kaen and Aura Perafi, and ensuring Borghart delivered on his promises.

'Wait here,' he told Nali, when they reached the wharf where the *Duce di Mundi* was now tied up. 'I need to find out what's going on.' He hurried onwards along the wharf and up the gangplank, where he found Sergio pacing the deck, Marika with him, fretting over her expanding belly. Apart from a few men on watch, the crew were ashore getting drunk.

Sergio came to meet him. 'What's happening?'

Largan leaned in and murmured, 'The bastion commanders want a word with our new friend, Jerome Baen.'

Sergio looked at him sharply. 'Just him? Not Aura?'

'Just Baen,' Largan lied. 'They know nothing about her.'

'Even though she was imprisoned in the north?' Sergio pressed.

'Order bastions don't share as much information as you think. Is Tonio back?'

'Not yet.'

He feigned disappointment. 'I've got to go back out. Wait here for Tonio.'

Sergio gripped Largan's forearm. 'Aura must not be harmed.'

I doubt Marika agrees. 'Don't worry, they have no interest in her.'

He retrieved his elobyne orb from his cabin before disembarking and hurrying along the wharf. Fortune was surely running his way, because he'd barely reached the promenade when he ran into Tonio.

'Whoa, there, my friend,' he said, planting a hand on his chest. 'What's the word?'

'Hands off,' Sergio's brother growled.

Largan didn't remove his hand. 'Don't worry, I don't find you in the least tempting. Where are Aura and Jerome?' He dangled a gold auroch in Tonio's face. 'Did they spot you? Are they still under observation?'

'I'm following them for Sergio, not you,' Tonio muttered, his eyes on the coin.

Largan added another. 'I'm acting for Sergio. Answer my questions.'

Tonio probably guessed he was lying, but he took the money, more than a month's pay. 'Aura and Baen took a room for the night at that hostel you always recommend. Shrem and Ramsey are watching them now.'

'Good work,' Largan praised. 'But here's the thing. The Order want Jerome Baen, so you and I need to guide them in, then collect the reward. I'll give you a cut if you stick with me.'

'Sure, but I have to report to Sergio. And he doesn't want anything to happen to Aura.'

Largan grinned. 'Be honest, Tonio, Aura's a bitch.'

The younger brother pulled a face. 'Sergio does crazy things when she's around. I hope the Order strings her up.'

'Oh, they'll do worse than that. Count on it.'

Tonio grinned savagely. 'Then I'm in.'

Largan found Nali and sent him to fetch Duenvost, then he and Tonio headed for the hostel, passing through the tangled morass of the Boussian, a bazaar dealing primarily in Abuthan goods. Very quickly, black faces outnumbered brown and white ones, and the turbans and robes became colourful and bright. Music engulfed them, insistent drums and shrill strings, enough to set fingers and toes tapping. There was an air of festivity about the city, because the hierophant was expected any day. Night was falling, but the city was coming to life.

The hostel, Dera's Hope, was run by a former knight; although open to all-comers, it gave a discount to retired soldiers and knights. Such places, though commonplace in the north, were rare here. They were usually tawdry, sad places, but good for gossip and blades for hire.

Largan let Tonio lead him to the back alley, where Shrem and Ramsey were sharing a hemp pipe. 'Are they still up there?' he asked.

Shrem pointed to a window three storeys up. 'I walked past their door a few minutes ago. There's a thumping noise, and a woman moaning. I reckon that northern bastard's giving Aura one up the gushy.'

'Sergio always said she was insatiable,' Tonio sneered. 'Dirty bitch.'

'Shall we move in on them?' Ramsey asked.

'We wait,' Largan told them. To emphasise his authority, he pulled out his elobyne orb and screwed it to the pommel of his sword. The others watched avidly, jealous of a power that would never be theirs – and grateful, in case Jerome Baen had a secret orb, too.

Which isn't impossible, Largan reflected. *This might not be easy.*

'What we waiting for?' Shrem asked.

'Some help.'

'Who?' Ramsey asked suspiciously.

'You'll see.'

Largan didn't have to wait long. Nali hurried up, took his fee and with a 'see you later' smile, vanished as Lictor Duenvost, Lictor Borghart and Exemplar Virago appeared, cowled and wearing cloaks over their Order gear. Giving the three sailors a dubious look, the Exemplar asked, 'Do these men know who we are and what we're doing?'

Largan shook his head, and turned to Tonio, Shrem and Ramsey. 'My friends are here to secure Baen and Perafi. We're just guides and back-up, understand?'

The sailors gave Largan a puzzled look – they'd been expecting him to be in charge – but they managed some rudimentary logic and realised that these strangers must also be Order, but still in active service. That had them tugging forelocks, even without knowing names.

'Don't Sergio want—?' Shrem began, before realising and shutting his mouth. 'Don't matter.'

'Where are they? Borghart asked. 'What's the layout?'

'There's four floors,' Tonio reported. 'The only entrances are front and rear. They're in that room there.' He pointed to the third window from the left. 'They're screwing, I reckon – going at it hard.'

'Then let's take them *en flagrante*,' Exemplar Virago said, wrinkling her nose. 'We'll enter from both sides simultaneously and trap them.' She turned to Duenvost. 'Take the front door, Lictor, as you're known here. I'll take the rear with Sier Largan. Yoryn, remain here, in case they escape via the window.'

'I could go in that window inside ten seconds,' Borghart commented.

'Better to take them unawares as they jump,' she replied crisply. 'Let's do this quietly.'

The lictor bowed his head, which clearly surprised the sailors, who didn't know who was who. Largan assigned Shrem to Duenvost and Ramsey to Virago, to guide them to the right room. 'Stay out of their way,' he told them. 'My friends here don't jag around.'

'We're not stupid,' Ramsey answered. 'You folk are all glyma-knights.'

And the rest, Largan thought wryly. 'Then let's go.'

He led the Exemplar, who was dressed like a commoner but carried herself like a warrior, to the rear of the hostel, where some Bedumi cooks were passing round a pipe of pungent tobacco. They took one look at him – he was known here as someone you didn't mess with – and waved him through. He doubted they'd be in any hurry to return to duties. He found the back stairs, waited until he heard a stir in the taproom indicating Duenvost's advent, then headed upstairs quietly. The Exemplar was a ghost behind him, one hand on her flamberge.

First flight . . . second . . . and then the third. He opened the door with a flex of energy, found the corridor empty and waited until Adu Duenvost appeared at the far end, put a finger to his lips then tiptoed to the third door on the left, Vazi Virago behind him.

A headboard was banging against a wall and a man was grunting furiously, in rhythm with the panting woman. Shrem was right, they certainly were copulating with some abandon. Largan chuckled softly, thinking that Baen – or Kaen – was a dark horse, because he'd not seemed the sort.

Then he drew on the glyma and shattered the lock with a sharp punch. The door burst open and he strode in, light rolling down his blade as he raised it. *'Don't move!'*

A man and woman were indeed on the narrow bed, locked round each other in a sweaty lather. They came apart in terror, grabbing sheets and pressing themselves into the wall, gaping at his glowing blade.

A Bedumi man and an Abuthan woman.

Largan stared, cursed then shouted, 'Damn it! Wrong room!'

He heard Duenvost and the Exemplar swearing, then they turned and began kicking in doors. Most were empty, some had sleepers and in a few they found men so far gone in opium they didn't flinch.

They checked and double-checked, but Jadyn Kaen and Aura Perafi weren't here.

Largan punched a hole in the wall, then whirled on Shrem. 'You said they were in here!' he roared, scared that the Exemplar and lictors would blame him.

'Boss,' Shrem quaked, 'I don't unnerstan'. We *saw* 'em go in!'

Largan jabbed a warning finger at him, then whirled on the naked couple, shouting questions in pidgin Bedumi, but he couldn't make himself understood. Then a furious Adu Duenvost strode in and grabbed the Bedumi man by the throat, shouting in his face.

The answers came in incoherent rushes, but finally they understood: Auranuschka Perafi had interrupted them screwing in the alley and offered them a room. Some kind of subterfuge had clearly played out, but the long and short of it was that Aura must have spotted Tonio tailing her and left this pair here as a distraction while slipping away.

'I should break your jagging jaw!' Largan told Tonio.

'That's enough,' Vazi Virago snapped. She cast a disdainful look at the naked couple, then opened the window and leaned out, calling, 'Yoryn, wait there.' Then she turned to Duenvost. 'I think I know where they're going. Let's get back to the docks. We need passage across the straits.'

8

To the Shadowlands

The Perils of the Shadowlands

Beyond the portali gates is a shadowy land of mist, broken ground and caves of impossible depth. There is no vegetation, no life and no colour. But those who traverse the Shadowlands speak of malicious voices, and being stalked. Every year, knights or men-at-arms are lost beyond the gates. Scholars tell us that ghosts don't exist, but offer no better explanation for this phenomena.

SIER BRETON BARTOS, GRANDMASTER OF TAR-VIRO, 1449

Foyland-Neparia borderlands
Autumn 1472

Keffrana was burned, her skin seared red in blistered patches that wept constantly, and half her hair had been singed away. Despite this, the erling chieftain was exultant. 'I've been wanting to put my axe in that prick's skull all my life,' she kept saying, cradling her immense belly and eating for two. 'If I can nail Grenfel too, I'll die happy.'

She meant it, Elindhu knew. The veneer of civilisation in her erling-vyr tribe – and all of Foyland – was very thin. But right now, she and her comrades were the toast of the village for enabling Keffrana's victory.

My own brother is a turd, Elindhu reflected. *I'd happily slap him . . . but no more than that.* He was in Tyr, the reigning monarch of the erling people, a title that meant little given most of their kind lived in hiding and the Talmoni empire controlled the region.

The celebrations in Keffrana's village were loud and savage, but this time Elindhu forbade Fyn to join in. Instead, she thanked their hosts and announced they'd leave immediately, which Raeldaran and Keffrana accepted as wise.

'We're grateful to you,' Keffrana said, 'but things will be crazy tonight.'

The erling gave them supplies and four wild-looking mounts that Elindhu wasn't sure were really horses at all. They also gifted Elindhu the elobyne orb they'd taken from Arghyl Goraghan's body, fixing it to a staff for her, and Keffrana generously gave Soren the flamberge he'd wielded in the battle for his own. He'd thanked her, although he was clearly uneasy about it. Elindhu made a mental note to ask him why.

As they readied themselves to leave, a string of giggling erling girls lined up to kiss Fyn off, leaving Soren mortified. But most of the village were already drunk and barely noticed them leaving. Gram was unconscious, strapped to a stretcher pulled by a horse Soren was leading. Elindhu had done what she could, scraping away the festering flesh and applying poultices to soak up the poisons. She hoped it would be enough.

Before they left, Elindhu took Keffrana and Raeldaran aside and cautioned them to be careful. 'I know that you've survived thus far by hiding, but there's a storm coming and you may have to choose a side. The Triple Empire seeks to enslave the world, even if they have to burn all of Coros to achieve their mastery. The vyr move against them, seeking freedom from oppression. You know which side you're on. When the call to arms comes, I beg you to answer it. No freedom comes without price.'

They rode towards another portali gate Raeldaran knew of, two days' travel away. The woods were dank and dark and it rained intermittently. At times they saw hill-top villages behind crude palisades of wood, but gave them a wide berth, and no one appeared to notice their passing. Fyn and Soren were surly, but Elindhu kept her nose out of that. Her concern was Gram, whose skin was beginning to heat up alarmingly. By mid-afternoon, she began to look for somewhere to shelter, worried that more travel might kill him.

*

I don't want to know. I don't care anyway. I hope you got the cock-rot and die.

Soren had been having a shouting match with Fyn all day, screaming insults and abuse.

But only inside his own head.

His imagination kept conjuring new insults and new arguments with which he devastated his private imaginary Fyn – while Fyn himself rode alongside in sullen silence.

You're just a bloody child, he railed silently. *I despise you!*

Not far out of the village, they found an abandoned watchtower, which turned out to be a giant bird's nest: they had to drive out a flock of shrieking crows, which were now glowering at them from the surrounding trees. The place stank of rotting wood and bird-shit, but the stone roof had kept the interior dry.

'Get Gram inside,' Elindhu told him and Fyn. 'I need to tend him.' She looked worried, flapping about like an anxious moorhen.

Soren cooked while Fyn kept watch and Elindhu saw to Gram. The trapper was sleeping uneasily, his wounds wept and he was hot to the touch.

'He's tough as old boots, Aunty,' Soren said, shuffling over on his knees and putting an arm around her. She was back in human form, her pale face anxious. 'He'll pull through.'

'Ar-byan, Obanji,' she said fervently. Then she blushed. 'Sorry, Soren! I do know who you are.'

He shook his head to show he didn't mind, but returned to his cooking feeling unsettled. A note in her voice had made his spine shiver, as if he were a ghost she'd conjured. When the stew was ready, he spooned it into four bowls, left her two, and took the others out to Fyn. He handed him one and settled nearby, his back to the wall.

'Are you still angry with me?' the erling asked quietly.

'No,' Soren lied.

Fyn snorted, and then in an eerie rush of energy and flesh became female, the change only really visible in the subtle changes to the curve of her chest and buttocks. 'I stayed male all that night,' *Fynarhea* said. 'I'm saving my womanly side for you.'

'You're wasting your time. I'm full of glyma and I can't be with you.'

141

'It's only a few years; just an exhalation of time,' she said, her usually hard voice tinged with notes of pleading. 'You think I have no restraint, but I do. I'd wait for you.'

Her declarations of affection left Soren even more confused. 'We barely know each other.'

'But we will,' Fynarhea replied. 'Anyway, how does anything ever start? You see someone you fancy and make a move. If it comes to something, you ride it out, and get to know them along the way. Or that's how it is for me.' She looked sideway apologetically. 'I wasn't even myself last night. I was in heat. Those erling girls meant nothing.'

'Nothing in the world means nothing,' Soren retorted, shovelling food into his mouth.

'Is that right? So what does sleeping with Aunty Eli mean?' Fynarhea sniffed.

'We didn't "sleep together" – we *slept*. She understands me – you don't!'

'Whatever. Go hide under her skirts – and have a good sniff of her fanny while you're there.' Fynarhea rose, and despite the rain, stalked away, peeling off clothes and pulling her wolf-skin up over her head. A few moments later, she bounded away on all fours.

His face burning, Soren stumbled back indoors, and found Elindhu at Gram's side, studiously bathing his forehead. 'Um, sorry if you heard that,' he mumbled.

'It's all right, dear, I've heard a lot worse,' she replied, not looking up. 'Fetch me my pack, please. This isn't going well.' Gram was sweating profusely, radiating heat, but his skin had gone pale. 'Hurry.'

For the next hour, he helped Elindhu bathe the Avas man, trying to cool him down, while she combined powders and dried leaves with water, then either salved the wound or poured the mixture into his throat, before setting up another batch. All the while it poured outside, the wind howling like the ghosts in the Shadowlands. Sometimes Soren was sure he heard Fynarhea, howling desolately, the sound swirling around them. But his fears weren't for her, but for Gram, who was going downhill fast.

'Wake up, Gram,' Elindhu implored the vorlok. 'Wake up and fight!'

*

Gram was caught in the mists, stumbling amid broken ruins where wraiths whispered from behind dead trees beneath a skull moon. The wind licked at his ribs and spine as if his flesh were insubstantial. Rats scuttled in his wake, thousands of them, seeking to bring him down and devour him alive.

But his beloved's voice drew him on. 'Romara,' he called after her, glimpsing her again through the trees, robed in white with blood-red hair, the horn in her forehead glittering like ice. 'Wait for me!'

'This way, my love,' she called, and led him through the maze of shattered stone dwellings beneath a sea of stars and that deathly moon, to a square where a well waited, oozing black liquid over its lip to pool and drain into the cobbles. The reek of iron and blood filled his nostrils.

The courtyard was empty: Romara had vanished.

Then his eyes were drawn to the overflowing well, where two hands had emerged and gripped the rim and an old woman's leering head appeared, her long hair thick with blood. Her eyes were moons, lifeless orbs old as time, and her face split into a hideous grin.

'*Romara? Mother?*' Then he realised and corrected himself. '*Urghul.*'

The Devourer tittered softly. 'Third time lucky.' She clambered from the flow of blood and faced him, just as ghastly as the plates in the *Book of Lux* his first pastor had gifted him at his birth-ceremony. In fact, just like them.

Exactly alike.

'I'm imagining this,' he blurted. 'This isn't real.'

'You think not?' Urghul the Devourer flowed towards him in a sight-defying rush, until she was suddenly right before him, filling his senses. The stench of blood was overpowering, her claws on his arms icy, her eyes boring through him. 'I'm the most real thing in Creation. All else is delusion.'

That didn't sound right, but then, nothing did here. 'What's happening to me?'

'You're dying, and I'm here to devour you, Vorlok,' the Queen of Evil told him. She leaned in, brushing cold lips to his, her breath so full of rot that he gagged. 'I can't wait to pick my way through your soul.'

She grabbed his shoulders, infinitely strong, and drew him towards the well. In moments he was staring down into the blood welling up over the stones and pooling around his feet, then with a gurgle it drained away and instead he faced a tunnel of pulsing flesh. The rim was made of jagged teeth, and flames licked up from below.

The Maw, where evildoers and unbelievers were devoured for ever and ever.

'Come down, and lay with me for all time,' Urghul purred. 'It's time, Gram.'

The hole beneath him pulsed wetly, whispering his name with the voice of his mother, and everyone else he'd lost. He bowed his head and prepared to fall . . .

Gram?

The stricken whisper, felt more than heard, pulled his eyes from that vertiginous hole in the universe and he saw Romara watching helplessly, her face shifting from the pale Miravian with auburn hair to the horned, skinless monster he loved just as firmly.

'Let her go,' Urghul rasped. 'You'll see her below.'

'But she's here,' he gasped. 'She's not dead.'

'Wake up, Gram,' a disembodied voice called. *'Wake up and fight!'*

His eyes flashed open as he shouted, *'ROMARA! ROMARA!'*

But she wasn't there.

Other people he cared for were, though: Elindhu and Soren, babbling encouragement and thanks to the skies, their tired, worried faces lighting up with joy and relief. He grabbed the magia and the initiate and pulled them to him, tears falling from his eyes and turning the world liquid.

'I met the Devourer,' Gram said weakly, his face awed. 'I looked into the Maw.'

'Yes, dear,' Elindhu murmured, stroking his forehead. 'Just rest. Try to sleep.'

'Holes in reality, leading straight to the fires,' the trapper babbled on, deaf to her. 'My mother calling my name. She's down there, being devoured . . .'

'No, dearie,' she replied. 'She's at peace, ar-byan. And you need to sleep.'

Please, she thought. *Rest. That fever just about killed you.*

Soren had stayed with her all through the crisis. Even Fynarhea had reappeared, surly and belligerent, to keep watch and bring water. They'd been here a night and a day already, and were looking at another night, and all the time, Romara was being taken further and further away. But Gram was too weak to move, despite his remarkable resilience.

'Sleep,' she said again, adding a touch of glyma to the command, and a few seconds later, he was snoring softly. She glanced across at Soren. 'Well done, lad. You get some rest, too.'

They shared a fond look; during the last twenty-four sleepless hours while they'd been working together, sharing stress and hope alike, he'd spilled his soul, telling her all about his family, the dead mother he'd loved and the tyrant father he'd loathed, and his fears for his sister, who was supposedly in a convent somewhere in the north.

That she constantly saw Obanji in the young man's face was troubling Elindhu. At times throughout their vigil she'd wanted to hold him again, a physical need for comfort, but the blurring of lines in her tired brain and the suppressed yearnings of a lifetime made her mistrust herself and her responses.

You're twenty years too old to be getting hot flushes over a boy, she scolded herself. *Especially if it's just because he reminds you of Obanji.* Though she knew she was lying to herself on that front, too: Soren was Soren, and her heart knew that.

It wasn't just the inappropriateness of this new weakness that fed her self-doubt, but what it told her about herself. Loss of emotional control was an urgent warning that her grip on the glyma was increasingly tenuous. She'd felt her control slipping as she fought Arghyl Goraghan, with Romara and Gram in sight but out of reach. During the desperate fight, her vision had begun to turn scarlet and she'd felt a ball of rage ripping at her insides. If Keffrana hadn't reached Goraghan and cut him down, she knew she would have lost control.

This journey is breaking me. It's destroying us all.

But she had no choice but to go on. Romara was still in the hands of their enemies and Jadyn and Aura were out there, too – if the Twelve were merciful – seeking Nilis Evandriel and the truth. Despite her weariness, she had to go on.

She rose and went out into the cool evening air. The rain had stopped and the Foylish Highlands were a vision of wet heather, purplish-crimson clouds and shafts of pale light.

'So, what's got into you this time?' she asked Fynarhea, who was moping on the porch. 'I asked you to shadow us, for our sake and yours. You did well at first, but of late you've been a proper pain in the arse, and I'm sick of it.'

'It's not my fault—'

'I'm also sick of people telling me things aren't their fault,' Elindhu snapped. 'We're on a life-or-death journey to rescue our friends, while you're plaguing us with your petty grievances, urges and ego. I know you think the world revolves around you – every *child* does – but it's time to grow up, or you can sod off back to Semmanath-Tuhr.'

Fynarhea hung her head. 'I'm sorry, Rann Elindhu.'

'As you should be. You're playing games with Soren, who's at a vulnerable age, and you're undermining me. It can't go on.' She put her hands on her hips and said firmly, 'So, you can grow up, or you can go home. Your choice.'

The erling was abruptly on the verge of tears. 'In Semmanath-Tuhr I knew who I was. But out here, there's so many people and places, and I don't who I am in it.'

'Then go home, dear,' Elindhu told her.

Fynarhea looked agonised. 'But Aunty, I *hate* it there. I *can't* go back.' She dropped to one knee. 'I'll do better, I promise. Just let me stay. *Please.*'

This journey is going to end in death, Elindhu thought glumly. *I shouldn't allow this.* But with Gram so sick and Soren inexperienced, she needed whoever she could get. 'Fine, but this is your last warning.'

'I won't let you down,' the erling girl vowed. 'I swear by the Twelve.'

Elindhu stifled a yawn, utterly exhausted. 'Keep watch,' she ordered. 'I need rest.'

She re-entered the watchtower, where she found Gram and Soren both deeply asleep. After laying out her sleeping mat across the fire from them, she took a moment to study their faces, unable to stop her eyes lingering on Soren's boyish features and notice yet again how like the young Obanji he was. Obanji had been twenty when they met, his accepting smile instantly captivating, as was his wry humour and wisdom. They'd forged an immediate friendship, always sensibly restrained and platonic; it had taken love years to creep up on them, the natural flow of emotions stifled by the poisonous nature of elobyne and the glyma, and the secret of her true race.

Oba, I see you in Soren, every day – but I see him, *too, and it's driving me mad.*

She rolled over and stared at the old stone walls instead, thinking how better life would be for them all, if only the glyma wasn't a chalice of venom. But exhaustion muddled her thoughts and now she found herself thinking of Gram's description of his death vision, of a well that went all the way to the Devourer's Maw.

She fell into torrid dreams of spells that went awry and flames bursting from her hands, burning a hole in the ground through which she fell, into a sea of fire . . .

Soren woke to pale sunlight creeping through the open door. Gram, sprawled on his back, was snoring like a bellows, while Elindhu was snuffling in distress, clearly caught up in a nightmare. He crawled to her side and shook her shoulder. 'Aunty, wake up.'

She mumbled, half-woke, then fell asleep again, her odd, homely face going slack and her body going still again. 'Oba,' she sobbed dazedly. 'Don't go.' Her grey braids had unravelled, but they suddenly curled up tight, reminding him of a child hiding from the world.

Choking at this glimpse of her inner sorrow, Soren tucked the blanket around her and held her until she settled again, her hair going limp once more, then he gently detached himself and went outside. Fynarhea was watching the sun rise, and after relieving his bladder, Soren joined the erling. When they grunted shy greetings, Soren felt like they were starting all over again, but perhaps that was a good thing.

'Do you need to sleep?' he asked.

'No,' Fynarhea replied flatly. 'Can we be friends again?'

Soren thought about that. 'Friends, yes. But that's all. Sorry, but it's the way the Order is.'

'I know. I mean, we have a few glyma-users at Semmanath-Tuhr, but I never understood what they sacrificed for that power. I just thought they were arrogant.' She glanced towards the door. 'I don't know how Rann Elindhu does it.'

'She's amazing,' Soren agreed.

'You love her,' Fynarhea accused.

'It's *collegial* love,' Soren replied quickly. 'We're Falcons: that's a real bond. But we all know the rules. Anyway, it's not like that. She's Aunty Eli and that's all.'

Although when she was in erling form, she was another thing altogether.

'What am I to you?' Fynarhea asked morosely.

Soren realised he needed to be honest, even if it hurt. 'You're someone I might have wanted to, um, learn about love with. But I can't, so we can't.'

'But you'll put your arms round Elindhu instead,' she muttered sourly.

'Because she's safe, and you're not.'

Fynarhea flinched. 'Thanks for nothing.'

'Sorry, but in the last few months I've lost my parents, my sister and the man I thought of as my mentor in the Order. I need someone to look out for me, guide me and keep me sane. Right now, that's Aunty Eli. She'll stop me doing anything stupid.'

'So you admit you might do something stupid?'

'Because I *am* stupid,' Soren agreed bitterly, thinking about Elindhu in erling form, lissome and mysterious, yet still reassuringly her. 'But I'm *smart* enough to know that.'

They fell silent as he reflected on the things he'd just confessed, deciding it was all true, and maybe even the right things to have said. But maybe he'd also wrecked this relationship.

With a heavy sigh, Fynarhea put her arm around his shoulders. 'Elindhu threatened to send me home, but I've persuaded her to let me stay, but I have to be good. So I will be.'

Soren patted her knee awkwardly, then they shuffled apart. But at least it was civil, and after a while, comfortable too. By the time Fyn went inside to join the sleepers, Soren felt that he'd passed some kind of a test, and maybe grown up a bit more.

With Gram still weak, they had to stay put. The day crawled by, with bursts of sudden rain and interludes of glorious sunshine. Once, Soren glimpsed a herd of deer on a nearby ridge, and twice he saw Foylish hunters, but no one came near.

Mid-afternoon, a still yawning Elindhu came out and settled beside him. She looked rested, and had some colour back. 'Gram's eating,' she reported. 'Ideally, I'd keep him abed for a few days yet, but we'll move on tomorrow. He says they were taking Romara and him to Tar-Brigida, the Order bastion at Folkstein, to put them on trial. That's a process that takes about a week, so we can still get there in time to ... well, do what we can.'

'Is there any hope?' Soren asked.

'Not much, but I have to try. Soren, you're just an initiate, so this isn't on you.'

'I'm still the best sword around,' Soren replied, with a show of bravado. 'And you and Obanji and everyone else have been giving me tips and I'm practising every day and—'

She interrupted him with a raised hand. 'Yes, yes, dear, but this is a suicidal gesture. We're not going to be able to get into the bastion, let alone get Romara out. And you've got your whole life ahead of you.'

'You can't get rid of me, Aunty. I'd follow you into the Devourer's Maw.' He grabbed her hand earnestly. 'You and the Falcons are my family now. I'm going everywhere you go, no matter what.'

'Oh, for the enthusiasm of youth.' She sighed and conceded, 'We'll go after Romara, do what we can, and then see. But honestly, dear boy, I fear that we're already too late.'

'Elan, you jagatai scum, your baby killed me,' a woman's voice wailed. *'It ripped me open and I bled away.'*

A baby shrieked a moment later, from the same direction. 'Papa,' it moaned.

'Who's that one?' Tevas grunted conversationally as they traversed the misty vales of the Shadowlands.

Elan Sandreth looked puzzled. 'You'd think I'd know, given she bore my child, but I really can't remember the silly get's name.' He shook his head. 'I remember she was dumb as a doe and didn't know shit about contraception. Died in childbirth – served her right.'

Yet again, Tevas silently questioned his choice of company. 'For her to be here, you must be feeling a little guilty about it. It's well known that this place plays with our subconscious.'

'Guilty? Not really. I mean, I've got a dozen or so bastards – that I know about – but Ma's policy is to deny all involvement. If there's no proof it's mine, it's not mine, right? That one was drowned by the midwife. Ma's orders. I always felt a little bad about that.'

Elysia on high, is that what passes for remorse among these highborn pricks?

As ever, Tevas was doing all the work. He'd had the unconscious Romara Challys slung over his back the whole time they navigated these treacherous mists. He was frightened he'd already deviated from the bearing he needed. Twice they'd had to work their way around holes that fell into nothing and his sense of direction was wavering.

'You'll walk with us forever,' murmured a half-familiar Abuthan voice.

Obanji Vost, Tevas realised. *A traitor – or just loyal to the wrong people?*

'Are these actual ghosts?' Elan asked.

'Some scholars say malevolent spirits haunt the Shadowlands,' Tevas answered absently. 'Others say they're erling ghosts. Or that this is the pagan Lands of the Dead. But the one I believe is that there's something out there that picks thoughts from our heads and uses them against us. So don't listen – and never follow them.'

You'll come to us eventually, came a dry female voice in his ear. *I'm waiting.*

He shuddered and closed his mind.

The mist reverted to whispering imprecations from the jilted lovers of Elan Sandreth, who didn't appear to be too concerned, though he did wince at some of the barbs about the size of his cock and what he did with it.

A man's insecurities are always telling, Tevas mused.

His own ghosts he could live with: men he'd killed; folk he'd seen die who hadn't deserved it. A man he'd cheated who'd hanged himself rather than face debtors' court. His sister, who he'd abandoned to fend for herself.

I'm a piece of shit, and one day I'll pay, he admitted.

You bet you will, the Devourer whispered. Or he imagined it. Who knew?

'Come on,' he said, 'let's pick up the pace.' He lengthened his stride and lifted his flamberge pommel to light their way. As he walked he decided it was high time he raised a genuine fear: his own safety and status.

'Milord, we have a problem,' he said, a while later as they rested on a hillock just above the fog, Romara lying senseless at his feet. 'You've promised to take me on as your bondsman, but we've had no opportunity to legally formalise that. So when we arrive at Folkstein, I will need your protection. My life is literally in your hands, and – well, I'm owed a share of the bounty. That's not giving me a lot of reassurance.'

Elan's fleshy face wrinkled in thought, then he gave Tevas a sidelong look. 'Listen, you probably think I'm a back-stabbing snit. Jagat, you're carrying a woman I've falsely married for her fortune! I'm a rake and a dastard, that's undeniable. But we all need friends, in high places and low. You and I, we've fought side by side, saved each other. I value you. There are plenty of people I'd betray in a heartbeat, but you're not one of them.'

'You sound like you mean it.' Tevas wondered if he did.

'Then I've not lost my touch,' Elan chuckled. 'But it's true. I'll vouch for you.'

He offered his hand, and Tevas shook it thoughtfully. 'Then I'm your man.'

With a groan, he swept Romara back onto his shoulder and they got underway again.

Navigating the Shadowlands was an exercise in staying calm and maintaining one's sense of direction as much as sense of self, but helpfully, the landscape was like a scale model of the real world and the known portali gates tended to be on hilltops. And once you learned them, the unmoving constellations above helped too.

With his little remaining glyma augmenting his strength enough to carry Romara, they strode on, and after about half a day in the darkness, he spied the distinctive low hill above a dried-up riverbed, topped by a ruined roundhouse of stone. The door was intact, and shut.

'This is it,' he told Elan. 'Welcome to Tar-Brigida, the bastion in Folkstein.'

There was a bell-rope hanging beside the door, but Elan didn't bother with that, going straight for the handle. It was locked.

'You have to ring,' Tevas panted. 'They don't let just anyone walk in.'

Elan grimaced, gripped the rope and tugged. The bell rang, an oddly dislocated chime as the sound penetrated the space between two worlds.

Wearily, Tevas put Romara down and checked her breathing. It was steady, although her face was swollen and bruised from his several blows.

Doing this to her was the right thing, but it felt all wrong. She was family and he had begun to regret his actions, regardless of the bounty.

Rom, I always thought you'd get out intact.

The door opened and a dozen men poured out, brandishing swords and, in two cases, a flamberge. One of those, a Bravanti knight, looked Tevas over, then demanded the papers giving him the right to wield his elobyne weapon.

'He's my bondsman,' Elan said. 'I'm Lord Elan Sandreth and I vouch for that.'

The magic word was 'Sandreth'.

Ah, the benefits of wealth, status, and having his mother in the archon's bed.

'Of course, Milord,' the knight said, then he looked hard at Romara. 'Is that who I think it to be?' When Tevas nodded, he grinned widely. 'Excellent. Let's get her in and I'll notify the Grandmaster. Welcome to Folkstein.'

9

Change of Heart

Draegar

There is a misunderstanding many have about fallen knights and the vyr. They are often mistaken for the same thing, but that's not correct. Fallen knights are trained in the disciplined use of the glyma, but when their control fails, they're a danger to all. So pity the fallen. But those knights who reject the way of Akka and embrace the vyr are worse: they become draegar, *and those we destroy without pity or remorse.*

RYSTAN GABRIEL, SCHOLAR, PETRAXUS 1392

Bedum-Mutaza
Autumn 1472

Oars kissed the water, the rowers strained and the longboat flowed sleekly across the black water. Behind it, Bedum City was a distant cacophony of drums, music and coloured lanterns, myriad celebrations blended into one. Ahead was Mutaza, quiet, except for the wailing calls to prayer.

Jadyn bent his back into the next pull on the oars, not too proud to help out the rowers when speed was of the essence. But his head was still spinning at their sudden departure from Bedum.

One moment he'd been sitting down to a meal in the hostel, when Aura – who'd gone off to answer nature's call, or so she said – had bustled in with a purse of coppers. In a few moments she'd hired not one room but two – both on the third floor, one at the back and one on the other side. She'd led him up to the third floor, saying – quite loudly – that they'd sleep there tonight, but before they'd stepped through the door, she was pushing in an obviously lustful couple who'd just arrived, looking at her expectantly. Before Jadyn could open his mouth, she'd rushed him to the other room, opened the window and leapt through and onto a neighbouring roof.

Without a word, he'd followed.

'We escape sneak Tonio,' Aura told him, as they climbed down some rickety stairs.

So I was right. 'Do you know why he's following us?'

'Not knowing. Only know must go.'

'Whose money was that?'

'Took from bad man,' Aura muttered. 'Not important.'

'But we just got here – how do you know he's a bad man?'

'Is rich; is bad,' she answered. 'That be how knowing.'

Twenty minutes later, she'd used some of that coin to cross the Jaws of Leos in this longboat. She sat in the stern, leaving Jadyn, the boat's owner, his brother and son to row manfully across the narrow strait.

Halfway across, the smuggler informed them that the Mutazan galley flashing a lantern at them would also require paying. Once that bribe had been handed over, on they went, into a canal winding into Mutaza, much of which was built on stilts. Jadyn was alarmed at one point when a crocodile rose beside them, but the smuggler broke off rowing to prod it away and the beast cruised harmlessly by. They passed hundreds of hovels where men sat drinking on ramshackle little jetties, then pulled into some stone steps behind a ruined stone building with a collapsed roof.

'Shukra, Sidati,' the smuggler called to Aura, once they were safely ashore. *Thank you, Lady.* He kissed the argent she gave him, the second half of the fee. 'Seelam Akka.'

'Seelam Akka,' she responded as the longboat pushed off.

In seconds they were alone beside the stinking canal.

Jadyn was worried. Unlike Bedum, which was firmly under the heel of the Triple Empire, he'd heard that Mutaza paid only lip-service to the worship of Akka, and that northerners weren't welcome. 'Where can we find a safe place to sleep over here?' he asked.

'Sleep?' Aura scoffed. 'No sleep: we be tasking.' She pointed through the trees and roofs to a distant gleaming dome. 'Tonight, we go to Heart of World!'

He caught his breath, excited . . . 'How will we get in?' he mused to himself.

She snorted. 'You be knight, I be Magic Girl. We go where we want.' She produced two lengths of cloth and tied one, a dirty brown colour, around his head, fashioning it into a Mutazan turban. The second, a colourful headscarf, she knotted around her piled-up hair, creating an exotic-looking tower. 'There, now: I be lady—'

'And I'm your servant,' he drawled, resignedly. 'Again.'

'Bueno, you catch on.' She beamed. 'Come, come.'

Stony-eyed house-guards watched them pass through the back streets, peering through iron-grilled gates, and passers-by gave them a wide berth, but no one molested them. 'Why's it so quiet here?' Jadyn asked. 'Bedum was a riot.'

'Hierophant stay Bedum side. Court in Bedum, all money, all power. This side left in decay and rot, so hate hierophant. Hate north.'

She paused by the remains of a street vendor's cooking-fire and pressed her hands into the ashes. 'Look at Aura,' she commanded, then she smeared the soot over his face. 'Make you darker, more handsome. Blend in.'

He couldn't help feeling she was laughing at him. But he still rubbed it in.

They had to pause to avoid Watch patrols, then pressed on towards the looming domus: the Hejiffa Dhouma, the holiest pre-Akkanite site in the Caliphates.

'Will it be open?' Jadyn asked.

'Always open,' Aura replied, 'but temple has guards.'

'How do you know? Have you been here before?'

'No, but all domus like this. Before Akka, domus be for Zynochi gods: twelve peoples with animal heads. Very strange. This one named for Dhouma, Lord of Fate. From him come northern words "doom" and "dome". Interesting, si? Aura very wise.'

'You are a living wonder,' he told her, amused but sincere.

She snorted. 'You flatten me, I think.'

'It's *flatter*. Words of praise are flattering.'

She pulled a face. 'Then what is "flatten"?'

'That's to, um, press you flat . . . flat to the ground or a wall.'

'If you be real man, you do both, eh?' She winked and sashayed on.

Ten minutes later, they were standing in the lee of a silent mansion, across the square from the Hejiffa Dhouma. It was massive, a match for anything Jadyn had seen on his one visit to Petraxus, but unlike those blockish edifices of shiny white marble, the Hejiffa was dark, time-stained and intricate, every spire and carved curlicue a sublime work of art, but discoloured, weathered and crumbling. It was lit by lamps in each minaret and corner turret, and the stained-glass windows were glowing from within. The dome itself gleamed in the moonlight; the entire surface was, according to Aura, covered in pearlescent seashells. It was breath-taking, even in the darkness.

They were not alone: the square before it was filled with a gentle hubbub of conversation from the hundreds of people gathered there.

'Homeless,' Aura told him. 'Forbidden entrance, but permitting outside.'

Smoky heat was provided by innumerable braziers, while priests went among the people, dispensing little bowls of food and water from big pots on wheels. On the main steps a holy man was droning out scripture from the *Book of Akka*, though his misplaced pauses and mispronunciations suggested he had no understanding of what he was saying. Red-clad temple guards patrolled the square, and more guarded the portals.

'How do we get in?' Jadyn asked.

Aura considered. 'Two things to know. One, woman not be permitted. Domus be for men. Two, up close they see you are white. So must enter not seen.'

'Women aren't allowed in?' Jadyn was shocked. 'Surely Akka is for everyone?'

Aura snorted dismissively. 'Zynochi people, nice. Zynochi priest, not nice. Woman pray in home, they say. Only men pray in temple. Is silly. Is wrong. But priests decide.'

'But *anyone* can enter an Akkanite church. Isn't this an Akkanite dome now?'

'Si, but Hejiffa Dhouma be "historic", so not convert. Hierophant angry, but caliph no back down.'

Jadyn looked at her thoughtfully. 'I didn't know that.'

'You learn seven languages, you become wise like Aura.' She patted his hand. 'Don't feel bad. Am sure Jadyn knows much of pig-farming and mud that Aura not know.'

'Probably,' he conceded. 'So, how do we get in? Is there a back door?'

'Many, but all have guards, am sure.' She looked up at the forest of spires surrounding the giant orb of the dome. 'Up, must go. Climb near building, cross to roof, get in. Si?'

He gazed about, noting that the domus was hemmed in on three sides by large buildings, with just a few paces between them. 'They look jumpable,' he agreed. 'Let's try it.'

They worked their way back into the maze of cobbled alleys until they found a darkened building backing onto the Hejiffa Dhouma. Aura picked a locked door and they slipped silently into the dark corridors of what looked like an administrative building. There was a guard room, but the men gathered round a fire playing dice didn't notice as Jadyn and Aura flitted past. They soon found a door and steps leading up to the flat roof, which jutted out to within a dozen paces from the decorative battlements of the domus.

They left their packs and bedrolls against a pile of debris that looked like it might have been left by builders, before peering over the edge. The cobbled street below looked a long way down.

'To make that jump needs glyma,' Jadyn pointed out. 'We have none.'

'We find other way,' Aura muttered.

Jadyn tried to engage the aegis, to see if it might guide them, but all that came to him was confirmation that an unassisted jump would result in broken limbs and smashed skulls. He went to the debris pile, hoping something there might help, but other than a few short planks, there was nothing, certainly nothing long enough to bridge the gap.

'We can't do it,' he admitted, returning to her at the ledge.

'Si, am feeling same. No way to cross, many way to die.' She sounded more annoyed than despondent. 'Aegis see result of act; but can't help jump.'

'Aye, that's the sum of it. I've traded superhuman athleticism for imperfect foresight of my weakness.' He settled back on his haunches. 'But remember the erling valley, the lake there? The Wardens found some way of making the water breathable, so that the erlings could build a whole castle underwater and live on the bottom of the lake, still breathing air! The aegis *should* have the power to change nature. It's not *just* a predictive tool.'

In fact, it's not a tool at all, he thought, trying to recall what he'd been told about it. *It's a state of grace.* But how to harness that insight, he had no idea. *How do you turn water to air? How do you change something's nature?*

No answers came to him.

Then Aura pressed her lips to his ear. 'Am remembering: in pirate attack, Aura be with Marika. She stab Aura – Aura make stop. *She tell knife not to stab.* It not stab.'

Jadyn hadn't realised things had got so deadly in that cabin. 'Why didn't you say?'

'It no matter, Aura fine,' she replied offhandedly. 'Thing be: how did Aura stop knife?' She produced one of her myriad hidden daggers – this one a stiletto from a sleeve scabbard – and handed it to him. 'You stab Aura.'

'*Uh, what?*'

She rolled her eyes. 'You stab – not *actual*, just trying to . . . what is word? . . . procreate the minute.'

'"Recreate" the moment?' Jadyn guessed.

'Si, that.' She gestured impatiently. 'Now try.'

He tentatively stabbed the stiletto at her chest, but when he stopped well short, she snapped 'Neya! Again. Like you want to hurt Aura.'

'But I don't.' He poked it at her half-heartedly – and felt momentary resistance.

'Si!' she purred, 'again!'

He stabbed properly this time, hilt first, but halfway to her breast the stiletto froze, his hand slipped on the handle and he lost his grip.

The dagger continued to hang in the air and Aura's face lit up.

Akka on High, Jadyn marvelled. *I'm not even sure how I'd do that with the glyma! Maybe a force grip, using the* Tenac *rune?* 'What's causing that? What did you do?'

She grinned like a cat with cream. 'Is thing I practise alone, after Marika and knife.' She placed her hand beside the floating knife and he realised it was actually dropping, but very slowly. 'See, this knife not stopped, but now falling *slow-slow*. But when we throw coins to each other, we move *faster* than normal. This aegis can be for fast *and* slow.'

'That's incredible.'

'No, is *credíbile*.' She plucked the stiletto from the air, tossed it up then stopped it again. 'See, credibile. Am Magic Girl.'

'I thought the only thing we could affect with the aegis was ourselves,' he marvelled.

'Now be knowing different.' Aura cast about, then scurried to the pile of rubbish, returning with some of the short planks. 'Have idea.'

Explaining oneself in Talmoni was irritatingly difficult, but sometimes actions spoke louder than words. That was one of Aura's hopes as she tossed the planks into the gap between the buildings, willing them to *stop*. She couldn't have said how, precisely, but it worked: she caught them at just the right moment and now they hung in the air, the nearest at her feet, the other three strung out across the gap like stepping stones, finishing beside the roof of the domus.

The question was whether they could take weight in this state.

Before Jadyn could prevent her, she stepped onto it and bounded across, now secure in the knowledge that she wouldn't fall and shatter herself on the cobbles far below, because the aegis was telling her so. It was a self-fulfilling prophecy – provided you were prepared to commit to the impossible.

She could feel all kinds of forces and energies working around and through her, none of which she understood. It didn't matter – she just had to know what she wanted and the universe provided. *Buena! This is how life should be.* She didn't need to know the hows and whys; all she needed from the world was obedience.

There would be limits, no doubt, but right now, who cared?

But even that thought brought awareness that the planks were fighting gravity, and were about to lose. 'Hurry,' she hissed across the gap. 'Jadyn Knight, *come!*'

He stared across the void back at her, and she realised that he was more frightened than she'd ever seen him. *Because he has no control here*, she realised. *He can only trust.*

She saw the moment he decided to do exactly that: he stepped from the parapet onto the first of the planks and launched himself . . .

And they took his weight. He wobbled, teetered onwards and leapt the final gap into her waiting arms. His heart was thudding painfully against her chest, and he was shaking in relief, but she saw exhilaration on his face, too. Then he kissed her with a passion she didn't recognise, a fierce devouring, while his body enveloped hers. He was fizzing with fear and hope and joy.

Ah, this is what I want from him: passion. She gave it back, and it felt glorious.

That's how she forgot the planks, which dropped and smashed into the cobbles below. Voices yelped in the alley below and she pulled away. 'Nice kiss, but must hurry.'

A flustered Jadyn went to follow, then groaned. 'We left our packs on the roof.'

'Neya problema, we find later.' She'd just felt another premonition: danger was coming. 'We go, *now.*'

The domus, as was traditional, was in the shape of a keyhole: a long rectangle attached to the round dome, aligned north-south. The roof was a steep 'vee' but had walkways on either side, leading towards the dome. They took the walkway on their side right up to the base of the pearlescent dome and found a door, closed but unlocked. Somehow they *knew* there were no guards or priests on the other side, and entered to find a circular passage, lit by oil lamps, that ran left and right around the base of the dome. Through the walls they could hear the chanting of priests somewhere below, in the prayer hall.

Go right, Aura guessed, but Jadyn, also attuned to the aegis now, was already headed that way. She felt a burst of pride for having guided him to that state. But she could feel that unidentified danger closing in . . .

It's almost here.

They came to another door to the outside and a stair going down, but neither would lead to revelation, her premonitions told her. 'On,' she started to say, just as a man loomed out of the dark. The startled temple guard went to shout, but Jadyn's right fist hammered into his jaw and he went down like a poleaxed bull. The sound of his armoured body thudding to the stone floor was alarmingly loud.

The danger she sensed didn't accelerate, but nor did it fade.

She darted ahead, running round the curve as future possibilities coalesced around a door leading to the inside of the dome. She found it, pulled it open and found herself inside the domus ceiling, on a narrow walkway with a low wall that ran right around the circular dome – and there above her was the famous mosaic, the map of the known world.

She had a vertiginous moment when she realised that the drop to the stone floor was over a hundred paces. She could see the altar directly below, covered in lit candles, with rows of scarlet-clad priests kneeling to twelve animal-headed gold statues – clearly pagan worship was alive and well here after dark. She looked for the Akka statue and found what she thought must be it behind the altar, shrouded in canvas.

The unknown danger was now imminent. *We have a minute at most*, she estimated.

Jadyn had caught up and was staring out at the mosaic, eyes gleaming. She gripped his hand and tried to study the map, but it wasn't easy: the mosaic was filthy with dust and smoke and festooned with what looked like decades of spider webs.

Couldn't these priests clean it occasionally?

Through the grime she made out an upside-down image of the city, with Bedum-Mutaza at the top, and around it, a stylised portrayal of the Inner Seas, Bedumassa and Zynochia. It placed this very spot, the Hejiffa-Dhouma, at the apex.

The Heart of the World.

But nothing chimed with her and she blurted, '*Che nessa ey!*' just as Jadyn said the same words – *This isn't it* – in bewildered Talmoni. Then the answer hit her, just as he spoke it: '*There's another mosaic underneath!*'

The acoustics of the dome caught their words and threw them out into the chamber below, and a hundred bearded faces of turbaned priests looked up, gasping in outrage.

'Ah, jagatai,' Jadyn swore.

Someone below was shouting in Mutazi, a challenge or an order, or maybe both. Boots thudding, guards came running, and she barely heard what Jadyn was saying because her premonitions exploded into vivid reality as the giant main doors of the temple crashed open and she heard a harsh voice direct from her nightmares.

'Stand aside,' Yoryn Borghart cried. 'This is the Exemplar herself!'

They're here. That fact reverberated through Borghart's mind as he and Vazi Virago strode down the aisle of the Hejiffa Dhouma, followed by Adu Duenvost and Largan Rameleau, accompanied by two dozen Vestal soldiers. The temple guards were shouting warnings, the priests shrieked indignantly at this invasion, but he didn't care.

Kaen and Perafi are here.

The worshippers fled, but a row of temple guards formed up in front of the altar and the priests. Everyone was looking bewildered, but the guards were resolutely locking shields and presenting spears. Duenvost and Rameleau kindled glyma, but Borghart and the Exemplar held back, in case it dimmed the aegis-premonitions that had led them here.

His eyes went to the altar plinth and the ancient statues of animal-headed men and women, the ancient gods of Zynochia. The image of Akka which should have been standing there had been pushed back and was covered by dark cloth. He seethed at the sight.

Damned pagans.

Then the khateeb, the senior cleric, stepped to the fore, impressively fearless, and addressed them in accented Talmoni. 'Who are you to defile this sanctuary?'

'Stand aside,' Borghart repeated. 'This is the Exemplar herself!'

The head priest didn't look at all impressed; he puffed himself up to deliver a tirade, but Vazi spoke first. 'Khateeb, I am Vaziella al-Nuqheel, the Exemplar,' she told him. 'We are in pursuit of vyr renegades. They are up in the dome, right now.'

Then she added a short burst of Zynochi, perhaps to remind him of her roots.

Rank and protocol demanded that the khateeb obey her, but centuries of mistrust between Order and Church, Talmoni and Zynochi, even men and women, argued otherwise.

Suddenly, there was a crashing sound from beneath the dome, and stone fragments started raining down amid a billowing cloud of dust. Those immediately beneath shrieked in alarm and took to their heels as a massive dust cloud enveloped the altar. Confusion reigned, and that persuaded the khateeb to part his men and wave the Exemplar forward.

Vazi broke into a run, Borghart beside her and their men clattering after them, as they headed for the calamity ahead. The air was clearing a little as the dust settled, revealing a pile of debris, mostly mosaic tiles, from what he could see. He looked up to see the world-famous map of Bedum-Mutaza had partially collapsed, revealing something beneath, a painting so faded and chipped as to be undecipherable.

There was movement at the bottom rim of the dome: Aura Perafi and Jadyn Kaen were there, at least eighty paces above, looking bewildered.

'There they are!' he shouted, casting about, and instantly, visions showed him ways up, as if he were sending shadow-selves rushing ahead like scouts and they were reporting directly to his brain. He realised he was finally opening up to the aegis. *Thank you, Elysia!*

'You and Rameleau go right,' he told Vazi. 'Duenvost, with me.'

She didn't question and he realised she was seeing the same things as him. She grabbed Rameleau and took him towards the right-hand door, while Duenvost followed Borghart to the left. They crashed through and found stairs spiralling upwards. The Abuthan lictor surged ahead, fuelled by glyma and zeal, and Borghart let him go, unwilling to use glyma himself in case he lost the aegis. Half the soldiers followed; the rest were chasing Vazi, he presumed.

Despite his lack of glyma-energy, he was only a dozen paces behind Duenvost as they reached the third level, a dimly lit curved corridor, stretching left and right around the base of the dome. The lictor went left, but Borghart's instincts took him right, where he found an inner door, skidded to a halt and kicked it open. He found the walkway Kaen and Perafi had been standing on just a minute earlier. The air inside the dome was still hazy with dust – and the fugitives were gone.

Duenvost appeared a quarter-turn around the dome and shouted at Borghart, asking what to do. Borghart went to reply when a flash of foresight intervened and he headed right, shouting for Duenvost to follow. The renegades were on the move, heading for the roof of the prayer hall.

He tore in and out of pools of dim lamplight, heard footfalls, and an urgent call – Jadyn Kaen to Aura Perafi – then he saw movement, and instinct took over . . .

He drew on his elobyne at last, the fiery energy boiling into him, and he *unleashed* . . .

'*Aura, did you do that?*' Jadyn gasped, looking at the ceiling collapse.

She shook her head. 'Neya, neya.'

Both pressed their faces into the crook of their arms to protect their eyes and noses from the rancid dust and sharp stone fragments, then as the air began to clear a little, they stared at the newly exposed layer of the ceiling mosaic, which *possibly* depicted a fish-tailed man and a sea serpent fighting above a blazing volcano. It meant nothing to him.

Then he heard boots hammering on the marble flagstones, weapons clattering and voices shouting. Through the murk he could see Vazi Virago and Largan Rameleau, heading for a side door.

Largan, you bastard, he thought, and grabbed Aura's arm. 'We'll be trapped – we need to get back to the roof!'

He could sense two columns of men running up the stairs on both sides of the dome – they'd be here in less than a minute, 'This way!' He ran to a door facing south, towards the roof of the prayer hall. His mind's eye was showing him Vazi Virago closing in on his left and Lictor Borghart on his right; followed by glyma-knights and men-at-arms. The noose was closing.

He burst through the door, Aura at his heels, shot across the curved passage and saw stairs leading straight up – to the roof spine, he realised. But as he crossed the space, he sensed glyma-light, red and angry. He dived forward, beneath the precognitive image of a livid blast of energy, hit the stairs and tore upwards, half-turning as Aura was about to cross that open space. Her face looked alarmed as another bolt shot past her nose – this one from the other direction – then she vanished back into the dome.

'*Aura!*' He went to go back, but a dark blur appeared at the base of the stairs, where Aura had been, a copper-skinned woman wrapped in a headscarf and wielding a gleaming flamberge. Vazi Virago.

'You take her, I've got him,' the Exemplar shouted to someone, and came at him.

Jadyn spun as she launched herself up the stairs, though strangely, she didn't unleash her glyma. He battered the door at the top open, lurched through and turned, pulling out the cutlass he'd worn since the pirate attack – but she'd stepped through before he could close the door.

Her flamberge was still not lit.

'You know how this ends if you fight,' she told him. 'We both do.'

He absolutely did – because foresight told him he was dead, whether he fought or ran. But he hefted the cutlass and cried, 'Without glyma, what have you got, *girl*?'

Mocking her was dangerous, but he was hoping to provoke a mistake. She scowled, marring her perfect features, and closed in.

As he backed up, he took in his surroundings – as he'd guessed, he was on the spine of the main hall, a sloped roof with walkways on either side. The outside of the domus, its shell decorations gleaming in the moonlight, rose majestically behind her. But he sensed sentries up here, too, rushing to investigate the noise.

He would be cornered inside a minute.

Before he could devise an escape route, the Exemplar reached him . . .

Aura had been so distracted by the older mosaic that had appeared beneath the new one that she'd ignored the oncoming danger. That was a fatal mistake.

She sensed a blaze of glyma-energy an instant before it carved the air in front of her, blasting the plaster wall. In some possible futures the exposed timbers caught fire and this whole structure burned down, but she blanked those, instead concentrating on her own survival. Sensing she could no longer cross that corridor and reach Jadyn, she backed into the interior of the roof dome again, as two figures appeared, between her and Jadyn.

The Exemplar went after Jadyn, but Yoryn Borghart turned her way.

Glyma-light ignited in his hands, lighting up his harsh face as he stared at her, then he declared, 'Finally, you're mine.'

She backed onto the inner walkway and went right. The air was still clouded by dust, Vestal Guards were pouring in on all sides, and another lictor, an Abuthan with a false mask of geniality, was standing between her and the next door.

There was nowhere to run.

Myriad futures, all culminating in death, played out in her mind.

She drew throwing daggers, inching along until her buttocks hit the low guardrail of the walkway, as Borghart stepped back into view and sent tendrils of glyma-energy towards her, to snare her and reel her in. If she was taken alive, she would die horribly.

There was only one way out, and she took it, flipping herself into a graceful somersault over the rail . . .

Vazi refused to succumb to the temptation to simply kindle the glyma and *erase* this stinking renegade. Not when the flashes of the future were so clear. She could beat him without the glyma, and she would. There was no need to ruin the aegis just when it was opening up for her.

So she attacked Jadyn Kaen, trusting in her prowess – and the knowledge that Largan Rameleau was only a few seconds behind her, with glyma and no reason to hold back.

Kaen was bigger than her, but she went in hard, all speed and aggression, which was usually enough to overwhelm most men. He proved to be a serious foe, though, reading her every blow, parrying with deftness, not being drawn into rash counters, giving ground but never letting her near.

The aegis, she realised, with a frisson of shock. *With it, he's as good as I am . . .*

Her premonitions took on a darker edge as the possibility of being wounded, maimed or slain began to intrude.

The narrow walkway on the spine of the roof had spectacular views across the harbour, but it allowed little room for manoeuvre. Kaen's greater size and strength began to assert itself, while her mobility was hampered. To her chagrin, he began to drive her back.

Then Rameleau arrived behind her, she felt glyma-heat flare and realised he intended to leap up over them both and take Kaen from behind.

'Jump,' she panted. 'Take him alive.'

Then she feinted an attack, forcing Kaen to deal with her, even as Rameleau launched himself into the air, catapulting himself over them both . . .

Jadyn sensed her intent as it formed, to pin him here as Largan used his glyma-enhanced athleticism to hurdle them both and trap him. Without the blinding speed the glyma would have given the

Exemplar, he'd been holding his own, but if Rameleau got behind him, he was finished.

With options limited, he leaped from the walkway, landing on the sloped roof while Rameleau was still in mid-air. Instantly he was sliding, barely controlling it, managing to get his feet beneath him just as a Mutazan temple guard on the walkway above the guttering thrust out his spear. Jadyn, anticipating his move, twisted aside, planted a foot in the man's belly and sent him over the edge, wailing, to crunch into the cobbles below.

Scrambling upright, he saw Vazi Virago slide on her feet, perfectly balanced, towards him, while Rameleau, silhouetted on the roof's spine, blasted at him with glyma-energy.

He rolled aside, straight into the path of another sentry, parried a blow and locked hilts, then grabbed the man's collar and pulled him around, shielding himself from Rameleau's next blast. The man howled as heat washed over them both and his back ignited, then Jadyn flipped him over the edge and gave ground to avoid Vazi Virago, who had landed flawlessly. She lunged at him, her perfect features lit with annoyance.

His possible futures closed in again, and all of them ended badly.

For Yoryn Borghart, drawing on the glyma after two weeks of abstinence was like being doused in fire. He felt strong and potent, his familiar righteous anger searing through him. He used that fury to reach for the Nepari trollop with a *Tenac* spell, to grip her, reel her in and *break her smug face*.

But shockingly, she cartwheeled backwards, flinging herself into the empty air, and his spell closed on nothing. Shouting in frustration, he shot forward and looked down, expecting to see her body splatter across the elaborately patterned marble altar below.

Instead, she was halfway down, floating – then she just stopped there entirely, as if standing on an invisible floor. Her eyes met his, her face alive with wonder.

What the jagging hell?

From around the curve of the dome he could see Adu Duenvost

watching, his face stunned. The men-at-arms who were pouring onto the curved walkway had also stopped dead too and were staring in awe. Not even glyma-knights could do this.

'Buonasera, Lictor,' Aura Perafi called. 'Come and get me.'

Her words were reckless, but Aura didn't care. She felt invincible.

A second later she was dropping again, avoiding two bolts of energy, four crossbow bolts and three spears that came at her from all sides. Plummeting, she kicked off a pillar and somersaulted back into the centre of the domus, arched away from more projectiles and landed on the altar, perfectly balanced.

She curtseyed for the benefit of the enraged Borghart, then began to move as the pre-images of more spells and shafts flashed through her awareness.

Just then, somebody shouted in Nepari, 'Por aqui!' *This way!*

Instinctively trusting the voice, she spun away from the next volley that flashed and cracked around her, rolled under the sweeping scimitar of a temple guard who'd charged her and kicked him in the face, then tore past a terrified pair of priests to a side door held open by a cowled figure. She flashed through and it slammed shut, then she saw the barrier shimmer.

A locking spell, she realised, backing away. Just seconds later, someone pounded on the door, the sound weirdly distorted, but it didn't even shudder.

She was in a narrow passage, illuminated by the lantern held by the brown-cloaked man. He dropped his hood to reveal unsettling mismatched eyes set in a sharp, clever face with an iron-grey goatee and straight grey hair slicked back. He wore the red robes of a priest, though his pale skin suggested he was a northerner.

'Hurry,' he urged, switching to Talmoni. 'Your friend's in trouble.'

'This door—?'

'Frozen in time – makes it hard to break. You could do it if you tried. Now, come!'

He hurtled away, his lantern swinging, Aura on his heels. The passage which ran around the circular domus was lit by occasional lattice-work holes in the inner wall, revealing flashes of the altar. But the stranger veered away down a short side passage and into a dark office stacked high with scrolls and parchments, covered in dust and spiderwebs.

'What a waste,' the man muttered. 'The fools don't know what they've got.'

He led Aura past the piles into an anteroom to a wooden door. He turned the key and revealed an alley outside the dome.

'But Jadyn—' Aura began.

'This way!' The stranger doused the lantern, the moonlight and street lamps providing enough lights, and Aura could see they were on the opposite side of the Hejiffa Dhouma from where they'd entered. The main doors were to the south, the dome to the north, gleaming beneath the triple moons.

'But Jadyn—' Aura tried again.

'Wait ... wait ...' The man looked up and she followed his gaze and saw the flash of glyma-light and heard steel crash ...

Then someone fell from the roof and plummeted towards them, out of control ...

Jadyn had a moment's premonition that the Exemplar had lost patience, and a moment later a livid burst of crackling energy burst from her fingers, accompanied by a shriek of fury. Above her, balanced on the spine of the roof, Rameleau did the same, intending to trap him, leaving nowhere to go.

The images he saw – of fire and flame and an agonising end – left him so disoriented, he stumbled, caught his heel and fell off the roof. The alleyway below flashed towards him as he howled, '*Nooo ... !*'

The universe heeded ... or someone else did.

He lost all momentum, hanging in space – only for an instant, but time enough to right himself and drop easily to the ground.

He was wondering how the jagat he'd done that when a man said, 'You're welcome.'

He spun and saw Aura beside a cowled figure, lit up by spell-light exploding where he should have been, in the air above. Then he heard Largan Rameleau roar in rage, and fore-images showed him the ex-knight leaping, landing and cutting them down . . .

Largan appeared a moment later, dropping towards them, blade raised – but suddenly he went still, hanging motionless in the air – until the hooded man made a forbidding gesture with his fingers, then inverted them.

Largan turned in mid-air, then in an eye-blink, resumed falling.

The ex-knight hit the ground head-first before he could even think to shield. His neck snapped on impact; with a wet *crack* his skull caved in, spraying blood and brain. Jadyn took an involuntary step backwards, appalled despite his years of combat.

Aura vomited noisily in the gutter.

He looked up and saw the Exemplar, silhouetted on the roof above.

In no future did the mighty Exemplar jump. Instead, as he and the stranger watched, she emitted an audibly shaky gasp and vanished. He heard her tearing along the walkway.

She was afraid to follow, and no wonder . . .

The cowled man said, 'Come, we don't have much time.'

'But—' Jadyn turned to Aura. 'Are you all right?'

'Is fine,' Aura told him, wiping her mouth. 'He's with us—' She broke off, looking worried. 'Our bags!' she exclaimed. 'Is on far side of domus.'

Jadyn cursed; anything they left behind was an opportunity for someone to scry them. But a wall of men-at-arms and temple guards were pounding around both ends of the domus and the decision was made. 'Run,' he told her.

Perhaps they won't find it anyway, he hoped. *Akka, make it so.*

He and Aura tore after the stranger, and because they were opened up to the aegis, it suddenly felt like everything in the world but them was moving through treacle. They were barely seen as they flashed through a maze of ancient alleys, courtyards and building sites and the pursuit died away almost immediately. Still they flowed onwards, to put as much distance between them and their enemies as possible, because if they could do this, surely the Exemplar and Borghart could too.

Finally, they fetched up against one of the many canals that laced Mutaza, like the one they'd been taken up earlier. There was an interlocking web of them, plied by boats in the day and stalked by crocodiles, monitor lizards and constrictor snakes by night. However, the stranger ushered them into a waiting rowboat, they grabbed oars and pulled away until the current took over, leaving them to pole past obstacles while they caught their breath.

As they rested, the aegis loosened and faded. They were all drenched in sweat, chests heaving and legs wobbling. Clearly the aegis didn't provide the superhuman energy of the glyma, though it could do such incredible things.

We performed miracles!

'Largan must have dobbed us in,' he panted.

'What is "dobbed"?' Aura asked. 'Is bad thing, si?'

'It means informing,' he told her. 'He must've tailed us ... he and Tonio.'

'And Tonio, he do what Sergio say,' Aura said stonily. 'All of Sergio's crew betray Aura in Gaudien. All hate me.'

She's right, Jadyn realised. *They wanted to give up crime, and were tired of her schemes, and of this Gostan, too, so they tipped off the Watch. Both of them were meant to die.*

Even though she was the criminal, he felt sorry for her, knowing she wasn't the same person now. *It was murder by proxy.* The callousness took his breath away.

When she showed up again, they must have considered killing us at sea, until Rameleau persuaded them to cash us in. Then the Exemplar showed up ...

That meant he really should have destroyed the note and the mirror, back at the lighthouse.

Though if they also have the aegis, perhaps they would have found us here, anyway?

'I'm sorry,' he murmured, squeezing her arm. 'I know you loved Sergio very much.'

She looked up, her eyes flinty. 'Not love. Never love. Aura never trust men again.'

He wanted to say, 'You can trust me,' but to his ears that sounded almost predatory, so he said nothing. Instead he faced the man poling the boat and said, 'Good to finally meet you, sir. But I have questions.'

'So do I, Jadyn Kaen,' said Nilis Evandriel. 'So do I.'

'Did you get Kaen?' Yoryn Borghart asked, as Vazi Virago rejoined him beneath the dome of the Hejiffa Dhouma. He'd been trying to interpret the older mosaic that had been uncovered, but unfortunately, it had continued disintegrating after Jadyn Kaen and Auranuschka Perafi had started their destruction and it was now beyond understanding.

She said grimly, 'They got away, and that mercenary knight, Rameleau, is dead.'

'Can we track them using the aegis?'

'The moment I drew on the glyma in the fight, I lost much of my foresight,' Vazi admitted. 'I could still anticipate blows – but so could Kaen. He held me off, long enough to escape. And when they ran . . .' She shook her head in disbelief. 'I swear they used no glyma, but they ran faster than anyone, even with the glyma, ever could.'

'That Nepari whore stopped in mid-air,' Borghart told her. 'It was unreal. Impossible.'

How in a just world can servants of the Devourer do these things? he wondered angrily. *How could these nobodies best us like this?*

'Do you have any idea where they're going?' Vazi asked him.

He shook his head. 'I resorted to the glyma before you did. I'm blind to the aegis again.'

'I thought we were making incredible progress,' the Exemplar said, 'but we were barely scratching the surface. They danced rings around us.'

'Can it be that the aegis is more potent than the glyma?'

She threw him a worried look, but shook her head. 'Don't forget, it was the Order who exterminated the Wardens, not the other way round. We've been using a sliver of the aegis all our lives without realising – you to see through lies, me in battle. They clearly can co-exist; we just have to learn how. And now we've been given a lesson in what's possible – hanging in the air, running like lightning – and the way they killed Rameleau . . .' She was clearly shaken. 'We need to work this out.'

'It's still a heresy,' Borghart muttered.

'True,' she sighed. 'Why did they destroy the mosaic?'

'There was another mosaic beneath the famous map of Bedum-Mutaza – far older, I'd guess. I wonder if that's why they came here? Surely someone will know what it depicted?'

'We'll find out,' she said tersely. 'Where's Duenvost?'

'He's calming the priests down, making sure they don't blame us for this mess. But he'll want answers.' Borghart met her eyes. 'We're caught between worlds, Exemplar. If I hadn't used the glyma, Perafi would've escaped without breaking sweat – but she still read my every move.' He clenched his fists. 'I'm going to *destroy* her. I swear it on my soul.'

'Calm down,' Vazi told him. 'Have you tried scrying her?'

'I'll do it now.'

Seeing Duenvost striding towards them, she added, 'I'll cover for you.'

She intercepted the Abuthan lictor, while Borghart stepped into a small recess to shield him from watchers, before engaging the glyma. He focused on his memories of Auranuschka Perafi – whose smugly pretty face he longed to pulverise – and demanded that the universe tell him where to find her.

For a moment all he got was a swirling, bewildering panoply of distance and direction that made him spin – and then he realised he was seeing *potentialities*, the places she might *go*. In the ten minutes since she'd vanished, it was covering half of Mutaza City. It led every-where, and nowhere. He snarled in frustration and released the spell.

They could be anywhere, and we don't have a jagging clue.

Nilis Evandriel poled the rowboat into a small dock at the end of the canal, where it opened onto the harbour. Bedum City gleamed across the harbour.

Hearing the distant music and cheering, Jadyn asked, 'What's that all about?'

'Don't you know?' Evandriel replied. 'The Hierophant's arrived to take up his tenure for the year. Bedum City won't sleep tonight.'

'The Hierophant is here?' Jadyn exclaimed. 'Why today?'

'Coincidences do happen,' the scholar assured him. 'Come, I have a ship waiting.'

'But we haven't found what we came here for,' Aura protested.

'Actually, we have,' Evandriel replied, as the boat nudged the dock. He tied it to a mooring post. 'That was well done, to realise there was a second mosaic. I would never have thought of it.'

'What are you saying?' Jadyn asked.

'I heard Aura say something about another mosaic, so I made the new one crumble—'

'How?' Jadyn wondered.

'With glyma,' Evandriel shrugged. 'There's a technique that allows you to use both glyma and aegis – indeed, some would say they're part of the same thing.'

Jadyn stared, his mind doing flip-flops.

Aura looked stunned. 'You mean I do glyma, too?' she exclaimed. '*Santo mierdo!*'

'I'll explain later,' Evandriel told them, hurrying them onto shore. 'Keep up.'

He scurried along the promenade, then along a dock where larger ships were moored. There was no outcry here; they'd outrun their pursuers, at least for the moment,

'How did you come to be there?' Jadyn asked Evandriel.

'I sensed your arrival and waited,' the scholar replied. 'I've been masquerading as a priest for two weeks, utterly stumped, but Aura solved it in seconds.' He beamed at her. 'A concealed mosaic – brava!'

She curtseyed. 'Aura be amazamenta, is true,' she said, as if admitting a secret.

'It was an act of vandalism on a priceless work of art, sadly,' Evandriel added. 'But the original was revealed long enough for me to know what it depicted, and where to go next.'

'Where?' Jadyn asked, as they headed along the wharf.

'Have you ever heard of the Sanctuary of Sherkaza?' Evandriel asked. When they looked blank he said, 'It's in the Pelasian Islands, the home of a Zynochi monastic cult. When the Triple Empire was formed and the Akkanite Church became the sole religion, all pagan artefacts were supposed to be destroyed – including the world-famous Library of Balkhezamun, which was intended to be torched. So it was, but the librarians had been forewarned, and the most important treasures were long gone when the fires were lit. Most are now in Sherkaza, guarded by the warrior-monks and the Zynochi Navy.'

'They know of mosaic?' Aura asked.

'They're bound to,' the scholar said airily. 'The archives of the Hejiffa Dhouma, where you might have thought that information would be preserved, were purged decades ago – that's why I was so stumped when I arrived here; all the clues had been destroyed.' He gave Aura an admiring look. 'I'm lucky to have met you.'

'All men be lucky if meet Aura,' the Nepari declared. 'Am pineapple of womanhood.'

'Pinnacle,' Jadyn corrected drily.

Evandriel chuckled, then halted and gestured expansively at a felucca moored to the dock. Such long shallow-hulled sailing ships were more normally found in the Inner Seas, which were calmer than the open seas. 'Here she is,' he said proudly. 'Can either of you sail?'

'Am Goddess of Sea!' Aura declared. 'And Jadyn Knight has muscle and sometime listen.'

She quickly displayed her skills, hauling determinedly to hoist the main lateen sail on the short mast and ordering Jadyn around as if he were her crewman. For a few minutes they all worked frantically to get clear of the dock and get the second triangular sail raised.

Then Evandriel took the tiller, nothing more complicated than a large bladed pole in the stern, and set their bow due south, towards the Jaws of Leos and the open sea. They couldn't avoid the dozens of witnesses to their departure, but they caught the southerly tide, the sails filled with a stiff wind and they picked up speed briskly.

Best of all, no one set off in pursuit.

There was a strong swell, Jadyn noted anxiously. 'Can this thing handle the open sea?'

'Don't worry, she's had a deeper keel fitted,' Evandriel replied. 'She'll outrun triple-masted vessels in most conditions.' He grinned broadly. 'Her name's *Nidamoro!*'

Aura pealed with laughter.

'What?' Jadyn asked.

'It mean nest of love!' Then she leaned in and murmured, 'Will show you this love one day, Jadyn Knight. This you have earned with kiss on rooftop. Am not forgetting.'

Jadyn, feeling himself go scarlet, was thankful for the darkness. But he also remembered how good it had felt to stop fighting his urges and kiss her like that. Scary, yes, but only for what it told him of his future.

It now belonged to her, no matter what.

In minutes, they were just a pale smudge against the dark bulk of the city, the wind and current sweeping them on into the gulf.

We're too late. Vazi Virago knew this even before Yoryn Borghart returned from the docks with news that that a felucca bearing three people had weighed anchor some five hours ago. All she could do was glare at the stars, berating Heaven.

Borghart didn't yet understand that the game was lost. 'Then we'll find another ship,' he declared. 'We'll take one of these damned Mutazi vessels and catch them and—'

'Calm down,' she interrupted. 'They're gone – they had the wind and tide behind them, but both are now turning, so we can't go after them for another eight to twelve hours. And we'll need an ocean-going vessel and crew. Do you want to sail with Mutazi men who hate northerners? No? Then we need to go back to Bedum City and commandeer a ship there.'

Borghart's face went puce, but as her reasoned words hit him, he visibly calmed. 'Those two have the Devourer's own luck,' he growled.

'Aye,' she agreed resentfully. *Why does the Dark One answer prayers, while Akka gives us nothing?* Perhaps she was being unfair to Akka, but right now, that's how she felt. Then she brushed superstition from her mind and applied some reason. 'Let's get back to Bedum.'

As they trudged morosely down the wharf, a runner appeared – an Imperial Courser. Much to Vazi's surprise, she bounded up, presented empty hands and dropped to one knee.

'Exemplar Virago, greetings!' she boomed. 'You are commanded to appear before the Throne of Sand at dawn. I have a harbour boat waiting for you.'

Vazi blinked and glanced across the straits to Bedum City, just a kylo away and alive with fireworks and the distant boom of powder and jangle of music, which suddenly made sense now. But she asked anyway.

'Who commands me thus?'

'The Hierophant, Eindil Pandramion III, may he reign for all eternity,' the woman answered. 'His Divinity arrived at the bastion by portali gate earlier this evening. When he learned of your presence here, I was despatched immediately to find you.'

Vazi took a deep breath, burningly conscious of the courser's eyes measuring her reaction. For her sake she feigned honour. Placing her right hand to her heart and lying through her teeth, she said rapturously, 'I am filled with joy that my eyes will behold His Divinity once more. May he reign for ever over all.'

Part Two
KNOWLEDGE AND POWER

The Throne of Sand

The Three Thrones

The symbolism of the three most sacred thrones of the Triple Empire are rooted in ancient times, well before Jovan Lux's time. The Zynochi Throne of Sand, in Bedum, was made by a philosopher to remind the ruler that all is transitory. The Abuthan Tiger Throne is a plain stool with a tiger skin hide cover, a symbol of virility and conquest. By contrast to these noble traditions, the Talmoni seat, the Throne of Pearl, was stolen from Zynochia by an Order grandmaster and is still a source of anger in the south.

SEMERO DHUMBASSA, KHETIAN SCRIBE, 1454

Bedum-Mutaza
Autumn 1472

Eindil Pandramion III sat on the Throne of Sand, disoriented and uneasy at being outside Petraxus. Taking a portali gate was harrowing – the voices of his dead were always chilling – and the change was so abrupt that he could never acclimatise quickly, mentally or physically. To go in hours from the crisp, clean, cool of the north to the heavy, sultry, stinking air of the south was unpleasant. The changes in architecture, the dark faces, the babble of incomprehensible foreign tongues, not to mention all the different customs, were aggravations to which he never adjusted. It was going to be an insufferable year.

People say Jovan was wise to institute these rotational visits, to ensure we have our finger on the pulse of all three kingdoms, but I hate it here. I wish

183

I could abolish it – Bedum-Mutaza is foul, and Dagoz in Abutha is my idea of the Maw.

Right now, an hour before dawn, it was already warmer than high summer at home. He was sweating beneath his robes, crushed by his crown and struggling from the debilitating sickness of travelling the Shadowlands.

Just let me sleep.

This was his third visit, having already spent the fourth and eighth years of his reign here. Great pains had been made to make the Imperial Palace in Bedum feel northern, and there was no shortage of different nationalities in Petraxus, but he still felt like an alien here. The Day Court was dominated by local men and women, unfamiliar voices and faces with strange cadences and obscure agendas. They were waiting outside now, squabbling for position in the queues forming to welcome him. His first day might be ceremonial, but sleep was still denied him until evening.

At least he'd been spared the Night Court for the time being, to allow him to recover from the travel. But they would soon be back, those dark-robed masked courtiers, the same faceless counsellors he sparred with in the north: they were inescapable, as all things in his life were.

The palace staff had just finished renewing their oaths to him, many weeping with joy as they were presented. They were filing out now, thankfully.

Eindil rubbed grit from his eyes and looked at Robias. 'What next, my friend?' he asked his stentor, hoping that *she* had already arrived.

Moments after learning that his beloved Exemplar was right here – or at least, in Mutaza City, across the Straits of Leos – he'd sent for her, desperate to see her wondrous face again. All through the night, in between the tedious audiences with local officials, he'd been given updates. There had been a fracas in the Hejiffa Dhouma, and she was pursuing those responsible. They expected her by dawn. He was as nervous as a boy, his pulse rapid and breath shallow.

The layout of the throne hall here was exactly like the one in Petraxus: a giant pillared room with big doors at the far end. At night, when it was dimly lit, the sides were lost in shadow and mystery. But there were differences – the windows weren't stained glass but delicate, sinuous grilles of carved stone that admitted the moonlight in ghostly shafts through which motes of dust danced. He could hear unfamiliar night birds and eerie Zynochi music, high and sinuous, and the distant rumble of the ever-present drums.

He wondered if his desire to master Vazi Virago was symbolic of his desire to master her homeland – then his fluttering heart thumped, because the far doors cracked open, a pallid glow in the pre-dawn light – and a slender figure was silhouetted there, before vanishing as they were closed once more.

It's her . . .

Boots clipped in a martial fashion as she traversed the hundred paces of darkness and he could scarcely breathe in that intervening period. Finally, *she* stood before him, her scabbard empty and her garb as disorienting as everything else here. His Exemplar had abandoned her Order tabard and armour and instead wore Zynochi silken robes and a headwrap that framed her perfect face but concealed the lustrous curtain of hair that Eindil so longed to caress and inhale.

'Great Lord,' Stentor Robias boomed, 'I announce the Exemplar of the Order of the Vestments of Sancta Elysia, Vaziella al'Nuqheel. She presents herself as commanded.'

From his clipped phrasing, Robias disapproved – not of her, but of what her presence signified. *He thinks she reduces me to a callow teen,* Eindil knew. *And he's not wrong.*

She stepped to the bottom of the dais and knelt, pressing her lips to the stone footprint of Jovan Lux – there was one in each of the imperial throne halls – then looked up at him. Seeing her kneel before him, her upturned face lustrous, was his nightly dream: supplicating, wanting – and entirely his.

'Great Lord,' she said, in a hoarse voice, 'how may I serve?'

By wedding me – by bearing me a child to succeed me on these poisonous thrones. By ascending with me to the halls of Jovan and dwelling with me for ever. By looking at me with a love that mirrors mine.

He had the ten Zynochi wives Scripture demanded, but he had

not yet replaced the worthless bint he'd had killed in Petraxus a few weeks ago. The lawyers he'd had look into the matter had deemed that an Exemplar could be viewed as an honorary Talmoni – but as there were protocols to be followed and discussions to be had before any formal proposal could be issued to an Exemplar on active duty, he must contain his ardour.

'It has been several months since the Throne was last blessed with your presence,' he said aloud, speaking as much to those listening as her – there were always listeners. 'You were seeking a *certain place*. We wish to know whether you found it?'

He'd *never* seen Vazi Virago flustered – but he saw her expression flicker between doubt and resolve, just for a moment. He'd grown up in courts, surrounded by those eager to hide their true intents, and he had long since learned how to read expressions, even of those who might have wished to hide them. 'I . . . there is . . .' She looked round, then lowered her voice. 'There are issues of security, Divine Majesty.'

That was just the excuse he needed to be alone with her, which was why he'd raised the matter. He signed to Robias, who at once clapped his hands. 'The Hierophant invokes his rights of personal sanctity. This audience will be resumed in the Qhaz al'Noor.'

The Qhaz al'Noor – the Cage of Light – was a metal cage blending art, metallurgy and glyma situated immediately behind the throne room. The iron cage had a throne in one half and a kneeler in the other, with a lattice partition between them. Runes of protection, silence and veiling protected it: the guards outside might not be able to hear what was being said, but they had a perfect view of what was happening within.

Eindil stood, brushing off the sand that filled his seat, giving it its name, and allowed Robias to help him down from the dais. They walked to the rear door and he entered the Qhaz al'Noor, where he sat, a little regretful that she'd be separated from him by the inner barrier.

Vazi entered her half of the cage, clearly uncomfortable, but graceful as ever she lowered herself onto the kneeler and faced the throne through the latticework. He noticed again her uncertainty, finding it alluring, accentuating her female vulnerability as it did.

She senses my adoration and responds, he thought excitedly. *Torn between her own desires and her duty to the empire, she senses she must soon choose between womanhood and duty.*

He treated his eyes with her visage, thinking that the cage symbolised his whole existence – the things he most wanted were spread before him, but unreachable.

But the chance to hear her speak, to drink in her glorious visage, that was a joy.

'Tell me of your hunt for Nilis Evandriel,' he said, 'and the lost sorceries of the Sanctor Wardens.'

Vazi Virago could scarcely contain her revulsion. From the moment she'd knelt before the Throne of Sand she'd been aware of the heat of the Hierophant's gaze, undressing her with his eyes – and that despite being at least twice her age and married to thirty other women. He had a lined, dyspeptic face that spoke of spoilt whims and indulged vice. Just imagining his touch made her think of slugs slithering over her skin.

But . . . he was the ruler of the entire world, a living god. He probably thought he honoured her by his vile regard.

And now she must speak, when she'd far rather remain silent.

Fortunately, the years since she'd first started winning tourneys in the Order had left her well used to the scrutiny of men of all ages and station drooling over her. She steeled mind and stomach, made her face into a mask and recited her story, leaving out everything of importance.

She told of the discovery of what *might* have been Vanashta Baanholt, deep in the Qor-Espina mountain ranges of Neparia, of how her century had been ambushed by the treacherous Falcon pentacle, who'd murdered her knights before escaping. Realising they also sought the renegade vyr scholar, Nilis Evandriel, she'd followed their trail, which had led her here, almost catching them at the Hejiffa Dhouma, until they'd escaped by sail. She made no mention of the aegis or erlings, and certainly no mention of anyone having the capacity for heretical powers. She concluded with her request for a ship with which to take up the hunt again.

The chamber fell silent and she tried to still her jangled nerves that were making sweat pool in her armpits and between her breasts and trickle uncomfortably down her body, despite being a child of the south and well-used to heat.

Elysia, let me wash after this, to rinse this man's gaze from my face.

'There was a lictor from the north reported to be with you: one Yoryn Borghart,' noted Stentor Robias, who was seated outside the cage, to one side. He clearly had spies of his own at the Dhouma, if he knew of Borghart. 'How came he into your company?'

'He was pursuing the Falcons – our missions overlapped.' She hesitated, then added, 'He was accompanied by Elan Sandreth, the son of Lord Walter Sandreth. We captured two of the Falcons at Vanashta Baanholt. I assigned them to escort the prisoners back to Folkstein.'

'Sandreth, Milord,' Robias prompted when the emperor stayed silent. 'The son of Lady Elspeth Sandreth, whom you may recall?'

'She wanted to confirm some dubious wedding, yes?' Eindil affirmed.

'Correct as always, Great One.' Robias turned back to Vazi. 'Did you destroy the Warden stronghold, Exemplar?'

Another mission would be sent to verify her story, so there was no point lying. 'There was no time, and such a task was beyond the few men I had left, after the treacherous attack of the Falcons,' she replied. 'We chose to pursue the remaining fugitives as a matter of urgency.'

'Sier Jadyn Kaen – and some Nepari woman, yes?'

'Yes. Auranuschka Perafi. She's also a vyr.'

'Eyewitnesses at the Hejiffa Dhouma said she *flew*,' Robias said. 'How can she fly?'

'She didn't fly – they used vyr sorcery in . . . *unorthodox* ways,' Vazi lied.

The stentor's eyes narrowed. 'They escaped – from *you*, the Exemplar.'

'They were all but gone by the time I arrived,' she replied tersely. *Akka, I hate this damned cage.* 'I barely had the chance to engage. And the locals were of no use.'

'Incompetence or treachery?' Eindil asked dangerously.

If I say the latter, he'll have those guards and priests disembowelled.

They were nothing to do with her, but it would cause uproar across the Straits of Leos and ferment between the three pillars of the Triple Empire. That could suck in Order resources that were badly needed elsewhere.

'Sometimes ordinary men face situations that are beyond them,' she said coolly.

'Ordinary men?' Robias echoed.

'Men without the glyma,' she clarified, reminding them that she had a power they did not.

Robias got the message. 'I have no further questions,' he said. 'Great One?'

Eindil smiled blandly, but gave no order for her to depart. Instead, he continued to stare at her like a lovelorn peasant boy, though his beard was almost white and his skin blotched by age, his shoulders slumped and his belly was pudgy – and his crown was ridiculously outsized.

'Who is your guardian, Exemplar?' he asked eventually. 'Legally, once you leave the Order?'

Such a question was a clear precursor to questions about marriage. Her heart sank.

I thought I wanted such a match. I don't think I do any more, she thought desolately. *Elysia, I beg you, give me at least a semblance of love.*

'My parents dwell in Vintab, the place of my birth,' she admitted, striving to keep her tone neutral. 'Vintab is on the—'

'The Hierophant knows where it is,' Robias interrupted. 'Exemplar, Lictor Borghart is authorised to take over the pursuit of these fugitives. A ship, a crew and soldiers will be provided to him. But the Throne wishes you to remain here at court. Is this understood?'

'But Divine Majesty, I—'

'There will be a feast tonight, to formally welcome the Hierophant to Bedum and bless his coming year upon the Throne of Sand. We warmly anticipate your company.'

She bowed her head. 'Yes, Great One. I am honoured, and filled with joy.'

The Hierophant beamed as if she'd already agreed to wed him.

Robias signed, the cage was opened and finally she was free to fly. But not far, and not for long. Her wings were clearly about to be clipped.

10

All At Sea

Pelas

The Sea of Pelas contains thousands of islands, many too small for settlements, though some harbour large populations, and the natives are the greatest seafarers alive. For centuries, the Pelasian kings dominated naval warfare, even terrorising the Inner Seas, the Mar-Ortas and Mar-Eras. Finally, the Aquini built their own navy and broke their power. Soon after, a volcanic eruption destroyed the royal island of Silas. Pelas never recovered.

TELVYN ARGO, IMPERIAL SCHOLAR, PETRAXUS 1462

Sea of Pelas (eastern waters)
Autumn 1472

The morning after their escape from Bedum-Mutaza, Nilis Evandriel's felucca was ploughing a furrow southwest, the arid coastline of Zynochia a fast-receding shadow behind them. As the *Nidamoro* powered along before a strong tailwind, the sun rose in a hazy glow, lighting the gleaming sea.

The felucca had a small open-sided canopy forward of the mast, just big enough to provide cover for a bedroll and a small metal box encasing a cooking pit. Beneath the shallow deck was a hold full of provisions, including way-food, kegs of water, coal for cooking, tools and gear.

As soon as they got out into the channel and realised no one was chasing them, Evandriel had insisted Aura sleep first. When she'd awakened at dawn, she'd sorted through the provisions and made a meal. Now the three of them were crowded together in the stern, eating eggs and bacon.

The scholar didn't look like a seaman, but he talked enthusiastically about the craft and sailing. He appeared to have opinions – and knowledge – on everything, and a hyena laugh when amused. He was less bookish theorist and more teenager, Jadyn decided, sitting glassy-eyed next to Aura, their knees touching. He was surreptitiously drinking in the way the sunlight lit her tanned skin and her lustrous black hair rippled in the wind. The air was summer-hot, but the wind kept them cool. He'd have given much to bathe, but their priority for now was putting distance between themselves and pursuit.

The only ships they'd seen were traders heading north to Bedum-Mutaza, but none of them doubted that the Exemplar would quickly commandeer a warship and give chase. The expanse of water might prevent scrying, but their enemies shared the same precognitive gifts, so they had to presume they might be able to follow regardless.

'Can we outrun a galley or a cog?' he asked Evandriel.

'In light seas and light to fair winds, yes,' the scholar replied. 'In heavy seas or strong winds, maybe not. I took this ship all through the Inner Seas last year, so I do know her strengths and weaknesses.'

Reassured, Jadyn turned his mind to more esoteric matter. 'Milord, is the aegis—?'

'Don't call me milord,' Evandriel interrupted. 'Scholars go by their family names, so call me Evandriel. And you are Jadyn Kaen and Aura Perafi – your names popped into my dreams a few nights ago, so I knew you were on the way. I was stuck, you see: staring at that damned mosaic and wondering what it meant. It never occurred to me to look beneath it!' He gave Aura a beaming grin. 'Beauty *and* talent, a combination few can withstand.'

'This be nice man,' Aura told Jadyn, her eyes twinkling. 'You listen, learn much.'

Jadyn tsked impatiently. 'We have a thousand questions and—'

'Of course you do,' Evandriel interrupted. 'Who would not? We possess a power that makes thrones tremble: we can see the future, we can step between moments and hold back time. And though aegis is called a heresy, I am convinced that some in the imperial hierarchy also possess it. I think your "thousand questions" is conservative. You must think of more.'

Jadyn grinned. 'That won't be hard.'

'Excellent,' Evandriel exclaimed merrily. 'But I'm sixty-eight, and I've been on the run for decades now. Let's take things slowly, one question at a time, eh?'

'You be too youthful for sixty-eight,' Aura said, in her *wrap-you-around-my-fingers* voice.

'Beauty, talent *and* perception,' Evandriel exclaimed. 'You are a radiant rose, my dear.'

'Am knowing,' Aura said, feigning girlishness, then fixing him with a stern eye. 'What be aegis?'

'Straight to the heart of things!' the scholar exclaimed, nudging Jadyn. 'Your companion is a diamond, my lad. Do not let her slip between your fingers.' Then he pulled a 'genius at work' expression, and said, 'In truth, I too am still learning. But I have had a head-start, and I daresay I have read more histories than you two.'

'Have not read his stories,' Aura conceded.

'I only know what the Order told us,' Jadyn agreed, stifling a yawn – he'd been awake a long time, going through exhaustion and out the other side. 'Can you give us the basics?'

'Of course. I'll make it as brief as I can, then you can rest,' Evandriel said sympathetically. 'So, let me tell you a story from another time. Indeed, it is a story *about* time – fast time, slow time, time past and times to come. It began a long, long time ago, before history, or our history, at least. There have always been people – albeit very, very few – with inexplicable talents: "Seers" able to glimpse fragments of the future; "Warlocks" able to do strange things with fire or wind, and so on. We would now recognise such talents as the genesis of glyma and aegis, the first "Gifted" people – but with no training or elobyne, their talents are weak, random and misunderstood. They were often persecuted, unless they were able to hide behind religion, claiming their talents were "God-given". Many were murdered, condemned as demonic or evil.'

'Then how could it have survived at all?' Jadyn asked.

Evandriel smiled at the perceptive question. 'It survived not because of a person, but because of a place: the *Talam-Argith*, or the Silverlight, now known as the Shadowlands. The erlings found it – a place they could use to traverse great distances in a fraction of the time it should take, because *time* flows differently there. No one knows *why* – but the erlings discovered that magically talented individuals had their Gift enhanced by spending time in the Talam-Argith – although not too much time, for the Silverlight had other perils. You could lose years there, thinking only days were passing.'

'How can time move differently there?' Jadyn asked. 'It makes no sense.'

'Still a great mystery, and not one I or any other scholar can yet explain,' Evandriel said apologetically. 'Some theorise that time is like a river, with eddies where it travels differently to the main current. Regardless, let's get back to the tale: we had a few people, erlings and men, trying to develop their talents under great suspicion and duress, until a group of Gifted humans achieved a breakthrough and formed an order of mage-knights. They took pledges to serve and protect all people, but it was only when they came to Talmont's rescue against the Kharagh that they became accepted. That was the Charge of the Sanctor Wardens, just two hundred men and women, who cut a swathe through the invaders by anticipating and evading every shaft and blade, then unleashing fire and force to destroy the invader.'

The Charge of the Wardens had always been one of Jadyn's favourite stories, but he'd not heard it told like this. 'I've never heard of the Wardens using glyma,' he protested.

'That part was excised from the records once the Vestal Order decided that glyma was solely a gift from Akka,' Evandriel replied. 'Don't overestimate what the Wardens were: the Charge was indeed a great feat of arms, but it was as much down to timing, foresight and cleverness as brute force. The Wardens' magic was very limited, unlike the Vestal knights who supplanted them. But against a poorly equipped and entirely unprepared enemy, it was enough.'

Jadyn hung his head. *Are none of the great tales what they seem?* he wondered.

'Nevertheless, the Wardens thrived,' Evandriel went on, 'until suddenly they were gone.'

'What happen?' Aura asked.

'First, let me demonstrate something,' Evandriel replied, fishing a lump of quartz from a belt pouch and holding it up to the sun. He moved it about until the light passing through it painted rainbow-coloured bands of light on the deck. 'It is a property of some crystals that they can fracture light. A prominent Warden, Jovan – he was yet to claim the epithet "Lux" – had begun to experiment with different types of crystal. He was working in the Talam-Argith, and being precognitive, he could anticipate the results, making his progress both rapid and precise.'

'*Jovan Lux was a Warden?*' Jadyn blurted. 'The founder of the Vestal Order, the first Hierophant?'

'Indeed he was,' Evandriel answered. 'Another fact the Vestals do not like anyone knowing.'

Is nothing I believe in real?

'Jovan went to Nexus Isle,' Evandriel went on. 'There was a key *vivalocus* there – a "place of life" that formed a power nexus, hence the island's name – where energy flowed most strongly from the Talam-Argith into our world. It was the primary energy source for all magicians in this region. Without it, I doubt anyone would have been able to use magic at all. But Jovan disrupted everything: the vivalocus was destroyed, his famous giant elobyne crystal was formed and the Talam-Argith quickly began to die, becoming as we know it now: the lifeless Shadowlands.'

Jadyn looked away, shaken to have all his youthful illusions about the Order broken.

Aura squeezed his hand. 'Why Jovan do this?' she asked.

'Well, consider the results,' Evandriel answered. 'He became ruler of Talmont, his allies formed the Order and his rivals in the Wardens were massacred. He subjugated the world and the Triple Empire was born. There is your why.'

Jadyn felt sick to the stomach, but he needed to hear the rest. 'What's any of that got to do with crystals and light?'

Evandriel drew out a sliver of a glassy bluish elobyne orb and held it up to the sun. This time the sunlight passing through didn't break into a rainbow but cast one colour onto the wooden deck. 'Elobyne is unique. It takes the components of light and narrows it to this one red hue, without any loss in intensity.'

'And so . . . ?'

'And so we come to Jovan's acts on Nexus Isle – how he created his giant piece of elobyne, the source of all shards and orbs in existence, and how he destroyed the Shadowlands. The Wardens by then were a dominant military force, but still vulnerable if trapped and outnumbered, and they had enemies. Jovan's stated purpose was to make them supreme by creating more *extreme* power, so that *no one* could stand against him and his people.'

'His "stated purpose" – but not his real purpose, I suppose?' Jadyn said morosely.

'I'm sure vanity and ambition were also a factor,' Evandriel said drily. 'Somehow he changed a natural vivalocus – a place of power – at Nexus Isle, making *glyma*, magical energy in its purest, the most potent form of magic. This meant those Wardens specialising in glyma became much stronger, while the other powers withered to almost nothing. Of course, Jovan, having precognition, had already anticipated this, cultivating those who were able to use glyma with promises of greater power and the riches that would flow from it. As soon as Jovan changed Nexus Isle, they struck: his rivals were destroyed, the King of Talmont bent his knee to Jovan, the Order was installed at the summit of the tree of power and the rest, as they say, is history.'

Jadyn felt crushed by the whole narrative, but he still had questions, thousands of them. 'Why do they now spread elobyne over the world?' he asked.

Evandriel grimaced. 'The Nexus crystal is still growing, getting bigger every year, and it's draining life from everything around it. Nexus Isle – in fact, the whole of the Gulf of Elidor – would be dead by now if they had not started removing shards and spreading them around the world. Because the Talam-Argith is now lifeless, Jovan needed another source of energy and the only option was our own world. The Order has ten times more knights than the Wardens ever had, and as it keeps expanding, more power is needed to support so many. The shards are planted in every possible place, all feeding energy back to Nexus Isle. It is a vicious cycle: Jovan has created an insatiable monster, one which will eat us all.'

'Then how do we have any precognition at all?' Jadyn wondered.

'And was not Jovan left blind to future also?' Aura put in.

'Good points, both,' Evandriel said, approvingly. 'Aura's question first: I am sure Jovan has kept a stream of energy for "aegis" magic – precognition and time-manipulation – for himself. Some of that power must still leak into our world: which is the answer to Jadyn's question. Not much, though: I believe we three would have been among the most gifted aegis-wielders of the Warden era, had we lived then. That's why we can function with so little raw energy to work with.'

Jadyn had never thought of himself as among the best at anything. 'But what of the other Wardens, Jovan's rivals?' he asked plaintively. 'Why didn't they see this coming?'

'Clearly Jovan outmanoeuvred them. The aegis has a veil-like property, and I imagine Jovan used that, hiding his intent until he had eliminated his rivals. He ensured the histories portrayed them as villains, with himself the hero of the whole sordid tale.'

'But some Wardens must have survived, to create the trail we're following . . .'

'So it appears,' Evandriel agreed. 'I do know that a few Wardens were still at large at least a decade after Jovan's power-grab. I imagine it was they who created the path we're currently following, to enable potential aegis users to identify themselves. I sincerely hope there will be something at the end of this path, but who knows?'

Jadyn sagged against the gunwale, thinking through this secret history of ancient betrayals, murders and ruthless greed, all completed unerringly because Jovan could foresee the consequences of his actions. *What chance do any of us have against that?*

'Thank Elysia he's dead,' he groaned, and Aura nodded emphatically.

Evandriel started to say something, then sighed and said only, 'Aye, but his heirs have perpetuated his legacy and strengthened it and it is they who rule the known world.'

Jadyn looked up, to ask perhaps the most important question in his heart. 'Master Scholar, I'm a former Vestal knight – in fact, I believe I still am, because I've remained true to my vows. They've left me, not the other way around. You appear to have high ideals, but I've seen the destruction the vyr have wrought in your name. Your rebellion has harmed millions of farmers and villagers and their lives and lands. You've unleashed destruction beyond anything the Hierophant's people have done. Isn't there another way?'

'You are presuming that everything done in my name was sanctioned by me,' Evandriel answered. 'You're also presuming that all other options were not explored. I wasn't the first to raise concerns about elobyne and its effects – scholars have been voicing doubts from the beginning. They were forced to recant, or were silenced, martyred in nameless dungeons, unheard by the masses, because they refused to back down. It was they, those people who refused to lie down, who began this resistance movement, not I. When a tyrannical power is out of control and accountable to no one, then it will do as it pleases. Against overwhelming might and the absence of truth and justice, only extreme options remain.'

Jadyn was unable to fault the logic, but as yet, he knew nothing about the alternatives. All he could do was watch and assess the man for himself, before coming to some kind of judgement.

What that said about the state of Coros broke his heart.

Aura raised her head. 'What we do now? Follow trail to aegis, si? Where does trail lead?'

'Beautiful lady, I have no more idea than you.' Evandriel stretched and yawned. 'But the need for action is now. The distribution of elobyne crystals has increased tenfold in the past twenty years. You know of those in Solabas and Neparia, yes? But do you know of the thousands planted in the Kharagh borderlands, or across the Abuthan and Khetian deserts, or deep into the Zynochi hinterland? They are leaving dustbowls in their wake, killing whole tracts of land. It's as if they no longer care about the future at all.'

'It sounds a lot like the End of All Things,' Jadyn said grimly.

'It does indeed,' Evandriel agreed. He yawned again. 'And there, I have crushed your will and exhausted my own endurance. Sier Jadyn, might I take the liberty of bowing to your relative youth and beg leave to sleep next. Sadly, old men like me can no longer go all night as I used to.'

Aura snickered mischievously. 'Jadyn Knight be young, but he not go at all. Too much Order honour and glyma . . . but I live with hope.'

Jadyn coloured, as usual.

Evandriel grinned broadly. 'Well, I will tell you one thing of great moment: those with the aegis – and no glyma – suffer none of the disabling issues of rage and destructive humours. We are free to live and love like all ordinary people. Is that not wonderful news?'

'Why is the glyma cursed?' Jadyn asked, not really expecting an answer.

'I suspect because Jovan's elobyne has made it too powerful. It was never an issue before he did what he did – with foreknowledge.' Evandriel patted Jadyn's knee and winked at Aura. 'I will give you lovebirds a little space in my floating love nest, eh.' He laughed merrily, then headed for the cabin, calling, 'Wake me in time to cook dinner.'

Jadyn was feeling filthy, exhausted and struggling to absorb what they'd been told. He'd been awake through the night, for the second day running, and wanted nothing more than to collapse. But the felucca needed their attention – the wind was lifting and the vessel was now ploughing through larger waves. Fortunately, Aura was refreshed and was soon merrily swinging on ropes and calling the course changes, so he settled for plying the tiller. They worked well together, using their vestigial aegis to anticipate the wind-shifts with increasing accuracy.

'I'm beginning to see why you love sailing,' Jadyn said when Aura returned from the rigging, sometime around the middle of the day. 'There's such a sense of freedom out here on the sea—'

He lost his thoughts as she leaned in and kissed him fully on the mouth.

He had to quell the instincts of a lifetime in the Order to not jerk away, and instead let his lips feel her softness, at first shy and tentative, gradually gaining confidence and responding – only to jolt when her tongue slipped inside his mouth . . .

'Hey, uh . . .' He was nose to nose with her and couldn't look away. The teasing challenge in her eyes was making his throat go dry. 'That's thirsty work,' he croaked, grabbing the water flask and gulping, then handing it to her. 'I'm wrung out and out on my feet, sorry.'

'Not like kiss?' she asked, arching her eyebrows.

'I like it very much, but I'd prefer to be awake,' he replied, trying for light-hearted but not sure he was managing very well. 'Aura, I don't want to make big decisions when I'm tired. Let's wait until we're refreshed, washed – and somewhere alone.' Then before she could react either way, he kissed her back, with emphasis.

She understood. 'Rest here,' she said and took the tiller, then pulled his head into her lap. 'You sleep, I steer. Sailing is easy today, so I can do.'

He didn't mean to, but he went out like a snuffed candle.

Bedum City

Yoryn Borghart stalked the corridor in the Tar-Luxium bastion in high dudgeon, Adu Duenvost on his heels. The Exemplar hadn't returned from the imperial palace yet, and when his request for a century and warships to pursue the fugitives was turned down, he'd enlisted his fellow lictor and was taking his demands to the top.

A secretary tried to intercept them when they reached the waiting room, but they shoved past and crashed through the doors to the office of the grandmaster, Rolf Rendreth. The old knight was in an armchair in the corner, his lap covered with parchments. He looked up sharply, his grandfatherly face stern.

'It's customary to wait to be summoned,' he said.

'It's customary to hunt down vyr renegades with all our strength,' Borghart retorted. 'But your staff are stonewalling: some fool said I have no authority to requisition that which I need.'

Lictors were trained to intimidate, be it against allies or enemies, but Grandmaster Rendreth stood his ground. 'My staff aren't the problem, you are. Sit down, both of you.' He indicated a pair of chairs opposite his armchair. 'There's water, but no wine. I don't drink before midday.'

Borghart was in no mood to sit, but Duenvost all but pushed him down.

'We want to help,' the Abuthan told him, 'but the Grandmaster has questions.'

I don't want your damned questions, Borghart thought, but arguing with a fellow lictor wasn't a good look. Trying to assert some authority, he started, 'These fugitives are my quarry, and the laws of pursuit are clear: I arrested both Kaen and Perafi, and I have the right to retrieve them – to continue the hunt for as long as I see fit.'

'We know and acknowledge that,' the grandmaster answered. 'And we will aid you. But three war galleys and a full century? We are already dealing with the Hierophant's security, the latest vyr activity and the refugee crisis on the Bedumassa coast. I simply cannot afford to send three ships and a century after *two people*.'

'You would if it were the Exemplar asking.'

'But it's not, is it?' he retorted. 'The palace was explicit: she's not part of this now.'

Duenvost leaned forward. 'Explain to us what makes this pair so important.'

This was the conversation Borghart had hoped not to have, but clearly he'd get nothing without revealing a little of what they faced. He just had to make sure none of it put his own head in a noose. 'Fine,' he growled, 'but what I say cannot leave this room.'

That got Rendreth and Duenvost's interest.

'Explain,' the grandmaster said shortly.

Reluctantly, Borghart gave them a pared-back version of the hunt so far, from Gaudien to Vanashta Baanholt – and the first mention of the *aegis*. 'At Vanashta Baanholt, I found Kaen and his cronies blithely lying to the Exemplar herself. I warned her of their iniquities, and together, we took them on. Somehow, this "aegis" enabled them to escape. We tracked them here, to the Hejiffa Dhouma, and again, they escaped. Exemplar Virago and I both fear a revival of this wicked heresy.'

'This does align with the report of our informants in Mutaza,' Duenvost put in. 'One reported seeing this Auranuschka Perafi *flying* – he insisted it couldn't be done with glyma.'

Rendreth scratched at his whiskers irritably. 'Aegis? But you speak of them as vyr?'

Borghart pretended ignorance. 'They're sorcerers and rebels – what else do we call them?'

'But the aegis?' Rendreth shook his head. 'I've heard eminent scholars swear blind it was all a lie, that the Sanctor Wardens were nothing more than men with swords and some war-craft. Now you say it's real – and has been used to elude the Exemplar herself? This is most alarming.'

'Which is why I need the ships and men!' Borghart exclaimed. 'But if it gets out that the vyr are resurrecting the aegis, there could be panic.' He leaned forward. 'You know what sort of irrational shit happens when the Day and Night Courts get scared.'

All three shuddered: that invariably meant disruption and upheavals, careers destroyed.

'What is the Exemplar telling the Hierophant's people?' Rendreth asked sharply.

'As little as possible, I hope,' Borghart replied. 'The palace leaks secrets like a sieve.'

'Isn't that the truth.' Duenvost chuckled humourlessly. 'Grandmaster, I support my colleague's request for aid – indeed, I wish most fervently that I could join him. But the city is in ferment and I'm needed here.'

Good, Borghart thought. *I wouldn't want you along, not with your keen eye for heresy.*

Rendreth leaned back, contemplating the elaborate ceiling murals.

'This is a weighty matter,' he said. 'The revival of an ancient sorcery by our enemies is no small matter. It needs to be referred upwards.'

'The archon himself sanctioned my pursuit,' Borghart said, stretching the truth somewhat. Corbus Ritter had been more concerned with silencing Romara Challys, and the aegis hadn't then reared its head. 'You need to decide fast – if I don't sail soon, it'll be moot.'

'Aye, I get that,' Rendreth grumbled. 'But a whole century? And three galleys? Can't the Exemplar use her influence? It's said the Hierophant hangs on her every word like a puppy.'

'The Exemplar's virtue is unimpeachable,' Borghart snapped, surprised to find himself angered by the insinuation.

Rendreth raised eyebrows and a placatory hand. 'I don't doubt it. But mark my words, she's destined for his marital bed. It's likely being negotiated now, and your mission forgotten.'

She'd better not ditch me, Borghart worried, then admitted to himself, *but it might not be her choice.*

'I've heard nothing since she was summoned to court,' he said. 'How about one ship, a pentacle and thirty marines? I won't sail until I hear from the Exemplar, but at least let me prepare.'

The grandmaster considered, then sighed. 'All right: yes, to the marines and a ship. But I'm not giving you a pentacle. If the Exemplar can secure you more manpower, then good for her.'

It's not enough, Borghart thought bleakly.

'Can you even trace Kaen and Perafi?' Rendreth asked.

Borghart smiled grimly. 'We had some luck. Someone remembered planks of wood dropping from the roof of a building. I went to see and found some possessions Kaen and Perafi had been left behind. I can use those to scry them, even across water.'

'Very good. Well, Lictor, you may go and prepare, and may Akka be with you.' They all rose, and the grandmaster scrawled an order, placed his personal seal on it and handed it to Borghart. 'See my secretary on the way out. He'll requisition the galley and crew for you.'

They shook hands and, unusually for Borghart, parted on good terms. *I must be mellowing.*

But as he left, his mind was on the Exemplar, not the pursuit.

What's she doing? he wondered. *Fighting to get what we need? Or feathering her own nest?* As the answer to that question was probably going to determine his own future, he couldn't help worrying. *If the Hierophant's people discover she's tainted by heresy, I'm in deadly danger. And if she prefers harem pants to armour now, she might even see me as a loose end . . .*

He hurried onwards, anxious now to leave as soon as possible.

Vazi Virago stared into the mirror in disbelief, not recognising the delicate creature staring back. It was five years or more since she'd last donned a gown and she'd forgotten how much she loathed them. That had been for some stupid Order ball that the archon had held after her first victory as Exemplar. She'd left as soon as possible, even though the celebration was in her honour. Having humiliated her so-called betters on the tourney field, she had no desire to be paraded before them like some prize, or to rub their noses in her victory. They hated her enough as it was.

The Hierophant had had her installed in a suite in a grandiose tower of marble and stone, one level below his own. It was, she understood, a monumental honour, placing her ahead of princes, lords and ladies, even his wives, who were kept out of his way in a separate wing. Her rooms were larger than entire barracks she'd slept in.

However much she might hate women's garb, she couldn't deny this dress suited her. The silk was the colour of a peacock's feather, all iridescent blues and greens, with a silvery sheen like sunlight on the sea. She'd been given seven to choose from, in every hue of the rainbow, all heavy with gems and embroidery, and leaving far too much flesh exposed. Her arms and most of her back and chest were bare – a style that would have scandalised the north, but here in the sultry south it was considered demure, according to the women who dressed her. They had assured her she would soon be grateful not to be trapped in layers of cloth.

She sighed to herself. *I'll still be just a captive bird for leering old men to drool over.*

The afternoon had been trial enough, when a small army of Bedumi women had descended on her, first putting her through a ritual bathing in rose oil in a giant pool beneath the castle, before shaving her legs and plucking the rest of her body hair, an excruciating palaver. She'd had her thick hair oiled and brushed out, a hundred strokes or more, until it was gleaming like satin. The ends were cut, then they plaited and curled and styled until it was a veritable tower of ebony locks. They'd enamelled her finger and toenails, used powders to conceal her scars, rouged her cheeks and lips and painted her eyelids in shades of blue and green. Finally, they'd dressed her in this glittering raiment.

She was exquisite, Vazi could admit that. But she'd have rather worn chainmail and a sword.

It frightened her, to be transformed into someone else's fantasy, but she did understand why the gaggle of women applauded rapturously when she was deemed ready. They'd been pitiless in their determination to transfigure her, but if they disappointed their master, they faced dismissal or worse. So she just stood there and feigned gratitude.

The doors opened to admit the Hierophant's stentor. The women dropped to their knees, pushing foreheads into the marble floor, but Robias kept his eyes on her, running up and down her body, examining her face and hair. His expression was unreadable.

Vazi had fought champions and faced rampaging vorloks, but she couldn't ever remember feeling such apprehension, such uncertainty. She didn't know the rules of engagement, the consequences of the merest slip, so she remained still, rigid and humiliated at the scrutiny.

'Are you comfortable, Exemplar?' he asked, after circling her thrice.

No, was the honest answer, but this man was more than a servant – he was the *first servant*, one of the most influential men in the world. The wrong word could have dire consequences for everyone here, including herself.

'I have never felt so perfectly presented,' she answered, which was also true.

Robias mused on that, then he told the women, 'Well done. You may go.'

The Bedumi rose, beaming with relief, then shuffled out.

The doors closed again, leaving her alone with the stentor. Robias was still staring at her, apparently unmoved. She wondered whether he preferred men.

'The Hierophant does you great honour,' he said finally. 'I trust you understand this?'

She nodded mutely. 'I am fortunate.'

'You have earned this opportunity with your talent and hard work. The Hierophant admires your fearless pursuit of excellence in what is primarily a man's world. He has followed your career closely.'

She bowed her head. 'I am not worthy of his attention.' *Nor do I want it, the regard of that tired, grey man with bent shoulders and acquisitive eyes.*

'Yet you have taken his eye, and you will be given the seat of honour tonight, at his right hand, and few will wish you well. Your every fault will be magnified, your every quality questioned. It's not easy to endure that scrutiny.'

'It's something I face every day as Exemplar,' she said stiffly.

'I expect so, but here the duels are in etiquette and influence. The thrusts are verbal, the feints are made with flattery and the killing blows dispensed in whispers. My task is to impart the basics to you – to fully equip you for this arena would take years. So come with me, and pay attention.'

He led her to the next room, where a table was set for one. He took her through the etiquette of the table – when to drink, when to eat, what implement to use, and how. How much to eat – a few mouthfuls at most. How to sit, who to listen to and which gestures achieved what result – summoning a servant or asking for her plate to be removed, and so on. It was similar to the more informal Order procedures, but she picked it up quickly.

'What is it the Hierophant expects of me?' she asked, when the stentor had finished.

'Ornamental beauty which enhances his aura of supremacy.'

'And that is all?' she asked, her skin prickling.

'Of course,' Robias said, frowning. 'My master is well aware of your status as a glyma-knight and all that implies. Your beauty and sanctity are to be celebrated tonight, not undermined. This is the highest court in the land, not the throne hall of some bandit king.'

She flushed. 'I meant no offence.'

'And none is taken. But you are right in suspecting that his Majesty regards you as a potential future queen: tonight's banquet signals that explicitly to the world. He *expects* that in the *very near future* you will announce your retirement as unbeaten Exemplar and undergo the rites of purging to free yourself from the glyma. At that point, formal negotiations will begin for your hand as his thirtieth wife. This will elevate you and your living relatives to the court, and should you give him an heir, that child may come to sit upon the Throne of Heaven.'

She sucked in her breath, shocked, even though she'd seen it coming. She supposed she ought to be grateful but only nausea rose inside her. 'I don't know what to say,' she managed.

'Something about joy and the culmination of your life would be appropriate, when the time comes,' Robias advised drily. 'I advise you practise in front of a mirror. In the meantime, be ready in ten minutes for your escort.'

He gave her a shallow bow and went to leave, but she called after him, 'I was expecting to receive a report from Lictor Borghart on his progress?'

'The pursuit of the heretics is no longer your concern.'

'I am still Exemplar,' she reminded him, before taking a deep breath and deciding to test her boundaries. 'Must I tell the Hierophant that I've been kept from my duties?'

Robias' eyes glinted dangerously. 'You are commanded to delegate your responsibilities whilst sojourning here at the imperial palace, as I recall.' He gave her a calculating look, then added, 'Lictor Borghart has been given a ship and sails on the next tide. I believe that is within the hour.'

As he told her this, she got the sense of a hook being baited. He didn't like her, that was clear, and she guessed he would be quite happy to see her fail.

But his voice remained neutral. 'Put it from your mind, Exemplar. Tonight you face a new battle in a far more dangerous arena.'

'I understand,' she murmured, striving to hide her frustration.

Robias took her acquiescence for surrender, and departed, looking pleased. It was a relief when he was gone and she was finally alone . . . with ten minutes to decide her future.

I've foreseen all of this, she reflected. *I've dreamt it all my life: I rise, catch a powerful man's eyes and ascend. This is my fate.*

But that destiny had always felt like something in the distant future, and right now that was where she wanted it to stay: not here and now, when she was still in her prime . . . and not when she was on the verge of something extraordinary.

One day, she knew deep within her, as her beauty and prowess declined, she'd be fighting nature, until the wolves tore her down. That was the time she'd planned to leave the Order to move into this other arena. To do so now was too soon for her.

But this could be my only chance to be a queen. Or an empress.

But what sort of life would that be? A caged bird, desperately clinging to status and favour, her whole existence revolving around keeping one old man besotted with her? What if she failed to please him?

I want to be me, as I am now, forever. That's what I want.

But no one could give her that.

'Jag this,' she snarled. 'Jag them all.'

They'd taken away her travelling clothes, leaving her just this damned gown. Cursing impatiently, she belted her sword-belt over her shoulder. Finally, she drew her flamberge, recharged at the shard in the chapel, pulled in a snarling torrent of glyma-energy and cut slits in her skirt so she could move properly.

Then she cocked her ear, hearing approaching boots in the corridor outside.

The city was spread below her like a twinkling tapestry, but she barely noticed as she vaulted to the next balcony down, startling a group of Aquini lords drinking – she snatched a goblet and drained it as they stared, gaping at this madwoman in an exquisite ballgown.

One started to draw a sword, but he froze at the touch of her blade at his throat.

'Gentlemen,' she said, 'enjoy your evening, but tonight's ball has been cancelled.'

Then she leapt again, while the palace burst into uproar around her.

Yoryn Borghart was giving the orders to cast off when the Exemplar came storming along the wharf, hurdling from the boardwalk to the deck with a surge of glyma. The galley's crew went rigid in alarm; the marines clattered to arms at the sight of a Zynochi woman holding a flamberge but dressed like a high-class courtesan. But she was radiating glyma and their confusion blended with fright.

'At ease!' Borghart shouted, before anyone made a fatal error. 'She's with us.'

He strode down the steps and on a whim, dropped to one knee and kissed her hand with more fervour than he'd actually intended. 'Milady, it's an unexpected pleasure. You're just in time.'

She snatched her hand away, then smiled shyly, an expression he'd never seen on her face. 'Fool,' she admonished him half-heartedly. 'Get up.'

He rose and turned to the crew, shouting, 'Cast off, hurry!'

Eindil sat on the Throne of Sand, struggling to contain his fury and despair. The weight of his crown so crushed his skull that he feared it would cave in.

He'd been about to rise and lead his entourage to the doors of the ballroom, where he should have been met by his guest of honour so he could escort her into the hall. The tables would be laden with all the splendid opulence of three empires, and the mightiest men and women of Coros would be there to see him and his prize. All would rejoice in his majesty.

But Robias had just told him that the Exemplar had gone. Lictor Borghart's ship was already rounding the heads with the wind astern, and witnesses had seen a gaudily dressed Zynochi woman leap aboard, seconds before it left.

I should hate her.

But he didn't – he couldn't – because he adored her beyond all reason. She was the pinnacle of womanhood, and all the things he most admired in her revolved around her capacity to defy convention. She was an undefeated Exemplar, despite being a beautiful young woman. She flew free, like a soaring eagle. All wanted her, none could have her.

Even me.

He'd never been denied anything in his entire life. Whatever he wanted he took – everything, except Vazi Virago.

I will have her, he resolved. *This just sharpens my taste for conquest.*

'Advise me, Robias,' he said.

The stentor didn't hesitate. 'Let it be known that Exemplar Virago is called to battle. All know that a dangerous vorlok desecrated the Hejiffa Dhouma – so you yourself have sent her in pursuit. This ball is now a celebration of the Vestal Order and their constant sacrifices for the Triple Empire.'

Eindil considered. 'It is apposite. Continue.'

'On her return, you will make clear your unhappiness. You will force her to submit to your will. You will make an example of her.'

For once, Robias' advice didn't speak to Eindil's soul. 'No, my friend, you misread the moment. She is behaving admirably, like a true warrior. I will permit her this longer leash. But I would have eyes upon her.' He rose, energised by purpose. 'Let our guests wait. I will confer with the stars.'

Robias' eyes flickered uncertainly, but he bowed and went to go.

'Tell me, my friend,' Eindil called after him, 'how did she learn of the lictor's departure? I expressly forbade anyone telling her of his ship's departure.'

The stentor hesitated momentarily, then said, 'This is Bedum-Mutaza, oh Most High. Even the walls whisper.'

He told her himself, to lure her into self-destruction, Eindil realised. *How disappointing.*

But Robias was too big a part of his life to cast off hastily. Such a move would require planning. So he muttered something about 'faithless Bedumi' and headed for the highest tower.

Ten minutes later, wheezing uncomfortably, he clutched at the rails at the tip of the minaret, still slightly dizzy from the narrow spiral stairs and dreading the journey back down, which he'd have to do backwards on hands and knees to avoid an attack of vertigo.

Finally he felt able to murmur, 'Lords of the Sky, hear me.'

There was a heavy rush of wings and a moment later, a winged man wearing just a loincloth landed on the rail opposite him and stepped lightly into the cupola.

Eindil groaned inwardly, to see that again, the Serrafim who'd come to him was his father. The term Serra meant an angel of Akka, but he knew they were really mortals, anointed as divinities. Genadius was no angel, in any sense of the word.

Genadius gazed back, his perfected face unreadable, shrouded in secrets and subtle contempt. 'My son, what is it you want?' he asked, with musical resonance.

Why did it have to be you again?, Eindil sighed inwardly. But there was no other choice, if he wanted "divine" aid. Only Alephi of his father's coterie could be trusted to aid him.

'The Exemplar has defied me,' he blurted. 'I wished to honour her at a feast, but she sailed away.'

Genadius' face didn't change, nor did his voice. But his whole being radiated affront. 'I will destroy the ship, drown all who sail with her and bring you back her head,' he declared coldly.

'No, no,' Eindil replied. 'I need you to protect her, in secret – to ensure she returns safely.'

The Alephi were forbidden to betray their existence to ordinary humanity, and had only been revealed to him the night before his coronation, when he was told he could call on them for aid and they would be bound to give it.

Genadius' lip curled, so clearly that aid would be grudging. 'She has too much power over you, my son. It's a weakness others will exploit, not least her. Cauterise this wound before you bleed out.'

Despite his fear of his father, Eindil found himself making excuses for her. 'She is driven by duty, not malice. There are vyr defiling our holy places and she pursues them. Go after her, protect her, and bring her back to me safely.'

Genadius looked at him frankly. 'Never enter marriage with some-one stronger than you, my son. She will exploit you until you are her slave. Women are like horses; you can't enjoy riding them until they're broken in.'

Eindil met his gaze squarely. 'I will do *exactly* that, Father. I have chosen her *because* it is known that she cannot be tamed. A ruler must do what lessers cannot. And a spirited horse is always the better ride.'

Genadius pondered, then smiled slowly. 'Good, my son. Very good.'

Eindil told him the name and type of Borghart's ship, and its last known position, and in a rush of wings, his divine father was gone. Then he let out his breath and sagged, wrung out by the brief encounter.

But if he aspired to join the ranks of the Alephi himself, as Scrip-ture demanded, he had to show that he was their equal. Today, for the first time, he felt he'd won the encounter.

I lied to him, and he never saw. I don't want to break her . . . I want her to love me.

11

The Interrogators

Fate and Free Will

Akka the Father created us, and all that occurs is according to His will. Thus says The Book of Lux. *Therefore, every life is fated, every decision preordained, every outcome known. Whether virtuous or evil, we cannot act other than according to Akka's will.*

EVARIUS IV, HIEROPHANT 1388–1392

My mind refuses to accept the concept of fate. I have choice in my hands in every moment. How I use that choice may seem at times inevitable, given the options available, but those choices remain.

NILIS EVANDRIEL, RENEGADE SCHOLAR, 1471

Tar-Brigida, Folkstein
Autumn 1472

Romara Challys gazed about her, feeling like she was inhabiting a nightmare, trying not to see the filthy wet walls, or the groundwater seeping through and pooling in the rushes, not to smell the stagnant rot that blended with the reek of her piss bucket . . . trying to ignore the guards watching through the bars with disgusted eyes.

She didn't blame them for their enmity: she was everything they'd been taught to despise.

She'd been dragged in semi-conscious, barely aware of the latter part of the journey through the portali gates. Her clothes were soiled and torn, she was covered in mud and blood, her red hair was matted and her face battered by the repeated blows Tevas had inflicted to keep her stunned and helpless. She was ravenous too, because they wouldn't feed her: hunger, it was said, made it almost impossible for a vyr to conceal what it was. When she was dragged before the justiciar, they wanted to expose her as the beast she'd become.

They'll destroy my identity, then burn the remains.

The guards watched stonily as she limped to the bucket and shat again, then gripped the bars and said, 'Can you empty the jagging thing?'

They shook their heads, smirking.

Groaning, she stumbled to the water pitcher, but found it empty. 'Come on, lads! Where's your hearts?'

'Where's yours, Vorlok,' one retorted.

'The same place it's always been,' she replied. 'Won't be much of a trial if I die first.'

'You'll make it to the dock,' the other man answered, 'and then to the pyre. They'll pick a windy day for it, too, so the smoke don't get you first. You'll scream all the way into the Devourer's Maw.'

That, she believed.

Blinking away tears – *I will not break down* – she slumped onto her damp, rotting mattress and stared at the mossy wall – until, just a few minutes later, the doors crashed open and a Justiciary magia with a shaven skull entered, and behind her, a lictor. The guards chained her manacles to the wall, then the magia cut Romara's remaining clothes away, whilst praying aloud for her soul.

Then she hammered a glyma-strengthened fist into Romara's belly and the nightmare truly began.

Corbus Ritter was newly arrived from the north, where he'd been visiting Elspeth Sandreth. He'd hurried home when he'd received the news that Romara Challys was captured and had been delivered to Tar-Brigida, his home bastion.

The journey via portali gate had taken a full day; as soon as he'd arrived, he'd approved a preliminary interrogation before her court hearing. The official purpose of such interrogations was to determine if there was a case; unofficially, it was to find out if there was anything that might be too sensitive for the public record. This case would be one of those, he already knew. Nevertheless, he had to go through with it now, and he needed Challys broken, so she'd confess nothing at the trial that might damage him. Having requested the most sadistic local lictors for the interrogation, he now sipped his wine and listened to their report.

The man delivering it was Lucien Hromboli, an Aquini lictor, and his assistant, a bald magia who'd taken the name 'Faith', but radiated fanatical malice.

'Siera Challys has considerable strength,' Hromboli was saying, 'but Sister Faith lacerated her flesh, then cauterised the wounds with red-hot irons, at which point she broke.' He consulted his report. 'The most interesting revelation was her claim to have found a place called Vanashta Baanholt in the Qor-Espina, and—'

'*What?*' Corbus stopped slumping and leaned forward. '*They found what?*'

'Vanashta Baanholt,' Lictor Hromboli repeated, and the magia Faith nodded. 'She confirmed it emphatically, and even described its location, citing the Exemplar as a witness to its existence.'

'*The Exemplar?*'

Corbus snatched the report and scanned it, picking out the key points: as well as Vanashta Baanholt and the presence of Vazi Virago, there was apparently evidence that the oft-denied aegis was *real*. An assertion that Nilis Evandriel was right, that the elobyne shards were destroying the world. And a denial of having ever married Elan Sandreth, an arrangement that Corbus stood to profit indirectly from.

I don't want any of this voiced in court, he thought, drumming his fingers.

'Who else knows of this?' he asked.

Hromboli leaned in. 'The Exemplar and Lictor Borghart, who are pursuing Siera Romara's surviving pentacle. The men who survived and escaped Vanashta Baanholt – most of them are still in Foyland. And the pair waiting outside your door, Elan Sandreth and Tevas Nicolini.'

Corbus considered that.

To shut this down entirely, Romara Challys couldn't be permitted to stand trial. Given the damage her testimony could do, he doubted the Exemplar would care. Borghart might be trickier, given the rivalries within the Justiciary, but Hromboli outranked him and should be able to silence him if it got rancorous. As for the soldiers – he could just leave them in Foyland and let the savagery of that cesspit do his work for him.

Elan Sandreth – potentially his son-in-law, in due course – would do as he was told. *But what of this Tevas Nicolini? And the rest of the Falcons?*

'So this magus, Goraghan . . . he believes some of Siera Romara's pentacle are alive?'

Sister Faith spoke. 'Siera Romara confessed to seeing them, in Foyland. She said one, Elindhu Morspeth, was an erling spy. I'd love to get my hands on that one.'

Erlings in the Order? He had heard rumours of such in the past. 'We'll double the bounty on their heads. The real question here is how best to proceed.' He tapped the parchment the two lictors had presented. 'These allegations are too serious to be heard in open court.'

Hromboli nodded. 'I agree, Milord. But my superior, Justiciar Fontenau, might not.'

Olia Fontenau, who led the chapterhouse of the Justiciary here, wasn't someone Corbus got on with, but she was pliable, and he knew her price. 'I'll talk to Fontenau about it. If she gives her dispensation, you'll have carte blanche to finish Challys off without interference.'

Hromboli nodded and Faith lit up like a child given a sweet. *Dear Akka, she's repulsive*, Corbus mused. *I wonder if she's ever been pumped? And did she eat the poor man afterwards, like those spiders down south?*

'Carry on,' Corbus told them.

'Do you mean "Carry on" as in, "Ask the prisoner some more questions"?' Faith asked hungrily. 'There's so much more I want to do to that woman.'

Corbus frowned. 'Not until I've spoken to Fontenau. We're obliged for now to keep her alive and intact enough to stand trial. But I promise, once we've arranged things, you'll get your wish, so long as it's fatal to her.' He waved a hand. 'You may go. Please send Elan Sandreth in.'

Tevas Nicolini cast a bleak eye about him. The bastion at Folkstein was known as Tar-Brigida, after an old saint, but it felt more like a museum. Relics of the Order were preserved in every nook and cranny – oil paintings blackened with age and soot, moth-eaten tapestries, tarnished weapons and armour festooned with cobwebs. The hour he'd waited in the anteroom had dragged by so slowly, he felt like a dusty statue himself.

He had no desire to be here; though he was now officially a Sandreth bondsman, the Order had never liked ex-knights who continued using elobyne. But Elan Sandreth had insisted. Now his new lord was glaring at the secretaries protecting the archon's door as if the long wait was entirely their fault.

The last man I want to parade myself before is the bloody archon, Tevas worried.

A bald magia emerged, finally, followed by a creepy Aquini lictor, who told Elan he could go in. 'At last,' Elan muttered, gesturing to Tevas to follow.

Fortunately, other than gesturing at him to sit, the archon paid him no attention. He spoke to Elan amiably, as if the fact that he was screwing Elan's mother – and cuckolding his father – was neither here nor there, and Elan didn't appear to care. The gist of it was that there would be no hearing for Romara Challys; she'd shortly have an unfortunate accident.

'You'll still get the bounty,' Corbus told them, 'provided you remain silent about this meeting and everything you've seen recently, in Neparia and elsewhere.'

So that's what this is all about, Tevas thought bleakly. *I should've just cut Rom's throat.*

But two hundred aurochs, his share of the bounty, was a princely sum. And Elan would still be entitled to take possession of the Challys estates near Desantium.

'I suggest you leave as soon as possible,' Corbus told Elan. 'I've granted you full power of attorney over her parents. You cannot take the title of Earl of Desantium until they die, but you'll have full executive authority. Move decisively to establish your command and secure the earldom for our faction.'

'I won't fail you, Milord,' Elan promised. 'I only wish I could watch Romara die.'

Corbus considered, then said, 'I can arrange that. I need to talk to Justiciar Fontenau first, which I'll do tomorrow; then we'll finish her off afterwards.' He and Elan clinked goblets.

Tevas looked away, thinking about Romara as he first knew her, a girl he'd loved like a daughter. She'd been dedicated and brave, capable of putting aside her privileged upbringing in the service of something truly noble: service to the state. That the vyr had seduced and corrupted her was a tragedy, not something to gloat about.

But these two pricks will have my guts if I breathe a word of this to someone with the authority to act.

He sometimes wondered if Akka and Elysia were asleep, letting the Devourer have her way.

Elan, in contrast, was full of the joys of life as they left the office, crowing about his 'future father-in-law' and how great it was going to feel to watch Romara die in agony. He proposed rounding up some of his noble drinking buddies for a night on the town, but Tevas, now feeling genuinely sick, cried off.

Accepting that with a heartless shrug, Elan strutted away without looking back.

Left alone, Tevas plodded mindlessly through the familiar bastion until he fetched up outside the chapel. When he spotted Siera Segara Verber there, he realised he'd been unconsciously looking for her, knowing she loved this place.

Not that Segara was pious, but she liked watching the sunset through the stained glass, when the dust motes turned into shifting shafts of coloured light and painted the pews and stone in gorgeous colour. He went in and settled beside her, just enjoying the sight of her worn, lined face and the way her long silver hair became glowing coloured filigrees in that light.

Only when that glorious light had begun to fade did she acknowledge him. 'Hello, Tevas,' she drawled, in that familiar smoky voice. 'I heard you were here.' She leaned over and kissed his cheek, then eyed his flamberge sadly. 'A shame you've still got one of those.' Then she looked at the scabbarded blade propped against the pew. 'Not that I can talk.'

The veterans often said elobyne was as addictive as opium.

He and Segara had always got on. She'd become a tutor after active service, training female initiates in glyma, combat and how to handle life in the male-dominated Order.

'I made mistakes when I left,' he admitted. 'I did some bad things.' It was pointless lying to her; she always knew. 'But I've managed to get a bondsman contract from the Sandreths. I'm getting my life back together.'

Segara scowled. 'That damned family.' She'd never been a supporter of the current archon and his reign – which Tevas realised was the other reason he'd come here.

Because it just wouldn't be me if I didn't sabotage my big opportunity.

He dropped his voice and said, 'Segara, listen. You know Romara Challys is in the dungeons here, of course. I've just come out of a meeting with Corbus Ritter and Elan Sandreth. The archon said he'd be going to Justiciar Fontenau, to prevent her getting a trial. You know the sort of thing: a lictor 'accidently' rips her heart out – and so her story is suppressed. I know you knew Romara; if you think she deserves a proper trial, tell someone who can make sure it happens.'

Segara swallowed, then quickly kissed his cheek again. 'There's a good man inside you, Tevas Nicolini. One day, he'll rise up and kill the bad one.' She pushed his shoulder. 'Now get out of town.'

He'd hoped to remain anonymous, to still be Elan's bondsman, but he realised she was right: nothing ever remained secret for ever, and the archon's people would learn who'd betrayed this one. But he was suddenly struck by the strangest impulse.

'Come with me, Segara. Let's get out of this losers' game together.'

She blinked in surprise. He thought she'd laugh in his face, but instead she blurted, 'Jag me, maybe I will? Meet me at Westgate, tomorrow noon. It'll take until then to get this in motion.'

Then she rose and strode for the doors.

Romara hung in her manacles, in a torn shift that stuck to her open wounds and burns and made her scream in silent agony whenever she moved. Worse even than the pain was the memory of the ghastly faces of the lictor and the magia, lit up in exaltation as they flayed strips from her back and belly, then seared the wounds with heated metal. She'd screamed her lungs out then, begging for mercy or death, knowing that nothing could ever restore her. Even now, hours later, those brands felt like they were on fire.

After that, she'd blabbed all she knew, just to make it stop. Her bowels voided liquid, her voice had cracked from screaming, her pride had disintegrated. There was only one thing she'd managed to cling to: she'd not fallen into her bestial vyr-form. It was the only form of rebellion she had left, her only triumph.

Now all she could do was to implore Akka and Elysia for an ending to this hell.

Instead, the doors to the corridor crashed open. The bald torturer had returned.

Sister Faith. She and Lictor Hromboli had broken her. Romara cringed from her like a beaten puppy, wailing inside. *No,* she begged Elysia, *no more.*

'How's she doing?' Sister Faith simpered happily. She strode in and cupped Romara's chin, her loathsome touch inescapable. 'You'll never see public trial, you heretic scum,' the magia said gleefully, 'so I thought you'd like to know that tomorrow night, I get to do to you whatever pleases me. I really cannot wait.'

'*Nooo!*' Romara found herself whimpering, which made Sister Faith beam – until a man in maroon robes marched in, shouting, 'Hold there! I am the appointed defensior for Romara Challys and I demand the prisoner be placed in my care!'

The magia's face contorted with thwarted desire. 'No. You've no right—'

'On the contrary,' the defensior said briskly, 'this writ summons the prisoner to appear before the High Council. You will release her into my custody, right now.'

Hromboli stormed in, shouting, 'What the jagat are you doing here?' The burly gaolers gathered around him and Romara realised that there was every chance that she and this defensior could shortly be sharing a grave – until a knight with an iron-grey beard and a skinny, querulous mage-scholar forced their way into the gaol cell, closely followed by a woman dressed in elegant silks and a velvet cape of sky-blue. With them were six men-at-arms.

In crisp, commanding tones, the lordly woman announced, 'By Order of the High Council, Siera Romara Challys is hereby summoned to answer charges of heresy and rebellion. She must be surrendered to the High Council immediately. The Justiciary's right to question her pre-trial is revoked.'

Romara knew her: Lady Augusta Martia, one of the High Council, the hundred-strong body who were the ultimate arbiters of the Order's doings. They'd appointed Corbus Ritter to his post; but such appointments were never unanimous, and Lady Augusta was Ritter's greatest critic.

The air crackled – then Sister Faith quelled her orb and thumped away, kicking the door angrily on the way out. Hromboli, scowling, handed over the keys for the knight and the defensior to remove the manacles from the wall-hooks.

'Keep those manacles on,' the scholar snapped. 'They're confining her glyma.'

The defensior turned to the soldiers. 'Find a stretcher. We have a room upstairs for her.'

Romara stared glassily as he unfastened his cloak and wrapped it round her, covering her ruined shift and exposed body, and when she was unchained, she collapsed into his arms. They took her up a level, to a much cleaner cell. There, a young nun fed her water, which was wonderfully reviving, even though she craved oblivion. She was horribly aware of every movement; even the press of the sheet on her wounds was agony.

'Don't try using the glyma,' the defensior said. 'The manacles restrain sorcery and I'm told it's painful to try.'

Up close he had a blockish, stubborn face scarred by old acne which had had left his whiskers patchy and his eyes mournful, but he looked her squarely in the eye.

'I'll prepare a bath,' the nun offered. 'And I'll re-dress her wounds.'

'Thank you, Placida,' the defensior said. 'Be gentle.'

Lady Augusta, the scholar and the knight were all watching from the door. 'I'll leave you to it, then,' the noblewoman told the defensior. 'Keep watch, day and night. You know what Corbus is like.'

'I surely do,' the defensior said, his tones ironic. He turned back to Romara, his dour face sympathetic. 'The use of torture is a stain on the Order,' he said, 'but there is no will to ban it. I asked for your case, and as no one else wanted it, I got it. That happens a lot, I'm afraid. I will fight to give you a fair hearing, and as painless a death as I can negotiate.'

Romara was past the point of endurance. Even as she sought a response, she fainted away.

When Romara woke, she was struck speechless by the beauty of the sunlight pouring through the one iron-bound window high in the wall opposite the door. Then she wept, because her whole body hurt so much. But there was a greenish unguent slathered on her wounds, and bandages over the worst. The pain, though shockingly bad, was surely numbed, perhaps by some kind of opiate.

For now, she could bear it, so she looked around, taking stock.

The yellowish plaster walls were clean, and there was water, and a bowl of something mushy. She wasn't hungry, though. The mere thought of eating made her queasy. Finally, she realised the defensior was there, sitting on a stool, waiting patiently for her.

'Good morning' he greeted her solemnly. 'How are you feeling?'

She had to think about that. 'My head's fuzzy. I can't see right.'

'That's the opium,' the defensior told her. 'Best I could get. You should eat.'

She didn't want to, but he made her, spooning the mush into her mouth and making sure she swallowed. The belief this might all be a nightmare, mutilated body and all, was the only thing that got her through. She tried to draw on the glyma, but the recoil through the manacles made her limbs turn boneless and she fell sideways, helpless for a minute or more.

'I did warn you,' he noted. 'Lie still and let your head clear. It won't kill you, if that's what you're hoping.'

She groaned at that. It was some time before she could marshal her thoughts enough to say, 'Why do you bother? I'm guilty an' I'll burn ... You know that.'

'Undoubtedly true,' he agreed. 'But a proper defence is mandated by law. We seek to understand evil, not just eliminate it. I've been a defensior for fifteen years now. Often what emerges from trials like this helps us understand what we're facing.'

'Yet somehow you didn' realise the vyr're right,' she slurred.

'We've heard multiple allegations to that effect,' he replied evenly. 'But we've seen little proof, and always the crimes outweigh any mitigating evidence. You think I don't know about Nilis Evandriel's claims?' He tapped some papers on his stool. 'I have a copy of the lictor's report. There's nothing in it about the vyr that I haven't seen before.' He frowned. 'But Vanashta Baanholt is another thing altogether. That's why Lady Augusta got involved, and ensured Justiciar Fontenau didn't let her people kill you on the sly.'

I suppose a hearing is the most I can hope for, Romara thought miserably. *Dear Elysia, is this what your mercy looks like?* At least this man sounded sincere in his desire to help her. 'D'e believe Evandriel?' she slurred.

He frowned, then tapped his ear. 'I'm sorry, I didn't hear you.'

We're being spied on, Romara realised, eventually. 'Uh, shorry ... wha'ppens now?'

'Once you're fit to travel, we'll take you by portali gate to Hyastar and you'll go before the High Council. Tomorrow, we'll go over your story. In the meantime, rest.'

He rose and headed for the door.

'Wait,' she managed, groggily. 'Wha's name?'

At first she thought he wouldn't answer, but then he sighed and said, 'Dranit. Dranit Ritter.'

'Ritter?' she blurted.

'Aye, Corbus is my elder brother.'

She felt a horrible sensation, as if the floor had just given way and the Devourer's Maw was open beneath. 'Jagatai,' she blurted. 'You bastar's leave nothin' to chance, d'you?'

Dranit shook his head. 'On the contrary, there's no filial affection, no affiliation and no collusion between my brother and me. I take my cases *despite* him. Our political alignment and our base morals are so polemically opposed, I've been disinherited and ostracised for opposing him. So, one: there's only me in your corner. And two: despite it just being me, I will fight for you, tooth and nail, and be with you all the way, from the courtroom to the pyre.'

Then with a curt nod, he was gone.

Church bells chimed the noon hour and Tevas Nicolini grimaced, feeling each toll as punch to the gut. He looked up at the Westgate, stroking the neck of his newly purchased horse, laden with saddlebags packed for the road. That morning, Segara had sent a note to say she was coming, and his heart was as light as it had been in a decade.

I've been directionless on my own, he realised. *Since I left the Order I haven't truly known what to do with myself. I've just stumbled into things, mostly bad. But Segara's always had a good head on her. We can make this work, maybe down in Aquinium, where bald-headed old fools like me are everywhere.*

But where is she?

The bells faded, the echoes swallowed up in the bustling streets around the gate. It felt like those big open doors were calling to him, whilst every rider who appeared down the street had his eyes jerking their way, praying it was her.

He gave it another five minutes . . . then another.

At last, he hung his head, unhitched his mount and swung up, then mournfully trotted for the gates, nodded to the guards eyeing him doubtfully as he passed, and faced the broad street lined, with brick terraced housing closing in on either side.

Moments later, four horses emerged from the alleys, two on either side. Two knights, a mage . . . and Elan Sandreth. 'There you are, you dirty turncoat,' Elan said.

Oh no, Tevas thought, more for Segara than himself. *Elysia, you bitch, where's your mercy?*

Elan looked as smug as ever, blithely sure he was the equal of everyone here, as if nobility conferred immortality. But the other three were clearly trained glyma-men alert for danger.

He contemplated running, but it dawned on him that Segara wasn't here because she was already taken.

So what's the point of running? What's the point of anything?

But he pretended to flee anyway, slamming his heels into the horse's flanks. The startled beast leapt forward, and instantly the spells came, bursts of flame and force calculated to cut him down as he broke for the open road ahead.

They would have, too, if he'd gone that way. But he was already wrenching his reins hard around and was careering straight for the knight protecting Elan Sandreth. He shielded his left flank, battered a blow at the man's head, forcing him to defend – but he didn't intend to kill the knight, just to evade capture.

This all started with Elan, the piece of shit.

Elan realised the danger a moment too late, but he still got his sword up, which might have been enough, had he not been facing a glyma-knight. His parry blocked the gleaming flamberge, but Tevas' sheer power and the radiant blade sufficed to smash Elan's parry aside and open up his defence. Tevas felt bolts of energy crackling into his back, but he was already driving his thrust down and in, straight through chainmail and ribs. Elan's fleshy face swelled with shock as light flashed inside his chest. He went rigid and began to fold.

'That's for Romara!' Tevas told him as he toppled, whimpering.

A moment later the knight behind him, who Tevas had wilfully ignored, intent only on reaching Elan, drove his flamberge through his back. Tevas saw the gleaming tip emerge through his left breast as numbing pain rocked him. It didn't matter; he'd done what he needed to – and he had nothing left to live for now, anyway.

He pitched forward, fell over his horse's neck then toppled, but the darkness took him before he hit the ground.

12

The Gulf of Leos

Erlings in the South

It's often said that erlings lived only in the north, but I have found relics on desert monuments in Zynochia that show clear signs of an erling presence, including the characteristic spiral motif. Some wall paintings may even depict erlings being worshipped by ancient humans. The truth is, they were everywhere.

KEES SCHRABER, TALMONI SCHOLAR, 1327

Sea of Pelas
Autumn 1472

The sleepless days prior to reaching Bedum-Mutaza, the energy expended escaping their enemies, the knife-edge of life and death they'd been dancing along, and the creeping exhaustion of stress and grief combined to knock Jadyn out like a blow to the temple. He vaguely remembering falling asleep in Aura's lap, but woke rolled up in a blanket on the deck. He sat up, looked around blearily, yawned and rubbed grit from his eyes, then stretched and sat up.

Aura was right above him, sitting at the tiller, her hair wrapped in a turban and wearing an unfamiliar eastern dress that fell past her knees. She smiled cheerily, lighting up his heart.

'Good morning – is it morning?' He felt refreshed, alive. 'Is it even the same day? Have you sailed single-handed all day?'

'It be tomorrow,' Aura replied. 'Jadyn sleep all day and night. Scholar and Aura do sailing.'

He was instantly mortified. 'Oh, jagat, you should've woken me—'

'Neya, is okay. Wind drop yesterday, so sailing be easy. We anchor at night, all rest.' She patted the seat beside her, where a platter of cheese and flatbreads waited. 'Better now?'

'Worlds better,' he answered, settling beside her and offering her the plate, then eating ravenously himself. 'I was done in. The aegis isn't easy, is it? You've got to be so alert – and running as fast as we did is more tiring than running normally. You must be just as knocked-out.'

'Was also sleepy, is true. But now good.' She waved at the clear horizon. 'Is tresa bella, si? Sun, sea, motion. This I love.' She gave him a warm smile that transfixed him. 'Am glad being here, with you.'

This time when she leaned in to kiss him, he felt clear-headed enough to put aside his earlier confusions and simply enjoy the sensation, the silken feel and the warm, bittersweet taste of her, a gentle pressing that became a slow feeding as they melted together.

She paused, lashed the tiller down and faced him. 'Scholar is asleep,' she whispered. 'There be just us. Am through waiting. Wanting is now.'

Then she sat on his lap facing him, cupped his face and kissed him again as his fears dissolved. His arms went round her, realising he was tired of fighting this losing battle against love and desire. He slid his hands up her legs and realised she was naked beneath the skirts. He caressed her skin, marvelling at the silken smoothness, until she pulled her mouth away and with a melting look, pulled her dress over her head, and guided his hand to her breast. All the blood in his body rushed to his loins and he felt himself go hard as she tugged at the knot of his breeches until she had it undone, then yanked the breeches down and climbed onto him again, looking at him speculatively.

'Do not move,' she instructed him. 'I ride.'

As he gripped her waist, she settled into his lap, guiding him inside, drawing them together. At the feel of penetrating her, he almost lost control, but somehow managed to hold onto himself, letting her lead this dance. She gripped his shoulders, pressed her breasts to his face and began to move, ponderous and powerful.

It was an earthy, intoxicating, sweaty, smelly, hot, fervent, animal experience, a constant striving to hold off the inevitable release; but it was also transcendent, glorious and joyous, to be holding her like this, to be giving her all of himself, a fulfilment of a love that had been growing over this journey, to feel himself becoming a new being, that was he and she as one.

It was beautiful, messy and wonderful.

There was a moment of regret as he held her in the aftermath of climax, that he'd never shared such an experience with Romara, but it was a brief moment, because right now, in this moment, he couldn't imagine wanting and needing and loving anyone else as much as he did Aura.

She kissed him triumphantly. 'See, not so bad, eh? Should be done sooner.'

'There was no moment, until now,' he countered. 'The waiting made it perfect.'

'Perfect?' she snickered, disentangling. 'Perfect be silk sheets, clifftop villa and Aura reach orgasmus. This just start. We do perfect later.'

Dazed, somewhat disbelieving but overwhelmingly happy, all he could do was grin foolishly, while reluctantly prising his eyes from her lush body, all lithe curves and mysterious tattoos, so he could check on the ship. They'd fallen somewhat off the wind, so they needed to dress again, then do some work to get back up to full-speed, all the while shooting hot glances at each other every few minutes.

It felt a lot like love.

The morning passed in a kind of reverie, an idyll of sun, wind and sea, stolen kisses and promises of more. But by early afternoon, they were forced to keep their minds on more prosaic matters as the wind swung round, blowing a wall of dark clouds in from the north, at first subtly menacing, then the waves grew heavier, rain closed in, the wind began to whistle in the rigging and spray began to fly. The felucca started dipping heavily into troughs and crashing against the oncoming waves, waking Evandriel.

Jadyn began to fear that the little craft wouldn't stand up to such harsh treatment as they fought to keep from being swamped and stay afloat. Despite the conditions, Aura climbed to the top of the mast where, from that precarious point, she sought land. The wind was snarling now, a hungry and vengeful ghost shrieking for their demise.

'This is too much,' he shouted to Evandriel. 'We need shelter!'

'We are hundreds of kylos from any harbour,' the scholar replied, 'but there are thousands of islands out here. We just need to find one.'

Jadyn glanced up at Aura, clinging to the mast, and he felt a flash of dread that she'd fall and they'd never recover her. Those fears doubled as rain began to lash down.

'We have to take in the sails,' he shouted. 'The winds are too much – we'll capsize.'

'We will lose all control if we do that,' Evandriel answered. 'We will be swamped, and if that happens, we will sink and drown.' The wind was howling now, the rain pelting; they were tired and shivering, blind to direction, and all their potential fates were closing in.

Then Aura shrieked, '*Tierra – land – see – see there!*'

He followed her out-flung arm and saw it, too: a lump of darkness off to the right, maybe half a kylo away. Evandriel, fighting the tiller, shouted, 'Aura, get down here—'

Jadyn tried to keep the rigging taut while Aura fought the battering winds, until at last she dropped the last few feet, grabbing the rail to save herself. She staggered towards him and together they set about unhitching and stowing the secondary sail, then resetting the mainsail, trying to slow the ship's headlong rush. Evandriel now had them skimming along on a cross angle to the waves, bursting through cresting breakers as the gloom deepened.

Jadyn caught sight of the island, little more than a glorified rock spire, looming above. It looked barren and hostile, but if they could reach the lee side, it might yet save them.

Another wave crashed over them and he lost sight of Aura momentarily, only for her to reappear amid the spray, soaked and shrieking at the heavens. The felucca had been taking on water and the decks were awash, so he grabbed a wickerwork bailer and scooped with all his strength, bitterly missing the glyma, because right now it felt like only supernatural strength could save them.

Suddenly, the island was looming up on them and he saw a burst of spray dead ahead. He spun and shrieked, '*Rock* – go left . . . starboard, whatever . . . *Turn!*'

Evandriel threw himself bodily at the tiller. The felucca fell off the side of a wave, almost tipping, the timbers screamed as the little ship scraped along the jagged rock and careered onwards. Jadyn pulled himself along the deck to the scholar and, together, they hung onto the tiller as the waves seemed to slow and the wind changed pitch. Time seemed to slow as his senses grasped all their immediate futures and discarded them, shedding the destructive courses and following a golden course of safety through the maze of rocks, making the precise changes needed almost blindly, until they crashed into a patch of relatively tranquil waters.

They had found a cove on the lee shore. Momentum took them up the sand, Aura whooping in loud relief. Evandriel threw up his hands to the heavens, while Jadyn just sagged to the deck, sitting in six inches of water, panting.

But that was just for a moment. The next few minutes they worked frenziedly, taking down the mainsail before the wind could catch it and flip them, then lashing down everything. Rain was still beating down, but the wind was no longer hitting them directly and the felucca had been driven far enough up the small beach that the waves weren't shifting it, though the stern was still in the water. Behind them was the rocky reef they'd traversed, and the storm-tossed sea beyond, illuminated by the flashing lightning as thunder rolled and the clouds boiled overhead.

Elysia have mercy, Jadyn thought. *How in hell did we survive that?*

But there was no time for reflection. He leapt into the surf and grabbed a mooring rope, lashed it around the nearest substantial rock, then found another and roped it too.

Aura ran up and hugged him, hard. 'Am alive,' she panted. 'Did not think we survive.'

He clasped her to him gratefully. 'To die today would be too cruel. I only just found you.'

Her body was warm, but their sodden clothing was plastered to their skin and there was no immediate shelter to be seen.

'We'll have to sleep aboard,' he called to Evandriel.

'There might be a cave or something above,' the scholar answered, scanning the dark silhouette of the rock pinnacle – then he shouted, '*Look!* Is that a fire up there?'

Jadyn followed his pointing finger and saw the flickering red glow on the underside of a rocky overhang. 'We saw no other ship . . . But that's definitely a fire . . .'

They say that pirates sometimes strand their victims – or their crewmates – on these islands. Marooning, they call it.

'I'll go and see.'

'Neya, together,' Aura said. 'Together now.'

'I'll watch the ship. Wait, though—' Evandriel clambered to the small storage hold and pulled out a pair of Zynochi scimitars. 'Best I could get, sorry,' he told them.

Jadyn swung the unfamiliar weapon, getting a feel for the weight, but Aura shook her head and handed it back. Producing one of her myriad daggers, she said, 'This, Aura knowing. Now we go.'

Jadyn led, picking the way carefully to avoid slipping on the water-slick rocky slope. As they climbed, the patch of firelight came into view, half a turn around the central cone that formed the core of the atoll. They approached at an angle, until they stood outside a hole some seven paces high and twice as wide, in the lee of a big boulder lit by the homely orange glow. They had passed plenty of driftwood caught in the rocks, so whoever was here had clearly collected it before the storm set in.

Trying to project assurance, Jadyn stepped to the front of the cave and called, 'Hello?'

At once, he heard a collective squeal of shock and glimpsed dark shapes in the shadows, shrinking back from the little fire, where half a dozen skewered fish were sizzling. The smell washed over him.

Holy Akka, what have we found?

Then his mouth dropped open as the boulder beside the cave mouth rose, huge limbs flexing, and a bulbous head turned their way. It grasped a rock the size of Jadyn's head and roared.

'Wait,' Aura squeaked, ripping open a belt pouch and pulling something out. Horrifying Jadyn, she dropped to her knees before the trulka, which was every bit as large as those they'd seen in Semmanath-Tuhr.

It reared above her, the rock in its fist poised to smash her skull to pulp – when a sharp voice from within the cave called something and the giant creature stopped. It plucked the thing from Aura's hand and held it up to view: one of the feather and bead tokens Elindhu had handed out before they'd entered Semmanath-Tuhr, to mark them as erling-friends.

Three figures came to the cave mouth: spindly erlings with hair like octopus tentacles and greenish-blue skin. They were naked and neuter. Two of them gave Jadyn blankly hungry looks, but the middle one was clearly curious, for it said something to its companion, then to the trulka.

Jadyn held his breath as the giant knelt and presented Aura's trinket back to her. He silently thanked Elindhu, then tentatively asked, 'Do you speak Talmoni?'

Everyone paused, and Aura added, 'Nepari? Solabi? Bedumi?' in a hopeful voice.

The middle erling eyed them both, then said in a rusty voice, 'Can Talmoni, little-little.'

Jadyn swallowed, trying to envisage just how these creatures got here. Given the diversity and mutability of the erling race, he could imagine the tale; abandoning the land for the sea. They'd glimpsed an erling family doing precisely that on the Solabi coast a few months ago.

How many of them are there in the world? he wondered. *Hundreds? Thousands . . . ?*

He went to Aura and pulled her upright, while the trulka tossed its rock away.

'We have a friend below,' Jadyn said to the spokesman. 'Please, may Aura fetch him?'

'Ysh,' the erling agreed, warily.

Aura didn't look happy to be leaving him behind, but she dutifully started retracing their steps. Jadyn waited in silence while the erlings studied him, and he them. Ten minutes later she returned with Evandriel, who was wide-eyed with excitement. Both were carrying bundles of food and blankets, and the scholar had a fiddle case over one shoulder and a small cask of beer lashed over the other.

The trulka sniffed, its eyes went round and it hooted, 'Ooowww, skoor naaf!'

It did a jig that threatened to bring down the cliff, then reached for the cask. Evandriel went to withhold it, then thought better, wisely. 'Food, drink?' He pointed to the fire in the cave. 'Shelter?'

The erlings looked at each other – but the trulka had already opened the beer cask and was glugging happily. 'Esuda skoor,' it belched. It went to drink again, but the nearest of the smaller erlings protested frantically, trying to reach the barrel, which the trulka held over its head, guffawing loudly.

'Friends,' the middle erling said in Talmoni. 'Friends now! Friends.' It advanced with outstretched arms, as weird a sight as Jadyn had ever seen, but he stood his ground, reflecting that maybe he looked just as alien to the erling. They embraced, and the creature tapped its own chest, saying, 'Neave, name is Neave.'

Introductions were made all round and food was shared. Two erling children the size of human toddlers but moving like adults emerged from the back of the cave and joined in the strange meal. It quickly became apparent that these erlings were nothing like the rational, calculating beings who commanded in erlhaafens like Semmanath-Tuhr, instead being ruled by their appetites – but it was also clear they loved the simple joys of life, one of which was sharing.

Music, nonsensical laughter, even dancing ensued. To Jadyn it felt bizarre and unexpected, but he got no warning flashes from the aegis.

At length everyone settled to rest. Jadyn set aside his disappointment that he couldn't spend his first night ashore alone with Aura, relieved to be alive at all. It was a small price to pay for shelter and safety.

Outside the cave, the storm continued to rage, with booming seas, thunder and lashing rain. They worried for their vessel, but the cove was as good a haven as they could hope for out here, and there was nothing more they could do. By midnight, the erlings were in a drunken heap, all asleep. One of the smallest was curled up in Jadyn's lap, snuffling like a child.

He winked at Evandriel and Aura and murmured, 'Get some rest. I'll take first watch.'

Aura blew Jadyn a tired kiss, rolled onto her side, Evandriel made himself comfortable and moments later, both were breathing gently. It had been another long, tumultuous day.

Somehow, Jadyn found the strength to stay awake, to keep watch through the night.

By the next morning, the storm had at last blown over, leaving the ocean dirty but smoother and the wind gentle. They gave the erlings the remaining beer cask in return for the trulka hauling the felucca off the beach and through the reef, while Jadyn, Aura and Evandriel used poles to keep them off the rocks. Neave and the other erlings cheered from shore, waving them off as they set sail.

With the risen sun and a fresh easterly at their backs, the sailing was easy at first, but as the days passed it became more challenging, with shifting winds and increasingly frequent islets and reefs to navigate through. But they were able to anchor in the lee of a different island each night, and Jadyn and Aura took to swimming ashore to seek fresh water, wash, and make love under the setting sun and the rising moons.

Paradise, Jadyn kept thinking, lying in her arms afterwards and basking in the glow of happiness – a strange kind of paradise, in which things he'd been raised to regard as terrible sins, were in fact rites of love and trust, tenderness and bonding. He felt like a new person, with a different view of virtue and sin.

This is all I want from life . . . this, and the aegis, the destruction of the elobyne shards and the end of misrule by tyrannies, not to mention a more equal distribution of wealth and happiness . . . But mostly this . . .

But the sun always rose and each new day demanded their attention, although the sailing was beginning to feel less a chore, more an increasing joy, and every conversation with Nilis Evandriel – about elobyne, the glyma, aegis or their world – was an education. Jadyn could almost forget that the scholar was the most wanted man in the Triple Empire.

Four days after the storm, the felucca sailed into a harbour, where a large town clung to the steep cliffs and a big blockish building dominated the skyline.

'Welcome to Sherkaza,' Evandriel called, from the tiller. 'That big building you see is the renowned Library of Balkhezamun. Let's hope it's all that the legends claim.'

The Gulf of Leos

The warship carved a furrow through the small waves, following the coast of the Gulf of Leos, while Yoryn Borghart used the clothing and possessions abandoned in Mutaza to find their quarry. He'd been scrying Auranuschka Perafi late at night, choosing her over Jadyn Kaen as she would be less likely to recognise the sensation, especially if half-asleep. It had nevertheless been a frustrating exercise, as her location shifted from moment to moment. Something to do with the aegis, he guessed. He was almost certain she was somewhere to the west, but he was not yet ready to commit to heading straight out into the ocean. The personal affects they'd found in Bedum-Mutaza were being used up, destroyed by the spells, and still they had no firm trace on their prey.

The need to scry meant maintaining his glyma levels, so his flamberge orb, which he'd recharged in Bedum-Mutaza, was beginning to run low again, and the glyma use was once again blinding his aegis. He resented that: Vazi Virago, who'd put the glyma aside, was once again outstripping him. Purging glyma normally took months, if you were in no rush and wanted to do it thoroughly, but he needed the magic right now, so he was stuck with it.

And despite that, I still can't scry them, he thought. *I'm wasting time and energy.*

Nevertheless, that evening he settled into his favourite spot in the prow, preparing the spell while brooding over the unfairness of it all. Then Vazi joined him, blithely unaware that he had no desire for her company. She was wearing men's clothing, spares from the captain's wardrobe, having arrived with nothing but a ballgown. It made her look somewhat boyish, but she still radiated cold authority.

'I'm hoping once we have a firm grip on the aegis, we can learn to use it and the glyma together,' she said, leaning on the rails with the wind ruffling her tightly pulled-back hair. 'I don't want to have to spend the rest of my life moving between the two.'

'Nor I,' Borghart agreed. 'The temptation to commit murder will become too much.'

'So, where's Kaen going?' she wondered. 'What's out there in the Mar-Pelas?'

'Pirates and other scum.'

'We need a scholar, someone who knows the history – they've already got one, if that was Nilis Evandriel we saw at the Hejiffa Dhouma.'

'I should have asked for one,' Borghart acknowledged. 'Not that Grandmaster Rendreth was very helpful, mind.' He cast about his memory, but Pelasia had never interested him. 'From what little I know, there are a dozen cities worthy of the name, and hundreds of pirate havens masquerading as fishing villages. The islands are the very definition of a backwater.'

'But it's where they're going,' Vazi observed. 'Even without scrying, I'm sure of it, too. This precognition the aegis gives appears to be a way of interpreting the evidence the world provides and predicting outcomes: that's why, short-term, obvious acts are easiest to predict and unexpected ones can be missed. Naturally, it's when they do the unexpected that I fear them.'

Fear them? It hadn't occurred to Borghart to fear Kaen or Perafi, no matter what they did. 'They're still fleeing *us*,' he reminded her.

'We just need to trap them somewhere they can't run. I want them alive, to extract every little bit of information from their brains.'

Their eyes met and he realised he no longer saw her as beautiful or desirable: she was just a comrade now, a fellow traveller on this dark road. He saw that she recognised this surprising kinship, too, like discovering a stranger was really your cousin.

'What drives you, Lictor?' she asked quietly.

'Nothing anyone boasts of,' he replied frankly. 'Ambition, jealousy and revenge, mostly.'

'Do you have any friends?'

'I have cultivated useful people, but genuine liking . . . ? No. I'm not a pleasant person to be around, and I've never needed others.' He snorted dismissively. 'I'm sure there's something wrong with me, but I don't care.'

'Strange. I feel much the same way, only without the anger. I've never felt more than shallow emotional connections. Everything I've ever done is purely rational. And I've never had friends either.'

He wondered at that. 'Is there anything you enjoy?'

'Succeeding. Winning.'

'I mean, do you like singing? Dancing? Drinking? Jokes? Good food? Is there any pointless pastime you do for the sheer enjoyment?'

She shook her head to all. 'I've never seen the point.'

'But our hearts and bodies have needs that sometimes we must bow to, for our sanity.'

'Mine don't,' she said flatly. 'And I am perfectly sane.'

You might think so, he thought, *but you're not human: you're like a predatory insect, or a shark. You exist to perpetuate your existence.* It struck him as both chilling and sad. *You're actually a long, long way from being sane. Much like me.*

'Well,' he said slowly, 'for my part, I find you a valuable colleague and I hope to continue to prove useful.'

'See that you do – and you can start by finding those damned heretics.'

Then she walked away, heading for the cabins below.

Glowering at her back, he resigned himself to another futile hour of failing to find his prey. Despite the personal possessions, which he was beginning to doubt were imbued with enough of their essence to be of much use, Kaen and Perafi remained elusive.

Scrying can't find them, he thought resentfully. *We need some other way.*

It was a little unsettling to find common ground with a man like Borghart; but in truth, those who thrived in the Vestal Order had always needed to have a strong sense of emotional detachment to survive the emotional loneliness, the glyma madness and a life of fighting and killing people, often just because you were told to. It was a competitive, macho and violent culture, for women as much as men. Vazi had always had that detachment, even as a child. Her parents had never understood her; they had called her cold and lavished their love on her younger sister. But she died at just fourteen and that triggered the Gift in Vazi, so she had to leave. Her mother was dead now, and her father had a new wife and new, more acceptable children.

The whole memory still tormented Vazi, and underpinned her dislike – indeed her horror – of physical or emotional empathy. But it was also part of what made her who she was.

'You've got no empathy,' a chaplain had once told her, and that rang true.

But now Yoryn Borghart was intruding on her inner world, because he inhabited the same emotional void as her. *He's got no empathy either*, she reflected. *We're similar that way.*

What to do with that bond, she didn't know, but for now, he was an ally.

She became aware that the ship had stopped moving, though the crew and marines were still singing, some interminable northern dirge that vibrated through the timbers from the main hold where they caroused every night. There were three cabins – she'd commandeered the captain's, the largest, which had shuttered windows beneath the stern. The captain resented being forced to take the smaller chamber opposite Borghart's, but as far as she was concerned, she was in command, so it was hers.

Too restless to sleep yet, she returned to the deck. The sails had been reefed and they sat at anchor in the lee of a low headland. Sailing at night was risky, the chance of striking rocks or a shoal too great, and it was increasingly unlikely that Kaen and Perafi were sailing south. All Borghart's scrying had got them nowhere, and her premonitions said they were off-course.

Once we've replenished our water supply in the morning, we'll turn west, she decided. *But unless we can pick up on them somehow, it's a needle-in-a-haystack search.*

There was only a light watch, just two men, bow and stern. She sent the one in the bow away and settled in the prow, where she was hidden from their sight by masts and rolled-up sails, and let the quiet settle into her bones. The peace was unsettling, as it gave her no distractions from the gnawing inside her bones: the glyma-craving eating her marrow.

Just draw in a little and you'll feel so much better, her treacherous mind muttered, but she fought the urge with stubborn determination. *Let the minutes pass you by,* she told herself, settling against the side of the ship. *When you wake, it'll be a little easier.* She closed her eyes.

Her dream was odd, because it was a lot like reality. She was right where she'd fallen asleep, propped against the railing, her head resting on her folded arms. But in the dream she woke and found a man sitting opposite, studying her. He was golden-haired, with a flawless ivory complexion and impossibly handsome features. People called her beautiful, but she had flaws aplenty – a slightly crooked nose, a chipped tooth, pores that clogged, itchy rashes beneath her hairline, broken nails and old scars.

But this being was *perfect*, his face symmetrical and his eyes radiant. He was robed in deep purple with Calvic squares embroidered in gold on the hem. If you looked at him in a certain way, you could almost see white-feathered wings furled on his back, though if you stared directly, you couldn't see them at all.

He was one of the Serrafim, a mighty servant of Akka, of that, she had no doubt. Which meant she had to be dreaming. So she didn't shriek in surprise.

'Who are you?' she asked, instead.

His voice was music itself, deep-pitched enough to send shivers down her spine. 'I am Genadius, Vaziella,' he replied. 'Akka sent me to guide you.'

When awake, she didn't believe in Serrafim or Akka; they were just constructs of the manipulative priesthood. But in her dream, she dropped to her knees, awestruck and afraid. 'Akka be praised,' she managed to croak.

'What is it you seek?' the seated angel asked her.

'Two heretics who fled Bedum-Mutaza on a Zynochi felucca,' she answered breathlessly.

The angel rose and laid a hand on her head and she instantly felt like he was pulling her brain out of her crown, a nauseating feeling, even in the dream.

'Ah, I see,' Genadius said. 'These are your quarry, yes?'

Her brain flashed images of Jadyn Kaen, then Auranuschka Perafi, though she'd barely glimpsed the woman, either at Vanashta Baan-holt or the Hejiffa Dhouma. 'Yes, them,' she panted, as a splitting headache tore apart her skull.

He sniffed the air, then he smiled. 'I sense . . . yes . . . west of here. West.' His eyes lit up. 'Do you wish me to destroy them for you?' he asked. His voice was flat, as if offering her a glass of water, not a double murder.

She went to agree, then thought about that, because despite the strangely overwhelming nature of this dream, she retained enough self-will to know she wanted to capture and question Kaen, Perafi – and Evandriel, if the scholar really was with them.

'Guide me to them,' she asked, fearing she was saying the wrong thing. 'I want them alive, for questioning.'

I'm imagining all this, she thought again. *This is my subconscious interpreting the world.*

'If you say so,' the Serra drawled. 'Fear not, I will find them. In the meantime . . .'

He suddenly bent and sucked the air from her mouth in an act that looked like a kiss but felt like asphyxiation. 'To help you see better,' he said, pulling away. 'And because I can.'

Vazi reeled as his glimpsed wings of light flashed and he vanished in a rush of wind.

She woke, folded over on the deck, holding her belly and dry-retching. The boat was utterly silent, then she heard boots and one of the watchmen scurried up the stairs.

'You a'right, ma'am?' he panted. 'I 'eard ye fall.'

She stared dazedly at him, than clambered to her feet, embarrassed. 'I'm fine . . . I must have fallen asleep and slipped,' she rationalised. 'Did you see . . . ?' Her voice trailed off as she decided against spouting lunacy about seeing angels. 'Never mind. Thank you.'

The watchman looked at her anxiously. 'You should eat more, ma'am.'

She gave him a frosty look. 'If I need advice, I ask for it,' she said tersely, unsettled by her lapse. Showing weakness in front of men was always an error. 'Goodnight,' she concluded, and hurried back to her cabin.

That night, she went to lock her door with a spell when she realised that she had absolutely no glyma-energy inside her at all. Perhaps that was why she'd almost fainted . . .

Did the Serra take it all when he kissed me?

She jammed the door closed, then lay on the bed, wondering what had just happened. But when she closed her eyes and slept, she didn't dream. Instead, she saw visions. Her aegis was truer, stronger than before.

And it was telling her that Genadius was no kind of angel.

13

Breaking In

What is Elobyne?

Jovan Lux claimed it was gifted to him in a dream by Akka Himself. But what is it? Though scholars have studied it for generations, no one can claim to know where it came from, what all of its properties are, nor why it's found on only one frozen island. What little they've learned, they don't share with the likes of you and me.

THE SHADOW HISTORY (BANNED), 1455

Folkstein, Miravia
Autumn 1472

The next day, despite Gram's continued exhaustion, Elindhu led her little group to the portali gate Keffrana had told her of, an old barrow believed to be the grave mound of an ancient chieftain. There she slapped their borrowed horses on their rumps and shouting aloud in the erling tongue, sent them home. They reared, bent at the knees as if bowing, and pounded away.

Gram was still horribly shaky, but the need to reach Romara drove him on. They entered the Shadowlands stealthily, and Elindhu led them safely through the deathly gloom without incident until they emerged among the hills north of the Osprey River, downstream of the Order bastion. The gate there, a shallow cave all but blocked by a rockfall, was unknown to the Order – but not the erlings, Elindhu noted with quiet satisfaction.

They rested until dawn, then ventured forth to find themselves overlooking the Osprey River, which flowed west towards the sea. The river was wide, a kylo across, and they could see barges being hauled along the well-tended banks and sailing vessels riding the currents in the middle of the flow. Their destination, Folkstein, was upstream, a large port on the river, which was itself a major artery for goods moving in and out of the Hytal heartlands.

Gram paused to soak up the fresh air on his skin, the wind rustling the trees, the rhythmic chanting of the crews of boats on the river and the distant cries of gulls which had followed the river inland. Not far off cattle were lowing and wood-smoke laced the cold, misty air.

It was a peaceful scene, but it failed to quell his inner distress. The tranquillity of ninneva remained inside him, but he could feel that calm eroding. The Order had held Romara now for days, and the lictors would surely have had their way with her. He'd asked Elindhu what Romara could expect, and the magia had been brutally honest. Though forbidden to damage her senses, her ability to communicate, or to cripple or violate her, they could still do awful things. Worry for her left him sick to his stomach.

He was thankful for Elindhu's support and dedication and Soren's unflinching willingness, but he missed Jadyn's earnest purposefulness and Obanji's calm assurance. He even missed Aura's spark. And he ached for Romara with all of his being. But logic said that the best he could hope for was to make her death count, to send a few lictors into the Devourer's Maw before he joined her in the hereafter.

If that's all, so be it. It will be enough.

They found a stream flowing towards the river. Even the small exertion of refilling his water bottle left Gram so shaky that he was grateful to drop down to drink as an excuse to let his legs recover. Elindhu knelt beside him, slaking her own thirst, while the two young ones sat side by side on the trunk of a fallen tree. Whatever lay between them was clearly a complicated swirl of youthful fascinations colliding with adult realities. The mutable gender of the erling made his head spin – he couldn't begin to imagine how he'd cope in Soren's shoes. He'd also seen homosexual men and women branded as sinners and hounded out of their homes, or worse. That was all too often how 'good people' dealt with things they didn't understand.

Surely it's better to just let people love as they will? But he couldn't tell if love was what Soren and Fyn felt for each other. They seemed uncomfortable, yet drawn together in spite of that.

'Are you ready to go on?' Elindhu asked quietly, and he nodded. His body wanted to plead for more rest, but the need to find Romara was imperative.

'It's a dozen kylos at least,' she went on. 'Romara will be held in Tar-Brigida bastion, inside the city. The Order, Justiciary and the scholars are all in the old inner keep.'

'Can we get in?'

'I hope so. The castle belongs to another age, so it's somewhat old and quirky.'

'A bit like you, Aunty Eli,' Soren called cheekily.

'I'll choose to ignore that,' she said, rising. 'Come, we've got a fair walk ahead.'

Before setting off, the two erlings made themselves look as human as possible, and Elindhu and Soren concealed their elobyne orbs. As it was, the country folk they met peered at them curiously, but that was all.

It was indeed a long walk, but they reached the city before midday and entered through the West Docks Gate, the guards barely noticing them as they filed in among the residents and visitors clogging the ancient cobbled streets.

The riverboat traffic meant southern faces weren't uncommon, so Soren didn't stand out. Fyn had concealed his most obviously erling features – his amber eyes and earlobes – and they were all dressed in the stained, lived-in clothing Keffrana had given them. But it wasn't impossible that the Order had circulated their descriptions, so they kept their heads down as they sought their goal, a contact of Keffrana's.

'This is it,' Gram murmured, checking out the ramshackle jetty on mossy piles jutting into the dirty brown river. Booths crowded the approach to the third wharf, where agents haggled with ship-masters over cargoes.

They queued for the third booth, reaching the front after a big man with a scarred face hurled a wailing velvet-clad fop into the river, leaving him to thrash his way to shore.

'What you want, ya big laggy?' the big man asked Gram, ignoring the kerfuffle he'd caused. 'If ye wan' work, we ain't hiring.'

'Someone told me I can source moonstones from Dagoz here,' Gram replied, using the words Keffrana had told them to say.

The man's face changed and he touched his fist to his heart. 'Well met, Brother,' he said cautiously, then he called over his shoulder, 'Korki, some folk here to see you.'

'Send 'em in and take over, Horto,' a woman's voice replied from inside the booth.

Horto clapped Gram on the back, then looked over the others and pulled a face. 'Elysia on high, let's get you lot off the street before someone with eyes works you all out.'

Gram led the way into a small office where a woman was seated at a desk, surrounded by piles of grubby parchment – what looked like bills of sale and purchase and shipping dockets. She scrawled something, poured blue wax and stamped a signet ring, then stood and looked them over. Gram was struck by her youth: she was in her early twenties, with a disfigured face, her right cheek burnt and the eye concealed by a patch, and her throat had a puckered scar from ear to ear. She'd obviously survived wounds that would have killed most. She was otherwise pretty, with jet-black straight hair, soft deep brown skin and narrow eyes. He couldn't place her race.

She reacted to their appearance with alarm. 'Akka's Balls! You lot come from Keffrana?' Clearly their disguises weren't terribly good. 'Let's get you out of sight.'

She ushered them downstairs into a large room piled high with bales and crates and stinking of damp and rat droppings. She studied them, hands on hips. 'If Keffy vouches for you, I'm at your service. Call me Korki.' Then she faced Gram and touched her heart. 'I'm honoured to meet you, Xaltos. Are you a wishart?'

'Sorry, I don't know these words,' Gram apologised. 'What's a xaltos – or a wishart?'

Korki frowned. 'Are you new to us?'

'Aye, and I've been in hiding ever since.'

'Ah. Well, a Xaltos – or a Xaltia – are what we call coven leaders. And a wishart is a word we use instead of vorlok. It means "wise heart".'

'Then I'm honoured,' he replied. 'My mother was a vorlok from Avas, but she didn't use those words.'

'They're mainland terms,' Korki replied. 'Avas? A hard-won victory, I hear.'

He didn't want to go into that, his feelings were so conflicted. 'Do you use the term "draegar"?'

Her single eye blinked. 'Oh, are you knight-trained?'

'No; but a comrade I lost was.'

'Ah. Draegar is a Kharagh word meaning *dragon's blood*. Only a knight-turned-vyr is called that. We see it as a term of great status.'

Romara would approve, Gram thought. 'Where are you from, Korki?'

She pursed her lips hesitantly, then said, 'I have Kharagh blood. When the wars ended, many of our people remained, unable to bear the long journey home. They became waggoneers, and eventually my clan settled in Miravia. My mother married local, and here I am.' She met his eyes. 'Her man was vyr and we joined a coven, but the Vestals discovered us – which is how I got this.' She brushed fingers over her marred face and throat. 'I was left for dead, but Horto found me and took me in.'

'How did you know what I am?'

'You have a musk that stirs the blood. A *wishart* scent.' She looked away shyly. 'But that's by the by. It is our duty to help you, so I'll do what I can.'

'That's much appreciated,' Elindhu replied. 'What news do you have of the city?'

'Particularly concerning one of our kind,' Gram put in.

Korki looked at him sharply. 'There's a rumour that the Order have caught a Xaltia.'

It's got to be Romara, Gram thought.

'It's hard to keep anything a secret in a city like this,' Korki said. 'Guards have family and friends – they talk.' She noted his anxiety. 'Is she your draegar friend?'

'Don't answer, Gram,' Elindhu put in. 'What she doesn't know, she can't be made to tell.'

Korki bowed her head. 'Horto always says I ask too many questions. Come, let me find you food and drink.'

She showed them to a room beneath the dock, and a boy brought in water, fresh-baked bread and a slab of butter, then scurried away. The room was dank and cheerless, and judging by the dampness of the floor, it frequently flooded – but the bread was still warm from the oven and the butter was a rare treat, as was the bottle of cider she opened.

While they ate, Korki spoke. 'From here in the docklands, Folkstein spreads north and east, towards Crow's Rise, where the nobs have their mansions. Tar-Brigida Bastion occupies the ridge. It's the archon's own home bastion, but his duties in the Order mean he's seldom here. His son Lancel manages the family's affairs.'

'Is there anyone who can help us get inside the bastion?' Elindhu asked.

'You need Shraedan,' Korki said. 'He's a hard man, but he has contacts inside.'

'Can he be trusted?' Gram asked.

'More or less. Shraedan plays the long game, so I've never known him to cash in anyone for short-term gains. His dark side comes out if anyone tries to double-cross him, but I don't see that from you.'

She gave them directions and schooled them in how to introduce themselves, including an elaborate set of passwords that Elindhu memorised. She slipped Elindhu some coin to pay Shraedan, then shyly hugged Gram. 'Don't throw your lives away,' she urged as they parted. 'I'm sorry, but if your Xaltia's in the lictors' hands, she's as good as dead already.'

The gnawing in Gram's gut was the fear that she was right.

*

The boy assigned to guide them to Shraedan took a winding path, nervous of city guardsmen and rival gangs alike. A skinny scruff, he barely spoke, treading the city like a hunter in a forest. But by midday they were supping with Shraedan, a disreputable-looking lank-haired Miravian, in a back room of a tavern.

'I don't need to know your names,' was the first thing he said, spitting betel juice onto the filthy wooden floor. 'I don't want to know where you're from or what you've done. Just tell me what you need and I'll tell you if it's possible.'

'There's a prisoner in Tar-Brigida,' Elindhu replied. 'Can we get her out?'

The gang lord's eyes bulged. 'Are you *insane*? You mean the fallen knight, I take it?'

'Can we at least get a message to her?' Gram put in.

'Impossible.' Shraedan leaned in. 'Listen, maintaining eyes and ears inside the bastion is risky, and my folk in there need to keep their heads down. The most I can tell you is that they've got the lowest dungeons closed off and they're only accessible through the East Tower.'

'I know it,' Elindhu said.

'You're best to stay away,' Shraedan said. 'It's a hornets' nest up there, right now.'

Gram bowed his head, but Elindhu asked, 'Does anyone have access to her?'

'Not unless you can get at a lictor, but they're . . .' Shraedan blinked and sat back. 'No, wait! There's one other fella who gets to see her: the defensior.'

'What's that?' Soren asked.

'An attornalus, a law practitioner, specialising in defending the accused,' Elindhu answered. 'The Code requires that everyone accused by the Order has legal counsel. That might sound unusually fair-minded of our beloved Order, but it originated because so few of the accused could speak intelligibly that the trials became a farce.'

'Most still can't,' Shraedan grunted.

'Who's her defensior?'

'Everyone's favourite: Dranit Ritter.'

Gram scowled and asked, 'Is he any relation to the archon?'

Elindhu gripped his forearm. 'He is, and it's good,' she chuckled. 'Dranit's feud with his brother is legendary. He'll do his best for her – not that he'll be able to do much – but Dranit loves to spit in his brother's broth.'

'Aye, Dranit's all right,' Shraedan put in. 'But he's very careful about who he sees. The lictors have him under constant scrutiny – they'd love to drag him over the coals, believe me.'

Gram looked at Elindhu. 'He's still our way in.'

She turned back to Shraedan, 'Can we meet Ritter?'

The gang-lord considered. 'Aye, but ye can't just walk up to him. I'll need money up front to make it happen, mind.' He named a figure, Elindhu paid him, and he rose. 'Wait here – drinks are on the house.'

He was gone an hour, leaving them in a constant state of worry that the next person through the door would be a lictor with a pentacle of knights at his heels, but when the door did open at last, it was Shraedan, followed by a solid Aquini man in his thirties.

'This is Lubano,' Shraedan announced. 'The rest is up to you.'

He left without another word.

Lubano sat, removed his hat to reveal a deeply tanned hairless scalp. The necklace flopping from his tunic had a chip of elobyne mounted on it. 'I'm Dranit Ritter's bondsman,' he said, in clipped tones. 'Basically, I look after his safety. I'm ex-Order, but I got out young when I realised what the glyma was doing to me. Now I protect Dranit, not just physically, but from conspiracy as well. No one gets to him except through me.'

Elindhu introduced herself and the rest of the group using the false names they'd agreed on, then brought up Romara. 'We understand your master is defending her?'

'Why do you ask?' Lubano replied bluntly.

'We're friends,' Gram replied, unable to keep the emotion from his voice.

Lubano's grey eyes fixed on him. 'Do you share her vyr affliction?'

When Gram didn't answer, the bondsman explained, 'Listen, Dranit does defend vyr on occasion, among a multitude of criminals, debtors and other aggrieved defendants. But he's not a sympathiser of the Vyr Rebellion and nor am I. He can't afford to be caught with your kind. The lictors watch everything we do.'

'Do they know you're here?' Elindhu asked sharply.

'I hope not. I know how to move undetected. But there's no way Dranit or I can get you into the bastion. His work is too important to risk jeopardising it for one case.'

Gram felt a flash of anger, but Elindhu laid a hand on his arm. 'We understand,' she said quickly, 'and we'll do nothing to endanger your master. But I believe we can help him, if we meet him face to face.'

Lubano leaned back thoughtfully. 'By rights I should refuse, but this case has touched my master's heart. I'll ask, and let you know. You'll have his response by evening.'

They spent a nervous afternoon, worrying over whether Lubano would return with Ritter, or if Shraedan would send them on their way – or cash them in.

But an hour or so before dusk, there was a discreet knock and Lubano, cowled and wary, entered and scanned the room. The travellers all rose, hands going to weapons. 'Pax,' the Aquini murmured as he signed behind him and another man, also wrapped in an anonymous brown cloak, joined him. He lowered his hood to reveal a pugnacious, acne-scarred face, worn and tired, framed by curling black hair that was going grey. But his eyes were alert and determined.

'Lord Ritter?' Elindhu asked.

'I'm not a lord any more, just plain Dranit Ritter, attornalus and defensior.' He chose a chair at the end of the table and sat. 'No introductions, please. I shouldn't be here, and if one of you is captured, you'll place me at risk.'

'But you're here,' Gram noted.

'I am, unwisely. I can spare you ten minutes at most – I'm expected elsewhere.' He tapped the table. 'So, Lubano tells me you have connections to Siera Romara Challys?'

'We do.' Elindhu replied. 'What's your impression of Romara's account?'

'I find her account of the machinations that have entrapped her in a fictitious marriage depressingly plausible. My brother's duplicity is long-established, as are his infidelities, his ties to certain dynasties and his belief that he is above all laws. Under his hand, the Order has become a tool for powerful men to enrich themselves further. I also know that Elspeth Sandreth travelled all the way to Petraxus to see the Hierophant himself, to have the marriage validated, so Siera Romara is now a Sandreth.' He steepled his fingers and smiled wryly. 'Or maybe not.'

'What do you mean?' Gram asked.

'Yesterday, Elan Sandreth was killed while trying to apprehend a former knight called Tevas Nicolini. Nicolini had tipped off Lady Augusta Martia, a member of the High Council, about Romara's arrival here, preventing her from being disposed of quietly, as my brother had intended. Instead, there's to be a trial in Hyastar, provided Augusta can get High Council approval. We're waiting news on that.'

Gram stared. 'Tevas Nicolini killed Elan Sandreth? But didn't they bring her here together?'

Dranit Ritter smiled grimly. 'I understand that Nicolini had a change of heart when he heard that Siera Romara was to be silenced without trial. He told a former colleague, Siera Segara Verber, who told Lady Augusta. But Nicolini was murdered and Verber's disappeared. The High Council is furious, and they are now doubly determined to hear Romara's testimony.'

'How does she fare?' Gram blurted.

Dranit was blunt. 'She's been tortured: she's in constant pain from flagellation, branding and burns, but she retains her defiance and clings to sanity, despite her vyr nature.'

Gram felt furious at her plight, but pride in her fortitude. 'She's a fighter.'

'Everyone breaks. They got a confession from her, containing allegations concerning her fictitious marriage, the finding of Vanashta Baanholt, a spell called Oculus Tempus and the true nature of elobyne.'

Dranit leaned forward. 'Augusta is trying to persuade her fellow councillors that her testimony is worth hearing. She's convened the whole council today – they use a system of mutual scrying, which allows voice-less communication, clever stuff – to get their approval. If she's successful, they'll move Romara to Hyastar for the hearing.'

'Can the archon veto that?' Gram asked.

'No,' Elindhu answered. 'He's appointed by the High Council. He answers to them, not the other way around.'

'Aren't they mostly his supporters?' Gram asked.

'No, not at all,' Dranit replied. 'He won the last election, but since then, his actions have alienated many. It'll be touch and go whether he keeps his job at next year's election.'

'So where is Romara now?' Elindhu asked.

'The Justiciary still hold her, but in supervised cells, well away from the lictors. If Augusta gains the right to grant her a hearing, she will take custody of her.'

'What if she fails?' Soren asked.

Dranit spread his hands apologetically. 'Then the lictors will reclaim her and we'll never see her again.'

Gram wanted to rage that these men weren't doing enough, but Elindhu, sensing his fury, forestalled it, saying, 'Thank you, Defensior. We pray to Elysia for you all.'

'Is that it?' Soren blurted angrily. 'After all we've seen and done?'

Dranit raised a placatory hand. 'I understand your frustration, but there will always be people who think it better to suppress unpleasant truths, rather than admitting that the system is flawed. It's that same attitude that sees nobles and officials protected when guilty, and the institutional covering-up of injustices.'

'Do you believe Romara's testimony?' Elindhu asked him sharply.

'Sadly, I do,' Dranit said. 'But Corbus has put it to the High Council that Romara's testimony is too incendiary to be heard outside a closed session – meaning only he, the imperial representative and the justiciar will hear it. If that proposal is accepted, she'll be muzzled, and likely dead by midnight.'

'But what about the Oculus Tempus spell?'

'Here's the thing: banned spells can't be taught, so even very well-trained mages don't necessarily know it. Only Justiciary mages with special permits are allowed to learn such spells – lictors, in other words. And any hearing will be adjudicated by a justiciar, for the sake of neutrality, so that probably won't happen.'

Gram hung his head as another thread of hope was slashed.

Lubano turned to Dranit. 'Milord, we're out of time.'

The defensior sighed and rose. 'I'm sorry, but I must get back to Augusta.'

'You've given us nothing,' Soren blurted. 'You cow—'

'Hush, boy!' Elindhu scolded him. 'He's given us much, and his work is vital.'

'Thank you for understanding, Magia,' Dranit said. 'You all have my sympathy, but I'm in a war of my own and this is but one battle.'

He and Lubano left, slipping out the door and closing it quickly. Their footsteps receded and were gone.

The four travellers looked at each other, crestfallen. Gram put his head in his hands. 'We'll never be able to reach her now.'

Elindhu turned to Fyn, who'd kept his cowl pulled up, a silent observer throughout. 'Well?'

The erling lowered his cowl, and Gram and Soren both gaped.

His appearance had completely altered, to the crinkled black and grey hair and features of Dranit Ritter. 'How is this?' Fyn asked, in the same gravelly tones as the defensior.

Gram's heart began to thump painfully. 'Akka on high, you can do that?'

'Scary, eh?' Fyn replied, with a hard smile.

Soren gulped audibly. 'Can you look like anyone at all?'

'While he's young and fully mutable, he can alter his entire appearance, more or less,' Elindhu answered. 'But the bigger the change, the harder it is to sustain.'

'I can keep this up for a decent while, though,' Fyn added, still in Dranit's voice.

Elindhu looked round the table. 'Well, what's clear is we can't wait on this vote, because she'll be whisked away, either by Lady

Augusta Martia, to be put on trial, then executed as a fallen knight, or by the lictors, to be tortured and executed. So it's got to be now.'

'We're really going to break into the bastion?' Soren took a deep breath. 'Fine.'

'With luck, the only people we'll need to hurt are the lictors and gaolers,' Elindhu said. 'But we must get in without raising the alarm. Fyn will be Dranit Ritter, but someone else needs to pose as his bod-yguard – we'll have to tell anyone who asks that Lubano is unwell.'

'That'll be me,' Gram said. 'It has to be me.'

Soren went to protest, but Elindhu was already nodding agreement. 'After what's been done to Romara, I doubt anyone else would be able to keep her this side of madness. But remember, she'll be in poor shape, so you'll have to carry her out.'

'We'll work something out – a distraction from without maybe, Magia?'

Elindhu winked. 'Leave that to Soren and me.'

'Who goes?' a male voice barked from a slot in the door of the bas-tion's eastern gate.

Gram, in an old priestly robe, had his hands clasped as if praying. He'd made the concession of having his hair and beard trimmed and now looked unrecognisable, or so Elindhu insisted. Beside him was Fyn, disguised as Dranit Ritter and wearing clothes appropriate to the defensior, purchased with the last of Elindhu's coin.

'Defensior Ritter, to see a prisoner,' Fyn said, through the slot.

The guard's eyes narrowed. 'Defensior,' he said, peering past him, 'I know you, but who's the fella with ye? Where's Lubano?'

'This is Friar Varch, a confessor from Sancta Baria Church, here to give a final blessing,' Fyn replied in Dranit's gruff voice. 'Lubano's got the flux.'

The guard grimaced, but said, 'Aye,' and pulled on a cord, jingling a bell that rang in the tower above. 'Open up!' he called. 'They're verified.'

As they entered, Fyn said, 'We know the way.'

The erling was doing well, but Gram was terrified they'd meet someone with whom 'Dranit Ritter' would be obliged to have a proper conversation with, at which point this would go very badly wrong.

And likewise, if it goes wrong for Elindhu and Soren, we'll be equally in the shit.

But they set off as if they knew their way, having memorised the route from the map Elindhu had drawn from memory, Fyn striding and Gram scurrying after him, mumbling prayers. At the back of the gatehouse was a spiral stair going down into the earth. Four turns down, they reached a landing, tried the lock and found the door open. As they'd hoped, this was the upper level of the underground complex, with grilled skylights providing a little illumination. Expecting guards, they proceeded anxiously, but it quickly became clear that no one was here.

'Jagat,' Gram whispered. 'They've moved her . . .'

'That's good, right?' Fyn whispered. 'The vote must have been favourable. They must be moving her to Hyastar.'

Gram wasn't so sure. 'It could also mean they've had enough "No" votes that they know it's lost and have pre-empted things.' He clutched his chest. 'They could have taken her back to the dungeons below . . .' He looked down at the floor, wishing he could somehow see through stone. 'We *have* to find her.'

Fyn looked dubious. 'Can you scry her? Aren't you a vorlok?'

'I have the talent, but not the training,' Gram admitted. 'I don't know how. We need to find her the old-fashioned way. If she's not below, we'll make someone tell us where she is.'

With that, they returned to the stairs and spiralled down another level, where the damp air smelled rotten and the landing was lit by a single oil lamp. Fyn stood in the pool of illumination and knocked on the ironbound door.

Gram readied himself for disappointment. *If they don't let us in, what the jagat do we do?* he wondered, as they heard a thumping sound, the clank of chains and, finally, footfalls approaching. The viewing hatch opened, glyma wards flaring around it to stop weapons being rammed through.

'Who is it?' a harsh woman's voice called.

'Dranit Ritter,' answered Fyn, who'd begun to sweat from maintaining his magical disguise.

A round-faced, florid woman's face appeared at the hatch, looking first at the false Dranit, then at the man in priest's dress. 'What do you want, Defensior?'

'I'm with Father Varch,' Fyn said, indicating Gram. 'He's here to give a final blessing.'

There was a pause, then the locks clattered and the door swung open.

Gram lurched as his senses were assaulted by a stinking wave of warm blood, fresh urine and faeces, the stench of burned flesh and the intangible echoes of screaming.

'I'm sorry, Defensior,' the bald woman smirked. 'You're too late. She's beyond prayers now.'

Gram's eyes tore from her gloating face to the room beyond, where six men in charnel house leathers were gathered around a table upon which lay a butchered body. He could tell she was a woman from her exposed groin, but she was otherwise unrecognisable, because the skin had been peeled from her chest and face and her ribs had been broken and pulled apart – the Eagle's Wings, torturers called this – exposing the still beating heart.

Around this horrific tableau stood further machines of torture: a rack, an iron maiden and stocks, and whips, manacles, chains and torture tools hung from hooks on the walls, along with monogrammed Justiciary robes of jet black. Beyond was a door, where another lictor, an Aquini with receding hair and a pale face, was loitering with a smile on his lips. They all looked to be enjoying their work.

Gram's ninneva shattered in a tidal wave of fury.

ROMARA! ROMARA!

Within his sleeves, his hands were already engorged with muscle and blood. Even as they erupted from the armholes, his talons grew, while his vision went scarlet.

The bald woman shrieked a warning and jerked an elobyne pendant from her tunic.

14

Choosing Sides

The Greatest Exemplar

Every Exemplar tournament, we ask the perennial question: who was the greatest Exemplar of all? There's no right answer to such tavern talk, but certain facts remain: only one man was crowned Exemplar in four consecutive tourneys: Voltan 'the Scythe' Karax, who served the Order for twenty years before retiring, thirty years ago. One wonders how this stripling Zynochi girl, Vaziella al-Nuqheel, would have fared against the Scythe?

GEDAS MEYER, ORDER HISTORIAN, 1469

Tar-Brigida, Folkstein
Autumn 1472

The postern gate, where the disguised Fyn and Gram had vanished a few minutes earlier, was tantalisingly near, just sixty paces across a cobbled stone square in the shadow of the bastion. There was a well, and the neighbouring buildings, residential blocks, solidly made of heavy stone, cut off most of the sky. But a guesthouse on the ground floor of one had outdoor tables, giving a view of the gate.

Soren waited with Elindhu, both nursing beers and fretting.

'It'll all happen quickly,' the magia muttered. 'They only have to go down one floor, find her and return. We need to be ready for anything.'

'But how will they get her out?' Soren worried.

'By force, if necessary. But hopefully we can do it quietly.'

They had a plan of escape – there was a canal nearby that cut between the buildings, offering myriad opportunities to hide under boardwalks or just to paddle down to the river, if they got out unremarked. But there were townsfolk coming and going, and off-duty Vestal men-at-arms in and outside the tavern.

This could get very messy, Soren worried. 'They'll be in the dungeons by now. What if—?'

'Forget "if",' Elindhu replied tersely. 'Deal with what is.'

They fell silent as a young man in a squire's Vestal tabard strode by, heading for the postern gate, and something about his silhouette and gait drew Soren's eyes, his memory pricked . . .

As if sensing his scrutiny, the squire glanced at Soren and stopped. 'Here, do I know you?'

Soren felt his jaw drop, because he knew the young man: it was the Exemplar's squire, Bern Myko, who'd almost certainly helped escort Romara here from Vanashta Baanholt, or maybe arrived here separately by portali gate.

Where we killed his century's knights . . . and Elindhu fought their mage and him!

'I don't think—' he blurted, as his mind flailed.

'You're that Abuthan—' Then Myko saw Elindhu. 'No . . .' he croaked.

Clearly the magia had left a deep impression on the young man, but his mouth flew open, his lungs filled – and Soren drove his fist into Myko's belly. He wasn't wearing armour, and his cry for help became a choked gasp as he folded over Soren's arm.

'Brother, are you well?' Soren said aloud, for people were taking notice. He shot Elindhu a pleading glance.

The magia darted in, touched Myko's temples and the squire's face went slack, his body limp. Before he collapsed to the ground, Soren caught him, still feigning concern.

'He's not well,' Elindhu exclaimed, as a pair of off-duty soldiers hurried up. 'It's all right,' she told them, 'we're with the Order. We'll help him home.'

'Too much drink, most like,' one of them guffawed. 'Young 'uns got eyes bigger'n their bellies. Want some help, ma'am?'

'We'll look after him. But thank you.'

'Come on, mate,' Soren told the limp Myko, propping him up. 'The bastion's just here.'

'He's out like a snuffed candle,' the other soldier said. 'Come on, I'll give you a hand.' He stepped in and took the other side, while his comrade hovered. There were a dozen more, ordinary citizens, mostly, watching curiously.

'He don't smell drunk,' the soldier helping Soren commented. 'What's 'is problem?'

Elindhu made some motherly noises. 'He's a squire, dear. He's overdone it, learning the glyma. Come on, lads, let's get him into the infirmary.'

What are we doing? Soren wondered, as they approached the postern. *How long will he be unconscious? What do we do if we can't get in? And what if we can?*

He threw another panicky look towards Elindhu, but she radiated calm, leading the way as Soren and the soldier hauled the unconscious Myko towards the postern door. She went to the bell, tugged on it and exchanged urgent words with a guard, who was protected by a heavy door. There were sentries above.

All the ways this could go horribly wrong clamoured through Soren's mind.

The door opened, revealing the space beyond where visitors could be trapped, assessed and if necessary dealt with. Elindhu entered and gestured for Soren to follow. 'C'mon,' he told his unwanted helper, and they walked the unconscious Myko through. The other soldier followed, clearly amused by it all.

This is it, he thought fearfully. *The sentries above have crossbows and there's nowhere to hide.* A crossbow at this range would punch through steel and rip through any glyma-shields – and even if they did get inside, what they would do after that, he couldn't begin to imagine. *Shouldn't we just drop him and leave?*

But the second door was opening too, and they hauled Myko through, into a cobbled courtyard where the door guard was standing. 'Whash hap'nin?' the guard asked, his voice slurred and expression vague.

Soren glanced at Elindhu. *She did something to his mind, just by talking to him.*

'Where's the infirmary?' the man helping Soren snapped. 'C'mon, sunshine, look alive!'

The guard just stared – then a sergeant strode up, calling, 'Oi, why's that gate open? What's wrong with that man?'

'The poor boy collapsed out there,' Elindhu told him. 'We brought him in for you.'

'Magia?' he asked. 'Sorry, I don't know you—'

Soren, preparing for the worst, his free hand already moving towards his flamberge handle, jumped when the alarm bells inside the main keep suddenly hammered into life.

Everyone turned and stared.

It can only be Gram and Fyn, he thought. *Now what?*

There could be no hesitation, and no mercy.

Gram's clawed hands made two raking chops; one took the throat of the nearest guard, the other ripped open the jugular of the bald woman lictor. He roared out a furious howl, so loud it shocked through the gaolers like a wave, freezing their reactions another vital instant, as his body, straining to catch up, completed his transformation.

The woman collapsed, blood arcing from her gaping neck, as Gram waded forward, a bunched fist breaking the next man's jaw and snapping his neck. Fyn lost control of his disguise and was wearing his own face when he drove his tuelawar into the belly of the next man. Three men and the woman were down, but three remained, including the florid Aquini lictor at the far door. That man began conjuring energy in the orb he wore on a chain around his neck.

The two remaining gaolers were finally moving, drawing their blades, and at the lictor's order, they attacked. Gram's sorcerous energy was fuelled by the ghastly state of the woman on the torture table, giving him the speed and strength to evade a swinging sword and rip the gaoler's arm off.

Fyn's opponent was doing better, putting his full weight behind some brutal slashes, forcing the lightly built erling to give ground. This gave Aquini lictor the chance to gesture at the right-hand corner, where a rope-pulley hung. The cord danced and muffled bells immediately rang somewhere above. He tried to slam the cell door in front of Gram, but the trapper caught it easily and smashed it back into the lictor's face. The impact sent the lictor reeling, and Gram advanced on him, talons spreading.

'Mercy!' the lictor croaked, backing towards the blood-spattered walls.

But above, other bells were chiming in, louder and faster.

We've jagged this up, Gram thought raggedly. *They'll trap us down here . . .*

But all he could do was go for the man, even though glyma-energy was surging in the lictor's orb. He felt the air about him congeal against his limbs. He roared, strained . . . and froze . . .

Our plan's gone, Elindhu realised, as the postern gate slammed behind them. People were appearing from all directions; someone was bound to realise they were imposters.

'Soren, go,' she snapped, turning with a speed that belied her plump build. Her staff flashed around, the iron-shod butt crunched into the jaw of the guard helping them, while Soren slammed a glyma-enhanced fist into the sergeant's face and toppled him. Then he threw himself at the inner doors, just as they swung open. He crashed into an officer and punched his sword hilt into the man's face, knocking him senseless.

'Aunty!' he shouted. 'Come on!'

Elindhu sprayed fire behind her, backing through the inner door and slamming it shut. '*Sigilum Osti!*' she shouted, and the locking spell fused the door and frame with energy, seconds before an arrow thudded into it.

Behind them was a spiral stairwell.

'Watch my back,' she told Soren, bustling to the steps and heading downwards.

*

Gram fought the lictor's spell, but he couldn't counter it, nor could he reach his foe in time ... but behind him, someone fell, then Fyn hurtled past him and went for the lictor. Forced to split his defences, the man's hold on Gram wobbled enough for him to stagger forward and bear him to the ground. He was all set to rip the man's head off – until Fyn leaned in, shouting, 'Where's Romara Challys?'

His words shocked Gram like a torrent of ice-water hurled into his face. He went rigid and stared. *She's behind me*, he thought. *She's right here, and look what they've done to her* ...

But Fyn laid his razor-sharp tuelawar across the man's throat. 'Where is Siera Romara?'

The stink of hot urine hit their nostrils, as the torturer lost control of his bladder. 'She's gone,' he bleated. 'The High Council took her away ten minutes ago. They're taking her to Hyastar. Please, have mercy!'

Ten minutes? Gram's eyes went to the poor woman on the table behind them. 'But who—?'

'She's Segara Verber, a lying treacher!' the lictor babbled. 'Thought she'd got one over us, but we got her alive. I was told to punish her ... Orders are orders ... Please, don't hurt me ...'

Gram felt a wave of utter contempt at the way this professional torturer could dissolve when faced with some of his own medicine. But mostly his brain clamoured at the thought that it wasn't Romara. *She's still alive. This is the poor woman who saved Romara's life. Segara Verber.* He would remember her name.

But bells were tolling and they were going to be trapped here, if they weren't already.

Clearly the High Council couldn't protect informants, and the archon appeared to have no compunction about destroying anyone who thwarted him. But Romara was only ten minutes gone ... He knew they had to go, but he had to ask: 'Who tortured Romara?'

'Sister Faith,' the lictor blubbed. 'She loves jagging people! I just took notes ...'

Liar.

'Kill him,' he snarled at Fyn – not because he was too squeamish

263

to do it himself, but because he feared the act might turn him savage for ever.

Fyn didn't hesitate, ripping his blade across the lictor's windpipe in one vicious motion, then returning to the hideously maimed Segara Verber. 'She's alive,' he croaked. 'Barely.'

Killing her is the only mercy we can give her, Gram realised, picking up one of the flaying blades on the table. He murmured a prayer and gently punctured Segara Verber's heart. She shuddered and went still – just as boots thumped down the stairs outside, the only way out. The door was hanging open and they lunged for it, scared of being trapped inside.

But it was Elindhu who appeared in the opening, puffing and red-faced. 'Ah, there you are,' she panted. Then she saw the body. Her clever face went white in shock. '*By the Twelve, no—!*'

'It's not Rom,' Gram told her. 'The Council are taking her to Hyastar – they left only ten minutes ago.'

'Then they'll be heading for the portali gate,' she exclaimed. 'We have to stop them.' She whirled back to the stairs. 'Come – I know the way.'

From the upper stairs, someone out of sight called, 'Hey, who's down there?'

Elindhu's face went ashen, but she called back, 'It's all quiet here – false alarm.'

It was scarcely plausible, but perhaps the man was relieved to have an excuse to *not* enter the lictors' lair, because he just called, 'Aye, thank ye,' and they heard him thud away.

They all sagged with relief.

Elindhu looked around. Spotting the black robes hanging from hooks on the wall, she muttered, 'At last, some luck. Time for us to join the Justiciary.'

Soren shared a glance with Fyn, who looked uncharacteristically solemn. *He's had to kill people*, he realised. He was oddly pleased that it affected the erling as much as it did him. He put a hand on his shoulder and their eyes met. 'Stay alive, brother,' he whispered.

The erling's amber eyes glinted in recognition. 'I intend to,' he breathed.

'You two go first,' Elindhu told them, pulling her hood over her tower of braids; it made her head look strangely misshapen. 'But I'll do the talking.'

Soren could hear Elindhu muttering under her breath as they climbed cautiously. Emerging into the ground floor chamber, six men spun to face them, but before they could speak, Elindhu had conjured a ball of soft rosy light, which every guardsman instantly focused on.

'I'm Magia Karena,' she breathed. 'You know me, and all is well.'

Six men went still, their faces slack. 'Aye, Karena,' they chorused. 'All is well.'

Just then, his Aunty Eli didn't seem quite so cuddly.

'Go below and help clean up,' she told them, and they dutifully trooped off.

As soon as they were gone, she faced Gram. 'The portali gate is in the south tower. 'Follow me.' She led them upstairs to a door opening onto the battlements. Alarm bells were still chiming, causing considerable confusion, Soren realised, looking around. From their vantage on the walls, they could see soldiers running in all directions, officers shouting contradictory orders and knights striding about aimlessly. Elindhu hustled them along the battlements, moving with confidence.

They passed a watchtower, where a sentry saw them and saluted, then hurried towards the squat South Tower. Below them was an outer moat, gardens to their right and majestic views over the city and the river. But their eyes were fixed on the South Tower, where a guard was protecting the open doorway. He looked alarmed to see four cowled lictors stalking towards him.

'Milords?' he called tentatively, perhaps surprised at the odd group: one huge man, a diminutive woman and two youths. Then he must have seen something about them that alarmed him, because he yelled, 'Jagat! *You're not Order—*'

Soren burst into a sprint, but the guard kept his head, slamming the door in his face as Soren launched himself at the closing barrier.

Click . . .

The door locked just as Soren hit, battering himself uselessly against the ironbound wood, jolting air from his lungs and all but breaking his shoulder. He staggered back, dazed.

Fyn tried, just as pointlessly, then Gram shoved them aside and started hammering at the barrier, also to no avail. Then Elindhu snapped, 'Stand aside and protect me. I'll get it open.'

When the bell in the tower began to boom, Soren cast about for dangers. The South Tower was on its own hillock, with a moat below and walkways left and right along the battlements. Above, but sixty paces away, on the looming inner bailey, sentries were peering down at them curiously, not yet understanding that they were the intruders – until armoured men appeared along both walkways, shouting and pointing before surging towards them.

Ah, jagat, he breathed. 'Come on, Aunty,' he begged. 'Get it open.'

Gram ripped off his robe, his body swelling into a shaggy monstrosity. Soren and Fyn were quick to follow suit, so they wouldn't get tangled in the material in a fight. Soren and Fyn took the right-hand walkway and Gram the left, leaving Elindhu with her hand on the door, locked in some arcane struggle. She was crackling energy into the lock, but Soren sensed someone on the other side doing the same, holding her off – for now, at least.

Soren glanced over the parapet: the hill on which the tower stood was steeply sloped, falling to the moat a long way down. 'You can still go,' he told Fyn. 'Jump, while you can!'

The erling looked down, then shook his head. 'I'm no coward,' he panted. Then he looked at Soren and smiled sadly. 'See you on the other side.'

Soren swallowed, then said, 'We'll make it. Stay close.'

He turned back to face a knot of advancing knights. They looked like giants, their orbs glowing like suns, while he was a barely trained initiate. Another group were approaching Gram's side as well.

'*Falcons Eternal!*' he shouted defiantly. '*Falcons Forever!*'

*

Opening the door was an infuriating contest, but at last Elindhu felt the tide turn her way.

Sometimes in magical duels, attack was better, especially in open combat where it was faster to act than to react. Protecting a barrier, however, with something solid and tangible to anchor spells to and no one able to reach you directly, favoured defence. To break such a barrier required skill and strength: identifying specific weak points and honing the attack towards them.

She was mentally engaging with the magus behind the door now – she could sense him, as he could her, and because he was bewildered to be facing an erling, he was overloading his spells, desperate to keep her out. His control was fraying.

Unfortunately, Elindhu was in a similar state herself, her control slipping as the urgency increased. But she put aside the thought that Romara might be so close, which made her scream inside, and instead re-focused herself, pressing her fingertips to the wood and summoning hatchet-blows of force. She felt her foe falter, but she was running out of time: the knights were closing in. She heard Gram's roar and the boys' muttered pledges.

'Falcons Eternal,' she heard Soren bellow, with youth's indomitable defiance.

I love you, boy, her mind blurted. *I love you all.*

Terrified of losing them, her vision bleeding red, she found a place where her previous spells had carved scars in the fabric of the defences.

Now—! she shrieked inside, blazing all her terror and anger into that one place.

A line of knights were steaming four abreast towards him. Gram roared out a final cry of defiance, one last call to Romara, to tell her that he fell fighting for her. His muscles tightened, ready to spring. Then he launched himself at the oncoming men, trying to shield Elindhu with his body, even as glyma-blasts flashed at him. Soren was shouting his own war-cry as the fighting began on the other flank.

His sorcerous vorlok hide was scorched and seared, though the painful blasts barely slowed him as he bounded towards his attackers, claws splayed and jaws open – just as something exploded behind him and he sensed rather than saw the tower door fly apart.

If he'd stayed put, he'd have been able to run.

Timing, he thought bitterly, crashing into the knights. *I never had any timing.*

Their blades scythed towards him.

Elindhu felt the door give way moments before her control did, and that tiniest pulling back saved her from tipping over into raging insanity. Her blood was up: she followed the blast by bursting into the chamber beyond to find her foe, a serious-faced young man with foot-long wooden splinters in his face and chest, still reeling from concussion. She unleashed another blast of energy that broke him completely – as well as the three guards huddled behind him, who'd been smashed into the walls, breaking skulls and limbs.

'Come on!' she shouted, spinning to aid her menfolk. 'Run – one floor up—'

But they were already engaged. She'd taken too long.

The knights coming at Soren and Fyn were readying glyma-blasts, so Soren took the front, shielding widely to cover Elindhu and Fyn. He might be new to this, but he'd practised shielding constantly under the tutelage of his Falcon comrades, and now his diligence was repaid, because it was coming naturally to him. He deflected the worst of the storm of energy upwards, remaining in control as the knights, dimly visible through the vivid blasts, came at him with terrifying speed.

Then he felt a shudder of power behind him and heard Elindhu shriek, 'Run!'

The door was open, but it was too late; he could only fight. The foremost two, a man and a woman, flashed towards him: knights just as he'd wished to be. He caught the woman's blade on his and slapped it away while dancing aside from the man's blow, then reversed his swing and hacked through the man's forearm. The knight howled and staggered away, while the woman, gasping in horror, took her eyes off Fyn – who took out her throat with a slash. She staggered, and toppled off the battlements.

The next pair closing in were clearly shaken by what had befallen their comrades. Soren leapt in, thrust his blade at one man's face while blazing fire into the other. The magia behind them launched a spell, unseen hooks that clawed his mind, but almost without thinking, he shouted '*Negatio!*' and broke that attack.

'He's a jagging demon,' someone gasped. 'Stop him!'

Fyn was shouting too. 'Soren – Gram – the door's open—'

Soren tried to drive the two knights away, seeking a chance to riposte then back up and get them both out of this. But he couldn't have eyes everywhere.

The deadly strike came from above.

Gram forgot survival: there was only battle now, until it ended.

He lashed out, breaking limbs, hurling men into each other, once even taking a man by the throat to use as a shield, until he threw that body at another hapless knight. Sword-tips and spearheads lacerated his hide, several plunging deep, causing explosions of pain, then a jarring weakness shot up his left leg and he staggered against the parapet.

He had no intention of fleeing, but in that moment the pentacle's mage, alarmed at the wreckage Gram had made of his knights, decided that the best thing he could do was to send this vorlok giant somewhere else.

Shouting, '*Pulso!*' the glyma-force propelled Gram through a gap in the battlements, sending him spinning head over heels into the air.

The ground rose as he flailed helplessly, then he landed . . .

Fyn felt the blow jolt through him, a flash of pain that instantly vanished beneath a fog of numbness. He staggered sideways as his legs gave way. He hit the side of the tower and looked down, craning his neck over his left shoulder, more puzzled than afraid.

There was a crossbow bolt in his back, angled diagonally into his chest cavity. It felt like it'd gone a long way in, and hit something vital.

That's where my heart is, he realised. *I think . . .*

He sought Soren, saw the young man turning his way, his beautiful face contorting in horror.

Goodbye, Fyn thought at him. *I wish—*

The blankness reached his mind and he pitched sideways.

Soren howled in denial, shields billowing from him against the volley of crossbow bolts from the top of the inner bailey, right above them. Survival became luck . . . as shafts flashed past his face and limbs, shattering on the stone. But the one that mattered thudded into the young erling's back and he went down.

For a moment time froze. His eyes locked with Fyn's, and all that could have been but never would hit him like a blow to the heart. Then the erling's face emptied, he slumped sideways and Soren felt his heart rip inside him. For an instant he hesitated, looking along the other wall, seeing that Gram had vanished, leaving a clutch of dazed-looking Vestal knights.

Then he sensed one of his own opponents closing in. He spun, and in a gesture that had less to do with survival and more about rejecting the world and all in it, he hurled his incandescent flamberge like a spear. It burst through the man's shields, pierced his breastplate and impaled him, hurling him backwards. For a moment everyone froze again.

Then Elindhu appeared in the door, her braids waving about like snakes. 'Soren,' she shrieked, panic in her voice, 'get out of there!'

It felt wrong to go on without Fyn or Gram, but he couldn't abandon her. So he leaped for her as an energy bolt scorched the place he'd just vacated and arrows tore around him. He burst past Elindhu, who sent a burst of smoke and dust outwards, hiding them.

'Up,' she shrieked. *'Go!'*

He was caught up in a frenzied denial of grief and loss, but cost and consequence would have to wait. He took the steps at a run into a round chamber facing what looked like a giant stone oven carved with erling runes. That had to be the portali gate.

Elindhu was right behind him; there was shouting and clattering below. He slammed the door and, shouting '*Sigilum Osti!*', Elindhu activated a locking spell. 'It'll only hold a minute at most,' she gasped. Facing the portali gate, she shouted words of entreaty. Emerald light burst from the runes and the back wall went dark. '*Appura –Appura,*' she added. 'Open!'

A cracking noise made his ears ring, then came a whistling of air pressure equalising. Elindhu pulled him towards the open gate. He stumbled through, leaving her to follow. He watched as she hammered on a stone containing a shining green sigil that abruptly went dark – and the portali gate crashed closed.

He caught Elindhu, who was swaying at the exertion. They were both crying, but her tears were bloody and he knew what that meant. 'Just hold on, Aunty, stay with me . . .'

They sagged to the cold ground as the light of the gate faded, leaving them in a lightless void.

'Hold on, Aunty,' he begged her again. They were the last people alive. 'I'm here.'

He couldn't have moved if a host of knights had broken through, but none did. They were alone in the darkness of the Shadowlands once more, empty-handed and shattered.

We failed . . . and now we've lost everyone.

Unable to deal with that thought, he buried his face in Elindhu's neck and sobbed, begging Elysia to show some mercy and sweep the world away.

Coming to Folkstein had always been a fool's errand, but Elindhu knew she would never have forgiven herself if they hadn't tried. In any case, no one could have stopped Gram – nor Soren, she suspected. The boy took everything to heart, which was going to kill him.

But Fynarhea, a princess of her kind, could and should have been sent home.

I did try, but I let her refuse. Her death is on me.

She felt utterly wretched, even though in her heart she had known this could only end in disaster. She'd let their invincibility up till now delude her. It was the curse of the glyma: it made you believe you could survive anything. And now she was finished.

I've almost lost control . . . I'm right on the edge now . . .

But she couldn't just abdicate responsibility, because she had Soren to care for. He was shaking and sobbing in his grief and all she could do was hold him, knowing full well how it felt to drown inside, to second guess all you did while the worms of 'what if?' bored into your soul.

I asked Fynarhea to join us.

She wondered if Soren would ever forgive her – and if she'd ever forgive herself.

I didn't even see what happened to Gram. One moment he was there, then he was gone. She could cling to a faint hope, because she hadn't seen his body – although that didn't mean he wasn't lying out there, stunned or dead.

We faced two pentacles – it's a miracle any of us got out.

But that was absolutely no consolation to them. They'd failed, and Romara had been taken away.

It was that thought which jolted her back to the here and now. However much she might long to give up, she realised she couldn't. So she kissed Soren's brow, rose to her feet, seized her staff, lit the orb with the barest touch of power and faced the darkness.

'Romara,' she shouted. 'Romara Challys! Be strong – we're with you, dear girl. *We're here!*'

Her voice fell flat and lifeless, swallowed up by the misty expanse of the Shadowlands.

She strained her ears . . .

Was it her imagination, or had she heard an answering cry, cut short?

Elindhu? Romara lifted her head in wonder. Even as the men leading her mount reacted, she threw back her head and keened, wailing like a washer-wraith – until someone grabbed her from behind, a gauntleted hand gripped her mouth roughly, squeezing viciously, and a man growled, 'Shut yer jaggin' trap.'

'Gag her,' the grey-haired woman leading them snapped. 'We don't want a vyr war-party up our arses.'

For a noblewoman and pillar of the Order, Augusta Martia was as foul-mouthed as a laggy. There were no illusions about her, either: once she had Romara's testimony, mostly to further her own ambitions, Romara could burn. Her men had been rough-handed and contemptuous: vyr got no pity and fallen knights were scum.

But Romara's heart beat a little quicker now as they moved through the mists. Elindhu at least was out there, and she'd said 'we'. *We're with you. We.*

It's not just her, she told herself. *It's Gram and Soren . . . Maybe even Jadyn and Aura . . .*

She was no longer alone in this terrible world.

15

Angel in the Storm

Combating the Erling Threat

Erlings once ruled the north continent, now known as Hytal. But they were never numerous, or well organised. Indeed, most are childlike, with a tendency to live in the moment, with little capacity for planning. Those few with a near-human capacity for reason are their natural leaders. We recommend those be eliminated first.

FEODERIC BUSTT, IMPERIAL SCHOLAR, TYR, 1439

Sherkaza, Pelasian Archipelago
Autumn 1472

Aura had high hopes for Sherkaza – mostly concerning thermal baths, silk sheets and fresh food, not to mention several days and nights of satisfying some urges with Jadyn. He might not have Sergio's captivating eyes and sexual braggadocio, but she could feel their souls entwining on this journey, and his boyish smile increasingly lit up her soul.

It's infatuation, she warned herself. *I've been here before.*

Experience told her that everyone was flawed. One or other of them would ruin it, inevitably. But it hadn't happened yet, and now they'd opened that door, she was ravenous for him.

And some people do find true love. Why not us?

Finding Jadyn and the aegis felt like the same path: to be a Magic Girl, not only with sorcery, but in her emotional life. To make right choices for once, find lasting happiness, even though the world was against them. Perhaps now she'd see the mistakes coming and avoid them.

'Port tack coming, get ready,' Evandriel called, interrupting her thoughts. She looked at Jadyn, throwing him a weary grin. They'd been working hard day under Evandriel's direction, sailing heavy seas and constantly shifting winds.

'We go in three ... two ... one ... now!' he called, and they swung the felucca about and entered the channel. A few minutes of plain sailing later, a pilot boat emerged from Sherkaza Harbour, rowed by a dozen men with sun-baked backs and hard muscles, to intercept them.

'Identificato!' someone called, in Nepari with a northern accent. 'Quesa pas?'

'*Nidamoro*,' Aura replied. 'Alla Neparia. Soya Nushka.'

The harbour pilot was grinning as they drew alongside, evidently finding the felucca's name amusing. He switched to Talmoni, the language of commerce. 'We don't often see a felucca mid-oceans! What brings you here?'

'It's all we can afford,' Evandriel replied. 'I'm a scholar from Aquinium, seeking the Library of Balkhezamun.'

'Seriously?' the pilot replied. 'Well, good fortune with that. The librarians are paranoid and the monks guarding them don't let anyone near. Hardly anyone visits these days, and those who do get turned away.'

'Why's that?' Jadyn asked.

The pilot glanced over his shoulder towards the big monastery. 'Many who came were thieves or spies, so I hear, so now nobody is welcomed. Some of the monks are Gifted, so ex-Vestals can't push them round. And even the ordinary monks can kick most fellas' teeth in.'

Jadyn sighed. 'I guess we'll just have to hope.'

'Truth is, this place is dying,' the pilot told him. He pointed back to the port. 'Half those buildings are empty. There's no money here, the caliphs have forgotten us and the empire doesn't care. Only ones left are those too stupid to move on.' The self-mockery in his voice said that he considered himself one of the foolish.

Evandriel had spoken of this place as a refuge for truth, but it sounded more like a graveyard to Jadyn. The scholar remained unconcerned, though. 'I'm sure they'll see us,' he said calmly.

Aura became aware that the rowers were feasting their eyes on her like she was the only flower in a desert. 'Hola, chica,' one called. 'Show us your mammies.'

Usually she liked some attention – if not so crass – but she had a lover now, so she just stuck an insulting finger up in response.

They laughed, the pilot growled at his men, then turned back to Evandriel. 'You can seek an audience with the monks,' he called, 'but I'll need to look your ship over, to make sure you're not imperial agents or smugglers. Which I presume you're not?' he added, winking.

'Not us,' Jady replied. 'Come aboard.'

The ships kissed bows, the pilot leapt nimbly onto the felucca and Jadyn went to meet him while Aura kept the tiller steady, enduring the increasingly irritating leering of the rowers.

The official peered into their little hold, declared it clean and turned to Aura. 'Apologies, ma'am. My men are all bonded criminals, sent here as punishment.' He gestured around the felucca, adding, 'I'm impressed you got this little thing all the way from Bedum-Mutaza.'

'We be born to sail,' she told him. 'And can look after selves.'

'I'm sure you can.' He turned to Evandriel. 'Thank you, sir. Please, follow us into port.'

'Where's the safest mooring?' Jadyn asked him.

'Up by the Zynochi naval ships,' the pilot answered, 'though they charge extra.'

'We'll do that.'

The pilot pulled a lugubrious face. 'Wise.' He clambered back to his boat, they hitched the towline, then set about transferring into the sheltered port.

The three of them studied the harbour as it grew closer.

'Sherkaza be back of water,' Aura murmured, as they took in the buildings clinging like barnacles to the rocky slopes. Every structure was in disrepair, with missing roof tiles, weeds growing in the gutters, broken or barricaded windows. 'It be dying, as man say.'

'It's not what I expected,' Evandriel admitted. 'But I'm sure the answers we seek are here.'

The pilot boat rowed right across the small bay to the east side, where two Zynochi galleys were stationed. An official permitted them to tuck themselves up alongside the warship. It cost a ridiculous sum, but felt worth it, given the air of menace about the public docks, where dishevelled sailors loitered, peering at them with calculating eyes.

They secured the felucca, gathered some overnight gear in the hope they would be made welcome by the monks – though that felt doubtful, now – and made their way up the main road to the top of the cliffs, where the monastery dominated the skyline. Their path took them through a series of steep switchbacks, past bedraggled stone houses clinging to the edge. Jadyn wouldn't have entered many, so rundown and precarious did they look. None of the repairs looked new, and the stink of sewage mingled with the reek of bird shit. The few men they passed were wary, and the women looked battered and scared.

'Horrible place,' Aura murmured.

'Indeed,' Jadyn replied. He went to the edge of the path where there was a gap in the barrier wall and peered down a sheer drop to the remains of old slips and rock-falls. From this height, the harbour looked poisoned by the waste outflows. 'Let's hope this goes well.'

'My premonitions said this was the right place to come to,' Evandriel commented. 'But I'm beginning to doubt myself.'

Jadyn led the way, experiencing a nagging sense of danger, but no one accosted them as they topped the steep path and reached a heavily fortified gatehouse and wall, fencing off the plateau from the town below. The gates were ironbound and pitted with old blades and axe cuts, but the metal was rusty and the portcullis was broken. A guard was sitting propped against the wall, snoring, an empty wineskin beneath his hand.

'Hello?' Jadyn called tentatively.

The man didn't move, and no one else responded. Through the gate they saw more buildings in a state of semi-collapse, the path winding into increasingly narrow alleys. Gulls shrilled above, the only sound except for the moaning wind and the distant waves.

'Be no one here?' Aura wondered. 'Except this man,' she added, peering at the drunk guard.

The man stirred, looked up blearily and slurred, 'Who goesh?'

'We're looking for the library,' Jadyn answered.

'Oh, fine . . .' The man jabbed a thumb upslope, then rolled over and went back to sleep.

Jadyn scanned the alleys, guessed he meant the middle one. He drew his new Zynochi scimitar. 'Shall we?' he said, leading the way.

The dilapidated buildings crowded in as they climbed onwards, but the air of menace never crystallised into clear danger and they emerged from the built-up area to see farms and fields along the spine of the long, narrow island. Smoke rising from chimneys suggested a few farms remained, and they saw people working the fields in the distance. No one approached them.

They kept going towards the monastery dominating the skyline, passing a ruined church where a marble angel brooded, his head resting on his chin. Despite grime and moss, the sculpture had a life-like quality, with blank eyes that followed them as they passed by.

Then a lithe figure emerged from behind the church, followed by five others, who quickly surrounded them. All wore dun tunics, with cloths wrapped tightly around their heads, leaving just eye and mouth-slits. They all carried bladed staves longer than their bodies.

The monks of Sherkaza, Jadyn guessed, his skin prickling with excitement. He'd had no inkling that they were lurking there, despite the aegis, and judging by their reactions, neither had Aura or Nilis Evandriel.

The lead monk called out in Pelasian, a polyglot language few outsiders knew.

'Do you speak Talmoni?' Jadyn replied, raising a hand in greeting.

The masked man who had spoken asked, 'Name and purpose?'

Jadyn was nervous about lying, so he stuck to the truth. 'I'm Jadyn Kaen and this is Aura Perafi.' He decided Evandriel could name himself. 'We seek the librarians of Sherkaza.'

'The librarians do not see common travellers.'

Aura lifted her head. 'We not common. Sail from Zynochia in felucca. Will see bookmen.'

'I'm a scholar, myself,' Evandriel put in.

The monk twirled his staff theatrically. 'We decide who sees the masters – and you will not.'

Jadyn went to argue, but flashes of the aegis showed him divergent paths: in one, they were battered by this group, then attacked by the thugs waiting on the steep path back to the port; in a second thread, leaving without contesting got them nothing.

But a third vision hinted that if they bested them, there was hope.

Which was the more likely outcome, he had no idea.

He looked at Aura and saw in her distracted eyes that she was processing the same visions.

'Well?' he murmured.

'Two each,' she breathed. 'No killing.'

Jadyn glanced at Evandriel, who was no warrior but full of surprises. They exchanged an expressive look, an unspoken *yes-no-maybe*, then Jadyn tried one last time to talk their way in. 'We have important tidings—'

'No one cares,' the monk interrupted. 'The outside world means nothing to us.'

Jadyn set his jaw, and said, 'We're coming in anyway.'

The monks glanced at each other, the leader nodded – and they erupted forward, their bladed staves whirling with sight-defying speed.

The leader came at Jadyn, whose vision blurred into the now-familiar pre-images of his foes and their intended movements: the rapidly spinning staves hitting his jaw as the man on his right went for his belly. He surged forward to meet them, slamming his scimitar into the path of the headshot while kicking away the blow to his stomach. His eyes and body were adjusting to the Gift of the aegis flooding his senses – he and Aura began to *flow*, while the monks looked to be wading through treacle as he moved between moments, pole-axing one attacker with his fist while Aura, moving at normal speed to his eyes but blindingly fast to ordinary sight, spun and kicked another in the face. The blows kept coming – these monks were damned good, hemming them in, again and again – but they had two down and the rest were starting to back off.

From the corner of his eye he saw Evandriel contending with two of the monks, though not in a conventional way. It looked like the two monks going for him were fighting invisible cords, straining to move, while Evandriel fought to immobilise them, simply by *wanting* to.

A thousand more questions about the aegis occurred to Jadyn, mid-fight – then a seventh monk appeared, this one holding a stave with an elobyne orb. He gestured and broke Evandriel's hold on his foes; one slammed the butt of his staff into the scholar's belly and he folded. Jadyn turned to help, lost track of his foes and took a glancing blow to his head. Aura crumpled beside him, holding her head as an elobyne light flared around her, then a gripping spell shoved Jadyn to the ground.

A dark figure loomed over him and punched his jaw, and he spun into darkness.

Sea of Pelas (eastern waters)

The Serrafim called Genadius came to Vazi in a dream the next night, by which time her warship was sailing due west, out into the Sea of Pelas. He'd been searching the oceans, he told her, in the dream. But one felucca in tens of thousands of square kylos was a needle in a haystack, even for him. *Be patient and keep heading west*, he urged and was gone.

She jerked awake, unsure what was real. Chillingly, the shutters of her rear window were open and rattling in the wind, and she smelled something like burned elobyne dust in the air.

All that day she was unsettled, pondering the dream, if that's what it was. Her personal cosmos didn't include Serrafim – in her world, she was the apex predator, not mythical beings whom only priests and fools believed in.

Borghart found her brooding in the stern and settled against the rails beside her. 'Why are we sailing this way?' he asked. 'Feluccas are coastal craft, not ocean-going vessels.'

'I had a vision,' she replied, which was true enough to satisfy his lictor truth-seeking skills.

His eyes narrowed. 'So they're ahead of us, out there somewhere? How is it you can find them, when my scrying can't?' he grumbled. He'd used up the personal materials of Kaen and Perafi fruitlessly and plainly resented the wasted effort. Now he was trying to purge himself of glyma and restart his aegis-learning.

'Maybe it's my youth, and greater aptitude?' she suggested tartly.

'One day you'll be grey-haired and wondering why everyone else is so much faster than you.'

'Mmm, but think how much worse it'll be for you by then, old man,' she said tartly.

'You're hilarious. Perhaps the Hierophant wants you to be his jester?'

When she'd told Borghart about escaping the Hierophant's banquet, he'd almost sounded impressed, but he'd also told her it was her noose, not his. Strangely, though, she wasn't getting a strong sense of danger when she thought of that bent-backed old man on the throne.

He won't hurt me, she decided. *He can't.*

But when she thought about the Serra in her dream, her blood ran cold.

What if he's real? she wondered. *What does he want with me?*

Nothing good, her instincts said. He was a predator, and he saw her as prey.

Or maybe he's just a figment of my imagination . . .

'Do you believe in Serrafim?' she asked Borghart suddenly, wanting to hear reassurances.

He blinked in surprise. 'Well, the Scriptures say they dwell on Nexus Isle, in a tower made of elobyne, or gold, or marble . . .' He added wryly, 'Or is it Bravanti cheese?'

'It's a serious question,' she grumbled. Jokes weren't her thing.

'Well, in the Scriptures, the Serrafim were created by Akka to serve Jovan Lux. But, well, the Scriptures . . .' He shrugged. 'They're written by liars to beguile children and fools.'

'You say that, but . . . Have you ever seen something you can't explain?'

He snorted softly. 'In a world where the glyma exists, and now the aegis too? No. Everything is explicable. I've never seen a "miracle" that couldn't be done by a competent magus. Why, what's on your mind?'

She was hesitant to discuss the matter with anyone, but she was also badly troubled. 'The aegis gives visions of the future, yes? I met a Serra in one, who told me to sail west.'

'That's just how your imagination interprets foresight,' he assured her, dismissing her worries. 'You invented the Serra as a voice for your subconscious.'

She pretended to accept that, hoping against hope that it was so.

16

Bringers of Justice

The Madness of Faith

What if you met your god? Do you think it would go well for you? Imagine such a being; he's not your creator, he's not your saviour. He's a being who feeds on your belief and has grown both fat and greedy. To him, you're just a needy sup-plicant, begging for something he can't give you. He doesn't want your hopes and dreams, he wants your reverence and praise – and to devour you, body and soul.
THE BOOK OF FREEDOM, KYRGINIUS (VORLOK SCHOLAR) 1326

Sea of Pelas
Autumn 1472

It began like a dream . . .

Vazi was in bed in her appropriated cabin, lying on her back beneath sheet and blankets. The sailing conditions, after the passage of the storm, were perfect; all she could hear on deck were the trudging steps of those on watch and those sailing them by moonlight. The shutters were open, moonlight pouring in, casting the rest of the small cabin into deeper shadow.

But didn't I lock the window? I thought I did . . .

Then her eyes were drawn to a shadowy presence in the corner and she went rigid with fright.

Genadius, robed in grey, his gold hair a mane about his leonine visage, was staring right at her, speaking in a sibilant whisper that found her mind while barely brushing her ears.

They are in Sherkaza. I have a spy there, keeping watch. Change course and sail southwest. You are only a day away – you will reach them if you sail all night. I'll be there to hand them over, intact, as you desire . . . Well, perhaps mostly intact, he amended drily.

He rose to go as she came fully awake.

He spun, a look of faint surprise on his perfect visage. 'Impressive,' he breathed.

An eye-blink later, he was bending over her, his liquid gold eyes boring into her soul.

She instantly began to sweat, her heartbeat thumping as she tried to rise. But he sat and pressed his cold hand down on her chest. It felt like a boulder, pinning her down.

'Few can break such a spell and fully awaken,' the Serrafim mused. 'But then, you're not ordinary, are you? Aegis and glyma . . . The lictor too.' His other hand stroked the hair from her face. 'No wonder you've caught the eye of my son.'

She almost forgot to breathe. *'My son'* . . . *Dear Akka, he's not just named after the former Hierophant – he* is *the former Hierophant. He's the Genadius that died decades ago . . . and whose son is now fawning over me . . .*

'Unfortunately, the existence of my kind is a privileged secret, so we have a little problem,' Genadius mused idly. 'Now you know I'm real, you have to die.' His cold hand drew down her blanket, pulled open her nightdress and cupped her left breast. 'Hearken,' he whispered, leaning in. 'Your heart beats so fast. Shall I rip it out and show you?'

Only a life of the utmost discipline prevented her from screaming, or worse, using the glyma, which would surely have precipitated her end. As it was, she just lay rigid.

'What a waste that would be,' Genadius mused. 'My son wants you as his concubine.'

She wanted no such thing herself, but right then she'd have pledged her soul to the Devourer just to live – she had a *destiny*, so for all the terror almost paralysing her, she *had* to live. That kept drumming through her skull.

'Killing you would break his pathetic heart,' Genadius went on. 'He poisoned me, you know, to hasten my end, not knowing I'd been

promised eternity. Oh, the pain I owe that worthless rag doll ...'
His grip on her breast tightened, his nails digging in, piercing skin.
'Shall I punish him with the gift of your head?'

She badly wanted to shriek, but he waved a finger mockingly.

'Hush,' he whispered. 'Nobody outside can hear us. You could
scream your lungs out and they'd be oblivious. There's just you and
me, Exemplar, and our little dilemma.'

Be still, she told her shaking body. *Think*, she begged her petrified
mind.

But rage was fermenting inside her, too, the fury of feeling helpless and violated. It took all her discipline not to lash out, however
suicidal the impulse.

As if he saw her inner struggle and wished to mock it, he leered
cruelly, tearing the rest of her nightshirt away, and rolled onto her,
his body cold and crushing. He licked his lips with a tongue that
looked too big for his mouth, a purplish snake that swayed above
her blindly, and ground himself against her.

'Strip away the glyma and you're just like any woman,' he jeered.
'Good for only one thing.'

She tried to fling him off, but he was immensely strong, far beyond
her. He simply crushed her, pressing his face to hers again, amused
rather than concerned, all with a calculating smirk that she *loathed*.
But she got her mouth free and snarled, 'You rape me and my glyma
will burn you to cinders. You'll be ash, I swear!'

'So, you have some spirit after all,' he mused. 'Girl, I'm *made* of
glyma. I can do *whatever* I like to you and the only one who dies is
you.' But he had stopped moving, instead contemplating her coldly.
'There is a way through this. Only the Blessed may know of us – so
what if you yourself were Blessed?' He stroked her face, calculating
and cruel. 'How would you like that?'

She didn't need to guess what he was implying. If it meant survival, she already knew she'd do it.

'If you want me, take me,' she croaked. 'If you want me to kill
for you, I'll do it. I have a *destiny*. I *have* to fulfil it – it's the reason
I'm alive.'

'A destiny? *You?* I think not ... Though with your Gifts of glyma and aegis, why not?' A cold smile creased his flawless face. 'You'd bite your own leg off to escape this trap, would you not?'

'Bind me to you,' she suggested quickly. 'Twist my brain so I have no choice but to serve you. Cast a geas upon me, break me – do whatever you will ...' She took a deep breath, fighting a tide of self-loathing, the tears she could no longer hold back pouring from her eyes as her pride broke. 'Please – I will do anything you want. Just let me live.'

I'm destined for greatness ... I just have to get through this ...

'Well then,' he breathed. 'First things first.' His head loomed over her, he pushed her head sideways, bared teeth like glassy spines and plunged them into her neck, then held her as she jolted, his breath cold against her burning skin, and slurped the blood that welled up, sighing. She could sense more than just blood flowing: she felt mental images and thoughts flowing too, as a thudding headache began behind her eyes and her bones emptied of marrow. It felt as if he was draining her into himself.

'That's so I can always find you, my little pet,' he purred mockingly, licking her blood from his lips with a satisfied sigh. 'You know, I think we can have a profitable partnership. You and I are alike in sharing both aegis and glyma. And your naked ambition is clear, and I like naked things.' He pulled the blanket off her and drank in her body. 'It would utterly destroy my pathetic son to spend eternity watching me parade you before him as my own concubine,' he chuckled. 'I wouldn't have to kill him; he'd do it himself.'

'No, please,' she countered. 'If I am to marry a Hierophant, I must be a virgin. They make you confess your sins to a truth-teller. Please, I have to be chaste.'

Genadius considered, then smiled slyly. 'Of course.'

But he didn't get off her – instead, his face swayed like a cobra lining up a strike, his deathly cold body smooth and heavy like marble, flattening her as he lowered his mouth to hers and kissed her, the taste of opium and elobyne dust on his lips.

She heard herself whimper.

That thick serpentine tongue slithered between her lips and filled her mouth until she gagged. She was forced to breathe through her nose in snatches as it rammed down her throat like a phallus. She began to black out, thinking she would die, but he pumped faster – then gave a sensual moan and something like icy milk flooded her oesophagus, the cold so shocking it numbed her.

She gagged, trying to vomit, but he kept his ghastly appendage inside her while she fought, trying to bite it as her vision swam. She must have fainted at one point, because she saw stars that winked out . . .

She woke seconds later to find him gazing down at her, licking spittle and a shining crystalline paste from his own lips and chin. That hideous purple tongue caressed her mouth again, but when she tried to throw up, nothing came.

His expression was one of slightly glazed satisfaction, and smirking conquest.

'Well, we solved that little puzzle, didn't we, my sweet *blessed* Vaziella,' he purred.

I'm intact, she thought numbly, the hate in her gut a boulder now. *But that was rape.*

'What did you do to me?' she managed.

'We took the first step in making you one of us,' he told her. 'My seed will conquer your body. And thanks to your blood, I can find you anywhere, sense what you see, even if you are a thousand kylos or more away. You're *mine*, essentially.' Then he smiled, a chilling sight. 'Welcome to the Blessed Alephi, the future rulers of Coros.'

Alephi? The word was new to her. *So he's not a Serra, but something from the Maw.*

'No, girl,' Genadius replied, answering her thought, 'there are no angels or demons; just the strong and the weak. The hunters and the herd. Be grateful that I have chosen to elevate you.'

Mercifully, he sat up, though his eyes never left her face.

She forced herself to return his stare.

'The End of All Things is here,' he said, with grim glee. 'Nine-tenths of humanity will perish. Only the strong will survive. Even

now, the lists are being drawn up. The time is nigh to burn the chaff.'
He stroked her frozen face. 'My son wanted to save you, but you are
mine now. I rather think it will break him.'

She wondered why Akka and Elysia couldn't destroy this beast,
but said nothing.

'For now, we will continue this mission – this pair you hunt, and
the rebel Evandriel, must be caught and made an example of. After
that, you and I will return to Bedum-Mutaza and you will wed my
son. But on the wedding night, it is I who will take your maidenhood,
and then together, we will torment him for eternity.'

'What happens to me now? To my body?'

'I have given you Alephi fluids, the key to eternal life. As they
colonise you, you'll become eternal, like me and my brethren. This
is a great gift, Vazi Virago. Be grateful.'

She was utterly sickened, yet still thinking, *Isn't this what I always
wanted?*

'I . . . I don't know . . . what to say,' she managed to whisper.

'The changes will be gradual,' Genadius went on. 'You'll absorb
glyma without needing an orb, your aegis sight will grow clearer and
you'll learn to move as we do. Inside a month, the transformation
will be complete and I will present you to the Master. After that,
Elysium awaits.'

Elysium: the Paradise Akka had promised to establish on Coros
after the End of All Things, which Genadius had said was imminent;
and if he was right, only beings like him – and now she – would
survive it.

'So,' Genadius whispered, 'does this please you, Milady?'

It terrified her – and so did he.

'Yes,' she managed. 'It's like a dream.'

He chuckled darkly. 'Aye, just like a dream . . . Maybe it was?'

He passed a hand over her face, she felt reality ripple and distort
and fell into a swoon . . .

. . . only to wake to find the dawn seeping through the flapping
shutters of her cabin window, lighting up her tangled sheets. Her
throat ached, her neck was raw and a wound was scabbing over and

she felt like the lowliest of whores. And in her belly, a sensation like creeping ice was spreading.

So not a dream: a nightmare . . . but horribly real.

But perhaps, the beginning of the fulfilment of her destiny.

Jadyn woke from a chilling dream in which marble statues crept through a darkened maze, hunting him, while he sought Aura. Then he burst into a chamber where Lictor Borghart was strangling her . . . and jolted awake.

The pain of the battering he'd taken from the monks hit him a moment later. His jaw was throbbing, his skull grazed and his knee swollen. He supposed he was lucky to be alive.

Or not, if these people are like the lictors.

Then he saw Aura, lying unconscious on a bunk against the opposite wall, beneath a barred window through which shadowy light seeped. He hurried to her side, made sure she was breathing and had no serious injuries, then looked out the window. Another marble Serrafim statue stood on the corner of the ledge outside, contemplating the coming dawn: for a moment, he wondered if he was still dreaming.

Then Aura woke and sat up.

He hugged her close. 'Are you all right?'

'Neya, be tresa infirma,' she groaned. 'Head, oh, head. Not be wanting.' She rubbed her stomach ruefully and added, 'Bad here. Arm too, very hurting.' She looked around. 'Where is here?'

'I don't know. But we're alive. That's good.' He looked around. 'Where's Evandriel?'

There was no sign of the scholar, but he did find a jug of water beside the locked door, with two copper mugs. They'd been left a piss-bucket, too, and a wash-basin and towels. They both drank, then took turns to rinse off.

'I hope it's still the same day,' Jadyn said, looking at the twilit countryside through the window. 'If we don't get back, someone'll steal our ship.'

'Not knowing,' Aura replied. 'Hurts to think.'

There were footfalls, and both fell silent. A key turned in the lock and the door opened to admit the same grey-haired monk-magus who'd crushed them earlier, with two of his fellow monks. He looked Pelasian, with dark weathered skin, a nearly white goatee beard and narrow eyes. They wore coloured bracelets that looked to have some significance of rank, as those with him had fewer. His staff was planted between his feet, the elobyne chip glimmering a warning.

Jadyn wondered how the elobyne was re-charged, having seen no shard here. *An orison, perhaps?* Or maybe it hinted at a relationship with the Church or the Order?

'I am Master Sendu,' the magus said, in Talmoni. 'You are Jadyn Kaen and Auranuschka Perafi. You should not have come here.'

'No one told us we couldn't,' Jadyn replied, as he and Aura stood. 'The people below said you'd give us a hearing, not set upon us like we were thieves.'

'The people in the port are nothing to us,' Master Sendu said dismissively.

'Why?' Jadyn demanded. 'Are you not the rulers here?'

'Does anyone truly rule? The complexities of authority and consent, of leverage, negotiation and dominion are complex. We exist alongside the port, but their doings are irrelevant.'

'Well, they shouldn't be,' Jadyn told him. 'Or have you abrogated all authority?'

'That is precisely what we have done. We have no interest in them, nor in pilgrims.' He advanced into the room, looking them up and down. 'The only one reason you did not wake up in a ditch is because during that fight, you moved in a way I have heard of, but never seen.'

Jadyn gave him an exasperated look. 'Here's a strange new thought: why not talk to strangers, instead of whacking them around the head with a stick?'

'We have tried it, but it does not work,' the magus said drily. 'We have been the targets of spies, assassins and thieves ever since the Caliph founded the Library here in 1283. That is two hundred years of people trying to fool us, threaten us or steal from us. From Zynochia to Abutha to Hytal, they all think they can just walk in and demand whatever they want. So we have been forced to break up the collection and sell it. There is little of value here now. I don't care how far you have come, you can go home ... Once you have told us how you moved like that.'

Aura stuck out her chin and said, 'Trade for trade. We give, you give, si?'

The magus narrowed his eyes, but said nothing.

'Where's our companion?' Jadyn asked, taking heart from his silence.

'Your friend Nilis Evandriel? Yes, we know who he is.' The magus pursed his lips, then in a more reasonable tone, said, 'Perhaps there is room for mutual gain here. Come.'

He turned and stalked out the door, and his monk guards stood aside. Jadyn went to follow when Aura plucked at his sleeve. 'Be trusting these?'

'Not sure,' he breathed. 'If the library is no longer here, why have they remained?'

'Am thinking same.' She patted his cheek. 'Have taught you well, youngling.'

They emerged to a long corridor, crossed the hall and entered a dining hall, where Evandriel was eating. At the magus' invitation they joined him, each grabbing a steaming pastry, but not sitting.

'It's all right,' Evandriel said quickly. 'I've explained who we are and what we're doing. We've come to the right place.'

'This place isn't on the path laid down for us,' Jadyn reminded him. 'We diverted here because of the mosaic.'

'I've not forgotten,' the scholar replied. 'But nevertheless, it's useful to be here.'

Jadyn faced the monk-magus. 'I'm not sure we can help you, Master Sendu. This thing we do is a gift, not something that can be taught.'

'You say that, but is it so?' he replied. 'You anticipated every blow and moved in a way that defeated the eye, as if you were not subject to *time*.' He mimicked a low parry then a high one, with grace and poise. 'You went from this posture to this, without an intervening movement. Incredible. And Master Evandriel held two people in place: the opposite skill.' He leaned in. 'What is this power?'

Having a strong suspicion that, like most mages, he could discern truth from lies, Jadyn answered honestly. 'It's aegis – like the Sanctor Wardens used.'

Sendu frowned, clearly thinking hard. 'Come.' He led the way into a dilapidated building, past doors open to dark, dank rooms filled with wrecked shelving, piles of old, damaged furnishings and the stink of rot. In some, the ceiling had fallen and wind whistled through broken windows. The sound of the cranes calling on the roof above was lonely and mournful, adding to the desolated feel.

'We expected to find a great library,' Jadyn commented. 'Is there nothing left at all?'

'We had to dismantle the collection,' Sendu replied. 'Sherkaza is the traditional home of our order, the Monastics of Myrokos. We are a martial order founded half a millennia ago, keepers of a tradition of living and training requiring total dedication. But against the Vestal Order, we were nothing. When the predators circled, the librarians decided to disperse the collection. You can search these premises all you wish, but you will find the ancient books are gone. If we mattered, we would already be dead.'

'Then we have wasted our time,' Jadyn concluded despondently.

Sendu glanced back at him. 'Perhaps. Let us see, shall we?'

Descending through the building, they found the lower floors less damaged, even a few books still leaning on the remaining intact shelves. There looked to be barracks for hundreds, though they counted only a few dozen of the dun-clad monks. Most were in the torch-lit central courtyard, practising kicks and punches and throws, shouting aloud with each blow. It was a style of combat Jadyn hadn't seen before, very poised and balletic.

'It is an ancient way of fighting, using speed and momentum, known as saenryu, the way of the wind,' Sendu commented. 'Saenryu is an art for all men, not those with a special "gift". I find "gifts" like your glyma abhorrent, in truth, despite possessing it myself. I wish we lived in a world in which all gifts were open to all who wanted them. Why should a few gifted people rule the world? I much prefer the openness of the saenryu, which anyone can learn, no special talents or breeding, such as the glyma or aegis need.'

Jadyn shrugged that off. 'We can't help what we're born with. But you're aware of the aegis?'

'Of course, but no one has seen it in action for generations . . . until today.'

'There's more to both glyma and aegis than waking up with a talent,' Jadyn pointed out. 'I've spent a decade living with the glyma and all it demands, and now I'm trying to learn the aegis – without being captured and executed.'

'Oh, I doubt not that the empire wants your heads,' Sendu replied. 'And Master Evandriel has explained his purpose: the destruction of the elobyne network. I can even sympathise . . .' He paused, then added, 'Which is why we will treat you as guests, after all. Come, meet my colleague Peralin. She and I run this monastery, protecting the remaining librarians.'

They arrived at a small office on the ground floor, where Sendu sat at a desk and indicated for them to take the chairs opposite. The guardsmen stayed outside, but a Pelasian woman, old and grey, but spry, entered and bowed. She had twinkling eyes and a dancer's poise.

'I am Mistress Peralin,' she said. 'Nilis, Jadyn and Aura, yes? What brought you here?'

They'd already decided that they had to trust the monks if they were to get anywhere, so Jadyn spoke about their journey from Avas, meeting Gram, the trail leading them to Vanashta Baanholt, on to the Hejiffa Dhouma, and here.

Then Evandriel took over the story, describing his own path to this point, from the fragments of lore that had shaped his thinking to his travels among the vyr, preaching the destruction of elobyne. 'I believe it's no coincidence that the three of us found each other on this journey,' he concluded. 'Precognition guided our decisions.'

'And it led you here?' Sendu asked sharply.

'We diverted here, hoping the Library of Balkhezamun contained

293

information about the older mosaic in the Hejiffa Dhouma,' Evandriel explained. 'The one the Akkanites covered over.'

The two monk-mages looked puzzled. 'There are probably a hundred other places you could have gone instead of here to learn this,' Peralin said. 'The mosaics of the Hejiffa Dhouma are a wonder of Coros, and much about them is preserved. Any priest could have told you of them.'

Evandriel pulled a face. 'Sadly, we were on the run, by then, and followed . . . other impulses. And we – *ahem* – damaged both mosaics, somewhat irreparably.'

Peralin and Sendu glared at him. 'You ruined *two* priceless mosaics?'

'We had no choice, and I sincerely regret the necessity. But if you put aside that loss, the concealed mosaic was of a man fighting a sea-beast near a volcano. Does that mean anything to either of you?'

The two mage-monks didn't look entirely willing to put aside the damage, but then turned to each other and conferred.

'To us, it means nothing,' Sendu replied tersely, 'but the librarians will know. I will have an answer by morning.'

'Why the wait?' Evandriel asked irritably.

'Communicating with the librarians, getting a decision out of them, takes time. There is no such thing as consensus in the halls of learning.'

Peralin nodded in agreement, then clapped her hands briskly. 'In the meantime, please relax – eat and drink, get some rest. We have better rooms than the one you woke up in.'

'What about our ship?' Jadyn asked. 'Is it safe?'

'We will send people down there to secure it for you,' Peralin answered. 'We have a friendship with the Zynochi Navy. Come, I will help you get settled.'

While Sendu hurried off, the old magia led them back through the ground floor, where some fifty young men and women, unmasked, but all wearing the dun robes, were eating and chattering away like excited students. They all paused to stare at Jadyn and his companions, then the sound welled up as they left the hall. Clearly, visitors were rare.

Peralin was as good as her word, providing a reviving meal. The hot, rich fish stew and wine were much appreciated, but they were all exhausted. Evandriel was spry for a man in his sixties, but even before the monks' attack, the journey had taken its toll. Jadyn and Aura were still aching too, so they were all content to retire to their allotted rooms, this time on the second floor. Evandriel took one, while Jadyn and Aura took the next, which had two single beds. They pushed them together once they were alone, though neither was in the mood for love. The real question was whether one of them should keep watch, but as neither could keep their eyes open, they decided to trust the master's words.

Jadyn went to the window and peered out, seeing another of those damned angel statues outside. *Odd*, he thought, *I never noticed them when we were outside.* But he couldn't retain the thought, shuffling back to his bed, kissing Aura then rolling away, promising her he'd be more lively in the morning.

'I hold you to that.' She yawned widely. 'Sleep, mi amor.'

Mi amor . . . My love.

Her words ensured he faded off to sleep with a smile on his face.

Aura woke, nudged by the prickling sense of impending peril. She was still fully clothed, as was Jadyn, lying a foot away and breathing slow and deep. She left him to slumber, went to the window and gazed out. Outside the dirty glass was a winged statue, covered in moss, gazing towards the impending sunrise.

Creepy, she thought, dropping the curtains, and concentrating on her precognitive awareness. *Is there danger?* she asked it. *Of what kind?*

There was no evidence of danger, but she couldn't shake her unease.

Then Jadyn started awake, instantly alert, which told her this wasn't just her own imagining. She hurried to him, brushed her lips to his, and whispered, 'Bad thing coming.'

He sat up and reached for his boots. 'Do we warn the monks? Or are they the danger?'

'Don't know,' she replied.

'Then let's first make sure we're not jumping at shadows.'

They dressed and girded themselves with weapons, his cutlass and her knives, then went to the door, opening it cautiously and scanning the hall, shadowy – and empty.

'Let's go to the ground floor,' Jadyn whispered.

They found some back stairs and crept down, finding a door opening onto a service corridor running to the back of the entrance hall. The sky outside was lightening perceptibly and the moons were sending pallid light through the upper windows, illuminating toppled and broken statues, torn tapestries and shattered sarcophagi.

'Dining hall be behind us,' Aura whispered. 'Those be main doors.' She indicated a half-open pair of tall doors. A dark figure was briefly silhouetted there, a sentry passing by. *One of the young monks*, she guessed. She put a finger to her lips, and tiptoed towards the opening.

'Aura?' Jadyn hissed. Then he went silent, for fear of betraying their presence.

In truth, she wasn't sure what she was doing, just that there was something to see. So she padded up to the broken doors and peered through. The young monk was a dozen paces away, facing the glowing eastern horizon. He looked like someone at peace with his world.

Everything's fine, she thought, but her unease wouldn't lift.

Jadyn came up behind her, and murmured, 'Come back to bed. But let's not sleep.'

Her pulse quickened at the invitation. *Yes*, she thought. *I want that.* But still she hesitated, as indeterminate fear clouded her mind . . .

Then that dread crystallised.

Through the open doors they saw something drop into sight, landing before the sentry. The young man responded with alacrity, gripping his bladed staff two-handed and trying to leap away from the newcomer's reach. But the hooded, winged figure was faster, unerring and brutal. A blade that lit up red materialised – and was instantly buried in the young man's chest, as easily as carving through parchment, spraying blood everywhere.

The attacker's hood fell back, revealing a face of ghoulish perfection, an angelic visage alight with hateful glee.

The boy collapsed, twitching, and the 'angel' looked around.

Aura emitted an involuntary gasp, so faint she barely heard it herself.

But the awful face of the killer turned their way: a male, redheaded, with a leonine mane, wearing white silk robes and a savage grin.

'*Help!*' Aura shrilled, gripping one door as Jadyn grabbed the other and they crashed them closed. Her hands blurred to the key and the lock clicked, but they still instinctively leapt aside, left and right, as another premonition struck . . .

—and a moment later, the doors were smashed off their hinges, flying through the room to mow down a statue of an old librarian.

Then the bloody-handed angel filled the doorway.

Aura saw only death if they stayed.

'*Run!*' she shrieked, inhaling power and energy from the very air around her, as she had when they ran from the Dhouma, trying to recapture that speed and make the world blur. But Jadyn had already drawn his sword, moving to protect her, and she hesitated.

The Serra flashed between them in a rush of wings, planting feet and slamming a two-handed blow at Jadyn's midriff. The blade broke his scimitar and crunched into his mailed belly, doubling him over, staggering, with blood welling through the torn metal mesh.

Aura heard herself scream, hurling a knife while drawing another as the speed she sought came. But the angel effortlessly slapped them away, then came at her with blade and fist. She somehow matched his speed, drawing her third and heaviest knife from her wrist sheath and making parries she could scarcely believe, holding the dagger in both hands and hanging on as the angel's sword smashed into it, and snapped the steel, hurling her backwards.

Jadyn, barely recovered, flashed *here*-to-*there* in an eye-blink, then charged back in with a halberd he'd snatched from the wall, raining in blows as Aura drew more knives – her second-last pair – and for a moment they held the angel at bay.

Then a pile-driving fist of force smacked into Aura's belly and she flew, struck the wall and emptied her stomach in a hideously painful gush. Jadyn got between them and took a kick to his already damaged knee, buckled and hit the wall beside her.

The fiend grinned, licking blood-red lips. 'Nice moves, you two,' he rasped. 'You'll be fun to play with.'

Aura tried to match the Scriptures to this thing. 'Bringers of Justice', the holy texts called the Serrafim. *Maybe he's here because we're heretics?*

She was sure they were doomed, but with a piercing howl, a young monk burst through the far doors, shrieking to Akka, followed by a wave of young students, with Master Sendu among them, shouting orders in Pelasian.

Aura skittered towards Jadyn, who was writhing, holding his knee. The Serra went to strike her down, but bows sang and even the winged angel had to spin away and flail his blade, twisting with sight-defying speed as he swatted arrows aside, then unleashed a wall of force that staggered the wave of oncoming monks.

But more were still arriving, flooding the hall, and the angel roared, furious now. It tried to go for Jadyn again, but the first wave of monks had recovered and were charging. Steel hammered on steel, and for a moment they had hope – until another male Serra flashed in, this one dark-haired, looking like a sixteen-year-old poet, and hacked one of the monks in two.

They move like we move, Aura thought hopelessly, *but with glyma too.*

Now Sendu himself was lighting up his elobyne and contesting with glyma. The monks converged, staves flailing in a storm with the two Serra at its epicentre, and all the spells the winged beings tried were fizzling against the magus' power.

Aura grabbed Jadyn's shoulders, shouting, 'Up – get up!'

'I can't – my knee—'

'Jagga your knee – you have to move—'

She got her shoulder under his armpit and hauled, her body flooding with energy as it had when they fled the Exemplar in Mutaza City. Jadyn grunted in pain as his right knee took some of his weight, but another monk, a young Aquini girl, took his other arm.

'This way,' the girl said, indicating a side door, 'is way out.'

She and Aura hauled and Jadyn hopped, using the halberd as a crutch, towards the side door. Behind them, the two Serra looked trapped ... but suddenly they weren't, flashing upwards on wings of light to hover above the room.

Red-Mane went at Sendu while the Boy-Poet came at Aura.

She had no choice but to release Jadyn, snatch away his polearm and try to fend it off. The Aquini girl tried to help, but although the Boy-Poet had only one sword, it was like facing someone with four arms, each holding a glowing blade. He was able to parry Aura and stab at the monk in the same instant. Aura tried to match that speed, but the girl was cut down brutally.

The angel, chortling in glee, turned on her.

It was coated in a white powder and its robes were streaked in slime and moss – and Aura realised it'd been here all along, hiding among the statues they'd seen. *How many*, she wondered. *And why?*

She tried to do as she'd seen Evandriel do, as she'd managed with Marika, willing the Serra to stillness, but it brushed off the attempt and its blade cleaved her halberd pole in half. Disarmed, she saw no escape ... but Jadyn, on the ground, suddenly lunged up and in, driving a dagger into the angel's groin. The creature shrieked and staggered backwards, glowing pale blood bursting from the wound. With a howl, he shot into the rafters, wings flailing, and clung there, wailing.

Then the side door burst open and Mistress Peralin was there, shouting to the young monks with her, 'Get Jadyn and Aura below! *Go!*'

It felt wrong to run, when surely these creatures were here because of them, but Jadyn was in no state to argue and Aura let herself be swept along. She glimpsed Sendu surrounded by protectors, but Red-Mane was merrily carving them apart. Then the doors slammed and they were in a darkened hall with Peralin and half a dozen shaking students.

'Where's Evandriel?' Jadyn gasped, as he tried to walk.

'Ahead of us,' Peralin answered. 'Now let me concentrate.'

She spread her hands and a tracery of light lit up the door frame, a locking spell. Aura looked at Jadyn, but his face was a blank of agony. *Twisted knee*, she guessed. *It could be bad.* But if they couldn't get out of here, that would be moot. She threw his arm over her shoulders again and got him limping onwards.

'Hold these locking spells intact as long as you can,' Peralin told a young Pelasian girl with a serious moon-shaped face, who, Aura belatedly realised, also had a magia's staff. 'You two, guard her,' she told the other monks.

Then she took Jadyn's other arm. 'Come, Sier, be strong,' she urged.

Peralin just sealed them all in with those demons, Aura thought. *Even Master Sendu . . .* She felt sick at the thought.

Jadyn cursed with every step, but they made it to some steps, where Jadyn gripped the wooden handrail and hopped down on his good leg, a feat in itself. Aura guarded his back, dreading the rush of wings, but though the sounds of fighting went on, muffled voices shrieking and shouting, the noise remained distant.

At the bottom was another barred door, but Peralin produced a ring of keys. Aura took Jadyn's weight and wiped his face, for he was sweating in rivers and clearly in pain.

'It's a strain, not a tear,' he panted. 'I just need ice . . . and about a week's rest.'

'Hold on, mi amor,' she exhorted. 'Hold on.'

After getting the door open, Peralin lit her staff, illuminating a large cellar filled with crates, most broken. Eyes flashed in the flare of glyma-light, then scattered.

Rats, Aura thought, but they held no terror for her tonight.

The magia locked the door behind her, added wards of glyma for good measure, then led Aura and the limping Jadyn to a large furnace with an iron door, big enough to walk inside, blackened by soot and ash, but empty.

Aura wondered why they'd come here – there was no visible exit, and no way out. But the sheet metal floor was warm, even felt through the soles of their boots. This furnace was dead, but beneath it something burned.

She went to ask, but Peralin hushed her with a finger to her lips, as the sounds above abruptly stopped and the whole building fell silent. *They're all dead,* Aura realised. *And we're next.*

*

The old man died last, as was fitting. Genadius gave him that honour, after slaughtering his protégés and acolytes one by one, taking his time to make each kill a display of technique, so they'd know that all their training, dedication and effort meant nothing, that their brief lives had been utterly wasted. And so the old man, who'd doubtless inflicted some pointless regimen of diet and exercise and discipline upon them, would also see that his entire life had been futile.

Then he disembowelled the fool and beheaded him, rolling his head over so the last sight his desperately flickering eyes would see was his own body, spewing its entrails.

This has been an absolute pleasure, he mused, gazing about at the carnage, soaking in the stench of blood, voided bowels and fluids and disbelieving despair on the dead faces.

But time was burning. His prey were somewhere ahead . . . *below*.

His two acolytes rejoined him. Slender, pretty Akkadeus sashayed through the carnage, dabbing his fingers into the wound in his groin as it closed, licking his fingers, while blonde, braided Saskia appeared from above, where she'd been slaughtering those hiding up there. She was a Vorska princess, the favourite of a past Hierophant, and fully at home with savagery.

'Where are those you seek, Master?' she asked, taking in the blood and death blithely.

He indicated the side door, where the fugitives had gone. It was irritating to have had them in his grasp, only to be forced to let them go, but it was a temporary setback.

He shattered the glyma-wards on that door, then burst through, cut down a foolish girl-mage and her fellows without breaking step, then he and his comrades waded through three more 'masters' who couldn't lay a blade on them, pausing only to drink their dying thoughts.

Those held a revelation.

There's some kind of cave below the building, some kind of bolt-hole . . . to the real *library.*

Genadius felt his face split into a broad grin. This place wasn't dying at all, and the library was far from dispersed. It had merely gone into hiding.

'Open!' Peralin called again – not a spell, but a request.

With a sudden grinding, the slabs at the back of the charred furnace split and swung backwards on hidden hinges, revealing light beyond. She led the way, leaving Aura to help Jadyn limp after her.

They passed through the concealed door into the arms of a crowd of young monks and robed, scholarly men and women of all ages and races, all with uniformly frightened expressions. Evandriel was with them, his face filled with relief to see them. But he was clearly too distracted by the contents of the room to come and join them.

Jadyn gazed around.

This is the real *library*, he realised. *They didn't really break it up at all. Once their foes became too powerful to fight, they just played dead.*

The chamber was long and narrow, with a great many side doors, running for hundreds of paces. The walls were lined with bookshelves. There were older men and women in orange robes moving among yellow-clad younger staff: librarians and trainees, he guessed. One bustled up, a grey-haired Abuthan in orange, his staff tipped with elobyne.

'My name is Iakolo Emboma,' he said briskly. 'What's happening up there?'

'An attack,' Jadyn answered, as Peralin closed off the back door of the furnace. He glanced around and saw ventilation grilles, and smelled cooking from the far end of the main chamber. *There's a whole other facility down here*, he realised. *Incredible.*

'Attackers be demons,' Aura added. 'Winged angel killers.'

'Peralin?' Emboma called. 'Is it—?'

'Alephi,' the old woman said tersely, 'just as we feared.'

'You know of these things?' Jadyn demanded.

'A little,' the Abuthan magus answered. 'We've been aware of a secret circle of mages for decades now, based on Nexus Isle. We sent spies, who saw things they couldn't explain – and heard long-dead names, too – but that can wait.' He turned to Peralin, who was opening a metal hatch. 'Has it truly come to that?' he asked hoarsely.

Peralin smiled grimly, revealing a pit of fire beneath the dead furnace they'd passed through. The heat that radiated from the opening was enough to make them reel. 'We have no choice,' she told Emboma. She turned to the monks hovering nearby. 'Feed the furnace and be ready.' She looked at Jadyn. 'I'm sorry, but this is our final chamber.'

'You've no other exit?' Jadyn demanded. 'Why not?'

'A way out is also a way in: another point of vulnerability and weakness. At some point, you must turn at bay.'

It made a certain sense, Jadyn acknowledged. 'Has this chamber been attacked before?'

'It's never been found,' she replied. 'Let us pray it isn't this time.'

The senior librarians were urging quiet now, as everyone became aware of the crisis. Jadyn realised that most were so locked into their studies or duties they'd not even noticed them arriving. But as the danger was made clear, their fear was palpable. These were mostly scholarly sorts, scrawny and underweight, and none had weapons.

'Alephi demons be here for us,' Aura whispered in his ear. 'Why?'

'They must serve the empire,' he guessed.

'Not be fair,' the Nepari woman muttered. 'Akka hate us.'

They backed away from the furnace to avoid the heat and get out of the way as student monks wheeled a coal-hopper forward and started shovelling black lumps into the fires. Jadyn slumped against a wall and stared about him, giving his hurt knee some respite as he took a measure of the place and the people. Everyone looked shocked as the realisation set in that they were all who remained of the legendary Monks of Myrkaza. He'd seen Vestal centuries in defeat – rarely, but it happened – so he knew a little of how they felt.

At the far end of that hall he saw something that pricked his curiosity: older men and women strapped to stone thrones, wearing leather caps festooned with copper tubes running into their mouths and ears. Facing them were lecterns upon which other librarians knelt, reading from books into speaking tubes connected to the caps of the seated ones. It was a bizarre sight.

Jadyn asked Evandriel, 'What's going on there?'

'I'm not sure,' the scholar admitted. 'We're trapped, you know. There's no way out.'

'We got in, we can get out,' Jadyn replied with deliberate calm. 'Do they have supplies?

'A month's worth, I'm told. But we don't have months, just minutes.'

Jadyn felt that too. He indicated the furnace, which was now closed. The door, he realised, was neither stone or metal, but something like glass, deeply clouded.

'It's volcanic glass, cut and planed into slabs and reinforced with the glyma,' the Abuthan magus, Emboma, told him. 'The rest of the furnace is made of stone slabs reinforced with tempered steel plates. If it can't hold these things out, nothing will.'

Putting it like that didn't feel comforting at all.

'We can regulate the temperature inside that fake chamber by stoking the real furnace, below,' Emboma went on. 'It's hot enough to cremate a body, and we've got a few more tricks up our sleeve.' He indicated some levers and an array of bellows cemented into the walls. 'We can intensify the heat using those, and even unleash poisonous fumes. Those levers control the doors, so once someone's inside, we can lock them in from here and incinerate them.'

Then he raised a hand in warning. Staring at the volcanic glass doors, Jadyn made out shadows moving at the far end of the furnace. The Serrafim were here – and if he could see them, they could see him. The far door hung open, a rectangle of light broken thrice, as the angels entered the dead furnace . . . above the live one.

'They'll feel the heat through the floor,' he warned. 'And they can fly.'

'And they see us,' Aura put in.

'Good,' Peralin replied. 'Let them come closer.'

The dark blurs resolved into human-shaped figures and a moment later a pale, perfectly symmetrical face pressed to the volcanic glass. It bared teeth and slapped at the glass.

The arrogance, Jadyn thought. *It's a clear trap, but they believe they're untouchable.*

'Do we know how many?' Emboma asked.

She shook her head. 'We saw two, and I'm sure I heard fighting on the upper levels.'

'If we miss even one, we may never get out,' Emboma muttered. 'But we can't wait any longer.' A few seconds passed, then he asked, 'Poison fumes, now?'

'Poison won't hurt them,' Jadyn predicted.

Peralin smiled grimly. 'It doesn't have to, so long as it distracts them.' She signalled, 'Now.'

The time-sapping yet ineffectual defences – the monks who sacrificed themselves pointlessly, the barriers thrown in their faces, the few who hid – served only to whet the appetites of the three Alephi. Saskia was chewing so hard on her lower lip that it bled, and Akkadeus was stroking his groin unconsciously. They'd been drawing on the glyma and unleashing it in swathes, a glorious orgy of inflicted destruction.

And now this . . . clearly some kind of trap . . .

'Caution,' Genadius told his acolytes, smelling something venting in. 'I don't like—'

Then he recognised it – a cloud of gas, debilitating for humans but not his kind. He sniffed the air and snickered, relaxing. But next moment the door behind them slammed shut and locks thudded, then the floor gave way, fire roared up from below and bellows blasted in more air to feed the flames.

They'd been braced for trickery, but they were high on the *jang* of the glyma and joy of killing. Even he, the coldest and most rational, was taken by surprise.

The wave of fire and smoke that enveloped them caused the poison gas to ignite, so that their reflex when the floor dropped – to shoot upwards – resulted in being caught in the sheet of fire that rippled across the steel ceiling as the furnace filled. They screeched as one as their silk robes ignited. The heat disintegrated cloth and crisped flesh, then Saskia and Akkadeus, lesser beings than Genadius, dropped screaming into the coals, striking them and going under.

It's only fire, Genadius roared at him, his ghostly wings pumping. *Fight!*

But they weren't him: he felt the Vorska princess perish first, and saw his beautiful Akkadeus become a charred skeletal wraith, then disintegrate into the coals. He shrieked in rage and smashed into the volcanic glass with all his remaining power, closing off his airways as heat and fire flayed him, burning away blackened skin and roasting muscle and fat beneath. He felt none of it, sustained by rage as he hammered at the glass barrier, screaming threats at those beyond, bringing to bear all his glyma-strength.

Then he sucked in the heat and sent it to his right hand, which went incandescent, a white-hot skeletal claw that he planted against the volcanic glass . . . which began to melt.

He drew back his glyma-blade and thrust it into the barrier with all his remaining power.

Aura couldn't understand how anything could survive that furnace, and from Jadyn's horrified gaze, neither could he. But one of these beings was still alive, clinging to the other side of the glass barrier like a giant insect as his body went black. She saw a glowing white skeletal hand . . . then realised the barrier was liquefying . . .

'Elysia on high,' Peralin gasped. 'He's coming through!'

'Cut the air!' Emboma shouted, taking a step back. 'Die, damn you!'

As if he heard, the Serra drew back his blade to drive it into the barrier.

In a flash, Aura saw what came next, and what would happen if it did: the explosion of glass ripping through the chamber, and the carnage as this deadly demon followed . . .

She reacted instinctively – and so did Jadyn, simultaneously slamming the palms of their left hands to the glass. It was so hot it blistered their skin instantly, but they did as they'd seen Evandriel do, *willing* the glass barrier's destruction to slow in time, to hold it intact, even just a few seconds longer.

She saw the Serra's face swell in hate as it saw them, and its incandescent blade crunch into the glass. Dark spider-web cracks formed . . . but the barrier refused to shatter, and the seconds she and Jadyn had purchased proved enough . . . Its bulging golden eyes exploded, the wings burst into flame and it fell, fighting time and howling, a deeply distorted sound as it drifted downwards into the bed of coals.

Fire flared and engulfed it.

She had to rip her hand to get it from the glass, leaving burned skin seared to the surface. Howling in mute agony, she buried her face in Jadyn's chest, clinging to him through the pain.

'Close the lower furnace roof,' she heard Emboma croak, and someone moved the required levers and wheels. She heard metal grind and then boom shut. 'Keep those hatches shut. Seal them. Let the bastards burn for ever.'

Agony. Utter, complete, all-encompassing agony.

Genadius screamed as his body fought the fire, but even he had limits. Realising he was doomed otherwise, he turned all his awareness inwards, to preserve his core while he could. Clinging on, he used his mastery of time to slow the heat that was eating him, sliver by sliver.

Hold on – hold on . . .

It reminded him of his final moments as an ordinary mortal, when he'd realised he'd been fed poison and tried to slow his heart and cling on, begging Elysia to send aid. But only his son showed up, the scum-sucking prick who'd given him the envenomed cup in the first place.

Had I not already begun the process towards immortality, I would truly have perished. And if Akkadeus hadn't arrived a second later and unknowingly prevented Eindil from finishing me off, I'd already be dust.

He'd rewarded the young poet with immortality for that deed. But it turned out that 'for ever' was over for his beautiful boy-lover.

But not for me. Never for me.

Rage sustained him as he clung on, screaming with his mind to his remaining acolytes, anyone in range upon whose blood he'd feasted, whose body he'd used. *Help me!* he screamed. *I'm in Sherkaza – help me—*

As the agony increased, it became a primal scream, calling over and over to the nearest of his seed he knew to be alive.

Vaziella! his mind screamed, the sound reverberating through the fabric of time and space. *Save me!*

Part Three
THE DEVOURER'S MAW

Wings of Shadow

A Loving God

All known mythologies have tales of Creation, but also prophecies of Destruction. Be it a fire that engulfs the world or a giant fish or serpent that devours it, a day of reckoning is a universal belief. Only those who are obedient to the gods will survive or be resurrected. Sinful unbelievers will be damned in some form of eternal punishment. The Book of Lux *claims that Akka loves humanity, but He rules by fear.*

ON TALMONI RULE, INCHALUS SEKUM, MATEZ, 1468

Bedum-Mutaza
Autumn 1472

Eindil Pandramion III, the Hierophant, God-Emperor of Talmont, shifted uncomfortably on the Throne of Pearl, his thoughts trapped in a spiral of dread, that the End of All Things was nigh. It was as if the room were filled with unseen crows whose cawing presaged universal death. Wings of shadow beat the air around him.

His fears were exacerbated every day: earthquakes in the Pelasian Archipelago were driving waves of refugees to the southern coast of Bedumassa, where the harvests had failed. The vyr were burning the abandoned fields and vast tracts of shards. Normal balances had collapsed in the face of a sea of displaced humanity.

I've been promised immortality, but will I survive to receive that gift? he worried.

Since dawn, the Day Court in Bedum Palace had been beseeching him to send aid to the affected regions – channelled through their hands, of course. As Robias put it, men and women you wouldn't trust to hold your beer were putting their hands out for thousands of aurochs each.

We are awaiting imperial inspections and will allocate aid on that basis, Eindil kept pushing back, with increasing irritability. *And I'll certainly give nothing to you lot,* he wished he could add. The hours had dragged on interminably, when he had so much more important things to worry about, starting with the whereabouts of his beloved Exemplar.

Where is she – is she safe? When will she return?

Most of all, he worried about having sent his father after her, when Genadius and he had been at odds throughout his entire life. *Mother had to keep the peace, and Father hated her for it.*

But any other Serra would be deadlier to Vazi than anyone she might meet, even if they were obliged under oath to protect her.

Father won't harm her, he told himself. *Even he must answer to higher powers.*

Finally, like the answer to a prayer, the great bell tolled and the Day Court was over. Eindil jerked back to full awareness to find himself blinking at a big Abuthan courtier who was now bowing, crestfallen, at being cut short. 'With your Majesty's permission, I could go on?' the man suggested hopefully, in heavily accented Talmoni.

'No, I need to rest,' Eindil told Robias curtly, and his wish became command. The courtiers were ushered out, functionaries rushed in, curtains were drawn around the throne and Eindil, leaning on Robias' shoulder, hobbled out on legs aching from yet another day of sitting on that damned uncomfortable throne.

'My friend,' he whispered, 'I do not think I can stand to see a wife tonight. And as for the Night Court – tell them I am unwell. All I want is a massage and bed.'

He'd given the same excuse for the past three nights. The Night Courtiers would be chafing, he knew, but he hated the thought of this hall at night, being lectured to and berated by those faceless, acidic adversaries.

'Milord, each day you don't see them is added to the end of your stay here,' Robias reminded him softly, as he helped him walk. 'You'll have to face them in the end.'

'Aye, and I will – when I'm stronger.'

When Vazi has returned, unharmed and ready to submit to me.

The stentor's face tightened just a fraction, the closest Robias would ever come to a criticism. 'As you will it, Great One. I will make the arrangements.'

Three hours later, Eindil entered his bedchamber, mercifully alone – if one didn't count Robias, or the courser with the latest dispatches, or the servants waiting to take his crown, undress him, refill his water and wine jugs, turn down the bedclothes, close the curtains and all those myriad other tasks that were more ritual than necessity.

Too tired to fight, he submitted to their demands.

'What news?' he asked the stentor, when they were finally alone and he was sitting up in bed sipping sherbet tea. 'Did anything good happen in the world today?'

Robias, standing beside the bed, scanned the papers. 'Do you like babies?'

'I abhor all squalling brats, especially my own,' Eindil told him, only half-joking.

'Then no, nothing good happened,' Robias replied drily. 'I'll add Lady Clervont's news to the Disaster pile. As to the rest, most of this concerns a series of earthquakes in the Kerat Isles, with some considerable loss of life in the low-lying villages.'

'The Kerats? Where are they? Why is that name familiar?'

'They're on the northern rim of the volcanic circle, not far from the heart of Old Pelas, which was lost in the eruption of 1187. We sent the Lighters there to explore the possibility of shard placements.' Robias frowned at the scroll he was reading. 'They insist they've tamed a dozen volcanoes there by planting shards to soak up the volcanic energy. It's been a huge success: the islands where they've placed their shards are the least affected by seismic or volcanic activity.'

'That's one in the eye for Nilis Evandriel and his lies,' Eindil smirked, before asking the only question that mattered, 'Is there news of the Exemplar?'

Robias shook his head. 'Nothing, Great One.'

'Then the rest can wait for tomorrow.' Eindil yawned.

The stentor looked up sharply. 'There is one you should hear now, Great One.' He raised a parchment bearing the seal of the Vestal Order. 'There's been a bit of a furore in Folkstein.'

'How poetic you are,' Eindil remarked, though his unease sharpened. Folkstein meant that snake Corbus Ritter. 'Oh, very well. What do my great and loyal knights want now?'

'The High Council have declared a hearing into a fallen knight, Romara Challys—'

'The one allegedly married to the Sandreth heir?'

'Exactly. She denies it, interestingly.' Robias frowned over the parchment. 'She also claimed to have discovered Vanashta Baanholt, spouted some nonsense about "aegis" and found Lighters erecting shard-clusters in Solabas, which no one's supposed to know about.' He folded the paper and half and concluded, 'The Order have decided to put her on full trial in Hyastar.'

'Is that good?'

'Archon Ritter fought against it, apparently to protect Your Majesty's reputation. But there is resistance to him within the Order's High Council. Majesty, this is serious: the archon may be deposed, and whilst Corbus is a snake, those wanting to take him down are idealistic fools.'

'Does that matter?'

'It could split the Order.'

Eindil looked up in surprise. 'A schism? Surely not.' If the Order split, his rule would be weakened, perhaps fatally, especially if the Caliph managed to co-opt half of the Vestal knights into his service.

'It's a genuine threat, Great One,' Robias replied. 'The Night Court will demand a full report.'

Eindil groaned, but he saw nothing he could do tonight. 'Keep me informed, my friend,' he murmured. 'Dear Akka, I'm so tired. I haven't slept properly since . . .'

Since Vazi left . . .

As if he sensed the thought, Robias' face turned stony, but he merely bowed and left.

Eindil lay back down, let the pillow take the weight of his throbbing head and prayed for sleep, but for hours nothing came but a dull moaning sound, too deep to hear properly, if it even was words. It was a mercy when oblivion finally claimed him.

He didn't know what woke him, whether it was some sound – or had someone whispered his name? But his eyes fluttered open and he jolted awake.

Three figures stood over Eindil's bed: two white men either side of their leader, whose ebony skin was a stark contrast to her pale robes and flickering wings.

His heart thudded against his ribs and his throat locked. For a moment he was utterly rigid with terror, convinced that the assassins he always dreaded had finally come.

'Great One,' they said, in perfect unison, and genuflected.

He sat up, his mouth dry as a desert. 'I . . . uhhh . . .' He was too scared to reach for his bell. They all wore golden-hilted swords, and had the same shapely, perfectly symmetrical faces as his father – and the same utterly remorseless expressions.

'We seek your once-father, Genadius,' said the angel with the jet-black skin.

'Is he here?' one of the males added.

'I . . . I know not,' Eindil stammered weakly. 'He's gone . . .'

'Why?' the woman demanded. 'He told the Trinity he was coming here to watch over you.'

The Trinity? The fabled three had been present when Akka gave elobyne to Jovan Lux. He'd never heard these beings from the Scriptures spoken of except by priests in pulpits.

'He left,' Eindil croaked, 'following . . . uh . . . following the Exemplar.'

The three Alephi looked at each other and though not a word was said, Eindil was certain they were communicating. Finally the woman said, 'Why should he follow the woman knight? His place is here. He requested this assignment, to be your guardian here in the south.'

Eindil regretted mentioning Vazi now, but was too afraid to lie, even by omission. 'I asked him to keep watch over her,' he admitted fearfully.

The three Serrafim exchanged glances again, then the leader asked, 'Where did she go?'

'Heretics in the Dhouma . . .' He realised he was babbling and tried to slow down. 'Kaen and . . . some Nepari woman . . . She pursues them . . . with Borghart . . . I gave them a ship . . .'

The three angels hissed as one and his throat seized up completely.

The woman leaned forward. 'Yesterday, we heard Genadius crying out in great pain. He is calling for aid. *Our* aid. But in his extremity, he also calls the name "Vazi".'

Eindil's brow bled perspiration. '*She's in danger?*' he blurted, then he remembered to add, '*My father is hurt?*'

The three angels surely noticed his slip, though the woman said only, 'Of her, we have no tidings. Go back to sleep, Great One. We will seek your noble father and bring him succour.'

Abruptly, they were gone – not quite instantly, for his eyes caught afterimages of pale blurs streaming out through the closest window, which flashed open and slammed silently.

For a few minutes, all he could do was pant for breath.

When he had calmed a little and was sure he was alone, he reached out and rang his bell.

In a few minutes, a bedraggled-looking Robias stumbled through the hidden door behind the bed, where his own chamber lay. Eindil heard a youthful male voice murmuring tiredly, but Robias shut his door and dropped to his knees. 'Great One?' he said, in a subservient voice. 'How may I serve?'

It felt cruel, as Robias was the one person who got less sleep than he did, but Eindil would have trusted no one else. 'I've had a bad dream,' he mumbled apologetically. 'Please, old friend, will you sit with me?'

17

Ever Onwards

Of Fire and Ice

Prior to the black and white polarities of the Akkanite Reformation, religion was nuanced, a balancing of natural cycles. Death was sad, but it wasn't 'evil'. Winter was as revered and valued as summer. The cycle was seen as a whole. But Jovan Lux reduced everything to simple mantras. The irony is, of course, that such is the complexity of morality, that Jovan's religious laws are a morass none can navigate.

IN DEFENCE OF THE OLD WAYS, RUELLA SHERNOVAR, 1448

Sherkaza, Pelasian Archipelago
Autumn 1472

'We cannot remain here,' Iakolo Emboma said in an empty voice. 'We have lost too many. The monastery and the library must move.'

Beside him, Peralin, her face set like she'd never smile again, agreed. 'We need to salvage what we have, then vanish. Others may come at any moment. I want us gone by mid-afternoon.'

Jadyn could well understand that. Of hundreds of monks and trainees, only fifty or so remained, the initiates who'd been in the final chamber with them when they stopped the Serrafim, and a score or so who'd had the sense to hide instead of fighting – and were now torn with the guilt of surviving as 'cowards', though nobody would ever have called them that.

Those concealed trainees had only just re-emerged, not knowing if they would confront more of the enemy. Instead, they'd found a heartbreaking scene of destruction and slaughter. The bodies were piled up in some places, while others had died singly or in small groups, trapped and murdered by impossible foes. Everywhere stank of death.

'Where will you go?' Evandriel asked Emboma. 'And how will you get there?'

'The Zynochi Navy has promised aid, and we will pay any reliable merchantmen to aid us, too,' Peralin replied. 'We will make for the Zynochi mainland and seek the Caliph's protection.'

Evacuation was wise. Jadyn doubted these Serrafim or Alephi or whatever they were would take the loss of any of their number lying down. He was anguished at the thought that this had all happened because of his quest – and he was just as anxious to leave.

'I don't know how to say this, but during the attack, it felt to me that they were seeking Aura and me, and Master Evandriel,' he confessed. 'We had no idea that such beings even existed, let alone were pursuing us, but the blame is ours.'

For a moment it felt like the air had been sucked from the room, but Peralin shook her head. 'The blame for a murder lies with the murderer, not the victims. You came here seeking wisdom, believing yourself free of pursuit.'

'You did believe so, yes?' Emboma put in, not so immediately forgiving.

'We evaded our enemies in Bedum-Mutaza and we had no reason to believe they had found us again,' Evandriel answered. 'In any case, we believed our enemies mortal. I've been a wanted man for decades and have never seen such beings. They are neither knights, nor vyr. They are not erling.' He looked at Emboma intently. 'You called them "Alephi". What do you know about these beings?'

Emboma flinched. 'As I told you last night, the few spies who returned from Nexus Isle spoke of "angels" who bore the names of past rulers and heroes. But that knowledge is third- or fourth-hand. Had you asked me yesterday, I would have said that I did not believe it.'

'Be careful who you tell at the court of the Caliph,' Evandriel warned. 'They are devout Akkanites: they will believe that if the Serrafim attacked you, it was justified. If I were you, I'd claim that pirates attacked you . . . and in fact,' the scholar added, his eyes glazing into a faraway look Jadyn recognised as foresight, '. . . if I were you, I would not go to the Caliph at all. Go north, into Hytal. Seek those who seek to rid the world of elobyne and these "angels". Seek Romara Challys, if she still lives.'

Jadyn shot the scholar a look, wondering what future he'd glimpsed.

Emboma and Peralin shared a hollow-eyed glance. 'We will consider your warning,' Peralin agreed, before looking around sadly. 'Our young folk are devastated. How will they get over this?'

'Day by day,' replied Jadyn, experienced in the trauma of loss. 'Keep them busy, but encourage them to talk, to you and each other. Rituals help, like ceremonies to inter the dead, and other communal acts. Keep them together – and don't let *anyone* blame themselves.'

Recognising the words of a survivor, both mages nodded solemnly and thanked him.

'Tell me about the thrones and the apparatus in that final chamber,' Evandriel put in, after a discreet pause. 'The leather caps and the tubes, what were they?'

After a moment of hesitation, Emboma said, 'Those you saw are "oracles": librarians with eidetic memories. We have had to sell many works to survive, but we keep them by committing them to the collective memory. We read to them, and they retain the books and scrolls, word for word.'

'Each oracle contributes to the library, and can access any other work by reaching each other mentally through a means devised for us long ago by the Sanctor Wardens,' Peralin added proudly.

'The Wardens again,' Jadyn breathed. 'You have historic links to them?'

'Of course, Emboma said proudly. 'We were allies, until the Order replaced them.'

'So, these poor peoples sit in dark all life, eating books?' Aura asked, sounding appalled. 'Am not wanting to be!'

'The sharing of knowledge and reading in of new texts is just part of their day,' Emboma was quick to reply. 'They enjoy normal lives – some even travel to augment their learning.'

'Do the Hierophants know of this?' Evandriel asked. 'Do the caliphs?'

The Abuthan smiled. 'No, despite some having an oracle embedded in their courts.'

'May I speak with one?' Evandriel asked eagerly. 'The questions we came here to ask are as yet unanswered.'

The two mages gave their consent and summoned the youngest oracle, a plump girl in her twenties, so pale she might be albino, with tangled wet hair. She wore a colourful shawl over her grey robe – and a blindfold, because she'd been born sightless, Peralin told them.

'This is Yvora,' the magus told them. 'Ask your questions.'

Evandriel introduced himself, Jadyn and Aura – but at his name, Yvora reacted. 'You are known, Nilis Evandriel,' she said, 'as a causer of strife and rebellion, condemned first by the Akkanite Prelature in—'

'Yvora, Master Evandriel has our blessing,' Peralin interjected gently.

The girl coloured. 'But why? In 1471 he sacrificed a young woman from Miravia to the Devourer and consumed her heart, and—'

'We get court reports on trials *in absentia*,' Emboma put in apologetically. 'Oracles are recorders; they do not critique. Yvora, please ignore references to Master Evandriel in Church and Court documents. You have our permission to speak with him.'

The girl frowned, but made a submissive gesture. 'Ask,' she said doubtfully.

Evandriel leaned forward. 'The mosaics beneath the dome in the Hejiffa Dhouma created two centuries ago to honour the ascension to the throne of Jovan Lux recently fell apart – revealing a second, older, mosaic. It appears to show a sea-god, a monster and a volcano. Do you know of this second mosaic?'

Yvora fell into a trance-like state, then recited, 'This is known. It was made circa 1068 to 074, recording a myth of the origin Pelasian people, in which the God Maka contested the rule of the sea with Ur-Krakos, his progenitor. To prevent Ur-Krakos from destroying the world, Maka slew Ur-Krakos with a burning trident lit from the fires of Kimusamusa.'

'What is Kimusamusa? Where is it?' Evandriel asked tersely.

'Kimusamusa is a volcanic island in legend, but in reality, it is not known,' Yvora replied flatly. 'There are no islands called Kimusamusa. In the legend it was destroyed when Maka cast the body of Ur-Krakos into the cone, forming the thousand isles of the Pelas.'

It's a creation myth, Jadyn thought blankly. *There's no such place . . .* 'Why would the Wardens direct us to a place that doesn't exist?' he wondered aloud.

Evandriel ignored him. 'Yvora, have you read texts in Khetian from the pre-Jovan era?'

'No such texts are known—'

'Thank you, Yvora.' The scholar turned to Jadyn, and murmured, 'Only original Khetian texts will tell us more on this subject, but I think we have what we need.'

'Uh, good,' Jadyn said doubtfully, not understanding.

Evandriel turned back to the girl-oracle, and said, 'Yvora, have you ever read a text of instructions on how to use the aegis?'

'No such text has been read to me.'

Clearly, faced with an actual oracle, Evandriel felt compelled to keep asking questions. 'Yvora, what is elobyne?'

'This is known. Elobyne is a crystal of unknown origin, found only at Nexus Isle, used by—'

The scholar tsked and interrupted. 'Yvora, why does elobyne energy cause battle-rage?'

'This is known. Elobyne energy causes a reaction in the body, which urgently seeks to expel it. This physiological response has psychological repercussions that profoundly affect—'

'Yvora, I understand that – but *why*? What is it about elobyne energy that causes these responses?'

Yvora replied in a despairing voice, 'The texts do not record definitively. Speculative work by Anderus Rolf postulates that—'

'He's a fool. Who else?'

'The theorem of Bekus den Ahrim suggests that—'

'I've read it,' Evandriel said. 'Anything else?'

'I have nothing else.' Yvora sounded on the verge of tears, as if her inner world had been destroyed and her self-worth shattered. 'I am sorry.'

Jadyn tried to imagine being her: existing in darkness, her only purpose the recording and recitation of the words of others. He wondered what sustained her, or brought her joy. Maybe it was something so mundane as being able to recall the right text at the right time – or poetry, perhaps . . . But if she'd been born blind, could she even understand the imagery? In her lightless world, did words like 'colour' have any meaning at all?

Peralin squeezed the girl's shoulder. 'The texts are not infinite, Yvora, you know that. You have eliminated lines of enquiry and that is often as valuable as finding answers.'

Yvora sniffed, as if trying to hold back tears.

Evandriel sagged, and in a gentle voice said, 'Yvora, I thank you. Be safe.'

He thanked the masters before taking Jadyn and Aura aside. 'We've got to get out of here. Those Alephi will be missed, and others will come – I've warned them, but the real danger is to us. Gather your baggage and meet me downstairs in ten minutes.'

'But they need our help—' Jadyn began.

Aura shook her head. 'No, Evandriel be right. We are danger to all. Must go.'

Jadyn took her arm and they headed for their rooms. His knee was bound but much improved, so too their burned hands, thanks to a slave and bandaging. They traversed the chaos of wreckage, passing survivors hauling crates and luggage to the main hall. A few of the oracles wandered amongst it all like ghosts, reciting aloud from apparently random works concerning engineering, or weather or sea travel. The senior monks and librarians were shouting commands, purpose overcoming the paralysis of despair. Jadyn was reminded of caged birds, born to captivity but suddenly freed.

They climbed the stairs, found their room and went in—

—and Aura slammed the door, seized him and pushed him against the wall, kissing him so hard she was almost biting, pulling at his clothes, and he caught her fever, tugging down her breeches and lifting her against the wall, pinning her body and thrusting inside, cradling her buttocks as she locked her thighs around his hips, his pent-up desires from days without her colliding with the relief of survival, and some primal urge to seize life from death.

He spent himself a frantic few minutes later, then caught her lips in a long, devouring kiss as humanity returned. 'Thank you,' he groaned. 'I needed that too.'

'Mmm, si-si-si,' she sighed, 'been wanting. Too long we wait.'

Jadyn sighed in accord. 'We never even got to use the bed,' he lamented as he lowered her to her feet. 'There never seems to be time.'

'Si,' she agreed, stroking his face. 'We have hunger, must feed, si? Am needing this. Every chance, we take, si? No more shy Jadyn Knight; you give me your macho bravado, compreya?'

He grinned while colouring. 'I'm not sure that will possible on our ship, but I'll take every chance, I promise.'

Peralin had assigned a few initiate-monks to start transporting supplies and baggage, and they escorted Aura, Jadyn and Evandriel down to the harbour. News of the attack had clearly spread, because many people were piling their lives onto ships and leaving.

They loaded swiftly, farewelled Peralin and her initiates and set sail. *I wish there was more we could do*, Aura thought guiltily, as they pulled from the harbour. *This was our fault. The attack happened because we came here.*

Within a few minutes, the felucca was streaming along with Jadyn, his knee bandaged, at the tiller, Aura flitting about the rigging and Evandriel calling the course changes from the bow as they left the now bustling harbour, caught a gusty wind and set out on a north-west bearing.

The skies were cloudy and the seas choppy, so the sailing was demanding. Aura was kept hard at work with the sails, already drenched in seawater and sweat, her muscles protesting and her gauntleted hands aching, but she had a broad grin on her face.

Part of her good mood was from her greedy little interlude with Jadyn, naturally, but the rest was down to the sheer joy of sailing.

The morning passed with frequent rain showers, until by noon thunder was rolling in the distance, with sheet lightning flashing occasionally on the eastern horizon, although there was no venom in it. She climbed the rigging and surveyed the little ship from where the giant spar met the mainmast, squealing excitedly as dolphins emerged from below and rode their bow wave, leaping and cavorting as if life was for play.

Which it is, at times, she thought, waving gaily to Jadyn.

The vessel was humming along towards the northwest on a steady wind and all was well, so she took a break, grabbing a rope and daringly swinging out over the water and back to land lightly on the deck, following the lines of probability her mind conjured. She lashed it down and bowed to the applauding men, then joined Jadyn at the tiller, greeting him with a hungry kiss.

We're a good team, she decided. Unusually for a man, he actually listened to people, rather than just imagining he always knew best. Sergio had been terrible for that. And she liked the way he tasted and smelled and felt – she was desperate to get him inside her again, so much that it was distracting. *I love being in love,* she thought warmly.

'Hola, scholar-man,' she called to Evandriel. 'Where go now?'

Evandriel made his way back to join them. 'We're heading for Lost Pelas,' he announced. 'Do you know the tale? At the height of their power, the Pelasian pirates were defeated by the Aquini Navy – then a devastating eruption destroyed their home city, Silas itself. The entire island was blown apart, leaving no survivors. The Kingdom of Pelas fell apart completely, as if it had never been. Now the islands, all that's left, are backwaters.'

'What's there for us?' Jadyn asked.

'Well, that tale the oracle told us, of the demigod Maka and the sea-monster Ur-Krakos, was clearly set in the volcanic circle at the heart of the Pelas Archipelago. No one actually knows the history, and you'll have noticed that I specifically asked Yvora about her understanding of Khetian and she had none. But for most of its early years, the Pelas Archipelago was Khetian, and even now their language is riddled with Khetian words and fragments. 'Kimus' is Khetian for *fire*. My belief is that when we enter the volcanic centre of the Pelas, we'll find an oral tradition that will enable us to identify Kimusamusa, the lost volcano on the mosaic.'

'Your "belief"?' Jadyn echoed doubtfully.

The scholar grinned and patted his shoulder. 'Foresight guides me also, Sier Jadyn.'

'Is that why you directed the librarians to seek out Romara?'

Evandriel shrugged uneasily. 'It was an impulse. If she is alive, she will be a focus, because of what she's seen at Vanashta Baanholt – that is all.'

Jadyn had hoped for more.

'What volcano to do with aegis?' Aura wondered.

'A good question,' Evandriel said. 'Hopefully we'll find out when we get there. I'm confident the aegis is leading us, and hopeful those pursuing us can't track us.'

'Ar-byan to that,' Jadyn said fervently.

Evandriel headed back to the foredeck to prepare a meal, while Aura settled beside Jadyn and examined his peeling nose. 'Northern man skin falling off in sun,' she chuckled.

He grimaced. 'While you just go a deeper bronze.'

She peered at her darkening limbs with displeasure. 'Si. People will think I am peasant.'

'I don't. I think you're a queen.'

'In Neparia we say, "Pigeon nesting in eyrie", for man whose lover be too beautiful for them.' Aura grinned slyly and patted her groin. 'This be my eyrie, you be my pigeon.'

'Harsh,' Jadyn smiled. 'So, will our children will be peagles?'

They shared a laugh—

BOOM!!!!

They jolted as a long, reverberating thunderclap cracked across the skies from somewhere to the northwest. Her eyes flew to the horizon, where she saw a flash of orange and scarlet, then a gushing plume of inkiness poured into the sky. A second later a shockwave slammed into them, cracking the sail back against the mast as the felucca's timbers creaked alarmingly. The wind turned instantly, stopping them dead in the water, and a dozen seams in the hull burst open, spraying water everywhere.

'Akka Alive,' Evandriel shouted, 'brace yourselves! There's been an eruption—'

Aura shot up the main mast as the sound echoed on about them. While Evandriel and Jadyn tried to block the worst of the leaks, she cast her eyes towards the horizon, watching the northwest fill up with darkness, while balls of fire shrieked overhead like comets. One arced down and struck the sea – a kylo away, at least, she guessed – sending up a massive fountain. Another fell even closer, almost swamping them.

The felucca was been rocking violently, but the wind had gone and a few moments later they were wallowing, becalmed on a flat, glassy sea. Then she saw something she didn't understand. A black wall of darkness had appeared on the horizon, preceded by a gust of unnaturally hot air that was ripping at her clothing and hair.

'What is?' she shouted, pointing, 'Evandriel, what is?'

Evandriel went pale. '*Aura, get down here now!* It's a seiche, a giant wave formed by the eruption—'

Aura scrambled down in terror, as Jadyn asked, 'Giant? How big is it?'

'Too big,' Evandriel replied. 'We must run with it, or we'll be swamped.'

Evandriel helped Aura reset the mainsail, while Jadyn turned the prow southeast. That hot wind was now hissing across the water, making their sails billow, but the giant seiche was filling up the horizon as the sea before it seemed to bend and sink. It bore down on them like an avalanche, and Aura calculated and recalculated its height by the second as it loomed ever larger. The ridge began to fray, white spray flying. They were racing now, as fast as they'd ever gone, but there would be no outrunning this mountain of water.

'*It's going to break,*' Evandriel shrieked. '*We must ride it – or we'll die—*'

Aura dashed back to Jadyn to add her weight behind the tiller, which was shuddering at the force of the water and the unprecedented speed

of their passage. All their possible futures unfolded amid the surging wave, crashing down, rolling them and swallowing them up . . .

. . . but *not* if they wrenched the tiller hard to port, *now*, bringing
the nose about as they arced across the wave's slope, flashing away
from where the wave had begun to curl and break, flowing across
its face in a frightening yet exhilarating rush. Whooping in hope
and fear, they surged along what was becoming a tunnel of curved
water, spray washing over them, the stern all but underwater, the
vessel about to founder . . .

. . . until they reached the very crest, then the breaking surge
flowed past them, and they slid alarmingly down the back side of
the giant wave, their sails filling again as the expanse behind the
seiche opened up, churned by lesser waves extending into infinity . . .

Aura grabbed Jadyn and kissed his face desperately, in case it was
her last chance to do so. A moment later, the next massive wave rose
above them, and they were fighting once more to survive beneath the
indigo sky laced with scarlet and propelled by howling winds. The
sun was gone: though it was only midday, blackness was surging in.

Aegis visions flooded them, and they followed the thin, shifting
thread that seemed to lead towards survival, with all their strength
and courage.

Borghart's warship entered the harbour of Sherkaza like a cat stalking into a rat's nest, and the few ships afloat scattered like rodents
before them. The docks that should have housed Zynochi galleys
were empty and there was an air of recent turmoil, like walking
into a room to find a burst pillow, the feathers already strewn on
the floor. Abandoned debris was piled everywhere, the local people
picking their way through it all squabbling over the prizes.

Vazi Virago wasn't here for them.

'Where do we moor?' the sailing master asked, in a surly voice. He
and his crew were still resentful about being made to sail all night
and half the day without respite. It wasn't yet midday, but they all
looked jaded.

'Anywhere,' she told him, gesturing at the empty docks.

The chaos was a surprise; she'd been given to understand that this place was a backwater, but she hadn't expected it to look like it had just been evacuated.

'Dock swiftly, then find someone who knows what's happening,' she told the master.

After a few minutes of reefing sails and manoeuvring with oars and poles, they found a berth, and a nervous-looking string-bean with bad whiskers approached.

'Are you in charge here?' she called, not believing he would be for a moment.

'I'm the duty pilot, ma'am. Who be askin'?'

She stepped to the rails, making sure he saw her gleaming flamberge and its orb and her newly washed Order tabard. 'I am Vaziella Virago, Exemplar of the Vestments of Sancta Elysia,' she announced proudly. 'Who are you?'

The skinny pilot visibly quaked. 'Jagga . . . uh, I'm, um, Meretens, ma'am, I mean, Siera . . . It is an honour to—'

'What's happening here, Meretens?' she interrupted.

Yoryn Borghart joined her at the railing, clad in his lictor's black, and the young man's face took on an even more sickly expression. But to his credit, he kept talking. A felucca had arrived the previous afternoon, moored up in the naval docks, he told them. The occupants – three of them – had gone up to 'visit they monks'. During the night there'd been unaccountable violence of some sort, and the next morning the entire monastery and all their remaining books had been packed into Zynochi Navy ships and sailed away.

'They went east, ma'am,' Meretens told her, with the disbelieving air of someone whose entire world had been turned upside down. 'There's no one left up there now.'

'What of that felucca and those aboard?'

'They left first, ma'am – sailed out ahead of all the others, headed nor'west.'

She scowled, staring upwards at the overhanging cliffs and houses that looked like they might at any moment fall off their perches and come crashing down into the cove.

'So all the monks and scholars have gone? Why?'

'I heard Imperials killed a bunch of them, an' they was scared more'd come,' Meretens replied nervously. Clearly, he was worried she was the 'more' who would come. 'That's what we was told. Nowt t'do wit' us, ma'am. They kept to theyselves.'

She glanced at Borghart and saw her frustration mirrored there. Their prey had escaped again. But she'd had a strange feeling for hours now that someone was shrieking her name in a slow, sonorous voice so deep it couldn't be heard, only felt.

Genadius was coming here . . . Perhaps he's up there?

She'd rather have ignored that feeling and left, but she dreaded the consequences if the Serrafim found out she'd done so. There were others like him, he'd hinted, and any one of them could take her apart. So she had to do whatever was required. And regardless, finding the felucca's destination might depend on what they discovered up there.

'How do I get up there?' she asked the pilot.

Meretens gave her directions, then gratefully fled.

She and Borghart and a squad of marines disembarked and made their way through the town, which appeared to be in a state of near-riot. Evidently everyone else had decided that with the monks gone, this place was going to die.

They were probably right.

At the top, they found the decrepit monastery. It had been damaged recently, and there were bloodstains everywhere, and recent graves in the gardens. Those they dug up contained Pelasians, young or old and grey, though they all looked athletic, even the ancients. They all wore terrified, despairing expressions, even in death.

Genadius, she thought again. *I would wager anything he killed them.*

Borghart detected sorcerous energies below ground, so they left the marines on the ground floor and went exploring. Eventually they found a back staircase leading to a large walk-in furnace, sealed closed. When they opened it, they found the air was hot, though there was no coal or ash on the steel floor, which was hotter than the walls.

'The real furnace is below,' Borghart guessed, going to the far wall and finding that it was made of interlocked panels of thick volcanic glass. Beyond was a suite of rooms, empty apart from the odd forgotten book on the floor or the otherwise emptied shelves.

'What was this place?' she wondered.

'Their refuge room, I imagine,' Borghart guessed.

That sounded right. But it was the furnace that interested her most. She turned and concentrated on the levers, laying her hands on each. She considered pulling them, but every premonition warned her not to do it: there was a lurking danger here, something driven insane by agony that would rip her to pieces the moment she opened the lower chamber of the furnace. The intensity of the warning took her aback, showing her a ghastly flayed man, wreathed in smoke and ash, ripping her apart and dousing his burns in her blood.

She came to herself in a daze, her stomach churning.

'What is it?' Borghart asked sharply.

'I don't know,' she panted, staring at the lever, knowing it would open the hatch into the lower chamber of the furnace and unleash some kind of demon.

She knew with certainty that she couldn't face it and live.

You're the Exemplar, she reminded herself. *You can face anything.*

But that wasn't true any more.

'Come on,' she told the lictor. 'Let's go.'

Borghart gave her a hollow-eyed look. 'I sense it too,' he breathed. 'It's like a vorlok's mind, when you're torturing them and suddenly they go rabid.' He faced the furnace. 'It's in there . . . Still alive.' Even he sounded appalled. 'Should we open it?'

She went to reply when her brain was stalled by a slow moan of pure agony.

' . . . ZZZZIIII,' she felt, rather than heard, 'VVVAAAAZZZIIIIIII . . .'

It was coming from the furnace.

Borghart stared. 'By the Maw, who is that?'

Genadius is trapped in there, she realised, *Trapped in time . . . and burning alive.*

'Vazi' – Borghart grabbed her shoulder – 'what do we do?'

'Don't touch me!' she shrieked back. 'Don't you *ever* touch me!'

He blinked, then turned back to the hatch. 'But—'

She stared as her premonitions played out again and she weighed her choices.

If I rescue Genadius . . . he might *be grateful; but he could equally slaughter me in his madness . . . And even if he is thankful, he'll still rule me . . .*

'Jag him,' she breathed. *I got all I wanted from him. His spit or blood or seed is already in me turning me to stone and power . . . I don't want anything else of him or his kind . . .*

She faced Borghart. 'He's beyond our help, whoever he is.'

'You know who it is, don't you? Who—'

Something snapped inside her again. *'Jagatai, Borghart, let the bastard burn!'*

Then she turned and fled up through the cellars and out of the old library entirely, ignoring her escort as she ran, unsure what impulse was now driving her. She arrived at a ledge overlooking the harbour, gasping for clean air to wash the smoke and blood from her nostrils and lungs.

Then she spun as a gigantic *BOOM!* reverberated through the skies, and in the northwest corner of the sky, she saw a towering plume of fire and darkness well up into the sky.

DOOM, the sound echoed, on and on, as if Akka had passed judgment on all her sins.

DOOM.

18

Aftermath

Vorstheim

In the pre-Akkanite mythos of the north, the Home of the Gods was Vorstheim – literally, 'First House' – where a pantheon of gods dwelt whilst creating our world. At the Day of Ending, so the old shamans preached, all that lives will return to Vorstheim and Coros will be destroyed. Then the Gods will make a new world, perfected by what they have learned, and the Blessed will dwell in it for ever. It will be called Elysium.

THE CHRONICLES OF HYTAL, 1311

Tar-Brigida, Folkstein
Autumn 1472

Dranit Ritter was in the Tar-Brigida bastion's Justiciary offices, taking the statement of a witness in the case of a widow allegedly forced into marriage by a rapacious business rival. He emerged to find Carid Theomore, one of Lady Augusta Martia's allies and her faction's lead scholar, waiting for him.

'The High Council voted in favour of a hearing for Romara Challys,' Theomore blurted. 'We won the vote!'

'She's my client,' Dranit reminded the scholar, 'and I should be with—'

Before he could finish, bells began hammering in the neighbouring fortress and soldiers started spilling into the corridors, wide-eyed and frightened. Confusion reigned as Theomore, Dranit and Lubano were made to wait in the interview room, fearing the worst.

Are these Romara's friends? Dranit wondered fearfully. *If they're taken alive, I'm ruined.*

He waited anxiously for more than an hour, until the doors crashed open and four knights burst in, seized the three of them and pinned them to the ground.

His brother Corbus, who had followed them in, towered over them. 'Dranit, you damnable traitor,' he shouted, as his men mashed their faces into the tiles. 'You got them inside!'

'I have no idea what you are talking about,' Dranit replied, twisting his head and glaring up at the knight holding him. 'Get off me, you meat-headed oaf!'

Corbus' red face loomed over him. 'You were admitted by the postern gate. Dozens of people saw you!'

'I haven't been outside the Justiciary block all day,' Dranit fired back. 'Ask anyone!'

'He was with me, Archon,' Theomore put in. 'Right here.'

'You're lying, both of you,' Corbus retorted, but he was no longer looking so certain. He stamped away, shouting something, then he re-entered, fuming. 'Damn it, how can you be in two places at once?'

'I wasn't,' Dranit said. 'Jagat, Corbus, this idiot has his knee in my back. Get him off.'

The archon ignored him. 'Someone impersonated you – *exactly* – explain that!' Then he grunted in frustration and said, 'Damn it, let them up.'

'Peace, Lubano,' Dranit warned quietly, as they were freed. His bondsman was a good man, but he didn't take slights lightly. 'Don't let them provoke you.'

The shaven-skulled Aquini, furious at being taken so easily, glared about as if memorising faces. *I expect there's going to be some severe barroom retribution in the next few weeks*, Dranit thought. He wasn't overly worried; Lubano fought dirty, and always won.

Carid Theomore looked shaken, but Dranit just felt irritated; it wasn't the first time Corbus had done this sort of thing. 'A claret, brother?' he asked with ironic cheer, walking to the drinks cabinet in the corner. 'The Justiciary keeps a good bar. It's a Denium red.'

'I don't drink with the likes of you,' Corbus answered. 'Who was it? Who could impersonate you, right down to your speech and irritating mannerisms?'

Dranit let the question hang, collecting his thoughts as he poured three goblets and gave one to Theomore and Lubano before draining the third himself. 'I have no idea, *brother*,' he said at last, 'but I'm a public person, Akka knows. I'm in front of people every day.'

Corbus' sour face fell further. 'Jagatai!' he swore. 'Damn you to the Maw.'

'So, what actually happened, if I may ask?'

'You may not.' Corbus snapped, then he realised Dranit would find out anyway. 'Your vorlok client was on her way to Hyastar when her former comrades – Elindhu Morspeth and Soren var'Dael, both Falcons – and her vyr lover Gram Larch, accompanied by an unknown erling – got inside the bastion. They almost reached her – they killed two lictors and their men and several of my knights, then escaped through the portali gate. The magia and the initiate did, at least. The erling is dead and the vorlok is still at large in the city.'

'Hromboli and Sister Faith are dead?' Dranit exclaimed. *There is justice, after all . . .*

'Aye,' Corbus replied. 'She had her throat ripped out and he . . . well, he died on his knees.'

'That's more than either deserved.'

'Just the sort of bilious nonsense I expect from you. They were highly effective upholders of law and justice, not that you care about such things.'

'They were sadists who perverted justice for self-gratification. But isn't it interesting that the Falcons remain so loyal to their captain? Maybe they believe she's more sinned against than sinner?'

The knights escorting the archon reacted to that with stony contempt, but Corbus went puce, no doubt considering the embarrassment of having renegades striking his bastion and escaping.

Enjoying his brother's discomfort, but conscious that Lubano was looking quite capable of knifing someone then and there, Dranit indicated the door. 'Well, I'm sure you've other places to be. If you need me, I have a table at Antonio's tonight.'

Corbus' nose wrinkled. 'Never heard of it.'

'That's because it's a family establishment in the docklands. But the cooking is good, the fish fresh and the wine isn't sour. Disinherited defensiors can't afford better.'

'Good. May you die in penury.' Corbus glanced at his knights. 'Let's go.'

They stamped out, Theomore sagged into a chair while Lubano followed them to the door then closed it, clearly seething. 'Are you all right, Lubi?' Dranit asked him.

'Those pricks. I should've—' Lubano bared teeth, scowling. 'I'm sorry, I let you down.'

'When they come raging in like that, it really is best just to lie down and take it. Fighting just makes it worse.' He poured more wine for them all, then sat. 'Holy Akka, this is getting deep, my friends. Things are unravelling, I can feel it.'

Theomore scowled. 'What it feels like is a disastrous mess, one which will give your brother an excuse to throw all the laws out of the window and impose martial law.'

'Maybe . . . or not.' Dranit gazed out at the window, wondering. 'Either way, we've got to go to Hyastar and help Siera Romara with her testimony . . . provided she makes it that far.'

When his back struck, Gram was already dead in his own mind, his spine broken and skull shattered. But instead, he hit water and went under. He'd forgotten the moat was there, but he was grateful for it, plunging into the filthy water, then thrashing to the surface, desperate for air because he'd forgotten to breathe.

He got his feet beneath him and floundered up the muddy slope. Looking up at the walls, he saw a few archers peering down; one shot at him, which got him moving, staggering until he sorted his limbs out. He tore towards the houses below, evading arrows until he crashed into an alley and out of range.

That they'd failed to rescue Romara tore at him, but he was sane enough to know he couldn't go back – maybe the others still lived, because there wasn't much pursuit, but seeking them would be suicidal. Letting his vyr shape fade until he was just a burly man in sodden clothing, reeking of stagnant water, he plunged through the city.

He had no idea where he was or how to get out, but the only place he knew was also the only one Elindhu and the others knew: Korki's house. If they were to reunite, perhaps they'd go there?

So he headed downslope towards the river, staying away from the main thoroughfares, where squads of soldiers had begun to appear, both Vestal men-at-arms and City Watch. Inside twenty minutes, he was knocking on the door of the tiny office on the third dock.

Korki looked up from her paperwork, her scarred face lighting up to see him, then fear clouded her face. 'Jagat, are all those bells 'cos of you lot? Get below, now!'

During a frightening next half hour, watchmen swarmed the docks, even searching Korki's premises and the warehouse where he was hiding – but they didn't open boxes, which was just as well, because Gram was sealed in one, surrounded by cheese and salami bound for the hinterlands.

Some time after they'd gone, he heard a tap on the lid and Korki whispered, 'Stay put and hold your piss in. We're moving you onto a barge.'

He endured an uncomfortable hour or more before the lid was prised off the crate and he found himself facing Korki, her friend and guardian Horto, and a malevolent-looking man with oily grey hair and whiskery jowls, who whistled and muttered, 'Jag me,' when Gram rose and towered over him.

'Who're you?' Gram asked suspiciously, looking around. They were indeed on a barge, being hauled along by a team of oxen along a wide river – presumably the Osprey. There was a mast and sails, but the wind was coming from directly upstream, so the canvas was furled and tied up.

'Folk call me Toad,' the ugly man responded, with a belch. 'An' you're Gram Larch of Avas, hmm? A fella what thinks he can smash 'is way into a bastion. A fella some are sayin' is in love with a fallen knight, one what knows Nilis Evandriel. I know some folk that wanna word wit' you.'

'What sort of word?' Gram asked.

'The kind that determines your future. The Queen of the Vyr wants to meet you.'

'There's a vyr queen? Agynea never spoke of one, and nor did my mother.'

'You think we tell everyone our secrets?' Toad sniffed. 'Be grateful, laggy-boy. There's some who'd rather a troublemaker like you was silenced before the Order find and break you. But if the Queen wants to meet you, it's an opportunity you daren't spurn.'

'He's right,' Korki put in, her marred face hopeful. 'This is a great gift, if you seize it.'

'If you say so,' Gram replied. 'Where next, then?'

'We disembark a kylo upstream. There'll be horses waiting, for you an' me,' Toad said. 'You'll be kneeling to the Queen by nightfall.'

Do not travel the shadows if guilt or sorrow are your companions, wise men said.

The Shadowlands were indeed a bad place to be when grieving a recent and powerful loss, but Elindhu had no choice. She kept Soren moving fast, drawing deep on her erling lore to find trails through the misty darkness and desolation, seeking another portali gate to get them out of here again before it became untenable.

They endured a harrowing couple of hours, mostly walking along a dead riverbed – the Osprey, in their world – while Fynarhea and Gram and Obanji and Soren's parents and her own myriad dead taunted or beseeched them from the mist. She held Soren's hand tight and kept her elobyne orb lit, despite her control being badly frayed. Without it, she knew they'd be prey to whatever ghosts truly haunted the Shadowlands.

'If you go to them, you never come back,' she reminded Soren – and herself – gripping the young man's hand tight when Obanji's voice called them.

All we've got left is each other.

Beyond seeing him to safety, she didn't know what to do next. Getting to Hyastar in time to witness Romara's hearing would be beset with difficulties: four hundred kylos in three days was a daunting journey, and without glyma the Shadowlands were too perilous. And what they could achieve if they got there, she had no idea. Beyond that, she'd run out of ideas. Jadyn might be still alive, but she doubted it, so all she had left was this one young man.

He's special, a fighter in a million, and he reminds me of Obanji so much it hurts. But the next time either of us use the glyma will probably kill us.

He'd lost his flamberge and she had to dispose of her staff as soon as she could. She couldn't imagine a future as an ordinary person, but once she'd got Soren to safety, that's what she faced. And he'd never become the knight he should have been. He was an outlaw now, and the Order was too thorough for him to join under a different name.

She wished to the highest heaven she and Obanji had retired when they could – but they'd been too committed to the Falcons to leave, and they'd believed time was on their side, that they could serve longer and still retire young enough to find a new life.

So much for that plan.

I have to get Soren somewhere safe, then let him go . . .

That was a heart-breaking thought too. She had come to care for him deeply, as one of her comrades – and then a bit more, for who and what he was, and for who he resembled. But the Order knew his name and hers, so nowhere inside the empire would be safe.

'Only I can give you peace,' the ghost of Obanji whispered in her ear. 'Come to me and let me show you.'

She steeled her mental barriers again, her attention snapping back to the here and now. 'Ah, here we are,' she told a silent, distracted Soren, leading him through thinning mist towards an earthen mound the size of a haystack – another barrow, the low gate smashed open.

Then she spun, realising he'd slipped from her grasp, and shrieked, '*Soren!*'

A tall Abuthan loomed out of the fog – for a moment she thought it was Obanji's wraith, but it was Soren, with a stricken look on his face.

'Fyn?' he blurted, gazing about blankly. 'Fynarhea? I heard her voice . . .'

Elindhu hurried to him and this time he saw her. His face went through loss, pain, disappointment and then recognition. He glanced over his shoulder. 'I heard Fyn call me . . .'

'He's not here,' she said, as kindly as she could manage. 'Come, this is the gate. We need to get out of this dead place and feel the sun on our skin.'

She led him into the barrow, opening the portali with a sing-song spell that soon had the sigils glowing a soft green. They passed through, clambering out of a small cave onto a hillside swathed in long grass, dun-coloured seed-heads bobbing in the breeze. Forested hills hemmed them in; Folkstein and the River Osprey were nowhere in sight. To the east, massive mountains rose: the Qor-Massif, in erling myth the home of the fabled Twelve. They slumped to the ground in relief, at no longer hearing the ghostly whispers of the Shadowlands.

Elindhu took off the lictor's robe she'd stolen, throwing it away despite its quality, then found a rock she could perch on to get her bearings. Soren joined her, putting an arm round her shoulders and resting his cheek against her tower of braids.

Their relationship had become as much about touch as anything else these past days, which felt dangerous. *I've felt my loss of glyma-control coming in moments like this*, she realised. *The warning signs are clear. I need to re-establish some distance between us . . . especially if we're to go our separate ways soon.*

'What are you thinking, Aunty?' Soren murmured.

She'd spent nearly two decades dealing with all the dramas of young knights trained to kill but forbidden love. She knew all the traumas they went through: the guilt, injury, bullying, lost limbs, lost friends, secret affairs, sexual repression, loss of nerve and suicidal urges. As a woman and a magia, it was expected that she – rightly or wrongly – would be a mentor for them all.

No wonder I never had children.

'I'm not thinking at all,' she muttered, then bucked herself up.

'Sorry, this damnable quest is killing us all. Fyn was my fault – I asked him to come. You are right to blame me.'

Soren squeezed her shoulder. 'I don't blame you, Aunty. Fyn told me you'd wanted him to leave, but he chose to stay. I blame the jagging Order and that stinking piece of shit on the throne and everyone in-between, but not you. It's all Akka's fault. He made the glyma evil. I hate Him.'

Some days, so do I, Elindhu thought.

'He's got a lot to answer for,' she agreed. 'Think what the Order could be, if the glyma didn't poison and corrupt everyone, and it didn't stop us from loving others.'

You'd have got to hold your Fynarhea, and I'd have married Obanji.

'All my life I wanted to be a Vestal knight,' Soren said morosely. 'But now, I honestly don't. Once this is over, I'll go north, find my sister and try to live a normal life.'

His words were hard to hear, even though she thought he was making the right decision. 'Soren, you're probably the most naturally gifted glyma-warrior I've ever met, and you can use the few mage-spells I've taught you better than some trainee mages. You could become Exemplar, if you set your mind to it.'

He shook his head. 'Even if they didn't know who I was, if I could re-enlist under a false name, I don't want to. To spend a decade or more suppressing every feeling and emotion? That will kill me, Aunty. I can't do it, I just can't.' There were tears running down his cheeks, for the dream he was casting aside.

She bowed her head and held him, to help him through the grief.

For a long while, Soren felt like he was still in the Shadowlands, but eventually the sun on his back and the warmth radiating from Elindhu's plump body revived him. He wiped his eyes, lifted his head and looked around, grateful she'd been with him when the ghosts called his name, because otherwise he'd have been helpless.

Soren, he could still hear Fynarhea whisper. *I'm waiting for you, in the trees.*

Elindhu's arm around his waist anchored him when guilt and longing threatened to drag him away. She was talking about finding horses so they could push on to Hyastar, then head north to seek his sister, but all he heard was Fynarhea wailing in the darkness. If he'd only moved faster, been more aware, he might have saved her. Elindhu thought Fyn had stayed out of loyalty; he knew the erling had stayed for him. This was his fault, not hers. The voices said so.

I mustn't go to her, he told himself, without conviction. He knew he would.

Eventually he realised Elindhu was looking up at him, her pink-cheeked, long-nosed face solemn, dangling a flask before him. 'It's Obanji's special liquor,' she told him. 'Two sips.'

He gulped down three, choked and blinked his vision clear. 'Pa drank, but he wouldn't let me. I used to sneak sips when he slept.' He winced at the bittersweet memory. 'I keep thinking of Fynarhea – just when I feel okay, I remember that she's dead.'

'It's survivors' guilt. We blame ourselves for not sharing our comrades' fate, and think we're dishonouring them by not constantly thinking of them. I know exactly how it feels.'

'Obanji?'

'Him, and many others over the years. You've seen the loyalty a pentacle feels for each other. In the Order, we often lose people, sometimes in the most meaningless ways. Death can be just stupid bad luck; other times, you see it coming and you can't do a thing to stop it. You just keep wondering if you could have done something differently, but the moment's gone.'

'I missed those crossbow bolts,' Soren said miserably. 'I should have seen them.'

'In the midst of a battle against four knights and a mage?' Elindhu remarked archly. 'You're being too hard on yourself.'

He hung his head. 'I suppose. But Fyn kept following me around and I never worked out how I felt about that. If I had, maybe he'd have been halfway home by now?'

'They say "don't speak ill of the dead",' Elindhu said, 'but we shouldn't mistake them for saints, either. Fynarhea was a confused mess, just like all young erlings, and insisted on staying. Remember the good things, the courage and friendship.'

'But if I could just see her again . . . But it was confusing. I never felt comfortable around her, the way I am now with you. At first I thought you were scary, but now I don't know what I'd do without you. Losing Obanji was awful, and I'd have died too, without you.'

'Sometimes, I catch you from the corner of my eye and I think you're him,' Elindhu said softly. 'It's your height and build and colouring, your voice, your beautiful smile. That accent. It breaks my heart.'

Then suddenly it was her crying and him holding her awkwardly. But he was grateful to be able to give comfort, not just soak it up. 'You were wrong, Aunty,' he said eventually. 'You said that the glyma stops us from loving each other. But I love you.'

She threw him a tart look. 'I love you too, Soren: as a *friend*. As your aunty.'

'I know,' he said gratefully. He took a breath and confessed the thing that troubled him most. 'I *wanted* to love Fynarhea, I really did – and it didn't really matter whether she was in male or female form. But it was like holding hands through the bars of a cell, not being able to do more. And she always made me feel like I was letting her down.'

'I know how it feels,' she told him. 'It's the holding back that drives us mad.'

'She got so angry that I wouldn't risk more, but I *couldn't*.'

'You're a good lad; you think of others first. But guilt doesn't become you. Sometimes luck runs out – that's what befell Fynarhea. I wish I'd kept her from harm's way, but I didn't.' She patted his knee. 'But neither Obanji or Fyn would want us to give up on life. They would want us to live and be happy. So let's do that.'

Soren felt the power of those words deeply. *To go on, yes. But not as a glyma-warrior.*

He said slowly, 'Do we . . . do we go to Hyastar?'

'To bear witness for Romara, but no more than that,' the magia said sadly. 'Without glyma, it's all we can do. Then we'll head for Beradin, find your sister and set you up somewhere safe.'

'What about you after that, Aunty?'

'I'm an erling,' she replied. 'It's time I remembered that.'

'You're a beautiful erling,' he said. 'It would be good for you to be your true self.'

To his surprise, Elindhu blushed. 'I've been disguised as a human most of my life. This is how I'm comfortable. But thank you, lad. You're very sweet.'

Then she rose, almost as if he'd got too close to something, and scanned the hillside. 'It's not good to sleep near these wild portali gates. The bastion ones are properly warded, but these aren't and sometimes the darkness slithers through. Let's put some distance between it and tonight's camp, shall we?'

They gathered their things and headed down the slope. They found a stream, which they followed to a larger river, a tributary of the Osprey, Elindhu thought. They decided to make camp while the light held. Elindhu found herbs and berries, and Soren, using the skills learned as a child from his father, managed to tickle a trout into his hands. They built a small fire, settled themselves around it and smiling at each other across the embers, ate their foraged supper.

Elindhu dozed off swiftly, but Soren couldn't rest. Even in her homely human form, Elindhu's face contained traces of erling, which reminded him sharply of Fynarhea.

'I'm sorry, Fyn,' he whispered, yet again. 'Why did you have to die?'

I didn't, the erling's voice whispered in his mind. *I'm waiting for you, by the river.*

He shuddered and jerked his head around, convinced he'd felt her cold breath against his neck.

'Soren?' Elindhu murmured dozily.

'Sorry, Aunty,' he murmured. 'It's okay. Go back to sleep.'

Exhaustion took her again and he gazed fondly at her sleeping face. She represented safety to him right now.

But she's losing it, Fynarhea whispered. *Her eyes bled. You're going to lose her, too.*

That truth chilled his heart.

I can't bear to lose anyone else, he thought numbly. *It's too much.*

Sleep fled entirely and finally, with a feeling of inevitability, he rose and shuffled into the trees to empty his bladder. The fire was all but dead, but the triple moons painted the night silver. The Skull had eyes tonight. They were watching him mercilessly.

The night noises went still and he became convinced someone was right behind him. But he dared not look.

There's no one there, he told himself.

Wrong again, Lover, Fynarhea whispered.

He felt a sudden chill and spun – and saw the moon-dusted silhouette of a wolf-headed woman, bare-breasted and wild, her amber eyes glinting in the moonlight. Right here, for him.

He should have looked away, but he couldn't. Their eyes locked and all thought trickled away, leaving him empty and mesmerised. He had no choice but to go to her.

19

Swept Along

What was the Aegis?

The Sanctor Wardens are gone, weakened by decadence, outlawed and eventually annihilated. The Hierophant forbids research into them, and ancient texts concerning them are burned. The official line is that they had no arcane powers. So tell me: why was the Hierophant so afraid of them?

URGAN FENNOKLI, HISTORIAN, BEDUM-MUTAZA, 1417

Sea of Pelas
Autumn 1472

In the wake of the seiche wave, the sea was dangerously lumpy and unpredictable, and for a time all the three of them could do was keep the felucca afloat and ride it out.

However, before long, things calmed down, the prevailing north-easterly returned and Evandriel and Aura began the painfully slow, tedious process of tacking back and forth, working through a smoke and brimstone twilight to get back on course. Jadyn plied the tiller, resting his knee, while Aura and Evandriel took turns working the sails or resting.

They heaved sighs of relief when they found an island before darkness swallowed the remaining light. Once safely anchored in the lee, they concocted a warming stew, which they ate with way-bread and washed down with water, then sought sleep. Evandriel took the tiller bench, wrapped in a blanket, while Jadyn and Aura climbed into the cramped canvas-walled cabin forward of the mast. He pressed himself to her soaking back, wrapped his arm around her, inhaling wet hair, and thanking Elysia for her mercy, toppled into oblivion.

Waking up was like emerging from beneath the waves and learning to breathe air again. Aura could feel the salt-water stiffness in her clothing and her body was chilled to the bone, except where Jadyn lay against her back, breathing softly. The air smelled of smoke and brimstone, foul to the nose and sulphurous in the mouth.

Perhaps the Days of Ending are here, she mused. *Wouldn't it be just my luck, to find love at the world's end?*

She wriggled free, clambered to the side, dropped her breeches and peed over the edge, then looked about. Evandriel had been asleep, shivering in his dream, but he woke at the sound of her footsteps and sat up, yawning. The island just a few dozen paces away was really just an atoll, barely larger than the one where they'd met the erlings, but there were a few wind-bent trees and scrubby bushes. The sea was flat again, the wind barely shifting their pennants.

She went find Jadyn awake; they hauled up the anchor together, then jumped overboard and waded ashore. They wrapped a mooring rope around a rock and with the help of the gentle incoming tide pulled the ship closer to shore and anchored.

'We find fresh water, maybe food,' she called, taking Jadyn's hand possessively.

'I'll make breakfast,' Evandriel replied, tossing them the water gourds to fill. 'Take your time, there's no wind, so we're not going anywhere soon.'

The interior of the island was surprisingly lush, and bigger than they'd expected, with welcome pools of rainwater and some fruit-laden coconut palms. Aura didn't wait to strip off, desperate to rinse the salt from her clothing – and give him something to lust over.

She watched Jadyn hungrily as he set about salvaging fallen coconuts and filling the gourds. He was looking good, despite being a pink-faced, white-bodied northerner. The privations of travel were making him leaner, defining chest and belly muscles and already powerful shoulders and thighs. He was getting better to look at all the time, she decided.

Finally the tasks were done and she pulled him down on a bed of fallen palm leaves she'd made, though she'd have done this on a bed of nails right now. And once she'd persuaded him to put aside the bad advice of priests and prudes and press his mouth to her lower lips, it got very good indeed.

'You like?' she sighed, in the aftermath of some real love-making, enjoying his heat against her side and the lovely post-coital ache in her groin and thighs. 'Is as you dream?'

'It's wonderful,' he said, beaming foolishly. 'You're wonderful. Even the . . . um?'

'Cunning lips, is called,' she answered, not entirely sure she'd got that right. 'Am liking tresa mucho. You want please Aura, this you do, until orgasmus. Then, you use her as liking.'

He coloured, but said emphatically, 'Whatever my queen desires.'

'Buena. But we must make talk now, of babies.'

He flinched in alarm. 'What? Are you—? I mean, if you are, that's wonderful, but—'

'No, am not with bebe,' she snorted. 'Am not so stupid. But we must talk, to avoid, si? Am not wanting bebe now, too dangerous, non posso, si? But am soon fertile, comprenez? Church say we abstain now, fourteen days, from tomorrow. No sexing this week, or in blood week.'

Clearly he'd been told a little about the rhythms of a woman's body, probably so he knew when to tiptoe around Romara to avoid being shredded.

He still groaned. 'Two weeks? I wish—'

'Si, Aura nor be liking neither, certa! But some men and women do other things, so to not go mad. More sins that priests forbid. You know these things?'

'Um, I've heard of them . . .' Jadyn said, his face going even redder.

'My thinking be this,' she told him. 'We be newly in love so no sexing will make crazy. Am knowing this. So I think we choose sin for now, si?'

She saw the conflict between his pure and disciplined training and the need to explore their new relationship. Despite the exhaustion of their long days of near-constant labour aboard the felucca, she thought he needed her as desperately as she needed him. It was as if every danger made their bodies blindly reach out for something life-affirming.

'I'm in your hands,' he told her.

Thank you Akka, for sending me this man, she thought warmly.

I didn't send you that man, Akka grumbled in her right ear as she and Jadyn dozed in another post-coital haze, sometime later. *He's nothing to do with me.*

Nor me, Urghul the Devourer interrupted, in her rasping serpentine voice. *Sergio's more my style. But I like what you're making of him.*

Akka sniffed. *A pure-hearted knight, corrupted and fouled by sin. I'm disgusted.*

Good with his tongue, too, Urghul snickered. *Some men are too proud to do that, but he's eager and malleable.*

'Are you all right?' Jadyn murmured.

Huh? Aura twisted to face him, slightly alarmed. 'Why?'

'You were making noises in your sleep,' he told her. 'Like in a dream.'

She found herself blushing hotly, a rare thing for her. 'Uh, did I say words?'

'Some, but it was all in Nepari so I didn't understand,' he replied, apparently truthfully.

She sagged in relief. 'Maybe best you no learn Nepari, eh?' she said, and changed the subject. 'So, where we go now? Why we sail still towards volcano? This be madness, neya?'

He stroked her cheek. 'I don't know. But it's probably time we went back and asked.'

Jadyn felt like Aura had ignited a radiance inside him. With her, the world felt perfect, and all his old conceptions of virtue, sin and morality felt not so much wrong as irrelevant. Each moment felt like pearls stolen from the Devourer's Jaws, precious, and far above such trivialities as Scripture.

They told us only Akka can make people happy, but I'll never be happier than this.

But life demanded they keep moving, so they reluctantly cleaned up again and returned to the cove where the felucca was anchored. As they had to wade through chest-high water to get back aboard, they decided that dressing was pointless. They passed strings of gourds and coconuts up to Evandriel, who was taking everything blithely in his stride.

'I hold the human body the most beautiful thing in creation,' he told them. 'But you can both get dressed now. You're making me feel old.'

Over breakfast and coconut milk, Jadyn asked about their next destination.

'The oracle told us that this island, Kimusamusa, was destroyed when Ur-Krakos fell,' Evandriel explained. 'She said there were no references to an existing island called that name. But men rename places all the time – every settlement on the Inner Seas has at one time or another had Bedumi, Mutazi, Zynochi or Aquini names over the years, and the isles are no different. So I'm aiming for the Sora-bellos Islands at the heart of the Volcanic Ring. We will find people there who will know the traditions and can point us to Kimusamusa.'

'But the clues said we were to seek the centre of the world?' Jadyn replied uncertainly.

'They did. And if you were a Pelasian, where is the centre of your world?'

'Pelasia,' Jadyn conceded reluctantly.

'Exactly. Listen, I made the same mistake as you when I arrived at that lighthouse. I interpreted the "centre of the world" as Bedum-Mutaza. But in the days of the Pelasian Sea-Kings, Pelas was the heart of the world. Our histories name them pirates now, but Silas was a legitimate kingdom and even Bedum-Mutaza paid tribute to them. That older mosaic dated from that period; which is doubtless why it was covered over.'

'So clues for centre of world mean Pelasia?' Aura put in, frowning. 'But Pelasia die before Wardens, neya? In Warden time, Pelasia non importanto. Is strange, this, si?'

'Ah,' Evandriel sat up, 'you might think so, but there was an overlap, for the earliest Wardens were living while Pelasia still ruled the waves. It was in their time that many of the principles of navigation and time-keeping were devised. Do you know what a meridian is?'

They shook their heads.

'A meridian is a point on a map showing a degree shift in longitude – those are the vertical lines on a map or globe. There are three hundred and sixty of them, but the scholars of the time made the first meridian – the *prime* meridian, which marks the dividing line between east and west – at the place *then* believed to be the centre of the world. They called it the Corossi: the Heart. It runs north to south through Vandarath, the Gulf of Foyland, Foyland itself, quite possibly Vanashta Baanholt, and the Sorabellos Isles, where Silas, the Pelasian capital, lay.'

'So the Wardens used the Corossi as the centre of the world,' Jadyn concluded.

'Exactly. And there was a warden monastery in the Sorabellos Isles,' Evandriel added suddenly. 'I'd forgotten that!'

'So Bedum-Mutaza was mistake,' Aura groaned, 'and Sherkaza was to fix mistake! Why Wardens not send us from Vanashta Baanholt to Silas, with no lighthouse in middle?'

Evandriel *tsked*, then said, 'I think that's my fault. I leapt to that conclusion and it was my note that guided you to Bedum-Mutaza. I missed clues, and caused you to miss them too.'

'So did we miss something vital at the lighthouse?' Jadyn wondered.

Evandriel stroked his goatee thoughtfully. 'Perhaps. Or maybe, if others had passed through before us, they removed clues – pulling up the ladder after climbing it, so to speak. I don't know. But we're on track now. He tapped his head. 'I'm sure of it – in here.'

'Do you think we might find real, living Wardens?' Jadyn asked.

'Che posso, si?' Aura exclaimed. 'Maybe they teach us, si? Teaching self be hard.'

'That's what I'm hoping, too,' Evandriel replied. 'We know now that when they went into hiding, they left the trail we're following, so perhaps there'll be a few waiting for us, or even if there's none, some repository of knowledge we can study.'

It was something to hope for.

'What about those "Serrafim" or "Alephi" or "angels", whatever they were?' Jadyn asked.

'I have theories, but I know nothing more than what Emboma told us: that they come from Nexus Isle,' Evandriel replied. 'But let's think on that: what's at Nexus? Elobyne. And who controls it? The Hierophant and his court.'

'So powerful people can make self into angel?' Aura said, in a sickly voice.

'Using energy stolen from nature and men,' Evandriel finished. 'Just so.'

'If more people knew,' Jadyn exclaimed, 'surely they'd rise against them.'

'Would they? The Vyr Rebellion began many decades ago, but nothing changes – in fact, it gets worse.'

They fell into a despondent silence, until Aura said, 'Maybe it be worse because evil angels are afraid? Maybe of aegis? Maybe of us?'

'Or maybe it's because the End of All Things is truly coming?' Jadyn suggested. 'But what can *anyone* do against creatures like that?'

'Much, I suspect,' Evandriel replied. 'Think about it: they still operate in secrecy – why? Surely it's because they fear the masses will turn against them if they're revealed. Mankind abhors difference, and we always tear down those who try to rise above us. Enough hungry rats can bring down a lion. And what they are is abhorrent: predators who drain our world to perfect themselves. So they must creep about in the shadows and divide us to conquer. If we can lay their existence bare, the tide may turn.'

'You mean *capture* one?' Jadyn asked. 'Even the monks' fire-trap barely contained them.'

'But it did, and so three of them perished,' Evandriel replied. 'It's possible.'

'You think we three could capture one?' Jadyn clarified doubtfully. Aura lifted her chin. 'Si, I believe.'

Evandriel smiled, and nodded. 'Aye, I think it can be done.'

'Then I do too.'

The wind was rising, and it was time to sail on, though the sky was still dark and the air tinged with smoke and sulphur. But there was no indication of aftershocks and the virulent orange glow on the horizon had faded away. Once they were safely underway, Aura went to sleep, leaving the two men to pilot the felucca into the heart of the darkness.

'Will there be more eruptions?' Jadyn wondered.

'I hope not,' Evandriel answered. 'Volcanism involves pressure building and being released. My hope is that this eruption has eased that pressure – though it may have destroyed that which we seek. We can only press on with hope, while hoping those pursuing us lose theirs.'

The explosive blast of the eruption triggered a torrent of alarming visions for Vazi Virago, of placid seas turning wild, and a storm that destroyed all in its path – including Sherkaza Island. But fortunately, the harbour where their ship was berthed faced south, away from the direction of the blast, and that offered hope.

Even so, foreseeing that the sea would rise alarmingly, so high that any ship tied to the docks would be dragged under by their mooring ropes unless they were cut free in time, she warned Borghart and they pelted down the road back to the harbour.

'A seiche is coming,' she shouted. 'We've got to get aboard and get out to the lee of the island.'

Still immersed in residual glyma, he was virtually blind to the coming calamity, but he didn't question her, just ran as hard as she. The harbour was in uproar from the boom of the eruption, but she had neither the time nor the inclination to save anyone but them-selves. They cast off and got out into the middle of the small bay just before the giant wave swept around and in, flooding the docks and destroying many of the low-lying buildings. Most of the anchored ships were destroyed, smashed against the sea wall, as she'd foreseen. The death toll was likely in the hundreds, even thousands.

They're just Pelasians, she thought stonily, *enemies of the empire.*

But she'd never felt less like the heroine of her own story.

Trapped in the harbour, riding out a massive shockwave and a torrid wind, they watched the devastation and its aftermath in silent awe. She refused to let the captain rescue anyone – they'd have quickly been besieged. After the first few were hurled back into the waters, the rest realised the futility and splashed away – or drowned. People were now streaming up to the plateau and the old monastery. She'd seen farms up there, but she doubted they were self-sufficient without the fishing boats and traders. Their suffering had only begun.

That's not my problem, either. Pirate scum.

'When will it be safe to move on?' Borghart asked, equally heartless. 'That pilot said Kaen and Perafi left on a northwest bearing – that's the direction of the eruption,' he noted, as they watched the already destitute town descend into chaos. 'Is that coincidence?'

'Are you saying Kaen and Perafi can make volcanoes erupt?' Vazi snorted. 'I don't think so. The real question is whether they rode out the seiche or are currently learning to swim.'

Their eyes met. She was purged of glyma, and he was trying to manage his levels down, so he said. Without the ability to scry – which had proved fruitless anyway – and unable to find their prey through the aegis because Kaen and Perafi possessed it themselves, they had only logic and luck to guide them. They needed a breakthrough.

'I've been thinking,' Borghart said eventually. 'When we try to find them, we get nowhere, because the aegis veils them. But we know they're hunting the aegis, just as we are. What if we concentrate instead on doing that: seeking the aegis?'

'But they clearly have clues we've not seen or understood,' she replied dourly.

'But we have: I saw that second mosaic as it crumbled. There was a volcano in it.'

'This whole archipelago is made up of active, dormant and extinct volcanoes, fool.'

His face hardened. 'But only one has just erupted. Let's go there.'

She went to scoff, but then thought, *Why not?* She had no better suggestions.

Concentrating on the aegis, she framed that thought as a question: *Should we seek the recently erupted volcano?* She felt that enquiry float out into the world, and then the visions began, of a blackened rock in the ocean, spouting smoke and gouts of orange flame. In her mind's eye she swooped in ... and saw an outcropping below the crater rim, an old stone building of the same architectural style as Vanashta Baanholt.

'Yes,' she breathed, 'you're right. We must find that volcano ...'

Their eyes met and she felt a strange, alien sense of communion, of shared thought and will, that struck her like an arrow, piercing her armour and binding them.

As if sensing her weakness, he laid a hand on her arm. With his intense eyes boring into hers, he said, 'I dreamt last night that you saved the empire. You cut down the Falcons, one by one, and saved us all.'

'It's my destiny,' she replied, awestruck by the sense that she wasn't alone ...

... and then recoiled in furious dread, because *nobody* ever got inside her defences. She backed away, saying, 'I'll find the captain, give him his orders.'

Then she spun and fled, before he saw through her completely.

I belong to no one.

The captain received Vazi received warily, still scarred by the escape from Sherkaza harbour. She'd saved his ship, but nobody else; he looked on her with fear, but no reverence.

My heartlessness is laid bare, she thought, watching him shudder in anticipation of her next command.

'Captain, I have fresh orders,' she told him. 'Northwest, as fast as we can sail.'

'But the eruption was that way! Fumes ... poison ... fire from the sky—'

'In a few hours, the northeasterly will regain impetus and push the smoke away. We will not be poisoned, and the danger of burning debris is already over. Our mission remains.'

He wanted to argue, to assert control, to turn back and protect his ship, the one thing in this world he truly loved. But he was terrified, and that counted for more.

They were tacking onto their new heading within minutes.

Enapara had once been a woman. Her mortal life had begun forty years ago, when she was one of the Hierophant Trejanus' concubines. Not a wife, because those thirty poor souls were chosen only for reasons of State – good birth, great wealth and military or commercial alliances. They shared Trejanus' bed once a month, for a few minutes only.

She took up the rest of his time, a wife in all but name.

I adore you, my honeypot, Trejanus would tell her. *I crave you constantly – your ebony skin and scarlet lips – your lush bosoms and booming laugh. But most of all . . .*

You like my cooking, she would giggle, and feed him another morsel, a sweetling, or a savoury parcel . . .

Mmm, that's right. He would laugh, slap her rump and devour the treat.

She'd been born a slave in Khetia, until the Prince of Dagoz had heard of the pretty, plump girl who was mistress of every culinary delight, a genius who could make one's mouth dissolve into ecstasy. He'd presented her to Trejanus when the Hierophant began his year on the Throne of Hide – and she'd become his, utterly.

The thirty-first wife, they quickly came to call her.

When the year was over, Trejanus took her north, already carrying his child. They'd grown old together, and when he ascended to immortality, he'd chosen her to join him in eternity, ahead of all thirty of his true wives – they had been walled up alive in his memorial.

The rites of immortality began with taking the sacred seed into her body and culminated in a night inside a cavern of pure elobyne, where the light disintegrated her mortal flesh and rebuilt it . . . if you could see it through. The process had almost destroyed her, but she'd emerged, no longer old and obese but slender as the girl she'd once been, her skin still ebony and her hair still black, but all human weakness gone: an Alephi, anointed by Jovan Lux himself.

To her great sorrow, Trejanus was a pile of charred bones.

If she'd still been human, she would have wept.

Instead, she found herself alone among her new brethren, the plaything of immortal predators, who bullied, used and abused her, for she had no protector and they were no angels. The cruelty she suffered was like nothing she'd ever known in her mortal life. She had often considered casting herself onto a pyre and burning herself to death, if only she could have found a fire hot enough.

But at her lowest ebb, Genadius claimed her – not as lover or cook, but as an acolyte. *You are of holy blood now,* he told her. *It's time to truly earn it.* He taught her to use the gifts her transfiguration had given her – mastery of glyma and aegis, flight and the blade. He became her protector, her true master.

But now her saviour was screaming – she could feel his agony and anguish, even smell his burning flesh, though he was thousands of kylos away. His cries, low and sonorous, drew her southwest, following the clues his treacherous son Eindil had given. But the trail of sound was imprecise and vague, she felt her master's anguish deepen as the hours passed, and still she couldn't find him.

Three days later, under starry skies and the triple moons, she heard a devastating blast, saw a giant seiche engulf atolls and coastal areas of the larger islands and found herself in a hot, sulphurous headwind, flying through smoke so thick she had to swoop low and in sight at times. She saw refugee fleets fleeing the vyr torn apart by heavy seas, and the ravenous schools of sharks which swam around them. But the only thing that mattered to her was her master, whose wailing cries tore at what remained of her heart.

She followed his pain to a long, narrow island, with towering cliffs and a crescent harbour at one end. There was a town there, hopelessly wrecked, the harbour choked with broken timber bobbing wreckage and bloated bodies.

But there were intact buildings on a ridge along the top, and farmlands were still being tilled. Her master's cries came from up there. She followed them into a recently abandoned building, where some refugees were sheltering – she put them out of their misery, then descended further, following the sound of her master's torment.

There she found the treacherous firepit concealed beneath the furnace, in which the charred husk of Genadius lay in still glowing coals, the flames gone but the damage going on and on, drawn out by his slowing of the passage of time through his body. What she drew forth appalled her: a blackened, sizzling pile of bones with the meat roasted off. Only the merest spark of life was preserved in his slow-beating heart and what remained of his brain.

Emotionally, she was unmoved, despite all he'd done for her. Pity had been excised from her, along with all other emotions. But he was her master, and exerting his will. She felt a compulsion as urgent as breathing to save him.

Sacrifices were required.

So she broke the threads of distorted time binding him, opened a vein in her left breast, just above her heart, and pulled his mouth to the blood flow. Unconsciously, instinctively, he sealed his charred lips over the wound and she felt the first steady, debilitating draw. She didn't care: to give him the succour he needed, she'd give every drop of her own cold, liquid elobyne blood, the holy elixir of Jovan. The Blood of the One, replete with shimmering power, was the panacea that could give one eternity.

Under the starry darkness, she suckled him like a child as he first took her blood and then, while she looked on dreamily, he ate the breast he drank from, and then the other, before burrowing into her belly, devouring as he went. As he did, the ash flaked from his charred bones and what was left of his ravaged flesh began to reform.

What will be left of me when you wake? she wondered as he fed. *Will you even know it is me?*

It didn't matter, so long as he lived. She faded away as he feasted.

Finally she was just bones, except for her face, which he left intact. It wore a beatific smile.

20

Akka Protects the Righteous

Blood Trials

Resolving court cases by duelling – Blood Trials – was once legal, but nowadays no civilised nation permits such travesties in which evidence, morality and reason are put aside in favour of legalised brawling. It only persisted so long because Akkanite priests had a traditional role in such combats, and wouldn't surrender the privilege. 'Akka protects the Righteous,' the Scriptures read. Only when the Church and Crown were united by Jovan Lux was the practice abandoned, though it remains on the statutes, at the Hierophant's discretion.

CHRONICLES OF THE NORTH, 1448

Miravia
Autumn 1472

Elindhu jolted awake, her instincts telling her that something was wrong. The grassy glade by the river was dark, the moons westering; only the ominous gaze of the Eye was above, the Skull and Dragon's Egg lost in the treetops. But that was enough to show her that the blanket on the other side of the dead fire was empty.

'Soren?' she called anxiously.

She lit her elobyne orb, very gently, just enough to see by and no more, knowing her control was hanging by a thread. Then she let instinct guide her, circling their little camp, calling softly. She found no sign of him, so she picked some of his black curly hair from his blanket and scryed with them. Even then, nothing came.

Which means he's either underground or under water, she thought. *Or dead.*

'Damn it, lad, where have you gone?' she asked the night.

But the only reply was the moaning of the wind in the pines, the river's murmur and the susurration of the long grass. Her voice, like her hope, died on the night air.

He's not here, Obanji's voice murmured from the woods. *You've lost him.*

'Oba?' she gasped, because in that moment, she did believe in ghosts.

Come to me, he whispered. *I'm waiting for you. Over here, in the trees.*

That's when she realised what must have happened. *Soren followed the shadow voices . . .*

Her throat constricted as she realised that she was too late, that she'd never find him now . . . unless she followed them, too.

Soren glimpsed Fynarhea at the river's edge, but she'd vanished before he reached her, only to reappear downstream among the willows, calling to him. She'd gone back to her wild erling shape, as she'd been when he first saw her under the moonlight in Semmanath-Tuhr, a wild thing, a bare-breasted woman with a wolf's head, magnificent and alluring. She'd stalked him then, tried to lure him away.

Now he was hunting her.

I should have gone with you then, his tangled thoughts kept repeating. *We'd have never left Semmanath-Tuhr, and you'd still be alive . . .*

He glimpsed her again, closer, a flash of amber eyes, sometimes her woman's face, sometimes her wolf visage. He caught the whispered words, asking him to believe in her, to follow, pleas he couldn't deny. He moved faster and so did she, down a gully, up a slope, around a hill and across a stream. Every now and then he'd catch sight of her: the silver of starlight on smooth flesh and fur, those entrancing eyes. *Imagine risking your life for pleasure*, he remembered her saying, that stupid day when he'd been offered the paradise of her body and refused it.

I can't be hurt now, she whispered from a copse of tall elms with carved trunks. *Here, we can do what we like.*

All reason was erased as the musky scent of her, wild and fresh, wafted back to him, enflaming him, driving him on. He began to run, bursting through into the circle of the trees, a bare patch of ground where nothing grew. He dashed into the middle, looking around wildly, calling her name—

The ground opened up and he fell through . . . into the Shadowland.

For a moment he floundered, trying to catch his balance, because the fall had been momentary, really just a *shifting* beneath his feet – but now he was in the Talam-Argith, on a flat piece of ground ringed by petrified trees wreathed in mist.

The dislocation restored his reason – he *knew* he shouldn't be here, that whoever he'd seen *couldn't* be Fynarhea, that this was a trap – until he saw her again, staring at him from out of the mist, naked and wanting and perfect, and all thought collapsed again. Crying her name, he stumbled after her. The mist closed in around him, hiding her, and he bumped into dead trees, then real vegetation, the first he'd ever seen in the Shadowlands, though he gave that scarcely a thought, because all that mattered was finding Fynarhea and giving himself to her.

Suddenly she was before him, one hand over her groin, the other reaching for him, her gaunt but alluring face focused entirely on him, her lips parted hungrily, her wolf-eyes alive with passion.

That instant, his mind froze his body, because she was standing on *thin air* above a hole in the ground which was glittering with stars.

She smiled. His flash of fear dissolved. He stared, awed by her, and offered her his hand.

She took it, and pulled him in . . .

This is a bad place, Elindhu worried. *Dear Elysia, tell me Soren didn't come this way.*

Akka's handmaiden, as was her wont, made no reply, but the wind whispered to her in Obanji's voice, promising her love and faithfulness, the home they'd dreamed of by the bay in Mardium, an eternity of joy and laughter. *Come to me, I'm waiting for you.*

Sickened, she knew that Soren must have succumbed to just such words, perhaps hours ago.

I'm too late, she thought bitterly as she hurried on, doing what everyone who'd ever entered the Talam-Argith was told not to do and following the voices.

Officially, ghosts were imaginary, and the voices were too. But no one who experienced the Talam-Argith doubted they were real. Every year, dozens of people who entered this dreary realm, coursers, knights and soldiers, vanished, despite being forewarned.

Tonight, Elindhu felt a greed in the whispers she'd not heard before, perhaps because they could see that she was hearkening. *And maybe their appetite is already whetted.* She scurried through the pines, following glimpses of a big black man in an Order tabard. His voice when he called warmed her heart and made her throat dry in fear and longing.

Then she saw elm trees, tall and leafy, with runes carved into the bark of the trunks, the secret names of the Twelve, and a bare space in the middle. *A portali gate*, she realised immediately. Obanji stood there, lit by starlight, gazing back at her. Her skin prickled and she risked a glyma-light, making the shadows shrink away.

It shone right through Obanji's body, and for a split-second she glimpsed something else, a dark and hungry *thing* – and then he vanished through the gate in a flash of emerald light. She stepped forward, bracing herself, and a moment later the ring of elms was replaced by petrified trees, the small space surrounded by mist.

This way, Obanji called from the edge of the fog. *The boy went this way.* Then he smiled, heartbreakingly. *It's so good to see you, 'Lindhu. I've missed you.*

She went after him, stumbling through the fog as the petrified trees became real, living ones, and that made her stop in wonder, pushing aside the strange myopic urgency she'd felt since hearing Obanji's voice.

Nothing grows here, she thought, planting her feet. *This place has been dead for two centuries.* The Talam-Argith had once been a living place, but it died when elobyne was discovered. The forests withered to dust and the streams ran dry. Of course the Order denied the discovery of elobyne and the death of the Talam Argith were linked, even as they captured all the Warden havens containing a portali gate and claimed them as bastions.

She touched the nearest tree, an oak, marvelling at the mossy bark and green leaves.

Elindhu, there's more, Obanji called. *Come, my love, it's this way.*

She gripped her staff two-handed and began to think like a mage again. She risked loss of control by just touching the glyma, she knew, but her fears for Soren steeled her resolve, helping her regain a measure of control. She conjured shields and advanced warily, as if into battle, following Obanji's silhouette deeper into this grove of living foliage, until she emerged into a dell of thick grass and clumps of graveweed, the violet flowers bobbing in unfelt winds.

Obanji awaited her there, standing on thin air above a lightless hole in the ground, his weathered face creased into a smile, his big hands open to welcome her.

'My dearest Elindhu,' he said in his resonant, beloved voice. 'Welcome to eternity.'

Tar-Vestallis, Hyastar

The journey to Hyastar took all night and the following day, marching through the Shadowlands on a night when the voices in the mist were especially menacing. Romara thought she heard Gram accusing her of betrayal, Jadyn hissing spite and Aura laughing at her wounds, but she ignored them and concentrated on staying mounted while Lady Augusta Martia's men led her horse through the gloom. Eventually, they reached a hill topped by a beacon and emerged safely inside the mighty Tar-Vestallis bastion, home of the Vestal Order.

She had been here before, of course, several times. The first was her induction as a knight, and she'd returned several times for big events, even attending an Exemplar Tourney once. Her proudest moment had been in this place, when she accepted command of the Falcon Century. Every visit, she'd felt part of a great tradition, an angel fighting on the side of right.

Now her life in the Order felt like a big lie.

Lady Augusta's group surrendered her into the custody of stony-faced knights and grandmasters who gazed at her with pitying contempt, mouthing phrases like, 'It always surprises you, who falls,' and 'Corruption lies deep in some.' She was locked in a cell that was at least dry and clean, fed gruel and given a piss-bucket. They left her in the manacles that deadened her to the glyma, but they didn't chain her to the wall and best of all, no lictors came.

No one at all came that first night, or the next day.

But the following morning, the grille opened and after she'd been warned to stay away from the door, locks clicked and it swung to admit Dranit Ritter, accompanied by Lubano. He had news that set her heart beating.

'Your friends escaped. The magia and the young initiate – Elindhu and Soren, yes? – got away through the bastion's portali gate. Gram Larch fell into the moat, then vanished. There was a young erling with them, though, and he died. We don't know his name.'

Romara frowned, not sure who that erling could be, though the news that her comrades lived rekindled hope in her breast. 'Elysia be praised,' she blurted, tears springing to her eyes.

'Not all my news is good,' Dranit cautioned. 'Those who brought your plight to our attention have paid the ultimate price. Segara Verber was taken by the lictors and tortured to death.'

Romara knew Segara Verber, who'd toured the western bastions giving advice and counsel to female initiates. 'She didn't deserve that,' she choked. 'She was a fine knight.'

Dranit hadn't finished. 'The former knight Tevas Nicolini, who tipped off Siera Segara, was also murdered, while trying to leave Folkstein.'

'Tevas?' she gasped, shocked and saddened. 'He had a change of heart?'

'Evidently,' Dranit said gravely. 'His last act was to kill his master, Elan Sandreth, which ended the Family Sandreth's claim to your estate, as Elan predeceases you.'

Tevas remembered himself at the end, she thought wonderingly. *Elysia grant him mercy.*

'There's a trail of death behind me,' she sighed. 'I never sought that.'

'However, not only the virtuous suffered,' Dranit concluded. 'When your friends broke into the bastion to rescue you, they found Lictor Hromboli and Sister Faith torturing Siera Segara. They killed both, and those gaolers helping them.'

The dark place inside her growled with pleasure. 'Perhaps divine justice is a real thing.'

'Perhaps, but it doesn't help you. The standing orders are that you will speak before the High Council, then be executed the following day. That's irrevocable. What I'm here to do is to help prepare your testimony.'

With that, they began work, refining her story so that it would best resonate with the High Council. It was an arduous task, as he insisted on detail and precision; over the course of the day, many, many sheets of parchment were covered, scored through, screwed up and discarded. Romara came to truly appreciate that Dranit Ritter was working wholeheartedly against his brother, for he was utterly tenacious in extracting every drop of outrage from her tale, turning it into a burning diatribe against Order corruption and the destructive aspects of elobyne. His motives appeared to be vengeance and righteousness, but he couldn't help revealing glimpses of growing up in the shadow of a tyrannical elder brother, with Corbus invariably getting the best of every clash. Their mutual loathing was clearly virulent.

His reaction to her tale was also instructive; he knew much of the vyr and fallen knights, and many aspects of her tale had him nodding sagely, having heard similar accounts before – although when she told him how Gram had been able to leech her glyma-energy to keep her from falling over the edge into blood-rage, Dranit's astonishment, turning to intrigue, soon had him bombarding her with questions. 'He actually *stole energy* from you? What did that feel like? Could you prevent it? Did he affect your comrades in the same way? What else can you tell me about it?'

She answered as best she could, hoping such anomalies would

interest the High Council just as much, and lend weight to her testimony.

He was visibly disturbed when she related Jadyn's reports of finding triple-shard clusters in Solabas that were palpably destroying the landscape. 'Nilis Evandriel is right about us,' she told him: the first time she'd admitted it to herself. 'We are the enemy of our own world.'

'Perhaps, but the Order lives and dies with elobyne,' Dranit reminded her. 'That fact overrides all others. Some in the hierarchy might privately admit it to be true, but they don't care enough to want elobyne use ended.'

'But it's the Order's future at stake, too – maybe our whole world's future!'

'The Order's future is secure as long as they have elobyne, or so they believe. The wellbeing of the empire's subjects comes a distant second to keeping hold of power and status, at least to those with that status.'

She carefully omitted all reference to Semmanath-Tuhr, because that would bring down the Order upon the erlings there, but she did speak of the aegis. Dranit was clearly fascinated by her account of Vanashta Baanholt and the Exemplar's presence there, but he doubted any of it could be used against Corbus. 'He'll brush it off as a matter for the scholars, and he's likely right.'

'You believe me about all this, don't you?' she asked.

Dranit pulled a wry face. 'Of course. I have no illusions about the Order: I've had to deal with the aftermath of many atrocities, such as when knights run amok and destroy ordinary lives, while the hierarchy covers it up. I've been threatened with ruin, even death, for standing up for victims of abuse and murder. I've been disinherited, seen my marriage collapse and lost many friends.' He sighed, then looked at her and smiled. 'And made one or two new ones.'

His words reminded her that it wasn't just Vestal knights who fought against evil, and there were many other forms of courage besides waving a sword around.

Before he departed, he told her that outside in the streets, Order centuries were parading about wearing armbands in support of either

Corbus Ritter or Augusta Martia, and there had already been some brawling. Sides were being taken amid growing anger, as fractures in the High Council spilled down the Order's chain of command.

'The Order is tearing itself apart,' Dranit said. 'Your testimony could ignite a schism – Corbus is trying to use that risk to shut your hearing down, but even he can't overrule the High Council.'

'What of the Hierophant?'

'Day Court emissaries have been seen at the Archon's Palace, where Corbus arrived yesterday. Rumours abound, but they've not made any public proclamations.'

'And the Night Court?'

'Nothing as yet. But they'll be watching, and they hold the real power.'

She eyed the door. 'Can we trust these guards not to do Corbus' work for him?'

'We have to. The Justiciary Legion is sworn to be impartial.' He swept up his papers, then sat back down, facing her. 'The key to all this, as far as I can see, is gaining permission to cast the spell you were told of. If Oculus Tempus does as you were told, providing proof that elobyne really is destroying the ecology, then we'll have achieved something immense.'

She looked at him helplessly. 'I don't even know how Oculus Tempus works.'

'Nor I, precisely,' he admitted. 'But I've done a little research and it's apparently an earth-based spell that shows geographical changes over time. I'm guessing your vorlok woman – Agynea, yes? – believed it would reveal the impact of elobyne on our world.'

That sounded hopeful. 'Will the justiciar allow it to be cast?'

'I don't know. Chances are they'll refuse it outright, as it's a banned spell. But they could permit it under a decree, compelling Justiciary mages to perform the spell. But either of those choices would be seen as taking sides. The third choice would be to grant permission, but place the task of casting it upon you.' He met her gaze. 'That would be cunning, because it would absolve the Justiciary of favouritism, while siding with Corbus, because such banned spells are only known to certain mage-scholars and something complex, like Oculus Tempus, requires several to perform it. Lady Augusta's faction probably won't be able to find the people to do it.'

She swallowed. 'Is that the likely outcome, then?'

'I'm afraid it is.'

'But it's our best chance of proving our point,' she said, fighting to contain her hopeless frustration. 'We have to perform it if we can!'

'We're doing our best, Romara. Augusta's storming through the arcanums right now, seeking mage-scholars willing to break ranks in the name of Truth. But most are afraid to take sides.'

She looked away, closed her eyes and clung to the calm centre inside her where memories of Gram dwelt. Knowing he still lived helped, but it also made her afraid that he or the others would try to rescue her again and this time get themselves killed.

Just run, she exhorted them silently. *Run, hide – and live.*

Miravia

A day of hard riding saw Gram and Toad reach a clearing where a caravan of Kharagh waggoneers camped. The hard-eyed descendants of the Kharagh nomads had once terrified eastern Hytal, but now dwelt on the fringes of society, eking out an existence as short-term labourers and small traders. Though they still called themselves "exiles", they were now fifteenth-generation Hytali and most spoke Talmoni.

The Kharagh remained a distinctive people, though, with flat-planed faces of dark copper, narrow eyes and straight black hair, although many showed traces of Talmoni, Aquini and many other races, evidenced by paler skin and hair, and eyes of blue or green. Some were strikingly beautiful, as Toad noted appreciatively as they rode in.

'Sometimes I hate bein' a vorlok,' he grunted, as a willowy girl with waist-length jet hair passed, swaying in the colourful skirts of her people. 'Wouldn't you love to eat her peach?'

She wasn't Romara, so she was utterly irrelevant to Gram, and he was tiring of Toad's crass remarks. But he owed the man for this chance, so he ignored him and concentrated on the men coming to greet them. They were as colourfully dressed as their women, clad in brightly dyed shirts and festooned with cheap metal jewellery, but all had blades to hand.

Toad swung from his saddle and casually drawled, 'Well?'

'Tem Toderik, welcome,' one man replied, with minimal deference.

'This is Gram Larch of Avas,' Toad said gruffly. 'Her Majesty's expectin' him.'

'No problem with him,' the exile replied. 'It's you we don't want here.'

'En't that a shame,' Toad replied blithely. 'Gram, this way.' He shouldered a path through, until he was blocked by the largest of the exiled Kharaghi. 'Ah, Jed Ling, good to see you. How's Chi?'

'Jag off, Arsehole.'

Toad bared teeth like a big cat. 'Don't push your luck.'

The exiled man grimaced but reluctantly stepped aside, giving Gram a hard look as he passed. 'Keep away from our womenfolk,' he advised.

'I have a mate,' Gram retorted, while making some uncomfortable guesses about Toad. *If he's a vorlok, surely he doesn't molest the girls here?* he thought. *He'd better bloody not.*

No one else impeded them as they left the cordon of men behind and headed for a wagon with an awning held up by poles. A plump, grey-haired woman of indeterminate age with a face like worn leather was stirring a pot of something deep red, adding greens and chunks of cooked meat. She was clad in widow's black.

'Go and visit your daughter,' she told Toad brusquely, waving him away. 'Gram Larch, is it? Sit. She won't be a moment.'

Toad bowed his head and sauntered off, whistling, while Gram looked in vain for somewhere to sit, then dropped to his haunches to wait for the Vyr Queen.

'How has Toad got a daughter?' he asked the old woman. 'He's a vorlok—'

'Not your business, lad,' she interrupted. 'But so's you don't go pickin' unnecessary fights, he fathered her a long time ago, before his Gift came in. The fellas don' like 'im 'cos he left her ma.'

'Oh . . .'

'I know what yer thinkin'; lucky escape, eh.' She stirred her pot while looking him up and down. 'Avas man, eh? I hear all the islands have fallen to our kin. Were you part of that?'

'No,' Gram answered truthfully. 'I didn't become fully vyr until afterwards. I mostly looked after my mother.'

'Fritha Larch?'

'That was her. She . . . she died.' He didn't like to think of that, as it was Jadyn and Romara who had killed her. It had been a chaotic time, and it was still raw.

'I'm told you went into Tar-Brigida bastion, killed a couple of lictors and got out alive.'

He blinked and re-assessed her. 'I had help . . . *Your Majesty*.'

He bowed his head respectfully.

The Vyr Queen might not look regal, but she had an aura of self-assured command and unyielding patience. 'Call me Quyan, she said, filling a bowl with stew and handing it over. 'Spoons are over there. If you need more spice, holler.' Then she crossed her legs, fitted some artificial teeth into her mouth and ate, while studying him. 'I'm told you're heart-set on some ex-Order bitch locked up in Hyastar?' she said eventually. 'How'd that come about?'

The tale took some telling, from his meeting with the Falcons, the complex reasons that caused them to flee the Order as renegades, and their awakening to the truth that their own Order was propagating evil, the discovery of Vanashta Baanholt, the journey to Foyland and his rescue by Elindhu and Soren, ending with the failed attempt to get Romara out at Folkstein.

Quyan listened attentively, then asked some pertinent questions about Vanashta Baanholt, the aegis and his relationship with Romara.

'A renegade knight and now a draegar?' she mused. 'She sounds formidable.'

'She is – and she's been taken to Hyastar to speak before the High

Council.' He met her gaze hopefully. 'What she says to the Order's leadership could bring down Corbus Ritter.'

The old woman's beady eyes bored into his, but her voice remained noncommittal. 'A schism in the Order would be nice, especially if one side is prepared to admit that elobyne is harmful. But Hyastar is a death-trap. We won't be getting involved – and nor will you.'

Gram felt his heart sink. 'We broke into one bastion – we could do it again,' he protested.

She shook her head firmly. 'The agents I have inside the city are too valuable to risk on foolishness like that. Moreover, any attempt to break her out is likely to reunify the factions within the Order. None of them are our friends, boy, not even those helping your woman. To them, she's just fuel to a fire they've lit. They'll all happily let her burn.'

'Please, at least let me try,' he begged. 'After she's spoken, I could—'

'No. Your woman's already dead, Gram Larch. Accept that.' She put her bowl aside and sighed. 'I've buried a husband and three children. Life is long, but nothing lasts. You won't forget Siera Romara, but you'll learn to love again. Accept that and walk away.'

'I can't.'

'You must. I'm sorry, but here's my word: return to Keffrana's tribe and learn our ways. Become a fully formed vorlok and make yourself useful. You've been shambling about like a Phaunt in a pottery stall, flailing about breaking things. Master your powers.'

'But—'

'Don't make me put you down, boy,' she said, with sudden menace. Outwardly she was still the weathered old woman working over a cooking pot, but suddenly her words and gaze had weight and heft. 'And don't *ever* think I can't.'

She slowly moved her fingers and he felt a sudden tightening in his chest, as if her hand were cupping his heart and at any moment might squeeze. He went rigid, genuinely and deeply afraid.

'Romara's my only love,' he croaked. 'Together, we found ninneva.'

Her eyes narrowed but the pressure in his chest eased. 'That's a lofty claim, lad. Can you prove it?'

He blinked, confused. 'Love exists in hearts. How does one prove it?'

'With deeds.' Quyan's disturbing eyes flickered to the cooking fire, a bed of glowing coals. 'Come, I'll show you.' She indicated a patch of ground opposite her, across the fire. 'Sit, here.'

Apprehensive, Gram shuffled over and sat, as she stoked the flames thoughtfully. After a minute she began to speak in a more reflective tone. 'My husband was the love of my life. I was still young, and somewhat pretty. Tuan, his name was. He was lively and bright, always positive, even though we were both vyr. We were playing with fire, to lust after each other like that, but we found a way through dangers and found an emotional place where anything felt possible. I only have to think of him and all the hurt of the world goes away.'

'What happened to him?'

'A Vestal pentacle,' she replied flatly. 'For a time I was broken, but I kept him inside me.' She tapped her breast and then her skull. 'His memory is so real to me that I can still see and hear him. He pulled me through. Why? Because we too shared ninneva.'

Gram nodded slowly, then with a wry smile, asked, 'Can you prove it?'

The old woman gave him a sharp look. 'As a matter of fact, I can. But let me ask you this: what is ninneva?' She held up a hand. 'I'll save you time by answering for you, so you don't have to waffle about true love and soulmates. Ninneva is a state of inner peace in which even the rage of glyma-energy doesn't destroy us. It's rare, but not as uncommon as you might think. Idealistically, we associate it with "true love". But someone at peace with themselves can also attain it. It's a state of inner tranquillity that enables our bodies to deal with the poisonous, corrupting rage with which glyma-energy infects us. Every time a knight draws on his elobyne, or we vyr pull that same energy from nature, it floods us with fury. Only those who retain inner peace can handle it – not just at an emotional level, but on a physical level. Our minds affect our bodies, Gram Larch: never forget that. Our minds are powerful beyond our knowing. They can master our bodies, and our world.'

371

'Are you saying that a lictor, utterly at peace with his mission, also has ninneva?' he asked, somewhat appalled.

'The lictors are sanctioned to torture, maim and kill. It takes madness to harm someone helpless, not inner peace. Those men and women don't have ninneva. I met one once who claimed to, but after I explained things to him, he hung himself.' She met his eyes. 'True ninneva is a state of love for something worthy of it.'

Somewhat reassured, Gram asked, 'How can I prove it to you?'

'I want to you to look into the fire and picture your love, your Romara. Think on her with all the respect and affection you feel. I will do the same, thinking of my lost love.'

He bowed his head, picturing Romara, her pale aristocratic face, her shimmering waves of red hair, her air of command, the surprising moments of softness, the way her eyes could melt into his. The way he felt when they touched, yearning towards a consummation that was always snatched away.

He had to fight off demons of despair at the thought that she was a captive, and the anger he felt for those *snivelling scum* who'd tortured her, but he pulled himself back from that and found inner serenity again.

'Well done,' he heard Quyan breathe. 'Now give me your hand.'

Electing to trust, he reached across the fire and gave her his right hand . . .

. . . and with shocking strength, she took it, and slammed both into the fire.

The searing agony was instant, his eyes flying wide open as he tried with his considerable strength to wrench free, but she was prepared and had steel in her limbs, because though his whole body jerked and pulled away, his hand remained locked in hers. He gaped as his skin went red and then split, the flesh and fluids beneath sizzling and crackling while mind-racking pain blasted through his senses. He roared silently, barely holding onto awareness as his nose clogged with the smell of burning meat and his whole body recoiled. His vision swam, the heat waves rippling as he saw his hand blackening . . .

But Quyan's hand was untouched.

'Think of her,' the Vyr Queen snapped. '*Only* of her!'

He tried with all his will to black out what was happening to him, to thrust aside the pain and the ruin being made of his hand, but he couldn't . . .

But then Romara's face appeared in the flames, her expression as ardently loving as he recalled, gazing into his soul and guiding him through the glyma's maelstrom.

He clung to that, finally feeling the energy inside him become soothing and malleable. Now that he knew what was possible, he knew what to do. The ability to heal oneself was rare and even vorloks and knights could barely manage it, because the glyma was so destructive. But it felt natural to channel his inner peace into self-restoration, to let his body right itself.

It didn't happen instantly, but the pain subsided, at first into numbness and then a throbbing core of *good pain*, like the wrenching of a dislocated limb back into place, or the bursting of a boil, and then he was flooded with a rush of soothing balm and the hurt of renewal.

He stared as his hand, still deep among the burning coals, regrew, recoating itself in flesh and skin, so that when he pulled it out again there wasn't even a scar. The calluses and tanned skin he'd had all his adult life had gone too. Now it looked pale, soft – perfect.

He stared as his racing heart slowed and his breath began to flow normally again.

Quyan nodded and removed her own hand, and it too was untouched, but for a smear of soot and the hairs on the back being burned away. She wiped her fingers clean, her face softening to sadness. 'Each year it becomes a little harder to picture my man,' she admitted sadly. 'But he's still inside me. That's how it will be with your Romara. Gone, but never forgotten.'

'But surely you'll help me now?' he blurted.

She gazed at him sadly. 'No, Gram Larch: there is more at stake than your love, however pure it is. This is a war, and we pick only the battles we can win.' Her face closed up. 'You will leave here, ride south and take service with Keffrana. She will teach you the things a vorlok should know, so that you can better serve the cause.'

No. I can't accept this, he thought defiantly. *I can't.*

But he bowed his head. 'As you will, Majesty. I will ride south.'

He meant that, at least. *Sort of.*

He held his breath, waiting for her to read his intent, snap her fingers and stop his heart.

'Leave tomorrow,' she said, 'and travel alone. Give my greetings to Keffrana.' She gestured dismissively. 'Ask Jed Ling for somewhere to sleep.'

He rose, bowed and left, feeling horribly let down.

Around them, the exiles' camp had been settling into what he assumed was a typical night; fiddles had been brought out, the air was scented with the spice of the stews over every fire and those who had finished eating were getting up to dance. There were two distinct zones to the camp, he noticed: one where presumably unmarried women and children were performing domestic tasks, the other where the married couples mingled. Still churning over the Vyr Queen's refusal to help him, he had no inclination to join the dance.

He was given a bedroll and space beneath the Ling family's awning and accepted a flask of clear berry liquor, at which point he rolled up in his blankets, blocked out everything but Romara's face and faded off to sleep.

Next morning he rode south.

He'd ridden for some five kylos when he found Toad waiting beneath a huge old oak, mounted, with bulging saddlebags.

'Listen,' the vorlok said, 'you think I'm a prick and that's fair enough.'

'I never said that—' Gram protested.

'Didn't have to. It's a given – everyone thinks I'm a prick, because I am.' The vorlok scratched his groin thoughtfully, then said, 'The Queen's wise and clever an' all, but she's too timid. She thinks she's fighting a long-drawn-out war, and to be fair, we have been. But not anymore. The harvests are failing all over Hytal and the south. There's no "long-term" now. You feel it, I feel it. This is a crisis, a tipping point, a crossroads. The time for patience is over.'

Gram stared back, his despondency lifting. 'What are you saying?'

'That I know all the queen's agents in Hyastar – including those chafing under her cautious approach. Why don't you and I go talk to them, and see what can be done?'

21

The Wound in Surapaka's Side

Maka and the Ur-Krakos

In the tales of the ancient Tomai people of the Pelas, the archipelago was formed when the hero Maka was assailed by a mighty sea-dragon, the deathless Ur-Krakos. After a long fight, Maka eventually dismembered the monster – those body parts formed the islands. The Tomai claim that one day Ur-Krakos will reform himself, and devour the world.

TILDI MANAKOS, SCHOLAR OF MYTHOLOGY, BEDUM 1458

Pelasian Archipelago
Autumn 1472

Genadius woke from a dream of childhood, a warm embrace from a nurse who he'd thought for many years was his real mother, because she loved him, while his alleged mother ignored him. But as his eyes regenerated, sight returned in a smear of scarlet and white amid a sea of darkness. Gradually, it resolved itself into a skeleton, festooned in shreds of tendons and flesh, stained by drying blood, with only the face and hair intact. The face was serene, even blissful: Enapara, one of his acolytes: a waif among the Serra, whom he'd taken under his wing and conditioned to give him absolute loyalty. That investment in time and energy had paid off.

The rest of her was in his bloated belly, gradually being remade into new flesh for his body.

Thank you, my child, he thought, closing her eyes. *You served me well.*

He rolled off her, looking down at his own body in mute horror.

What little skin he had left was blackened and burned to a charred crisp, but the organs and muscles beneath were sufficiently reformed to allow movement. His belly was like that of a pregnant woman, a nauseating mass of raw meat and gristle, his limbs skeletal, scarcely functioning yet. He didn't need a mirror to know that his visage was hideous.

He looked round to see that Enapara had brought him out of the library to the nearby clifftop. The building looked empty and no one was near. Then he sent his awareness further afield, seeking another whose body and soul he had entered, one whose psychic imprint was engrained on his psyche.

Where are you, Vaziella, you jagatai bitch?

A moment later, he saw, and rage became energy that became wings of light and darkness.

Maimed and in agony, he still had the strength to rise up into the air and glide westwards, while his mind boomed out a summoning cry, one that all his own acolytes would hear.

From a dozen directions, near and far, joyous responses resounded, and his mind's eye showed him their beautiful, cruel faces, rejoicing to hear his voice, their wings banking in the high airs as they arched above land and sea and streaked towards him.

On the second day after the eruption, the *Nidamora* began to encounter refugee fleets – ramshackle clusters of fishing boats, rafts and canoes, piled high with the remnants of people's lives. Jadyn was horrified – even the evacuation of Avas had been nothing to all this. Every island they passed looked devastated, as if a hurricane had blasted through. Some were burning, ignited by volcanic debris.

Among the native Tomai, there were refugees of every other race. Pelasia was a melting pot of people, languages and culture, mostly those fleeing the Triple Empire. They were unified now by disaster and glassy-eyed shock. One boat tried to heave to and board them, but it moved too sluggishly, while another fired arrows, shrieking at them to stay away. Most just stared at them blankly, locked in their interior horrors.

Eventually, they found a canoe with a family of four, rowing stoically, who were prepared to talk to them. They drew alongside and Evandriel conversed with the father in halting Talmoni, while Jadyn and Aura kept the felucca steady. Aura was gazing at the black-skinned wife, wild-haired, broken-toothed and utterly exhausted. Seeing the children big-eyed with hunger, she plucked a bunch of bananas from their stores and threw them to the woman, who caught them and waved her thanks before sharing out the prizes, all the while weeping in distress.

'We are from Isla Junadu,' her husband called. 'Eruption was next isla, Huntaru. Was dormant, all my life. We were promised all fire islands would sleep forever.'

'Who promised?' Evandriel asked sharply.

'Order of Akka's Light,' the man said reverently. 'Holy mages, quieting the restless mountains. But Devourer woke Ur-Krakos against them. Days of Ending are here.'

While Evandriel reassured the man in his own tongue, Jadyn murmured in Aura's ear, 'The Order of Akka's Light – that's the Lighters, who plant the shards. What are they doing here in the islands? This is outside the empire.'

'Empire do what empire want,' she muttered back.

That's true enough, he thought bleakly.

After thanking the man, they sailed on. Jadyn gazed back at the little craft, which looked incapable of surviving any kind of bad weather. 'Where will they go?'

'Any island that can take them,' Evandriel replied, his voice not quite dispassionate. 'I told them to work their way along the chain of islands, foraging what they can. May Elysia have mercy.'

The rest of the day passed in intermittent encounters with displaced people, and the picture grew clearer: the dormant volcano of Isla Huntaru had exploded, and was still erupting, sending lava pouring down its slopes and noxious gases sky-high. Neighbouring islands had been devastated, hit with burning debris and pummelled by the seiche. Hundreds had died, maybe thousands, and now the survivors of those already precarious settlements were trying to leave.

What was becoming clear was that the members of the Order of Akka's Light were still present – fighting to subdue the volcanoes, some said; though others claimed to have seen them removing shards and taking them aboard big transporter ships.

They're abandoning us to die, some said.

'Damn,' Evandriel grumbled, as they cast off from an encounter with a fisherman and his extended family, two dozen crowded aboard a ship scarcely bigger than their own felucca. 'It looks like we might have Lighters to deal with.'

'Which place we go?' Aura asked. 'Have learned now, si?'

The scholar brandished a chart and his compass. 'Yes, I have. We are now right on the prime meridian, and that fisherman just explained the meaning of "Huntaru" to me. It is a shortening of a much longer name, meaning "The Wound in Surapaka's Side" – Surapaka being their Earth Goddess. In their mythos, it is the place where Ur-Krakos will return, bursting from the earth to devour the world. He said Ur-Krakos' skull formed the island when it fell and crushed Kimusamusa, closing the volcano's vent.' He waved an arm at the distant plume of black smoke pouring skywards, still a hundred kylos or so north. 'In other words, Huntaru is Kimusamusa, and that is where we must go.'

Aura looked at Jadyn in horror. 'E Cara, we go to erupting volcano itself? *Insanito!*'

Jadyn felt no different. 'She's right: that is crazy. And why would the Wardens site their base on an active volcano?'

'That, I do not know,' Evandriel admitted, 'but it was dormant until now, and I am sure it is where we are meant to be.'

Jadyn looked from Aura to Evandriel. Logic said it was insane, but his own aegis-senses agreed. 'What do you think?' he asked his lover.

'Am not being sure,' Aura replied, 'but there be only one way to find out.'

They had to pass Isla Junadu, which was also volcanic, if quiescent at the moment. The port on the southwest side faced away from the eruption on Huntaru. It was still devastated, mostly by fire, and looked largely deserted, though a last straggling flotilla of boats was setting sail as they arrived. Few of the vessels looked seaworthy.

There were imperial ships docked there too, flying the colours of the Order of Akka's Light, and the slopes of the Junadu crater were covered in shards – not just single shafts, but forests of crystalline spikes glittering under the sullen skies, their light flaring and fading as they fed energy to the master crystal so far away on Nexus Isle.

A sweep with Evandriel's spyglass revealed that two smaller islands in easy reach were similarly forested. The dozens of imperial vessels moored off each island were for the most part big, sluggish transporter ships. *Removing the shards, in case they're lost in further eruptions,* Jadyn surmised. *There have to be thousands here, more than I ever dreamed existed. It'll take months to remove them all.*

Then Isla Huntaru, their proposed destination, hove into view. It was a forbidding sight. The sky above the broken-topped conical peak was belching sullen clouds, slate-grey and ominous, lit by lurid flashes of fiery light. Massive rents in its sides belched rivers of molten lava, flowing sluggishly like veins of fire towards the sea, sporadically causing massive bursts of steam when the red-hot liquid hit the water.

It really is like paintings of the End of All Things, Jadyn reflected. *As if the artists foresaw it all – as if they too saw with the aegis.*

'The only island with no shards is the one to erupt,' he pointed out to Evandriel. 'Are the Lighters right? Do the shards soak up the fiery humours and prevent eruptions?'

The scholar pulled a sour face. 'More likely the opposite. The world's core is composed of molten fire, driven upwards by heat from below. By plugging other volcanoes, the Lighters did not lessen that pressure, they just redirected it to the most vulnerable point. They did not make an eruption here less likely – they made it *inevitable.*'

'So what we do now?' Aura asked. 'Still go to island?'

'I think we have to,' Evandriel replied. 'We need to be prepared for anything, though – poison vapours, smoke, further eruptions, perhaps even Lighters.'

'What are we looking for?' Jadyn asked.

'I'm not sure,' he admitted, 'but I am hoping there is something the Wardens left behind, maybe akin to the stone circle in the Qor-Espina, or the chamber below Vanashta Baanholt. Something which will tell us where to go next.'

Jadyn glanced over his shoulder, wondering how close those pursuing them were.

'Any insights about the Exemplar and Borghart?' he asked the scholar.

'They are veiled to me. The ocean, the aegis distortion – they could be anywhere . . . including right here.'

'So what do you think?' Jadyn asked Aura.

'We go ashore and see,' Aura said, her expression far away, but resolute. 'Something awaits, am knowing. Something dangerous, but needful.'

Yoryn Borghart was in his usual place of vigil, in the prow of the Vestal warship, as it churned through sluggish seas, having sailed day and night since the eruption, trusting to the sailing master's seamanship and Vazi Virago's precognitive instincts to avoid rocks, even in the dark – although once they'd mown down a much smaller vessel, some refugee family they'd crunched through and left to drown.

The whelps of pirates and rebels, Yoryn Borghart had thought at the time. But as the true scope of the devastation caused by the eruption unfolded, even he felt a sliver of sympathy. *They likely welcomed the Lighters with open arms and the bastards have destroyed their lives.*

The captain of the Lighter ship they'd encountered the previous day had been bewildered as to how this eruption could have happened when they'd been planting shard forests on the volcanoes to leech away the heat and energy from below. But even with his limited knowledge of geology, he was thinking they'd precipitated this disaster themselves – and experience had taught him that the Lighters were a pack of lying bastards in any case.

Pick the usual suspects and you'll be right nine times out of ten, a lictor had told him years ago.

But he'd gained one valuable snippet of information in talking to their magia. He'd asked, as if just in passing, if the Wardens were ever there, and she'd told him they'd once had a base on Huntaru, the island which had erupted. That fortress was now a ruin, overlooking the wreckage of an abandoned port. The Tomai natives held the island sacred and cursed, believing the island's spirit had destroyed the Wardens for their hubris in settling there.

Assuming it doesn't erupt again, he mused, *we can search that fortress and see if it's the place we need.* The Lighter mage-scholar had insisted there was nothing to be found there. 'All heretical relics were destroyed centuries ago,' she'd told him. 'There's nothing left of the castle's sinful past, Akka be praised.' Her smug piety had been grating, but Borghart didn't care. *If the aegis is sinful, so be it. I still want it.*

He was pulled from his reverie by the clip of the Exemplar's boots. He'd not seen her for over a day, as she'd been below, apparently scouring her cabin clean as if erasing a crime.

'Exemplar,' he greeted.

'Lictor.'

She'd aged in the short months he'd known her. At a cursory glance, she was still the same preternaturally beautiful woman he'd met at Vanashta Baanholt, but he could now see beyond that, noting her haunted eyes and brittle tension. Another thing disturbed him: she was oddly pallid, despite all the time she'd spent in the sun – and there were gold flecks in her eyes he was sure hadn't been there before. Something had happened to her, perhaps linked to the creature they'd found in the furnace at Sherkaza . . . But he knew better than to ask.

'According to our good captain, he can get us to the old docks on Huntaru before dusk,' Borghart told her. 'He's not happy, though. He thinks the volcano will erupt again.'

'I don't give a damn for his happiness.' She brushed ash from her hair and gazed at the uniformly dull sky, frowning. 'What time is it?'

He pointed out a lighter patch of dark cloud. 'It's mid-afternoon, but if you didn't know which way was west, you'd not be able to tell.' He dropped his voice. 'Are you all right?'

He didn't expect an answer, but got one. 'I got sick of the stench of that cabin,' she fumed. 'Maybe men are immune to bad smells, but I am not. Damn, I hate sailing.'

'As do I,' Borghart agreed, wondering what was eating her.

He didn't have to wait. 'Can you smell these rodents who sail with us?' she snarled. 'Don't you want to retch at their fish breath and the piss and shit smears in their smallclothes and the sweat they never wash off and the rot in the bilge? Elysia on high, I hate it all.'

'Is there anything you want to tell me?' he asked, his voice pitched for her ears alone. 'Sometimes women suffer heightened senses if . . . erm . . .'

Her expression switched to scathing contempt. 'If what? Menstruating? Pregnant?'

'If there's something you've done—'

She gripped his collar, pushing her furious, anguished face into his. 'That *I've* done? Damn you jagging men, for thinking that I did *any* of this. *What about what was done to me, eh?*'

Done to her? He swallowed, mastered his own flare of temper and said, 'I'm sorry. I have no idea what you mean. If someone here has harmed you—?'

'Harm me?' she snarled. 'I'm beyond *everyone*, including you, Lictor. I am the Exemplar, and I am . . . I am—'

You're on the verge of a breakdown, he saw. Taking a massive gamble, he laid a hand on the fist that she'd bunched in his collar and murmured, 'Whoever was in that furnace, he's dead now. He's gone forever.'

She didn't deny anything, just kept looking at him with those wounded, gold-flecked eyes, which were no longer furious but terrified. 'Is he, though?' she asked, her voice cracking.

He stiffened at the thought, and asked, 'Who was he?'

She hesitated, then said, 'A Serrafim . . . He called himself Genadius.'

It was an unusual name, except in *one* family. 'Like the old Hierophant?'

'He *is* the old Hierophant,' she whispered. 'That's what he told me. Before he . . .'

Before he . . . what?

Borghart stared, wanting to reject it all – impossibly alive

Hierophants stalking an Exemplar? – but she was clearly convinced. 'I'm sorry,' he said awkwardly, and risked enfolding her into his arms, for the first time since childhood endeavouring to give comfort, if only to head off some crisis that would end in blood. *Probably my own.*

To his complete surprise, she didn't pull away.

'It never occurred to me before that those jagging rebels might be right,' she mumbled. 'I thought they were deluded, jealous losers, the sort of people who know they're weak and are destined to achieve nothing, so they lash out. I thought their ranting against the empire was just propaganda. But there's a hierarchy of creatures above us, and they are *diabolical.*'

'What creatures?'

'Immortal demons,' she croaked. 'He came to me in dreams – I *thought* they were dreams – but it was real. *Genadius.* They pretend they're Serrafim, but they're *evil.* He spoke like he'd never died – and he hates Eindil, his son. He told me he was watching over me, he pretended to help, but then he ... he ...'

Borghart knew then he was completely out of his depth. 'You don't have to say it,' he said thickly. 'He's dead now. He has to be ...'

But Serrafim ... can they even die? Holy Elysia ...

Abruptly, Vazi remembered herself, pulling away, all her barriers reforming. 'We go on,' she snapped, with an anger he was sure was directed at herself. 'My destiny demands it.'

Then she pulled away, spun on her heel and walked off, brittle and closed-in as ever.

At least he recognised her again.

But what she'd told him filled him with dread. What was some kind of 'angel' doing existing, let alone following her around? What had it done to her to make her skin and eyes change like that? Could it truly be the old Hierophant? If so, how? And why?

And what am I doing, caring about what happens to her? he wondered.

For a few seconds he'd felt weirdly protective, something so against his nature that he barely recognised it. It wasn't affection or desire – the Exemplar was jagged as broken glass, barely female to him.

It's just this quest, he decided. *We need each other to succeed.*

But this mission was changing him too, in ways he hadn't anticipated. Her struggle moved him, and that just didn't happen.

Uncomfortable with that notion, he concentrated on watching the land off the starboard beam slide by. The volcanic peak was studded with a veritable forest of elobyne shards, twinkling like diamonds in the midday sun – then his eyes shifted to the island brooding on the horizon, pouring smoke into the air and lava into the sea swathed in plumes of over-heated steam. Huntaru was the only isle in this chain of volcanoes not forested with crystal shards, and the only one to explode. That did not feel like a coincidence.

The Lighters scholar said it erupted because they'd been forbidden to plant elobyne there.

So the truth is probably the opposite . . .

Huntaru was a forbidding pile of bare rock with at least three lava rivers that he could see, all pouring from the fractured cone. The crew were scared and Borghart was worried the captain would bolt as soon as he'd set them ashore. They'd had to promise him a rich reward to remain. Whether that would hold if there was another eruption, he couldn't say.

They docked in the old port, an abandoned township now just a cluster of broken chimneys, fallen roofs and wrecked ships below the waterline. There were no lava rivers on this side of the island and the old Warden fortress was nearby, on a spur running from the cone. The walls had mostly collapsed and the towers were broken stubs.

Vazi reappeared as they docked, wearing her burnished armour with her hair tied back severely and her face taut with concentration as she surveyed the ruined town and the castle above. She strode down the gangplank the moment it was lowered and marched off.

Before he followed, Borghart went to the captain, 'You will wait for us, or I will ensure you and all your kin are tortured and burned in open trial, understood?' he said softly.

The man went pale. 'Aye, Lictor.'

Still not entirely trusting him, Borghart hurried after Vazi, catching her up as she marched along what had been the esplanade, looking for a path up to the ruined fortress.

'Are you sure what we seek is up there?' he asked.

'No, but the trail leads here,' she said tersely. 'My visions are clear on that. Yours?'

After his enforced glyma use, his aegis was slowly returning, but he was still largely blinded to premonitions. 'I have no idea.'

'Then follow me and do as you're told,' she said curtly, striding on.

He had to take a breath to avoid a flash of temper that she might interpret as a threat, but this new empathy he felt for her told him she was wounded and lashing out at the nearest person.

I can take it, he resolved, *if that's what's needed to get us through.*

Vazi Virago had never felt so brittle or vulnerable in her life. Her emotions were a mess, and she knew that if she tried to engage the glyma, there was every chance she'd implode and fall. To step onto this island, where even the ground was untrustworthy, only heightened her dread. But this was where they had to be, of that, she was certain.

Borghart's presence hardly helped. When he'd shocked her by giving comfort earlier, she'd actually *needed* him – not sexually, but emotionally. She was falling apart and had been grateful to cling to him, even just for a minute. But never again.

We're both under siege: having to confront facts we thought were lies, and enduring failure. We're having our entire understanding of the world altered.

But she couldn't afford to rely on others, not even the lictor. *I have a destiny; he does not.*

Ever since she'd been corrupted by Genadius, her body had been changing, as he'd promised. A weird numbness affected her skin, like she was turning to marble. There were gold flecks in her eyes, and a sense that her heart was crystallising, her blood turning to ice and her thoughts too, a sharpening of that emotional detachment she'd had all her life. Her senses were heightened and her dream-visions and waking premonitions were growing clearer, but they only brought more dread. She could still hear Genadius howling, and other voices too, dispassionate murmurings she couldn't quite catch. They were more Alephi, she was certain, connected to each other, and now to her. She dreaded encountering them.

386

Her glorious destiny had never felt so fragile and endangered.

Another sharp earthquake pulled her awareness back to the present. She and Borghart had left the rubble of the town, clambering through gaps in the old walls, and were picking a way up towards the ruined monastery. They held their breath while stone slid and loose rocks fell all around them. Her premonitions showed another eruption coming: liquid fire bursting upwards into the heavens, boulder comets shooting through the sky, and scalding vapours enveloping the island. The island's wrath was not yet spent.

'Hurry,' she told Borghart, picking up the pace herself. Everything was ruined and desolate; even the tenacious tussock grass, the only vegetation around, was withered and dying. The dark sky was smeared with flashes of scarlet, reminding her of the scenery in famous paintings by lunatics of the so-called 'End-All Movement' who painted the Devourer's Maw: profane images of fornicators, murderers and unbelievers being abused by demons, ghastly images sanctified by their religious context.

Behind her, Borghart was a simmering, reptilian presence, but he wisely stayed distant. Angry at herself for her earlier lapse and ready to lash out, she pushed on without waiting for him, leading the way through the ruins to a trail beneath the old Warden fortress. Steam vents were active here, and the sulphurous stench felt menacing. She wrapped a scarf around her nose and mouth, noticing Borghart following suit, and resumed the climb up the remnants of a cobbled road. It was a slog, sweltering in the heat under the oppressive twilight skies. Looking back, she could see, with some surprise, that their warship was still at the dock. The conical peaks of the nearest island, Isla Junadu, were a murky silhouette over the gloomy waters. In an hour or two, Vazi estimated, it would be dark.

And something was prickling at her awareness, a sense of danger closing in. Then the ground rumbled and shook strongly enough to unbalance them.

'It's going to blow again,' Borghart worried. 'We should go back.'

'It may well,' she told him, 'but we are going on.'

He grimaced but said nothing more, following her onwards,

clambering around places where the road had collapsed, sidestepping volcanic rocks, some giant and clearly newly ejected from the volcano itself, embedded in gashes in the ground and still hot to the touch. Shards of glassy granite sharp as knives were strewn about.

When they reached the old gatehouse, they found the arch and much of the outer wall had collapsed, and the courtyard within was strewn with debris from a fallen tower. The well was dry and the whole place was dusted in grey flakes.

'I'm not sure there's anything here,' she muttered. 'I sense nothing.'

'The chamber at Vanashta Baanholt was underground,' Borghart replied. 'And the standing stones portal led to a cave network. We should go downwards.' He hesitated. 'Although going underground during an earthquake or eruption strikes me as foolish.'

He's not wrong, Vazi acknowledged to herself. She tried to probe using her foresight, playing a *What If?* game – what if I went that way? – to see if she gained any insight, but nothing came, just an uneasy sense that something was slipping by her.

I'm not sure, she muttered, backing away to the broken arch and peering upwards to the crater rim, just a few hundred paces above over broken ground. The air felt hotter and there was a throbbing sensation coming up through her feet, jangling her nerves.

We should go, she thought. *This is the wrong place . . .*

Then movement away to the left caught her eye, up on the high slopes below the broken crater – and she saw three distant figures emerge downslope from the smoke clouds, also climbing. They were too far away to identify by sight alone, but a flash of foresight revealed them to be Jadyn Kaen, Auranuschka Perafi and Nilis Evandriel.

'Jagat,' she breathed, 'they're here!'

'Let's finish this,' Borghart started – then he grabbed her shoulder, his expression oddly uncertain. 'I'm still blind to the future . . . Exemplar, do we survive this?'

For a moment, his doubts infected her. All her premonitions were telling her right now was that the dangers were myriad – and he wasn't the least of them.

'I don't know,' she admitted hoarsely, 'but I believe in destiny!'

My destiny.

She slapped his hand away. 'Come, or don't – I don't jagging care.' Then she spun and tore towards her prey, not knowing whether he followed or not.

22

On Trial

Justice and Society

A dangerous thing happens when the lines between Justice and Entertainment blur. Perpetrators can be glamorised or demonised or made to look the victim, while the true victims are forgotten. Heroes and Monsters are created and slain for our gratification. A clever speech has more weight than facts. Popularity can save a miscreant and the lack of it can damn an innocent. When we administer justice, we hold up a dark mirror to ourselves.

TORMAN GUDURSSON, SCHOLAR, HYSK 1454

Folkstein, Miravia
Autumn 1472

On the morning of her hearing, Romara's door was flung open by an Order magus, escorted by four guards. She couldn't stop herself recoiling in fear, but they offered no harm. The magus replaced her anti-glyma manacles with a neck-ring that had the same function, then the guardsmen marched her into the torch-lit corridor, down the hall to a tiled room, where a tub of lukewarm water awaited her. For a moment she worried they were going to shove her head under and hold her there.

Instead, they withdrew, leaving her to the mercies of a pair of hard-faced women, who made her shit and piss in the bucket in the corner, then washed her, towelled her down and dressed her in an ill-fitting grey penitential robe. Then she was led to the interview room, where Dranit Ritter was waiting, attired in his heavy maroon coat. His acne-scarred face was serious as he checked to see if she had any fresh injuries, while she devoured a bowl of warm porridge, struggling as her fingers were so badly mangled she could barely hold the spoon.

'Here's what to expect,' he told her. 'It's almost the tenth hour; shortly, we'll take you to the Rose Chamber, where the High Council meets. A justiciar will preside: Djana Bespari, who's an ex-lictor, but a stickler for the law. It's as good a choice as we could have hoped for.'

She'd expected worse. 'Who'll be there?'

'Officials from the Day and Night Courts, of course. Anyone within the Order with the appropriate status, both serving and retired knights and mages. And any lictor or scholar who wishes to attend. But only the High Council can vote on any motions proposed from the hearing. Corbus has the largest faction, then Augusta, but there are plenty of neutrals who are persuadable, if you're credible. Enough to swing the vote. They asked to hear your testimony, and many are furious that the archon tried to suppress this hearing.'

Romara cringed at the thought of being marched before these people, many of them her peers, knowing they would see her as broken, cowardly, failed, an animal, a traitor. She stared at her mangled hands and spilled her spoon.

Dranit recognised her anxiety. 'Romara, Hromboli and Faith are dead. They died like the scum they were. Your man took revenge on them, and he is still at large. Last one standing wins, and it wasn't them.'

She tried to grasp that, but those two were still alive in her mind, still laughing at her as they carved her open, then slammed red-hot iron to the wounds. The stench of sizzling blood and burnt flesh still lingered in her nostrils.

'I'll try,' she croaked.

'Face the gallery, head high: not hostile or proud, but not broken, either. Be regretful, not just of your fall, but that the Order has also fallen. You were proud to serve, but your leaders have let us all down. Show them that failure pains you more than your wounds.'

She nodded numbly.

Dranit took her hand. 'Romara, be strong. The world may seem a terrible place to you now, but not all goes badly for your people.' He dropped his voice to a murmur. 'I've learned of an incident that occurred a week ago: Jadyn Kaen and Aura Perafi were seen in the Hejiffa Dhouma, in Mutaza. They damaged an ancient mosaic and fled. Exemplar Virago and Lictor Borghart were pursuing them.'

'I'd thought they were dead,' Romara admitted, lifting her eyes. 'What happened?'

'They escaped – some say by flying.' His eyes flickered uncertainly. 'Even a mage can't do that. Is it . . . is it aegis?'

Jadyn flying? And Aura Perafi, the most irritating woman alive? Romara couldn't really credit it, but the thought of them running rings around Vazi Virago brightened her inner desolation. 'I don't know,' she answered honestly. 'I don't know what the aegis is.'

'And Gram Larch, Elindhu Morspeth and Soren var'Dael are also still at large. Don't despair, Romara. Fight your fight, for them.'

'I just pray they don't try another rescue. I don't want them on my conscience.'

'It would be foolish of them to come here, and it wouldn't help your cause.'

'What do I say if they question me about them?' she asked.

'The truth,' Dranit replied. 'The most damaging thing you can do is be caught lying. Don't give them any excuse to prolong your suffering. I will be seeking a quick death for you after this hearing. I have a good record in securing prompt executions with no torture.'

She gulped, and asked, 'What would it take to overthrow your brother?'

'After you've spoken, Augusta will move a vote of no confidence in the archon – provided your performance warrants it. If that motion passes – it needs half the members of the High Council to support it – there'll be a formal vote of no confidence at the next quarterly sitting, in three weeks' time. That will require a higher threshold: more than two-thirds of the vote. He was elected with a majority of three-quarters, but that was years ago and his support has definitely ebbed since. But it also requires a specific accusation of malfeasance.

That's something my brother is good at avoiding. He always gets others to do his dirty work.'

She hung her head. 'Well, I guess I wasn't going to be around anyway. I hope my ghost gets to see his fall.'

'I hope so too,' Dranit muttered.

She studied him. 'What happened between you and him? Did he used to pick on you when you were kids?'

He smiled grimly. 'Something like that.'

They fell into silence, then bells chimed, the door opened and a knight in the halved black and white tabard of the Justiciary Legion appeared.

'It's time,' he said curtly.

The Rose Chamber, the judicial hall of Tar-Vestallis, was a semi-circular amphitheatre named for the pale rose-gold hue of the marble seats shaped as petals where the officials sat. They faced the justiciar's throne, in front of which was the prisoner, chained to a giant anvil of stone and steel. It was a deliberately grand setting for High Council hearings, intended to impress and intimidate, and it worked. Romara felt her stomach clench, feeling small and lost.

Above her were ranks of serving and retired knights, a small knot of lictors and a crowd of brown-robed scholars. Facing her behind the judge's seat were rows of grey-clad older men and women, the High Council, who gained that status through quadrennial elections among veterans. She counted: there were more than eighty, a clear quorum.

As she was manacled to the anvil, known as the Forge of Justice, the audience throbbed with murmurs and whispers, their eyes staring down at her with a blend of disgust and contempt. Clearly the women present felt she'd let them all down, although she did see pity on a few faces.

She had to stand throughout this ordeal.

Dranit sat to the left of the justiciar's throne, with the accusatory legalus, a lictor named Erlfriede Vandari, on the judge's right. Erlfriede was a tall, thin woman in her forties with grace and an aristocratic manner. Her name meant 'erling-friend', but there was nothing friendly about her cold eyes.

'Rise for Justiciar Djana Bespari,' a stentor called out, and everyone stood for a black-clad woman with skinny limbs and a plump belly. She had deep brown skin and grey-black hair cut short, a southern Bravanti, judging by her elaborate necklace, ear and nose-rings of precious stones. She had an earthy face, but a dignified air.

Archon Corbus Ritter took a seat above and behind the justiciar and gazed coolly down at Romara. Most of the audience were gathered to his right in a show of support. He had a confident, unassailable air, even though he was effectively on trial here as well.

The justiciar sat, a chime sounded and the stentor announced that the court was in session.

Romara felt the weight of every eye on her, but her fragile inner peace held. She'd seen courts where captured vyr shrieked and raved like animals; she dreaded making such a display. *That could still happen*, she reminded herself. *Stay calm.*

The stentor introduced the accusator and defensior, and then turned to her. 'Before you stands Romara Sindra Challys, of Desantium, since 1460 a member of the Order of the Vestments of Elysia Divina,' he announced. 'She is attested as having fallen from grace and was captured in vyr-form by Exemplar Vaziella Virago. Her crime is not in question here. She will be executed the day after this hearing ends. That is the Code. Ar-byan.'

'Ar-byan,' the massed ranks of knights, officers and elders chorused, as Romara felt the marrow seep from her bones. It felt surreal to spend her last days speaking before these people, knowing her last sight would be a masked lictor.

'The purpose of this hearing is to learn how this came to be,' the stentor continued. 'It has been requested by the High Council at the behest of Lady Augusta Martia, to understand this knight's fall, and whether the Order failed her. *Our people must trust us.* So spake Jovan Lux when he founded this Order almost two hundred years ago. We are the backbone of the Triple Empire and must be judged to the highest standards.'

With that, the stentor hammered his stave into the floor and Dranit was invited to guide Romara through her testimony. He rose and faced her, his expression solemn.

'Are you Romara Sindra Challys, aged twenty-nine, born in Desantium, and the widow of Elan Sandreth of Hyastar?'

'I am Romara, but I am not a widow. I never married.'

'Untruth,' Erlfriede snapped. 'Her marriage to Sandreth is legally attested.'

'It never happened,' Romara retorted. 'It was a lie to rob my family, concocted by Archon Corbus Ritter and his lover, Elspeth Sandreth.'

There was a hungry stir in the audience – this was what those who disliked the archon wanted: scandal and skulduggery. Corbus' supporters loudly decried Romara as the liar.

'Perhaps this should be determined, *invictus excrucius*?' Erlfriede suggested: the right to further torture.

'Contested,' Dranit shot back. 'The validity of her alleged marriage is not at issue here. And Sandreth's dead, as noted. He got what he deserved and their petty scheme came to nothing.'

'See how he gloats over the death of a man slain trying to capture a traitor,' Erlfriede said rhetorically.

Justiciar Bespari cut in, 'The defensior is correct, this marriage is irrelevant now. Proceed.'

Romara glanced at the archon, who returned her hostility with contemptuous calm. But she was sure that Elan's death had been a blow to him and to his lover, Lady Sandreth. She hoped it had poisoned their relationship.

Well done, Tevas. I forgive you all else.

Dranit faced her again, saying, 'Siera Romara, let's begin.'

He started by going through her service record, including testimonies from former soldiers of the Falcons century, naming her 'the best knight-commander we ever had' and bringing a tear to her eye. How the defensior had obtained so many in three days, she had no idea. 'Siera Romara was a model knight and commander,' Dranit concluded. 'Do not let anyone convince you otherwise.'

He then led her through an account of her final days on Avas, and the journey that became the aegis quest: from losing control on Avas in the final fight; the wedding plot in Gaudien; rescuing Jadyn, Gram and Aura and escaping; to Solabas and the triple-shard clusters Jadyn and Aura found; and her sorcerous bond with Gram that helped delay her fall. She also spoke of Agynea and her words concerning Nilis Evandriel and the mysterious Oculus Tempus spell. Accusator Erlfriede interjected at times, but Dranit skilfully dealt with her derisive comments and claims of falsehood, until Justiciar Bespari told her to restrain herself or forfeit the right to ask her own questions.

As the testimony progressed, Romara felt a change in the atmosphere of the chamber. The veterans and serving members of the Order became quieter, taking in the revelations with interest, even if they remained sceptical. Meanwhile, the scholars were murmuring with clear interest. Romara reminded herself that most were like her, people who genuinely believed that the Order was – or at least should be – on the side of right. This was likely hard for them.

It helped that the Vestal Order had little liking for the Order of Akka's Light, the Lighters, who had greater access to the Hierophant's courts and were effectively their rivals. Everything she said against them was well-received.

When the tale reached Vanashta Baanholt and the aegis, the whole hall fell silent, taking in her words with utmost attention. The Sanctor Wardens had a mythic quality, even to knights of the Order. Sensing this, the accusator tried to attack.

'These are the words of a fallen knight, a corrupted liar!' Erlfriede called. 'It's pure fantasy!'

'I will hear this,' Bespari snapped. 'You're on your last warning, Accusator.'

Erlfriede risked one last try. 'The aegis is an attested falsehood, Justiciar. Therefore her testimony is a lie. Let us get a statement from her under *invictus excrucius*. A few hours in our care will determine the truth of the matter.'

Another attempt to take me back to the torture rooms, Romara thought, chilled.

'Denied,' Justiciar Bespari answered. 'No more interjections, Accusator.'

At this, Corbus Ritter shouted, 'This testimony affects the security of the Triple Empire. It's above us all, Justiciar. Close this charade down and send her to the Night Court.'

Romara flashed a look at Dranit, who was looking concerned. Clearly this was a realistic option for the Justiciar to take, an abdication of responsibility that would help her avoid appearing partisan.

'If it's that important, then it's twice as necessary we hear it,' Lady Augusta Martia retorted, from her seat on the left. 'We've not heard the whole tale yet. Sit down and listen, Corbus!'

There was a split reaction, but most appeared to agree with her. They were intrigued.

Justiciar Bespari rejected the archon's demand. 'We're here to determine if this is truth or falsehood. Those of you too fragile of faith to hear words that contradict their beliefs should perhaps leave. Defensior, continue.'

She's not on my side, but she's not on theirs, Romara realised. That was heartening.

Dranit turned back to Romara. 'Tell us of the Exemplar's involvement.'

Everyone leaned forward, craning necks and straining ears.

'She was at Vanashta Baanholt ahead of us,' Romara replied. 'On behalf of the Hierophant – not the Order.'

That revelation made everyone look at Corbus, who squirmed. He was the Exemplar's commander, but rulers sometimes took liberties, and this made him look weak.

Romara resumed, once the audience had taken that in, 'Exemplar Virago hadn't heard that we were outlawed and we forgot to tell her,' she said drily. 'They'd learned of the site through other means, and had been commanded to go there and investigate, then destroy it. The aegis is a heresy, they said, and understanding it was unimportant. I imagine they're doing that right now.'

There was a hush, then a rush of noise, some defending the

Exemplar, but most, especially the scholars, demanded an investigation, and for the Exemplar's mission to be suspended.

The stentor hammered his stave down and Bespari shouted, 'Silence! This hearing will continue.'

Everyone looked expectantly at Corbus, who wavered, then stood and affecting a grand manner, called out, 'It's the justiciar's call, and on her head. If this must continue, then let us listen civilly. These hearings aren't supposed to be a comfortable listen! We will determine the truth in due course. Please, all of you, sit and listen.'

Romara was surprised, but then she realised that Corbus was in damage-control mode. It was a politician's stance, not an honest response but an attempt to appear reasonable. She felt a surge of triumph, but reminded herself that it was an illusion: she'd still die tomorrow, and in any case, she was nearly finished, and she still had to face the accusator.

'I was brought to Folkstein by portali gate,' she went on, at Dranit's prompting. 'I was tortured, forced to give a statement, then brought here.' Her eyes swept the galley, then focused on Corbus. 'I am not and never have been married to Elan Sandreth. The man I love is Gram Larch. Some of you know of a state called ninneva, in which the inner peace of love transcends glyma-rage. The Order deny it exists, but I have experienced it, and it sustains me. You think of the vyr as beasts, and so did I, but I found love among them.'

The auditorium fell into a sombre, disturbed semi-silence, treating that claim with less hostility than she'd believed possible.

Dranit nodded thanks, then addressed the auditorium. 'Let me summarise,' he called. 'The accused and her pentacle were driven into fugitive status over a highly debatable interrogation, an incident that could have easily been passed over. But Lictor Borghart was compelled by Archon Ritter to accuse them, to gain leverage over Siera Romara for reasons of pure greed, and to please his adulterous lover. The Falcons had no choice but to run. They did not go renegade; the archon forced them to run, or face his so-called justice. In doing so, they encountered proof that elobyne is ruinous to the ecology, and that the aegis is real and beneficial. All of this, Archon Ritter wishes to silence. It is no wonder the accused turned to our enemies, when she has been victimised by corrupt men of an institution she has devoted her life to serving. Make no mistake, this is a blight on the Order, another example of blindly dogmatic, venal and immoral leadership that is bringing shame upon us all.'

Corbus' people hissed threats, Augusta's supporters cheered.

Dranit pointed at Lictor Erlfriede. 'Speaking of blind dogmatists, I now hand over to the accusator. Some advice: listen hard to what she does and doesn't ask, and disbelieve every conclusion she makes.' He bowed ironically to Justiciar Bespari. 'An honour, as always.'

He nodded encouragingly to Romara and took his seat. He looked exhausted.

He fought hard for me, she realised, *even though it gains him nothing except enemies.*

Accusator Erlfriede approached, and just having a black-robed lictor before her triggered a visceral response in Romara's gut as she remembered Hromboli gleefully smashing her fingers, and Faith's joyous face as she branded her. She went into cold sweats as Erlfriede looked down her nose at her, then faced the audience.

'Lord, ladies, noble knights and mages, learned scholars,' she began. 'We have before us an example of the most insidious of evils: *a plausible liar*. And that's just Defensior Dranit Ritter,' she quipped, raising a laugh among Corbus' partisans. 'The accused is even worse. A pretty face with a serpent's tongue – but don't worry, we'll pull it out in due course. It will be the first part of her tossed on the pyre, to protect our citizens from her falsehoods and half-truths.'

The relish in her voice made Romara shudder, and the beast inside her bared teeth.

Erlfriede saw. 'See the fury, brothers and sisters? See the hate? That's her true face – well, her *human* one. She has a vyr face too, now: an animal in human form. A child-eating monster.'

Romara almost snarled a retort, but realised she was being goaded for just such a reaction.

Gram, she whispered. *Be with me.*

399

'You're here to ask questions,' Dranit reminded Erlfriede. 'Not cast insults.'

'Agreed,' Justiciar Bespari said. 'Get on with it, Accusator.'

Erlfriede did so, turning on Romara and beginning her line of questioning; portraying the interrogation that had begun this journey – of Gram on the ship leaving Avas – as a sign that she'd already become a vyr, and had rescued Gram because of that. She produced documents from supposed ex-subordinates claiming she'd been a vicious, cruel century-commander, who tortured prisoners and openly carried on a sexual relationship with Jadyn.

'Ridiculous! Siera Romara was a fine knight and commander,' Dranit interjected, waving his testimonies. 'Did I not say, "let no one convince you otherwise"?' he asked the audience rhetorically. 'Justiciar, let it be noted that yet again, the Order's refusal to permit live witnesses in these hearings impedes the process of justice.'

'He says, then I say; but who's credible here?' Erlfriede sneered. 'I'm a sworn seeker of truth! What are you, Defensior? Someone who scrapes a living defending evildoers: the bitter, disinherited sibling of a great man.'

'And what are you but a sadist with a royal warrant?' Dranit shot back.

'Enough!' Bespari shrilled. 'Get on with it, Lictor.'

Erlfriede turned and swanned back towards Romara, leaning over her, face to face. 'This animal's tale is full of uncorroborated lies,' Erlfriede declared, deliberately spraying spittle at Romara. 'There are no shards in the wilds of Solabas – I have this from a local Lighter—'

'You accuse us of lying, then quote a Lighter?' Dranit jeered, winning applause.

'Typical small-minded partisanship,' Erlfriede sniffed. 'We in the Justiciary are above the petty rivalries between Vestals and Lighters, as you all should be.'

That drew grumbles, but Erlfriede, in her arrogance, didn't back down. 'If the Lighters, who are answerable to the Hierophant himself, are doing as alleged, then who are we to question it?'

Most of the room made exasperated noises at that. Order resentment of the Lighters was as old as the Triple Empire. The knights felt they were propping up thrones for little reward, while Lighters were invariably ennobled on retirement.

We've always hated those pricks, Romara thought. *Don't the Justiciary know that?*

The accusator finally realised that her words were turning the gallery against her, but – typical for a lictor – she ploughed on. 'The Lighters are your brothers, serving the same master,' she lectured the crowd. 'Petty rivalries undermine our beloved Triple Empire, whose strength lies in unity. In the words of Jovan Lux himself, "If there is resentment in your heart, look in the mirror for its cause." There is the potential for evil in us all.' Then she whirled upon Romara and snapped, 'This vorlok whore is an example of that. How dare she suggest that she is capable of love, let alone truth? I would suggest this "love" she claims to have for this Gram Larch is some sordid bestial fantasy. Do you lie with dogs, Siera Romara? Do you tup with goats?'

'Lictor,' Bespari snapped, 'that is enough!'

The lictor's face hardened, but Romara could see that she was just trying to goad her into losing control. She'd attended a few trials of captured vorloks and draegars, and always the vyr had been reduced to ravening creatures, losing all sympathy.

Thoughts of Gram kept her sane, soothed the barbs and fear of what was to come.

The accusator's face tightened in frustration. She turned to Bespari and apologised. 'I am sorry for my temper, Justiciar. It is just so difficult to hear such lies spewing from her mouth. She says she has never married – but she did. She says she's seen shards in Solabas. There are none. And as for the aegis? The Scriptures are clear: the aegis is a myth! Siera Romara has no proofs and the character references supplied by the defensior are spurious lies paid for with bribes. So all we are left with is a knight who has fallen, and worse, become a vyr. Her true nature is clear. She's here out of malice, the catspaw of Augusta Martia, a woman so bitter that she was not chosen to be our archon that she undermines the whole Order. Today we have learned nothing of substance, save proof yet again that vyr lie.' She waved her hand dismissively. 'I have no further questions. May the Devourer take her.'

She had been thwarted, everyone would see that. She'd failed to get Romara to break down. But she was also right: without proof, this was just an interesting story. And she'd deliberately not asked about the Oculus Tempus spell, presumably because to do so would give it credibility.

Dranit was on his feet instantly, to ensure it wasn't overlooked. 'Regarding proofs,' he said loudly, 'I have applied for a dispensation for the banned spell "Oculus Tempus" to be cast before the High Council. Now that you have heard the testimony, do you agree to permit it, Justiciar?'

Romara knew he'd much rather have raised this on the back of more compelling evidence so the audience would be united behind the request, but as it was, the response was warm. The factions were entrenched, but the neutrals were engaged and curious. Romara sensed a majority wanted it to go ahead.

But it wasn't their decision: that lay with Djana Bespari.

The Justiciar was scribbling rapidly, presumably the outline of her summary. She lifted her head, studying Romara with an unreadable face, then rose and walked to the lectern.

'High Councillors, veterans and serving members of the Vestal Order, these hearings are intended to be instructive,' she began. 'The guilt of the accused is not in doubt, but we're here to consider her tale, and learn from it. This is an unusual case, both for the coherency of the testimony, and the deep matters raised. The tidings of triple shard clusters in Solabas, the finding of Vanashta Baanholt and evidence of the aegis are indeed concerning, and worthy of further enquiry. That can proceed without delaying her execution. But the matter of Oculus Tempus should be resolved now.'

Romara's eyes sought Dranit, whose scarred face was taut with hope and fear.

'Certain spells deemed too dangerous or damaging for general use are banned by the agreement of the Imperial Courts,' Bespari reminded them all, 'but the knowledge of how to cast them is preserved by the Justiciary and mage-scholars, and the discretion to use them in a hearing such as this is in the purview of the presiding justiciar. I can command my people to perform it . . . but I do not see a compelling case here for doing so. If the High Council wish to see this spell, then let them find people willing and able to do so. I give you that dispensation, and the amnesty of anonymity, if any are willing to come forward.'

Dranit winced and dropped his head, which told Romara all she needed to know. Clearly, the lictor saw it as a victory, and the archon looked pleased enough. His supporters were nodding their heads too, while Augusta's people looked uncertain.

The session was adjourned until the following day.

Romara, back in the holding cell, asked Dranit, 'I presume Augusta hasn't got enough allies able to cast the spell, as you warned me?'

'That's correct,' the defensior said tersely. 'It's not just a case of someone powering up their glyma and shouting "Oculus Tempus" – those words are just a label for something long and involved that will require skill and practice to perform correctly. Such spells often require several mages – not knights – and Augusta at this stage doesn't have enough mages in her ranks willing to risk the archon's wrath. I have asked for a deferral but a day is the most we'll get. So without some fresh faces coming forward, we probably can't do it.'

Romara felt her hope ebb away. 'Then what have we gained today?'

He could have pointed out the little gains, but he spared her that. 'Not as much as we hoped,' he admitted. 'I'm sorry. I let you down.'

'I don't see how you could have done more,' she countered gloomily. 'The hearing was skewed against us from the outset, and Bespari was looking for excuses not to be involved.'

So much for my beloved Order and its dedication to Truth and Justice.

After overseeing the return of Romara to her overnight cell, Dranit, with Lubano at his heel, headed back up to the daylight. Most of the attendees had dispersed, but a few lingered, some of his brother's adherents wanting to tell him that he was a shit-smear and a vyr-lover who was going straight to the Maw. He ran that gauntlet stonily, letting Lubano keep the worst at bay, and headed for the Stone Garden, where Augusta's faction were gathered. He was a little alarmed at how quickly they'd shrunk to just the hard core.

'Corbus has already made it known that any mage-scholars who involve themselves are endangering their souls,' Augusta told him, as she walked with him, through the rows of statuary that adorned the garden: dead knights and mages, heroes of the Order. 'By which he means their chances of getting his endorsement for future postings or funding are jagged.'

'That's intimidation,' Dranit noted. 'Tell Bespari.'

'I did, but she told me – rightly – that it's not a Justiciary matter.' Augusta flapped indignantly. 'I'd participate myself, but the problem is, we retirees have been purged of the glyma and not used magic for years, even decades. We need service-age people, and they all have their careers at stake.'

'Do we know how many mages it takes to cast the spell?'

'Nine. I have four willing to help, and a few I'm still talking to; but we won't get enough.'

'Nine?' Dranit groaned. 'Then we really are jagged.'

Augusta's lined face was downcast. 'I'm sorry, dear. I know you're impressed by this fallen knight, and on hearing her tale, one can't help but sympathise. I'd like to slap Corbus silly for pushing her people into going rogue. But we're out of options, unless you can find five mages willing to sacrifice their careers for her.'

He bowed his head. 'Then I presume our chances of a no-confidence vote aren't good either?'

'No chance. Not without Oculus Tempus.' She sighed, and patted his shoulder. 'There's always a next time, dear. Do join us tonight for dinner.' Then she walked back her people.

Dranit forewent the offer of dinner, opting to sit in his rented room, trying to blank out the drunks in the streets outside while he re-read his notes on another case – until Lubano interrupted. 'Dranit, there's folk at the door.'

It was too late at night for any visit to be social. 'Who is it?'

Lubano came over and murmured in his ear, as if he feared there were spies listening – which wasn't out of the question, 'It's a certain trapper from Avas.'

Gram Larch – here in Hyastar? Is he mad? 'You said "people"?'

'There's another man with him, unsavoury sort. Larch I trust, but not the other.'

Dranit stroked his stubbled chin, then said, 'Allow them both in. I doubt they're here to cause trouble with us – we're the closest things they have to allies.'

Lubano returned with two men, the familiar shaggy bulk of Gram Larch, and a squat, ugly man who introduced himself as 'Toad' and scanned the room as if looking for something to steal.

'What the jagat are you doing here?' Dranit asked Gram.

23

The Eye of Time

The River of Time

There are as many theories about time as there are scholars. Some posit that it is possible to step in and out of it, and point to the distorted reality of the Shadowlands as proof, but even there, time still only goes forward, just at varying rates. The River of Time has many currents, eddies and branches, but it only flows one way. To which sea, we have yet to learn.

NILIS EVANDRIEL, RENEGADE SCHOLAR, 1437

Tar-Vestallis, Hyastar
Autumn 1472

Romara woke to noises outside her cell, feeling like she hadn't slept at all. All night her body had ached from the sharp pangs and throbbing in her mangled, broken hands and feet to the weeping wounds on her torso and the deep-rooted burning from the brands. A medicalus once told her that burns went on searing flesh beneath the skin for days. 'That's why they're the worst injury of all,' he'd said. She certainly believed him now.

She'd also been kept awake by her brain reliving the questioning, constantly second-guessing her answers, wondering whether she could have said more, and worrying about today. *There'll be no Oculus Tempus*, she thought gloomily. *Just my execution.*

It was a shitty way to spend her last night alive.

Then she heard movement outside, turned over and sat up as the door swung open, admitting Dranit Ritter and Lubano. The bald

Aquini bondsman was eyeballing the guards as he closed the door in their faces.

Dranit sat with her and with a slow smile, said, 'We've got enough mages for the spell.'

She reeled at the unexpected good news. 'I'm so grateful,' she blurted. 'Please, give them all my heartfelt thanks.'

'Well, it took some doing, and we had some unexpected help,' the defensior replied. 'But Bespari's guarantees of anonymity encouraged some people to come forward who otherwise would not have risked it.'

He couldn't say more, as the whole subject was a dangerous one. In any case, they had no time to dwell on it. She was taken to the tiled room for cleansing and dressing, then they made their way under escort through the fortress, a rabbit warren of stone and marble, courtyards and gardens, monuments and graveyards, this time to an open-air amphitheatre large enough for the Oculus Tempus spell to be performed.

Several times they passed clusters of men-at-arms who snarled abuse at her, but her escort kept her safe. *I threaten their sense of stability and rightness*, she thought. *I might have reacted like that, too.* But she hoped she'd have withheld judgement until the truth was revealed.

Their destination was an oval-shaped jousting arena: the Field of Kantarus, named for a mythic half-man, half-horse of Aquini legend. This was where the quadrennial Exemplars' Tourney was fought, and she recalled coming here to watch Vazi Virago defeat all-comers. How she'd cheered at this slip of a girl, overcoming all those big, powerfully built men.

I didn't know what a cold-hearted bitch she was.

Today, the stands were nowhere near packed, although the soldiers outside formed an intimidating cordon, ostensibly to keep the public away. But as they approached the gates, she was startled by shouts of support, and saw a knot of men on a balcony overlooking the press. She recognised Argon Roper, Sec Perryn, Medicalus Burfitt and others of her old Falcon century.

'We believe in ye, lass,' Roper was yelling. 'We's with ye!'

It was wonderfully heartening, but she was terrified for them, and hoped they had strong doors to shelter behind. Breaking down in the face of their support, she stumbled the last hundred paces through a smear of tears, then the entrance swallowed she and her escort, and they entered the dark halls beneath the oval stadia.

Many wearing armbands in Corbus Ritter's colours had crowded in, until Dranit and Lubano clearly feared a lynching. Having hundreds of angry men screaming, 'DIE BITCH!' was terrifying, but her brave escort kept her safe and got them through.

The next hour passed in a blur, until at last she was led forth again, not into the middle, but to a place beneath the presiding official's box, right below the justiciar's throne. To her right were Corbus Ritter's adherents; on her left was Augusta Martia's faction. The buzz of eager speculation filled the air.

Before her lay the arena: hard-packed earth, with no grass. A compass rose had been traced in the earth, at every tip and in the middle, and a flamberge had been stabbed into the ground at each point, the elobyne orbs glowing, there to help empower the spell.

The trumpets blared, the stentor shouted, 'All stand for Justiciar Bespari.'

A grudging approximation of quiet ensued as the black-clad judge entered above and behind Romara, bowed to the amphitheatre, then went to her lectern for her opening address.

'Honoured Members of the Order of the Vestments of Sancta Elysia, I thank you for your attendance on this historic day. This is only the twenty-third time that a banned ritual spell has been sanctioned to help us understand our world. Yesterday, you heard testimony from Siera Romara Challys, claiming the vyr rebels believe themselves justified in rebelling because they believe elobyne, the sacred crystal that upholds the Triple Empire – a gift from Akka Himself to our holy founder, Jovan Lux – is harmful and dangerous, both to humanity and our world. They claim that this spell, Oculus Tempus, or The Eye of Time, will prove their assertions.'

'It'll prove nothing,' someone in Corbus' entourage shouted.

'*Silence*,' the stentor boomed.

Bespari tutted, then went on, 'Oculus Tempus is based in earth-magic, a complex ritual spell in which nine casters attune themselves to the earth, extending that connection outwards while delving into the layers of the soil and the fauna rooted in that earth, interpreting the layers in times of past events that left a mark on the world. Those standing on the compass points are in a state of trance, feeding what they find to the central mage, who renders it into a visual illusion that will fill this stadia. From your seats, you will see – if the spell is cast correctly – a visual impression of hundreds of years of change in the landscape.'

'It'll be jagged-up lies!' a woman shrilled. 'And we'll not forget who did the casting! We'll find out who you are, you jagging traitors! You're all finished!'

'*Silence*,' the stentor shouted again.

'I have said it is delivered in a state of trance,' Bespari said sternly. 'This is not a spell that can be deliberately falsified. *It sees what is there to be seen.* And I should not have to remind you that those who have put themselves forward to cast this spell are protected by anonymity and an amnesty. *There will be no retribution against them.*'

Some hope, Romara thought gloomily. *Corbus and his people don't forget slights, that's clear.* She threw a worried look at Dranit, hoping he wouldn't come to regret protecting her.

'I now call the spell-casters forth,' the justiciar concluded. 'Let the casting begin.'

Bespari returned to her throne, as nine robed and hooded figures entered the arena, emerging in a line then parting to go to the nine embedded flamberges, placing their hands on the orbs and bringing them fully to life. There was a murmur of discontent from those in Corbus' ranks who wanted to see faces, but their clothing was so shapeless Romara couldn't even determine gender. Some were tall, some squat, some thin and some fat. Only two noticeably moved like women, but two others might also be female.

Whoever they were, and wherever Dranit had found them, the fate of the Vyr Rebellion, and perhaps the future of the Triple Empire, was now in their hands.

Not that I will see any of it.

But despite her fatalism, Romara was gripped by the fascination of seeing this mysterious ritual. Putting aside the future, she focused on the nearest of the mages, a big, masculine figure who'd taken up the compass point nearest to her. As she watched him move, taking in the set of his powerful shoulders, an uneasy sensation gripped her. He glanced her way for a beat and her heart almost stopped, even though the hood concealed his features.

It was Gram.

Blanking the presence of the woman he loved, chained to a seat just a dozen paces above him, was almost impossible, but Gram had been drilling this spell all night. It was their one chance, and he was determined it would be done right.

Including him was unplanned, but they hadn't been able to find a ninth willing mage. Despite the justiciar's repeated promises of anonymity, most of the Order people had been unwilling to risk retribution. In the end, Gram had to step forward, even though he'd never cast a ritual spell in his life.

Fortunately, eight of the nine roles were essentially passive, conjuring energy and linking it to the spell. Only the ninth person, anchoring the middle of the compass rose, did the real work. That fell to Lady Augusta's chief ally, Carid Theomore, who was now chanting the initial phrases, calling them all to attention.

Gram turned inwards, mercifully putting his back to Romara, who'd clearly recognised him, and poured all his fear and love into this act. The arcane phrases meant little to him, but Theomore had been drilling the group, a mix of Order men and Toad's people, enemies come together in service of truth, all night.

Chanting the ritual words, he channelled glyma-energy into the ground and rode the wave of awareness pulsing from Theomore, his mind's eye flowing above the landscape, travelling northwest through Miravia, over the Qor-Skorio Mountains into Vandarath and out towards his homeland. They'd given him this point for his ability to anchor his untrained mind to a place he knew. Around him, he felt the others' consciousness shift and widen, while Theomore constantly murmured corrections and guidance into their minds.

A shimmering web of light and shadow formed above their heads, masking the audience from sight, but he could hear murmuring, even some gasping.

'Now anchor,' Theomore called, 'plant and delve!'

His inner eye showed him his beloved Avas, giving him a full sensory impression of his old farmstead, now desolate and ruined, the homestead a pile of charred wreckage and the soil dusted with ash. Smoke still lingered in the air, but he heard birds singing and saw green shoots pushing up through the earth.

He followed them down, through layers of dirt and ash, the husks of insects nested in the ground, the worm and bugs, to the stones beneath, deeper and deeper, until it swallowed him up and he forgot everything else.

Romara soaked up the sight of Gram, his build, the way he stood, the sound of his voice amid the chanting, both longing to go to him and wishing he'd never come.

A vyr in the heart of the Order – they'll cut him to pieces, regardless of the amnesty.

But for now, all she could do was try not to betray him, and watch the spell unfold. As it progressed, it engaged her entire attention. A murky gloom manifested above the mages, filling up the low-lying arena, but giving those in the circular tiers of seats above a perfect view. Gradually, it took on colour – predominantly green, with grey seams and white and blue patches – and shapes they all recognised: Miravia, on the western side of the ground, and southwest Talmont to the east. It was a giant map with Hyastar at the middle, brought to life in colour, with all the contours shown.

My home, she thought, caught up in the vision despite her terrors.

The illusory map grew constantly as the casters took its scope wider, now encompassing Vandarath and the Isles, in the area nearest her, stretching out to reveal Talmont, the Gulf of Elidor and Nexus Isle to the north, the Qor-Massif to the east, with the sprawling plains beyond, and south to Aquinium, the Inner Seas, Zynochia and Bedu-massa, Bravantia, Neparia and Solabas and the northern Sea of Pelas.

There, the vision halted.

Romara could see that every single person in the amphitheatre was drinking it all in, even those who'd not wanted the spell cast. The unique views it gave them overcame their reluctance and commanded their awe as the image was brought to sharper focus by the central magus, taking in what the other eight gave him, and interpreting it.

Raising his voice, that magus announced, 'The spell is now ready. I caution that you will not see full detail – things like trees, pools or streams are too small and brief-lived to be captured in this way. Large cities will be seen as dark brown or grey stains. Small-scale events, like a localised flood or fire, may also not be seen. This is the big picture over a long period, channelled from my colleagues through me. The spell paints in broad strokes, based on what my colleagues find in the sedimentary layers: signs of flooding, layers of burned or rotting wood and other residues, including magical. I am not interpreting anything, just channelling. And to make it clear: I am certainly not interfering with it – I wouldn't know how.'

There was a doubtful murmur at this from a few of Corbus' adherents.

'What you now see is the continent of Hytal,' the mage went on, 'from the Isles to Elidor in the north to Pelas and north Zynochia in the south. *This is Hytal, a thousand years ago.* Aquinium rules the south and the north is too divided and underpopulated to matter. Note the forests: trees cover almost all the lands north of the Qor-Massif and all of Vandarath. The plains of Bravantia are too infertile to sustain large-scale agriculture, but the Aquini are great engineers, and they've built aqueducts from the Qor-Massif to water their farmlands. Bedu-massa is green in the interior, you'll notice, unlike today. Zynochia is arid but densely populated, and Bedum-Mutaza is the greatest city, rivalled only by Mardium, in Aquinium.'

The audience was silent now, awed by this ancient vista.

The central magus chanted in Runic again, then called out, 'We roll forward in time, through the Pelasian Sea-King era, the Aquini and Mutazan Ages and the taming of the north. See the spread of farmland across Talmont particularly, and the shrinking forests. Humanity flows north, like water into a basin. See the browning of Bedumassa and Zynochia as overcrowding and destructive agriculture affects the land during the last recorded "Age of Fire". Note the red flares in the isles – volcanic eruptions, including the one which destroyed Old Pelas. See also the browning of southern Aquinium as the decline of their empire causes the aqueducts to fall into disrepair. It is now 1100 and Zynochia dominates the Inner Seas, founding coastal colonies everywhere. There are more cities, especially in the north, as power begins to shift.'

It was like having a mighty tapestry being woven before their eyes, and Romara wished she could cast herself into it and meet these people who were shaping Hytal by the sweat of their backs and their visions of a better future.

'We now approach 1200, and the advent of Jovan Lux,' the narrating magus announced from beneath the carpet of light. His voice was tense, and Romara remembered he'd never seen this spell either. He sounded eager and worried to see what transpired.

There was a collective intake of breath, then a gasp as a brilliant starburst appeared at Nexus Isle, then washed over the landscape as if glowing dust had been deposited everywhere.

'This is heresy,' someone shouted. *'Unbelievers!'*

'Heresy is a point of view,' Dranit snapped back. 'Why don't you pipe down and enjoy the privilege of seeing something your betters don't want you to see.'

The heckler responded by drawing a finger across his throat, the threat clear.

The narrating magus paused to let them digest the view, then resumed. 'Now see the spread of elobyne shards as the Lighters begin planting them throughout the landscape, in and around the major settlements of the north. Though small, they are constant, like twinkling stars. See them spread – and watch the colour of the land around them . . .' His voice trailed off as his brain tried to catch up with what he was seeing.

413

They could all see the shards spreading across the landscape, but there were two phases: the first, when they sited in and around Talmoni settlements, but the landscape went visibly darker – and the second phase, when abruptly most of the glittering stars moved to the wilds, away from the major settlements.

'Er, what we are seeing is a policy change, no longer siting shards in the heartland of the north, but moving them to the wilds,' the narrator said. 'Most likely this is a reaction to local concerns at the effect on the land. There are smaller shards in local churches still, for orison purposes, but the bulk have now been moved to the wildlands.'

The audience murmured as the sea of stars grew; big clusters of shards were now apparent along the icy coasts of Elidor and Vorsk, on the northeast Vandar coast. There were also arrays south of the Qor-Massif, and around the abandoned Aquini palace-city of Qorium. And also, startlingly, in the interior of Bedumassa and east of Lenziu – all places where no shards existed – or so the official records asserted. And *everywhere*, the land was changing visibly from lush green to pale dun, emptying of life.

'Er, I . . .' The narrator was stammering as he pushed on. 'Note the . . . um . . . deforestation . . . in Neparia, Solabas . . . This *not* an Age of Fire – see how the polar caps remain steady . . . but northern Aquinium is barren now . . . Elidor is also fading, with nothing left for the Shards to draw out . . . Ah, it's now 1400 or thereabouts, and only now do we begin to see the fires of the Vyr Rebellion . . . but the ground was already dying. There's no question of that! And there's shards in the Pelas . . . ? When were they sanctioned?'

The Oculus Tempus froze as it reached *now*. There was an awed silence as the carpet of coloured light and images faded, revealing the nine mages beneath it, leaning heavily on the flamberges which had helped empower the spell. Romara felt a twinge of irony, that elobyne had been needed to reveal what elobyne had done.

Her eyes flashed to Gram, dreading that he'd rip his flamberge from the ground and try and reach her. *No*, she thought urgently, shaking her head as his cowled face turned her way.

She sensed hesitation, then to her relief, he bowed his head and joined his eight fellows in trooping from the arena into the maze of corridors below.

Leave tonight, she urged him. *Don't watch me die tomorrow.*

The stadium was abuzz all around her. She looked around, trying to assess the reaction. Corbus Ritter had his head bowed, listening to his mage advisors, who were probably devising some excuse to discount all they'd seen.

But Augusta Martia was first to stand and speak. 'I call upon the High Council to debate a motion of no confidence in Archon Ritter. He should have seen this wanton destruction happening! He sups at the teat of the Hierophant and he should have known of this . . . *Down with the archon!*'

The cry was taken up by many, but she'd gone too early and most, still processing what they'd seen, were yet unwilling to commit. But then some of the neutrals rose and backed her call, until it became apparent that Augusta Martia had the numbers to force a vote – but not necessarily the numbers to win, which would require two-thirds of the High Council to agree.

Corbus was clearly no longer so sure of himself, though, as he rose and made placating gestures. 'I hear your calls,' he said, trying to project statesmanship, not factionalism. 'I too am shocked – we of the Order have been blindsided by our rivals, the Lighters, and elements in the Night Court – that much is clear. I have as many questions as you!'

There was a burst of derision at that, not just from Augusta's people, but among his own.

'There you go, blowing with the wind again!' a veteran knight in his own faction bellowed. 'Show some backbone!'

'I do not blow with the wind!' Corbus retorted haughtily. 'When the facts change, a wise man changes his thinking. This is a time for calm reflection, not hot-headed demands. Justiciar, we need a recess.'

Romara had to admit that this once, he was right. Everyone was in shock, overwhelmed by what they'd seen. They all needed to take a deep breath and think. Justiciar Bespari seized on the suggestion like a lifeline. She signalled to her stentor, whose trained voice cut though the din.

'Thirty minutes' recess! Please remain here. We resume in thirty minutes!'

Most remained seated, huddling together to debate, but Corbus vanished down a stairwell with his closest advisors. Romara was fearful for her own safety in this amphitheatre filled with angry knights – although why it should matter when she was scheduled to burn, she didn't quite know – but Dranit and Lubano got permission to move her. There were still plenty of men and women who snarled abuse as she passed, calling, 'Your stinking friends are destroying the Order,' and 'You'll still burn tomorrow, traitor.' But no one tried to accost her.

They reached her cell, where a guard sergeant insisted on locking her to her seat again, but with Augusta's people protecting the door, they were at least able to draw breath. Dranit looked stressed, but Lubano was his normal phlegmatic self.

'Get Gram out of here,' she told them urgently. 'Make him leave, I beg you.'

'All the mages involved in the spell are being protected and we'll get them out as soon as we can,' Dranit replied. 'They'll be gone from the city within the hour.'

She was appeased by that, though she didn't trust their enemies not to try something before then, or to track the carriage and attack them outside the city.

'How did he come to be here?' she demanded. 'How did you find him?'

'He found me,' Dranit replied. 'He appeared last night, wanting to see you, but when I explained the situation, his comrade – a somewhat disreputable-looking fellow called "Toad" – offered vorlok aid in casting Oculus Tempus. We had no choice but to accept.' He gripped Romara's forearm. 'I don't like to hold out any hope that may not be fulfilled, but if the archon is overthrown, I will fight to have your execution delayed or commuted to imprisonment, if that's your will?'

'Thank you, but I don't want to grow old in prison,' she replied. 'Just get Gram out of here, please!'

The defensior nodded gravely, then he and Lubano left and she was alone, with nothing to look forward to but one night, and then execution in the morning.

But at least I saw that spell, she thought numbly. *We are in the right.*

24

A Barbaric Travesty

Crowning an Exemplar

Every four years, the regional champions of the Order meet on the tourney field, to determine who will be crowned 'Exemplar', the greatest knight alive. Though they fight only until one yields, to avoid maiming or death, every bout still carries great risk, for these are the deadliest fighters alive. Indeed, the greatest Exemplar of all time, Voltan Karax, was dubbed 'The Scythe' for the number of rivals he slew on the tourney field.

THE TALE OF TALMONT, JENAS FYLE, SCHOLAR, 1468

Tar-Vestallis, Hyastar
Autumn 1472

Corbus Ritter sat, head bowed, listening as his circle of advisors argued among themselves. Some were just venting, while others proposed various strategies – everything from flat-out denials to pinning the blame on the vyr, to trying to ride out the storm by arguing that he was the only one who could negotiate with the Hierophant.

He lost patience with them and sought sanctuary in a neighbouring chapel, with two trusted knights at the door to keep anyone else out. He wasn't here to pray, though, just to work through his slender options. He sat in the front pew and closed his eyes to better think.

He'd been fighting a rearguard action for days, ever since his attempt to suppress Romara Challys' testimony backfired, triggering this hearing. Now, with more than half the High Council prepared to put his status to the vote, he could feel the cold breath of his enemies on his neck. And Elspeth Sandreth had distanced herself – probably wisely – but he missed her wisdom.

With the Oculus Tempus spell having clearly shown a link between elobyne and the country's ecological destruction, he'd been left looking at best weak, and at worst, complicit.

'We need to shut this down,' he muttered aloud. 'It's ripping us apart.'

'Our very thought,' a muffled voice said behind him.

Corbus rose, groping for the sword he'd had to leave outside this shrine.

Two cloaked figures stood at the closed door. He hadn't heard it open, nor heard their footfalls, and his skin prickled in fear. Their appearance did nothing to alleviate his anxiety: they were cowled in black and wore silver masks, fantastical and ornate, one a moon, the other, a bat.

Emissaries of the Night Court, Corbus realised anxiously. *How'd they get past my guards?*

'Sorry to alarm you, Archon,' Moon said. 'We come in friendship.'

'My Lords,' Corbus whispered. 'This is an honour.'

He didn't feel at all honoured, only threatened. Had the Night Court decided he was a liability? His heart thudded faster as a side door opened and a third Night Courtier appeared, a woman in an owl mask, leading in a worried Justiciar Bespari.

'Sit,' Moon told Corbus and Bespari.

They obeyed without a word, and Moon effortlessly moved a pew to face them, while Owl conjured veiling spells. Bat, the only one openly armed, sealed the door with a warding sigil, then took up a guarding position there.

Corbus glanced at Bespari, whose dark face had a sheen of sweat. He couldn't blame her for her fear; he felt it too.

'The Most High is concerned at this unfolding farce,' Moon declared. 'It undermines the unity of our empire, when unity is needed. We must stand together, not let petty matters divide us.'

Corbus tried to get onside with him, saying, 'My people have been saying that—'

'Yet opposition to you grows,' the Owl woman interrupted. 'Damaging allegations are taking root. If you are brought down, a schism may occur. That must be prevented.'

Not wanting to be seen as blind to all this, Corbus answered quickly. 'We're prepared for adversity. I have the crowd primed outside, ready to be let in if the vote goes badly—'

'A mob?' Moon sneered. 'The Most High does not side with *mobs*. Rulers rule and the herd obey. There will be no riots here. There is no place at the high table for rabble-rousers. Do you understand, Archon?'

Corbus felt his blood chill. 'Yes ... yes. I erred, I misread the moment, but I can—'

'Hush,' Owl interrupted. 'We have this under control.' She faced Bespari. 'As for you: how *dare* you permit a forbidden spell to be cast in your court? Do you serve the vyr rebellion, Justiciar? Or Augusta Martia's faction?'

The grey-haired Bravanti woman was shaking. 'I thought they'd embarrass themselves – and my advisers told me the spell was harmless, that it wouldn't prove anything ...'

'Fool,' Owl jeered coldly. 'If we had heard sooner of this farce, we could have prevented it. These spells are banned for reasons. Let us be clear: what you saw today wasn't truth. *It was all a lie.* That is the *fact* you must make clear to everyone out there.'

Bespari quivered. 'Yes, Lord, but ... How?'

Moon jabbed a finger at her. 'You will declare the Oculus Tempus spell to have been corrupted and arrest all involved. You will declare it inadmissible, part of a vyr conspiracy to unseat the archon, and use that declaration to arrest and destroy Augusta Martia's faction.'

Corbus felt sweat beading his brow. While this was a godsend, one that might save his career, even he was horrified that these people could march in and tell his Order that night was day and which of their comrades they must kill. But he just nodded mutely, too scared to react any other way. He dared not deny the Night Court, the Hierophant's uttermost allies.

Indeed, there were some who thought they *outranked* the God-Emperor.

'Then there is the matter of Siera Romara Challys,' Moon went on. 'By permitting her testimony to be heard, it is now on the record, a stain on your Order. Her words give credence to the vyr rebellion. Your inability to silence her undermines not just your own standing, but our empire. So her words must be erased.'

'How? Even I can't—'

Owl leaned in so that he could see the beautiful, intricate detail of her polished silver and ebony mask and her eyes of golden-flecked lucent pearl. 'There is an ancient law, still on the statutes, left there by the all-seeing and all-knowing Most High. It permits direct action against those whose baseless accusations impugn the Hierophant. That law allows the Hierophant to call for Trial by Arms. You will invoke that.'

'A Blood Trial?' Bespari blurted, her legal mind appalled at the notion. 'But that's barbarism! It was Jovan Lux Himself who ended Blood Trials, to prevent the courts from being ruled by gladiators and hired killers—'

'And yet he left them on the statutes, at the Hierophant's discretion,' Owl replied. 'Such is the foresight and vision of the Most High. He left the provision there for exactly this circumstance.'

Moon pulled out a parchment and thrust it across the table. 'The Hierophant has already approved the Blood Trial. Romara Challys' attacks on the integrity of the Vestals, the Lighters and the Exemplar amount to an attack on the Throne itself. The Hierophant wants her lies erased, but the only way that can happen is for her to recant. In a Blood Trial, the defeated combatant is automatically deemed to have lied and their testimony is erased. So that is how we will proceed. She will be challenged, and if she fails to recant, she will be thrown to the arena and made to.'

The droplets of sweat on Corbus' face became a film. *It must have taken these three at least half a day to get here from Petraxus, even using portali gates. So the Hierophant prepared this directive even before Oculus Tempus was cast . . .*

Clearly they'd predicted this moment, even from afar. What else had they foreseen? And how would it play out for him? Would showing that he had highly placed backers strengthen his position? Or would it paint him as a tool, a mere catspaw? The Order *hated* being used as a plaything by courtiers in Petraxus.

The High Council will see this Blood Trial as an act of tyranny, and me as a catspaw of the Night Court. But if I don't go ahead with it, I'm finished. He didn't need to be told that he and Bespari only left this room alive if they agreed to this plan.

He still tried to protest. 'A Blood Trial will turn more people against us. Such a heavy-handed response risks giving Challys' words more credibility, not less. We're going to execute her tomorrow anyway.'

'In public, where her last words will be passed mouth to mouth among the mob,' Moon replied dismissively. 'That is just as dangerous. The Most High has seen where this leads. Voices of dissent must be silenced, and the Blood Trial is how you will do it. Once the people see that you can call down the wrath of the Night Court, your position will be strengthened.'

Corbus looked from Moon to Owl, seeing only implacable will. *They're wrong, but I dare not say so.* His own foretelling was that this would end in schism, and he'd be the focus of hatred from all sides. *There's no surviving this . . . unless . . .*

A plan came to him, and he glanced at Bespari, praying she'd back him. 'Justiciar?' he asked. 'I'm in agreement. Are you?'

Are you ready to go to war against Augusta and her faction and risk destroying the Order?

She winced, but nodded.

Well, I guess we're allies now.

He faced Moon. 'If Justiciar Bespari and I do this, we'll need to retire into positions of impregnability. We need to be elevated to the Night Court.'

The masked man's gold-flecked eyes blinked once, then he said, 'Agreed.'

Corbus rocked back in his seat, stunned – he truly hadn't expected instant agreement. But his heart was racing now. From his carefully constructed future collapsing about him, suddenly all his dreams could come true, a reward all his hard work and courage warranted.

I deserve this, he decided, *more than any other man.*

Djana Bespari just looked stunned, her entire horizons altered in a mind-boggling way. But she looked appreciative, too – as she damned well should.

I just got her seat at the highest table in the world – I own her, he told himself.

'The Blood Trial must happen as soon as possible,' Moon said, bringing Corbus back to the here and now.

'Tomorrow, midday,' Bespari said absently. 'Trial by arms traditionally takes place exactly a day after the court taking the decision began its sitting.'

Moon and Owl exchanged glances. 'Very well,' said Owl, 'make it so.'

'Who will champion our cause?' Corbus asked.

'I will,' the man in the bat mask replied, the first time he'd spoken.

His voice and accent made the hair on Corbus' neck stand up. He *knew* that voice, though he hadn't heard it in thirty years. It had belonged to the man who'd led his first ever century.

'Sier Voltan?' Corbus blurted.

The Night Courtier lowered his cowl and mask. 'Corbus,' Voltan Karax said gravely.

Elysia have mercy, Corbus thought, wondering if he was delusional.

Corbus served in Voltan 'The Scythe' Karax's century for a short time, until the Bravanti won the Exemplars' Tourney and went on to have a glorious undefeated reign as Exemplar. *Thirty years ago.* Incredibly, the man hadn't aged a day – if anything, Karax looked younger. His face had lost its scars, his nose had straightened, the teeth evened and his hair was jet-black again.

Corbus didn't know whether to rejoice or run screaming. 'It's a joy to see you,' he blurted, as survival instincts took over once again. *If this is the Night Court*, he thought wildly, *let me in now.* 'But surely some . . . er, younger knight should—?'

'It needs to be me,' Karax interrupted. 'An ordinary knight would struggle against an Order-trained draegar like Romara Challys. Only I can guarantee victory.'

Yes, you can, Corbus thought. *You were a reaper – an army on two legs.* 'But Sier Voltan Karax is supposed to be dead, and you look so young . . .'

How? he wondered. *Are you immortal?*

The hard-faced former Exemplar smiled ironically. 'I have maintained a fictional identity as a younger kinsman. I will be introduced as Enzo Karax, a legitimate persona, so I can be named as your champion without issue.'

He faked his own death and he hasn't aged. Dear Akka, what am I getting myself into?

Karax replaced his mask. The three courtiers faced Corbus and Bespari and saluted. 'We'll see ourselves out,' Moon drawled. 'Set it in motion.'

When they opened the chapel door, Corbus saw the two knights he'd assigned to guard the door standing stiff and unmoving – which was, he supposed, better than lying in a pool of blood. Then the door shut again and he finally remembered to breathe.

Was that even real? But their promises made his soul sing. Clearly, his ruler valued him, and now all his dreams were coming true.

As long as Romara Challys dies.

He turned to Bespari. 'Well,' he said, 'we're in this together. Are you up for it?'

She looked shaky, but she too was a political animal. 'I don't like it,' she admitted, 'and I like it even less that our futures are now resting on "Enzo Karax" and his blade. Everything I've heard of Romara Challys suggests a fighter of skill and tenacity. And as a draegar, she can channel far more glyma than an ordinary man.'

Corbus shared that fear, but not to the same degree. 'Don't forget, she's been tortured and had her hands broken. That'll stay with her, even if she shape-changes – which I hope she does, to show everyone the monster within. If she chooses a champion instead, that person won't have her training, even if they're a vorlok or draegar; and by doing so, she'll look craven. Anyway, I've seen Karax fight. He's a whirlwind of destruction.'

Or he used to be . . . and he doesn't look a day older.

Bespari gave him an uneasy look. 'Actually, I've seen him fight too – I was there when he won his last Exemplar Tourney. But how is it possible that he's survived so long without ageing?'

'I don't know,' Corbus admitted. 'But with luck, you and I will find out, first-hand.'

I rather fancy immortality, and I bet you do too.

Justiciar Bespari recalled everyone to the arena and read her incredible, unprecedented decision to a disbelieving audience. To Romara, chained to her seat beneath the Justiciar's plinth, it was as if she'd been placed onstage in the middle of a play set three centuries ago. The proposal – *a trial of arms, for Akka's sake!* – was a barbaric travesty, but apparently legal: a writ from the Hierophant himself said so.

The powers upholding the empire were showing their true colours now: blood-red.

Amid all the shouting and fury that greeted the proposal, she clung to memories of Gram to tide her through the turmoil. She hoped he was already gone, but if her enemies could do this, then the amnesty offered to those who cast Oculus Tempus was probably worthless, too.

Dranit Ritter was on his feet shouting, Lady Augusta was crying out above the din, while more than five hundred former knights and their retainers, unarmed but still lethal, were roaring at each other. The stentor, shouting for order, was hammering his stave hard enough to crack the flagstones, but no one hearkened.

Then Corbus Ritter rose, arms spread like a returning prophet, calling for silence.

'Let the archon be heard,' the stentor called plaintively. 'Hearken!'

Finally, everyone fell silent – but that was because two figures had emerged from a stairwell near Corbus, robed in black cowls and wearing silvery masks. Romara had never seen such attire, but like everyone else, she knew who they were.

Night Courtiers – what in Coros are they doing here?

Members of the fabled Night Court were *never* seen outside Petraxus, or even outside the royal palace – and never, so rumour said, in daylight. That they were here now was chilling.

Did you truly believe the great powers would let you undermine them? her brain sneered. *This is what you get for sticking your neck out, fool.*

The Night Courtiers said nothing, but suddenly Romara could hear every rustle of paper and cloth, every footfall. The entire assembly gaped as the archon waited, too composed for this to have surprised him. Clearly, he'd been fully briefed on Bespari's decision and knew who was backing it.

'Thank you for hearkening, my brothers- and sisters-in-arms,' he drawled. 'We welcome the representative of the Hierophant to our deliberations.'

The Order was supposed to be independent of the Throne. *Everyone* knew that.

It was the combative, forthright Dranit Ritter who reacted first. 'With every respect,' he called, coming to his feet, 'this is a hearing of the Vestal Order. Representatives of the Hierophant have no place here.'

'Don't you presume to speak for the Order,' Corbus sniffed. 'You're here due to legal process and no other reason. Sit down and shut up.'

'Who now can claim that Corbus Ritter represents the Order?' Augusta Martia broke in. 'He speaks for no one but himself – he goes crying to the Night Court rather than face the just accusations of his peers. Shame on you, Archon, shame. *This is an infamy!*'

'*Infamy!*' her cry was taken up – but only by her faction. Everyone else looked thoroughly cowed, and the calls died quickly in the intimidating atmosphere of the arena.

'Thus speaks the Hierophant,' Corbus retorted, brandishing a parchment, then reading from it. 'Any who assail my beloved Vestal Order, the Order of Akka's Light, or the integrity of the Night Court, assail the throne! Baseless accusations that cannot be proven are a poison which destroys our society. They are assassin's blades, delivered from contemptible safety. This is why the Blood Trial laws still exist: Jovan Lux foresaw this moment, when a treacherous demagogue would use court privilege to lead good people astray.' Corbus pointed dramatically at Romara. 'Behold the vyr-witch, clinging to the skirts of dissidents and hurling her venomous blades. See the hate in her

426

draegar eyes – there is our enemy, thinking herself protected from justice—'

The crowd rose again, both sides shrieking at each other, some defending Romara, but most happy to swing with the wind, now that the Hierophant had taken sides.

'Let the witch stand before us and recant her lies,' Corbus shouted. 'Recant and have them struck from the record – erased from history, as they should be! Or let her back them in the arena: that is the choice placed on her. How speak you, Vyr-Witch? Will you recant, or fight?'

His challenge was taken up: '*RECANT OR FIGHT! RECANT OR FIGHT!*' Angry faces, scared of the Night Court's intervention, were frightened enough to trample on tradition, justice and even decency. '*RECANT OR FIGHT!*'

Recant? They're going to kill me anyway, Romara thought. *Jag them all.*

Dranit hurried to her, speaking in a low, urgent voice. 'This is illegal – we will appeal, so say nothing.'

Her anger refused to let her contemplate that, even though right now she was a broken-handed cripple, still reeling from blood-loss and system shock. 'Recant?' she hissed. 'They're going to kill me anyway.'

'Please, no,' Dranit replied, as everyone strained to hear. 'This has to be resolved by legal means, or it sets a precedent that will plunge us back into the Dark Ages.'

I know. But I have no choice.

'You had plenty to say yesterday, Siera Romara,' Corbus shouted theatrically. 'Back when you thought yourself safe to lie as you pleased – so what say you now? Come on, name your champion and let's resolve this.'

Jag them all, Romara thought again, throwing off Dranit's arm and rising. 'I will back my words,' she cried, 'with my own body against whomever you damned well like.'

Corbus Ritter's smile never faltered. 'Challenge accepted,' he purred. 'I name Sier Enzo Karax, nephew of the late Exemplar Voltan Karax, to represent the Order. Let the combat take place at noon tomorrow.' He turned to the Justiciar. 'You have my leave to end this hearing.'

Again, a storm of protests rose as Augusta's people tried to have the decision stalled or thrown out, but now they were sailing against both wind and tide. The Hierophant had intervened, the Night Court were here and everyone could feel the change in the air. The Order prided itself on its independence from the Crown; but that was revealed as an illusion: clearly Corbus had only to point an accusatory finger and no one was safe.

'It's not the end of this matter,' Augusta was telling her supporters, but Romara could that see no one believed that. Corbus could clearly arrest her at any time, and after her, who'd be next?

As that realisation spread, those who weren't cheering lustily began to slink for the exits.

At least now I die with a sword in hand, Romara told herself. *It's better than I'd thought.*

After completing the Oculus Tempus spell, Gram, Toad and the three other vorloks who made up five of the nine spell-casters were herded to a carriage waiting in a courtyard behind the arena. The flamberges they'd used for the spell had been taken from them and they were now wearing scholars' robes. They were hoping the promises of anonymity and immunity would be honoured, But there was a delay, some kerfuffle going on back inside, so they waited anxiously, praying no one would recognise them as vyr and lynch them.

Toad and the others were eager to leave, but Gram, having thought himself reconciled to losing Romara, wanted to see what was happening that had everyone so wound up.

So he tapped Toad's shoulder and muttered, 'I'm going back to see what's going on.'

'You can't,' the squat vorlok retorted. 'If they arrest you, you'll reveal the Vyr Queen.'

'Then get her to move,' he said. 'Oh, and thank you.' He stalked away.

'Jag you,' Toad called after him. 'Your woman's doomed – come with us.'

Gram waved him off, then walked back to the arena entrance,

where two guards, hands on hilts, blocked his way. 'Oi,' one growled. 'You can't come back in.'

'I just want to know what's going on inside,' he said quietly.

The two men glanced at each other, conscious that he was a mage. 'We got told you lot have to leave. You need to get in that carriage.'

'Bring the defensior, if you can't let me through. It's a matter of life and death.'

'Whose?' then man said truculently.

Gram narrowed his eyes. '*Yours.*'

The men visibly quailed. 'Hey, we're jus' doin' a job here, fella,' the spokesman said. 'We don't want no trouble. I'll jus' call someone, yeah?' He backed a step and yelled, 'Siera Farina! This magus-fella wants back in.'

A burly blonde woman knight loitering near the door stalked over, looking up at Gram with apprehension. 'Yes?' she asked, her fleshy face uncertain.

'What's happening in there?'

Farina wasn't keen to talk, but must have seen something in Gram's demeanour that persuaded her otherwise. 'The jagging Night Court just marched in and declared a Blood Trial.'

'A what?' Gram looked blank.

'Exactly,' Farina growled. '*A what?* It's a trial by combat, from the jagging Dark Ages.'

'Who's fighting who?' Gram demanded, and when she shook her head, he said, 'Please, let me see Dranit Ritter.'

The woman frowned. 'Weren't you part of that spell? You don't look like any mage-scholar I've ever seen.' Then she thought better of that line of thought. 'Jag it, follow me.'

She took him past the guards, down a series of corridors until they arrived before a locked door lit by a flickering oil lamp. Gram wondered if it was a trap, but Dranit Ritter answered her knock himself, saw Gram and waved him in. Siera Farina marched off, clearly washing her hands of the matter. Gram could hear voices through the next door, but Dranit stopped him going through to seek Romara.

'Gram, you shouldn't be here,' Dranit warned.

'What's this about a trial by combat?' Gram demanded.

'It's jagging unbelievable,' Dranit exclaimed. 'Three Night Courtiers have just forced Justiciar Bespari to declare a Blood Trial. One of them is going to fight Romara to the death, to have her testimony declared invalid and erased.'

Gram stared in disbelief. '*What?*'

Trial by combat was so antiquated he couldn't believe it was legal. Talmont prided itself on being civilised; the only nations that still practised such barbarities were outside the Triple Empire. But the Hierophant had not only sanctioned it, he'd made Justiciar Bespari and the archon obey his wish.

Gram's need to see Romara became imperative. 'If you don't let me,' he said urgently, 'she's doomed.'

'She's doomed anyway,' Dranit pointed out. 'This doesn't obviate her death sentence: even if she wins, she'll still be executed. It merely preserves her testimony. And if she loses, she avoids torture and burning, so in some ways, she's better off fighting and dying, even if her words are officially recanted.'

Gram groaned. 'You people are beyond belief . . .'

'She's a condemned vyr,' the defensior reminded him. 'That hasn't changed.'

'Then let me see her – by the Maw, I'll fight in her place—'

'She's refused to let anyone champion her, even though she can barely hold a sword. She won't let anyone else die in her place, and she can't be made to accept a champion unwillingly.'

Gram winced, because that was so very like Romara. But he didn't relent. 'Then you must let me see her – at least I can help her fight.'

Dranit gave in. 'Fine, come with me. Augusta persuaded the justiciar that we had to keep Romara ourselves to prevent someone trying to murder her, but if she commits suicide or tries to escape, that's on us. So nothing stupid, you hear?'

He took Gram to another cell, where a Vestal knight stopped them, asking, 'Dranit, who's this?'

'He's one of the mages who cast the Oculus Tempus for us.'

The knight looked Gram and down, and said, 'He's no mage . . .'

Then his eyes bulged. '*Akka's Balls, Dranit, are you insane? He's a bloody . . .*' He raised a hand, taking a fast step away. 'No, don't tell me. Are you sure you vouch for him?'

'I'm here to speak with her,' Gram growled. 'Nothing more than that.'

The knight winced, and Gram could sympathise. He was firmly caught between duty and decency, and if the archon found out, he might end up in a cell as well. But he looked at Dranit and muttered, 'For all you did for my brother,' and stood aside.

Dranit shook the man's hand, then ushered Gram into the cell. Romara was there, sitting with a soldier with grey, receding hair who was examining her hands. *Healer Burfitt, from the Falcons,* Gram realised. That touched him, to see one of her old century helping her. He took in how pale and drawn she looked, and the mangled mess the torturers had left of her fingers – each one crooked, bruised black and trembling.

Anger welled up and he blurted, '*Rom—*'

She looked up, saw him and croaked, 'No, no, you jagging fool, get out of here—'

He ignored her words, instead striding up and sweeping her into his arms, wrapping her close, stinging tears streaming from his own eyes, and holding on as she struggled then surrendered. She kept protesting, but he ignored that and clung on.

If the End of All Things is coming, he thought, *let it come now.*

The seconds stretched to minutes and his tears cleared to see the healer and Dranit were watching them, their expressions awed and anxious. Romara was shaking like she had a palsy, telling him he was an idiot and to get out and damn well let her die.

'You're not going to die,' he told her. 'That's why I'm here.' He looked at Healer Burfitt and Dranit. 'Could we please have a moment?'

Dranit shook his head. 'She must be with someone at all times. I'm pushing the rules as it is.'

Gram accepted that and faced Romara again. There was more grey hair, deeper lines on her face, and fear in her haunted blue eyes: fear for him.

'I recognised you, during the spell,' she whispered. 'But you have to go. One of us has to live.'

'We both live, or neither of us,' he replied. 'Let me fight for you.'

'No, no and no,' she answered. 'Nobody is taking this fight from me. It's mine.'

'They'll kill you and erase your words,' he reminded her.

'But those present will know I never recanted. The truth won't be lost.'

He could scarcely look at her, chilled by the desperation for death he saw. He couldn't comprehend it – but then, he'd never been tied to a rack and tortured, helpless in the hands of sadists. What he saw most clearly was that nobody on Coros could persuade her not to fight.

'Then let me help you,' he said.

'Burf's here to bind my hands. We're going to splint the fingers, then wrap my hands round the hilt of a flamberge and tie it in place—'

'That'll last about three seconds,' Gram interrupted, glaring at Burfitt.

The healer pulled a face. 'Aye,' he conceded, 'but there's jag all else I can do. It's about defiance, and earning respect.'

'Even if I take on vyr-form, my fingers and toes will still be broken,' Romara admitted. 'And I don't want people watching to see that side of me, anyway. All they'll see is the monster.'

Gram ignored that. 'Look. I need to show you something.'

He got her seated, pulled another chair round the table and faced her, then took her broken hands in his. She was looking at him like she wanted to fix his face in her memory for ever, but her expression was utterly devoid of hope. He pushed the presence of Dranit and Burfitt from his mind, focused entirely on her and with his eyes locked on hers, whispered, '*I love you.*'

'I know,' she croaked. 'I . . .' Her filled with tears again. 'I want to feel the same, but they took that away from me . . . I'm sorry.' Her face crumpled.

'Hush,' he whispered. 'No one's blaming you for anything they did. I'm here to help you heal. You think you're broken, but you're not. If you were, you wouldn't be fighting for truth against these torturers. You wouldn't fear for others more than for yourself. You are still yourself, Romara, no matter what they did to your body.'

In the face of Gram's determined adoration, Romara had no words. His rough-hewn, battered and beautiful face filled her sight, shining with courage and conviction and compassion. His voice, the strongest sound she'd ever heard, filled up her senses. His big leathery hands felt broad and sturdy enough to cradle the world.

I love you too, she thought, and a dam burst inside, not of tears this time, but hope, pent-up and buried deep where it couldn't hurt her. Now it flooded through her fears, though she couldn't rationalise why, only that everything felt possible when this man was here. *I love you too*, she thought again, then she was finally able to say the words aloud.

'I love you too.'

Rationality returned in little waves, like a turning tide, along with the realisation that time was passing. Dranit and Burfitt were watching anxiously, but Gram's eyes were full of import.

'There's something I've recently learned,' he whispered. 'You know the thing we shared, that moment of love before you were captured? That was ninneva.' He held up his left hand, his fingers splayed. 'I need you to see what's possible if you have that love and the glyma.'

Then, before she could react, he gripped his little finger with his right hand – and *snapped* it.

She winced, recoiling in shock, while he groaned, arched his neck and back away, his face contorted as he took the pain.

'What in Akka's name . . . ?' Then she gaped.

He gestured and the finger bent itself back into shape, then he exhaled and flexed the hand.

'*What the jagat?*' Burfitt breathed.

Dranit just stared, speechless.

'Love heals the soul and the soul heals the body, that's how it was explained to me,' Gram said, his eyes boring into hers. 'What that means is that someone at peace with themselves can tame the glyma and use it for more than just destruction.'

At first, Romara felt utterly inadequate, because this was just impossibly unfair, to come in here and demand this of her: a demonstration of love she was incapable of matching.

How dare you demand these miracles of me?

But being within the ambit of his unquestioning love enabled her to push through that and instead feel the sense of possibility. Legendary knights and mages couldn't do what he'd just done – but he said she could do it as well, so maybe she could.

She had forgotten the necklet locked round her throat, which burned the moment she unconsciously reached for the glyma. She recoiled, swallowing a gasp of pain. 'I can't even try until they remove this thing,' she told him. 'I'll have just seconds to manage it.'

'That will be enough, my love,' Gram replied. 'Just *believe*. Clear your mind of doubt and fear. No matter what happens, the world will go on, and one day these tyrants will fall.'

That was what she needed to hear, because it removed the pressure she'd felt building in herself. 'I'll try,' she told him, 'I will try.' It was the most she could give him.

Then Lubano knocked on the door. 'Sir, there are marshalls coming to move her to the overnight cells. The visitor needs to be gone.'

Dranit turned to Gram. 'Master Larch, you need to go. Siera Romara will be held in comfort tonight, and she'll be moved to the tournament fields tomorrow morning. The bout is at noon. You've given us hope, but we can't afford to have you found here.'

Gram groaned, kissed Romara's forehead and then wrenched himself away. There was a creak and a slam, and he was gone.

She swallowed, and remembered to breathe.

A minute later, two armoured knights and a magia appeared, solemn-faced and grim. 'Siera Romara Challys,' the magia said, in a severe voice, 'we're here to see to your confinement. Come with us.'

25

Behind the Shadows

Land of Light and Shadow

The Erlings say that the Talam-Argith – the Shadowlands – were once a benign place filled with light, where the greatest danger was the desire to linger too long. Time passes differently there, swiftly for those with purpose and slowly for those with none. Tales are told of men stumbling into the Talam-Argith, falling asleep and waking years later. No one ever dwelt there, as the perils were too many, even before it fell into darkness.

HELION TAMASK, SCHOLAR, DENIUM 1446

The Talam-Argith (Shadowlands)
Autumn 1472

Elindhu knew it wasn't Obanji floating before her above a shaft of darkness that went downwards forever, although by the Twelve, it was tempting to pretend it was, to surrender to the illusion, lay down her arms and let all this fear and grief float away.

But Soren was here somewhere, as was some unseen menace she could feel creeping about, a tenebrous presence reeking of hunger and need. The ghostly image of Obanji was part of it, but not the whole. The real threat had yet to make itself known.

She stepped to the edge of the hole, which was almost thirty paces wide. Hoping a simple spell wouldn't threaten her precarious control, she kindled a dim light in her orb and glanced down the rough-hewn shaft. There was a faint glow far below, backlighting what looked like an immense vertical tunnel hung with spiderwebs.

At first she thought there were dark rocks protruding through the webs – then she realised that they were spiders, as big as wolves. As her eyes adapted to the low light, she could made out tunnels too, openings in the shaft.

Then she looked beyond those hideous shapes and saw Soren.

He was tethered across the shaft about a hundred paces below, limbs outstretched and trussed up by ropes of spider silk like a meal laid out for these ghastly creatures. Looking more closely, she could make out bones caught up in the webs, too. If they were human, as she suspected, they were the remains of dozens of people.

She had to stay and fight, no matter what the cost.

Her eyes returned to 'Obanji', hanging before her in mid-air over the hole. She raised her staff, called more glyma to the orb – and Obanji's ghost, if that's what it was, flinched . . .

The illusory form faded, revealing a massive arachnid as big as a horse, with pincers like swords, cringing in the light of her glyma spell.

Those below, maybe alerted by the glow of her staff, began to swarm up the shaft towards her, while the monster before her hissed evilly and tensed, ready to spring.

Twirling her staff, she sent a stream of fire and force, first at the giant spider facing her, then at the strands of ropey web festooned across the hole, which caught fire, forcing the giant before her back to the far side of the shaft opening and making the advancing arachnids below shriek and recoil. Several dropped, catching themselves on new-spun silk thick as rope – then they all began to climb towards her again.

The giant facing her shrilled, crunching its pincers together, then it reared and sprang—

She met it with another burst of force and fire, but it wasn't enough; her orb was too depleted. It arced towards her, smashing her backwards, her head and spine slamming into the ground as she thrust her staff despairingly at its snapping maw. The tip, and her orb, punched through teeth and was engulfed by its mouth as she lay there, winded and panicking.

The resultant instinctive blast of force exploded from her orb, and the monster's head burst apart, its milky blood igniting, turning her staff into a burning torch with elobyne at its heart. The body lifted, limbs flailing, then fell back into the pit, taking a few of its fellows with it.

She sucked in air and somehow got to one knee in time to drive the flaming stave into the face of a dog-sized arachnid appearing over the edge, sending it tumbling back into the pit.

'Soren,' she wheezed, hoping against hope he was conscious, 'I'm here!'

More came at her, and she flashed off energy bolts and light spells, her vision beginning to turn red, but she was holding her own—

—until her extended senses screamed, a heartbeat too late, for something was bounding from the mist behind her. She whirled as a pony-sized cockroach six-foot long slammed into her, its massive hind legs and chittering jaws snagging in her robes. Jagged spurred forelegs tore painfully at her face and body, sending her toppling over the edge with the creature clinging to her and ripping at her, shredding her robes as well as the skin of her belly and thighs. Teeth clashed near her face; she felt something slick like saliva spraying her, but she thrashed her arms free and rammed the burning tip of her staff into its abdomen. It screeched, a disgusting spray of sound and muck, but she'd tensed her leg muscles and now lashed out, kicking free and flying sideways, her body becoming snared in a weft of sticky threads as the giant cockroach spun away shrieking into the dark below. It missed Soren by inches, vanishing into the iridescent murk below.

She was caught only a dozen paces above Soren, who wasn't moving. The shaft of pale light shining up from below silhouetted his naked, spread-eagled body, and the thick strands of cobweb binding him across the shaft.

She peeled herself free painfully, tearing off her shredded robes until, clad only in her smallclothes, she was clinging to a small rocky outcrop on the side of the shaft. She removed the strain of maintaining human form by morphing to her more athletic, limber

437

erling self, then she balanced herself and blasted fire at the nearest giant spiders.

No sooner had that blast dissipated than more of the monsters came pouring out of the side-tunnels, dozens of eye-clusters glinting in the light of her burning staff, not just giant spiders, but cockroaches and other predatory insects too, most of them the size of dogs or cats, all clambering towards her, wary but implacable. The earth here was riddled with holes, a honeycombed underworld beneath the desolation above, but she could see nothing to eat except each other.

They must be cannibalising themselves to survive in the most lifeless place on Coros.

If she didn't move, she'd be engulfed. Casting about, she spotted a ledge right beside where Soren was stretched out like a sacrifice. She leapt, landed, and brandished her staff threateningly.

The creatures froze.

She suddenly remembered that they'd used *words* to lure her here. 'Stop,' she shouted, 'or I'll burn you all!'

They hissed and chittered, but they did at least stop advancing. Then the light around one of the giant crouching arachnids shimmered and a likeness of Obanji overlaid its form: an illusion, insubstantial, but chillingly real.

'Elindhu, you'll never escape,' a voice, so very like his, said. 'But we can make it painless – pleasant, even. My little brother, the blue-back reaper, has a bite like opium. We can make this easy for you.'

She knew the reaper spider and its venom from her scholar days, and she could see some of them here, as big as mice, quivering on their webs just a dozen paces away.

They could be on me before I knew . . . but they fear me, as well. Or they fear my fire, at least.

'I can burn this shaft like you've never seen,' she retaliated. 'I can incinerate you all.'

'Not all,' the false Obanji replied, but his tone betrayed definite unease.

'Let me rouse Soren and we'll leave you in peace,' she offered, not believing for a second that they'd accept. She tried to draw in more glyma, but her orb, critically low now, barely responded, and her control was fraying. This impasse couldn't last.

The spiders and insects withdrew their attention somewhat, as if conferring wordlessly. Even in her fear and desperation, they intrigued her. What she needed was a plan, but nothing came to her. This place was an impossible death-trap.

Then she noticed the way the shaft was lit from below. The pallid light seeping up from below was illuminating Soren's skin as if coating it in some kind of residue, like pale, luminous drops of light. She dropped to one knee and realised the whole underside of his body was already coated – and it was seeping into him.

There's something shining upwards, from the centre of the world . . . But this isn't our world, it's the Talim-Argith . . . What in Creation is doing this?

Tentatively, she extended her left arm, allowing the light to strike her hand. Immediately, the same liquid light struck her, clinging like luminous dust. She jerked her hand back and examined it. It didn't hurt, didn't smell, and had no discernible effect as it sank into her skin.

What have we found? It was as if she were on the outside of a giant eggshell, and this hole puncturing it was revealing the light from within.

Then she realised, *It's a vivalocus – a place of life, a nexus of magic!*

Such places were rare, almost impossible to find. This was a treasure beyond price.

Realising the predators above her were silently creeping closer, she sent a warning flash of light into their eyes. 'Who are you?' she asked the monstrous horde, because even faced with imminent death, such mysteries intrigued her.

They went still, only their swaying antennae, rubbing mandibles and forelegs betraying life. Again, she sensed some kind of unheard communion, then the illusion of Obanji said, 'We are fragments of a fragment of the guardian of the Talam-Argith.'

She took a moment to process that, drawing on ancient lore from the histories of the erlings, the tales of Jovan Lux and the learnings of scholars since.

One of the Twelve, Kalledene, was Lord of the Talam-Argith, the source of Life. He infused it with light and made it beautiful . . .

But Jovan Lux was gifted or created or found elobyne, a giant crystal on Nexus Isle; and in that same instant that the Talam-Argith was swallowed up by death and darkness.

Elobyne: a crystal infused with energy that feeds glyma-energy to the Gifted . . .

Put together, the inference was clear: Jovan *did* destroy the Talam-Argith when he created elobyne – but these creatures, or their ancestors, oversized intelligent predators capable of illusion and speech, must have survived that moment.

'What do you want?' she asked the horde. 'What's your purpose?'

As she spoke, the film of light on her left hand seeped into her skin and faded. She felt it still, though, inside her, flowing through her like elobyne energy, but without the edgy irritation. Soren's body was taking on more radiance as she watched.

But the insects didn't attract this radiance, and nor did the web.

Only we interlopers from another world are affected by it . . .

'Our purpose is to live,' spider-Obanji replied, finally. 'That is the purpose of all living things: to live and multiply. That is life's only purpose.'

Soren stirred then, arching his back as the light intensified around him. Elindhu's heart thudded in relief and dread as his mouth fell open and light shone from it, a dim beam as he rolled his head back. He moaned with both pain and a kind of sensual pleasure.

'What is the light doing to him?' Elindhu demanded.

'Your otherworld bodies capture it and transform it to energy for growth,' Obanji's ghost replied, though it sounded nothing like Obanji now, more like an *erling*. 'He dies in bliss, returning to us all the nutrients of his body, purified.'

'Why do you do this?'

'We imbibe your light-purified bodies to strengthen us, then pass the waste into the soil above, so gradually we restore life to the Talam-Argith.' He blinked mournfully. 'You have seen the trees and grass around the mouth of our lair. In time, we will restore my realm entirely.'

'*My realm*', she thought, as erling legends coalesced for her. 'You are Kalladene, Guardian of the Talim-Argith and God of the Underworld.'

He paused, then said, 'Once, I was Kalladene,' in a hollow, haunted voice. 'My children rebuild me, piece by piece.'

They've managed a few dozen paces of life in two centuries, she thought, stunned and horrified at what he'd become, and how little he'd achieved. *They've likely killed thousands over the years, for a few square feet of regrowth . . .*

'We were beneath the ground when the Bright One destroyed the surface of the Talam-Argith,' Kalladene told her. 'We survived when nothing else did. We delved deep and found the Pure Light, which enabled us to survive and grow, to mimic your kind and lure them in: fresh goodness for our bodies and the soil. Now we can even project into your world, to attract you here. All this is for the Talam-Argith, in the service of life and light. In death, you will contribute to the restoration of life and be reborn among us.'

He spoke as if this were something noble and right, not the luring of fools to die to keep insects alive in a desert.

But in following his words, she'd missed something else, until she felt an itch, looked down and saw a mouse-sized blueback reaper on her right calf. She swatted—

—as it bit.

She slapped it away, but the spiders and cockroaches hissed and began to close in on her again, coming from above and below.

'It was good to talk to you,' Kalladene breathed. 'I'm sorry you have to die.'

Her leg began to go numb.

Stretched out over the void, Soren moaned sensuously as his body lit up brighter . . .

No, she thought, *no, no . . .* Then a wave of dizziness struck her, followed by the beginnings of a beautiful sense of warmth and wellbeing radiating into her from her left hand, the one she'd bathed in light.

She had only moments left, so she gave up on control.

'*Flamma—!*'

She unleashed with all she had, spinning her staff and aiming it at the wall of monstrous insects descending from above, forcing them to give ground or burn, destroying the strands they were clinging to, but there was no remaining here, for more were swarming up from below and she had only moments left.

She did the insane, darting along the strand holding Soren's leg, then as her balance frayed, leapt and landed astride his belly. The impact made him convulse; his eyes flew open as she summoned more fire with the last of her control, spinning her staff in a circle to direct her final fires at the strands holding him. As the bonds burned away, she and Soren dropped, leaving the lashing mandibles and snapping claws of the insects and spiders behind . . .

Then the blueback's venom hit her and she went into rapture, clinging to Soren, now awake and staring up at her, light pouring from his mouth. In a state of delirium, she kissed him, drank the light from his lips as they fell, her filigree hair glowing pure silver as they burst through the webbing at the base of the tunnel and out into a vastness she couldn't comprehend, feeling herself come apart as the venom fizzed through her.

Clinging to each other as they fell, they gaped about in amazement, despite their impending end. They were dropping from inside a great hollow sphere of broken rock, plummeting towards a wide pool of liquid light that reflected a beautiful erling woman with tawny eyes: one she recognised as Aryella, one of the Twelve erling Gods. The descent seemed to take forever, but it was filling her with a gentle potency utterly unlike glyma.

One final thought struck Elindhu through the venom's delirium, her amazement and the terror: *This is the power that Jovan Lux destroyed when he destroyed the Talam-Argith.*

They struck the surface as Aryella's mouth opened to devour them, then plunged beneath, and her awareness burst apart.

26

Mastery

The Warden Mythos

The Sanctor Wardens' core philosophy concerned adaptability – 'Only Change is Permanent' – but this nebulous concept failed them. Jovan Lux aligned himself with the black and white teachings of the Akkanite Church, whipped up hatred against the Wardens, annihilated them and made himself Hierophant. The lesson is this: simple 'Truths' are more potent than complex philosophies. They need not even be true – lies are more powerful, in fact. Ask any despot.

INCHALUS SEKUM, ZYNOCHI SCRIBE, 1465

Isla Huntaru, Sea of Pelas
Autumn 1472

Jadyn, Aura and Evandriel anchored their felucca in a cove on the west coast of the island, the far side from the old Warden monastery, their provisional destination. With so many imperial warships around, mooring any closer felt risky.

Once ashore, Jadyn led the way upwards through a shattered landscape where rocks had rained down from the sky, lava had carved burning furrows and ash blanketed everything. The climb was exhausting, not helped by the hot, sulphurous air, barely kept at bay by the scarves wrapped over their mouths and noses. The ground quivered constantly, and every so often the dark clouds pumping from the crater flashed scarlet. Being there felt suicidal.

About an hour after setting out, climbing through shifting clouds of foul-smelling smoke, they rounded an outcropping and got their first view of the port and the old Warden castle. Not a single building had a roof left, or four standing walls. The castle had survived best, but even then the curtain walls were down and the watch towers fallen.

From their vantage point, they could see an Order galley in the port, so they'd been right not to seek mooring there. Then Jadyn was struck by a vivid flash of foresight and his eyes flashed back to the broken fortress, half a kylo away. In that vision he saw Vazi Virago and Yoryn Borghart, searching the interior of the ruins. He let go of that vision like it was a snake's tail, announcing, 'The Exemplar and Borghart are down there!'

The other two weren't even listening. 'There,' Evandriel was exclaiming, 'beneath the rim—'

He pointed upwards: where the crater rim remained intact, when everything around it had collapsed, stood an archway. Incredibly – and intriguingly – it looked as if the doors were intact.

'Are you listening to me?' Jadyn interrupted, pointing at the fortress. 'The Exemplar and Borghart are down there.'

'*E cara mia*,' Aura groaned as she took in his words. 'Now what?'

'Ignore them, my friends,' Evandriel said. 'That's just a ruin. We need to go up there.'

No one had any better options, so they turned their attention to the slope, using hands and feet to clamber upwards. The ascent was becoming steeper, the rocks were hotter and the clouds of noxious fumes washing over them, though occasionally broken up by a vicious wind from below, were becoming thicker and more unpleasant. Then they found steps carved into the stone leading to the archway, which was indeed miraculously untouched – as were the big iron-bound wooden doors coated in carved sigils.

No, not a miracle, Jadyn thought, peering at the runes, which were like those he'd seen at Vanashta Baanholt. *This gateway leads to the Shadowlands – because it exists in two places at once, not even the eruption could destroy it.*

'This is it,' Evandriel said excitedly, pointing to the pillars and the sigils matching those imprinted on their palms. 'This was made by the Wardens – it is the next step on our journey, perhaps even the final one.'

They all stared as the enormity of their discovery struck them. This could be their final destination, the end of their quest for the aegis – and the start of something far larger.

Jadyn shifted his gaze to what lay beyond – a shimmering scarlet lake of molten rock lay below, boiling and bubbling like a witch's cauldron. The platform of stone before the arch, just a score of paces across, reached out over the lava pit. The heat was unbelievable.

'Why would the Wardens place a test in an active volcano?' Jadyn groaned. Then he snorted and answered his own question, 'Because four days ago it wasn't active.'

'And hadn't been for centuries,' Evandriel added. 'The monastery was just a place to sleep, eat and distract enemies. The real aegis site is through this gate.'

Suddenly, they became aware of a new, imperative threat. When they turned, they could see two figures were charging towards them from the monastery – even at this distance, Jadyn could recognise the upright stance of the Exemplar and the lictor's glowering presence. They were still four hundred paces or more away, but running like the wind.

They'll be here in moments, he realised.

Evandriel went to the archway door, and tried the handle, but Jadyn was struck by the dread that time had run out for him and he'd never hold Aura again. He grabbed her arm.

'I love you,' he blurted. 'You know that, yes? In case—'

'Neya? Verite?' she grinned, as if in surprise. 'You love me?' Then she patted his cheek and said, 'I feel this too. But we have years ahead, mia amora. Have seen this. Be no fear.'

He looked into her eyes, and the churning inside him faded.

He believed.

Aura had never felt like this before, not even with Sergio, the blissful glow of total love, and the determination to fight for it. She would protect her man or die trying, and by Akka and Elysia, she intended to fight. All her life she'd run away when things got difficult, but now she was the Magic Girl, with weapons she was only just discovering.

She'd also just lied – all her premonitions were of disaster – but Jadyn didn't need to hear that. He needed reassurance and a future to fight for, so she had no regrets.

While Evandriel was trying to solve the riddle of the archway, she walked to the side of the arch and peered into the crater, down the jagged rock face to where foul-smelling lava boiled, a vivid red and orange cauldron of creation and destruction so hot her vision swam. The heat washed over her skin, down her throat and into her eyes, leaving them parched and sore. She reeled back dizzily, clutched at Jadyn and held on.

Evandriel found the sigils he sought, symbols carved into the Sanctor Wardens' triple knot, beside the handle, and touched them with his marked palms. 'Opperio,' he breathed.

Aura glanced back and saw the two dark figures closing in on them, their silhouettes blurring through the smoke clouds below. 'Be nearly here,' she warned. 'Open!'

Jadyn drew his cutlass as Evandriel grasped the door handle and tried to turn it. It wouldn't budge. He slammed his fist into the door, then cast about, seeking further clues.

Yoryn Borghart and Vazi Virago, just two hundred or so paces below, were facing the steepest part of the broken slope, after which they'd reach the foot of the stone steps. Jadyn went to the top, preparing to meet them, while Aura joined Evandriel. The heat was rising, searing the sweat from her face. 'Can open?' she asked. 'See, is keyhole!'

'But no key,' Evandriel wailed. 'No key – I have missed something . . .'

The Exemplar and the lictor were alarmingly close now, at the foot of the steps and powering up. They had seconds, at best.

Aura glanced at her own marked palms. *At Vanashta Baanholt, these opened the doors. But this must need more . . .*

For want of any better idea, she dropped to her knees, fished out a loop of lock-picks from a pouch and with the stiletto dangling from a cord between her breasts, she tried to pick the lock.

*

Jadyn looked at Evandriel, seeking hope, but the scholar looked flum-moxed. Aura was trying to work the lock with a knife and some thin metal rods, but clearly that wouldn't work: this had to be a test of the aegis, a way to determine who was worthy of entrance.

And we're failing that test, he thought bleakly. Virago and Borghart were storming up the steps now. *Twenty seconds*, he guessed, *then we're fighting for our lives.*

That hadn't gone well last time beneath Vanashta Baanholt: he'd lost the rest of his pentacle in a few deadly seconds.

'Can you open it?' he called over his shoulder. 'Last chance . . .'

Evandriel, who had been poised and confident all the time they'd known him, was unravelling. 'I do not know what I have missed!' He pummelled the door. '*What?*'

Aura just kept jabbing at the lock, her fingers a blur.

Jadyn winced, then commended his soul to Akka and prepared to face two of the deadliest fighters he'd ever seen.

This time they die, Vazi Virago thought, as she reached the foot of the improbable stairs leading to a stone platform jutting out over the crater lake. It was just thirty paces above. The heat was intolerable, the scorching air barely breathable, but there was a doorway there, which they had to reach before their quarry opened it and escaped again.

They reached a landing midway up the steps, where she drew her flamberge. Borghart did the same. 'This time,' she panted, 'we will get them.'

Then Jadyn Kaen appeared above and she levelled her blade at him, calling, 'Yield!'

He was holding a crude cutlass which wouldn't survive her first blow, but he planted his feet defiantly. Beyond him she heard the scholar Evandriel shrieking imprecations at himself or the door or the gods or all three. Auranuschka Perafi was out of sight somewhere.

She contemplated drawing on the glyma, but decided she didn't need it.

These are our much-vaunted enemies? she sneered, as she took to the final set of stairs. *They're dead already . . .*

Aura was going to get a sword through her back in a few seconds, she saw that clearly, but as she worked, she glimpsed the answer: the tripartite knot was the key. She worked her stiletto and pick into the lock again and moved them in that pattern, making the tumblers click . . .

. . . and the lock opened.

'*JADYN!*' she shouted, turning the handle and bursting through the door, tumbling across a flag-stoned courtyard. Evandriel stumbled in behind her and moments later, Jadyn flew past, even as the Exemplar appeared at the top of the steps, a look of savagery on her face.

Evandriel slammed the door, the latch clicked shut – and the door jolted from the Exemplar's impact. Then the handle rattled – but didn't budge. It'd locked again.

Aura looked around in amazement.

There was no boiling lava pit here, no dark fumes pouring skywards, no fiery scarlet light. Instead of stinking of sulphur, the air was crisp and cool. The courtyard was between an outer wall and the keep of a graceful castle, modestly sized, with tall towers, artful buttresses and ferocious-looking gargoyles. It reminded her of the erling keep beneath the lake at Semmanath-Tuhr, but this was no abandoned ruin, for they found themselves surrounded by people staring at them in stunned surprise.

She rose cautiously to her feet, pocketing the lock-pick loop but keeping her stiletto in her right hand, and went to Jadyn's side. He was limping on his damaged right knee, but he lit up with pride in her, gripping her shoulder and murmuring, 'You are wonderful.'

Evandriel joined them, still facing the door as something smashed into it again, but although it rattled a little, it didn't buckle.

'Hold there!' a sharp female voice snapped. 'How did you three open that door?'

They turned to face a grey-haired woman in a knee-length chainmail vest and an emerald-green tabard, who strode from the doors of the keep, backed by two young men in similar gear. Around the courtyard, the two dozen people already surrounding them had clearly been midway through lugging crates of gear to some half-loaded wagons.

They're leaving, Aura realised. *They're abandoning this place.*

'We are pilgrims, seeking the aegis,' Evandriel responded.

CRASH! The door rattled again, even more forcibly.

'I told you I heard something, Reina Lenedha,' a mailed youth called.

Most of them had drawn swords – erling-style tuelawars, Aura noticed, curved and graceful. But the grey-haired woman merely placed a hand on her sword hilt as she scanned the newcomers.

'Yes, Camryn, point made,' she said tersely, then she said, 'Master Evandriel, I presume.' Her eyes swept over Aura and Jadyn. 'You two as well,' she added, as if surprised. 'Kaen and Perafi, yes? I am Lenedha, Reina of this haven. How did you get in?'

'I pick lock,' Aura replied defensively. 'Che buena, si?'

'No, it's not good,' the woman retorted. 'The door is a test. You were *supposed* to have found the words on your journey – the lock is just a failsafe for our use.' Then the door rattled again and her expression clouded. 'Who's out there? I can't *see* them . . .'

'The Exemplar, Vazi Virago,' Jadyn told her. 'And a lictor, Yoryn Borghart.'

'The Order and the Justiciary?' Lenedha yelped. 'You brought them here?'

'They follow, not our fault!' Aura told her crossly.

Lenedha muttered to herself, then strode past and laid a hand on the door. 'This is made to withstand the glyma, but it's not impregnable. It also contains one particular emergency set of key movements, in case one of us need to get through without using power. That's how you picked it, somehow interpreting the required movements.'

'Si,' Aura told her. 'So maybe Aura pass testing, after of all?'

'Hardly,' Lenedha fumed. 'And you've led enemies to our very door. That's a failure of catastrophic proportion.' She snapped fingers at her young protégés. 'Disarm these intruders.'

'We mean no harm—' Jadyn began.

'But you've managed it regardless,' Lenedha snapped. 'Do not resist.'

Jadyn put a warning hand out towards the young man, Camryn. 'Don't.'

The tension ratcheted up, while someone kept slamming against the door again, and again.

'You should have been capable of unlocking that door without resorting to thievery,' Lenedha said – then she threw up her hands in defeat. 'But we ourselves erased some clues, because the Order were closing in on us, so it's just as much our fault.' She indicated the wagons. 'Anyway, we're going, due to the eruption. We don't have time for new initiates.'

'We're coming with you,' Evandriel said firmly. 'We crossed half the world to find you.'

She glowered at him, then hissed and relented. 'Fine. But we've hours of work to do before we depart. If you pull your weight, you can come with us.'

'You may only have minutes,' Jadyn told her. 'What we can do, those two out there can.'

Lenedha cursed again, and turned to Camryn, evidently her second. 'Camryn, your cohort guards the portal. The rest of you, load those wagons, now. Bridle the horses. We'll leave with what we've got; the rest we'll do without.' She threw Aura, Jadyn and Evandriel a sour look, but said only, 'You three, follow me.'

Jadyn's knee was still painful, but he limped after Reina Lenedha, Evandriel and Aura, listening to the grey-haired Warden barking orders at her people, men and women of all races, all much younger than her. Crossing the courtyard, he looked up to see that despite it being as bright as day here, the sky was black as night, with stars strewn across the firmament like spilled diamonds.

We're in the Shadowlands, he realised, recognising those constellations from the bridge beneath Vanashta Baanholt. *Or somewhere like Semmanath-Tuhr, rooted in both realms.*

He wished Elindhu were here to see it and marvel.

Lenedha led them into the fortress' entrance hall, where a trellis table had been set with food for her labouring protégés. She offered them bread and cheese, all the while shouting to her people to hurry up and get the wagons loaded.

'"Reina" is a Warden title, from the erling word for prince or princess,' Evandriel commented, looking as excited by that snippet as anything else here. 'Reina Lenedha, what is this place?' he asked.

She interrupted her task to reply, 'It's a training haven, partly in the Talam-Argith. Our predecessors discovered a way to blend the two worlds, which can create some extraordinary effects – breathable water, hollow mountains, tree-top cities and the like.'

Jadyn, remembering the castle under the lake in Semmanath-Tuhr, winked at Aura.

'This haven was created to greet those with the skill and instincts to follow our trail of clues,' Lenedha continued. 'It's a simple concept: if you can get in, you're good enough. That saves us the risk of using agents in the outside world to find new blood. However, we closed the path last year – or we thought we had.' She glared at Aura. 'Your blasted lock-picks shouldn't have worked, girl.'

Aura shrugged. 'Not be Aura's faulting.'

'I suppose not,' Lenedha sighed. 'I don't have time for long stories, but how the *jagat* does the Exemplar of the Vestal Order come to be right behind you?'

'We thought we'd lost them at Bedum-Mutaza,' Jadyn told her. 'But it's possible – well, probable, in fact – that they've found us because they've got the aegis Gift as well.'

'*The Exemplar?*' Lenedha exclaimed. '*And a lictor?* Well, I'm surprised, but I guess it's not impossible. If they've found a way to reconcile their use of elobyne to their latent precognition, it would be a considerable advantage in their careers. What manner of people are they?'

'Murdering fanatics,' Jadyn spat.

'That's unfortunate,' Lenedha sighed. 'To have such highly ranked foes abandon the Hierophant and join us would have been . . . Well, never mind. Unless they have a hundred glyma-knights with them, that door is impassable.' Her eyes trailed over Aura. 'Or it should be. Was it luck or intuition?'

'Not luck. Saw symbol, so knowing pattern for using.'

451

The reina's gaze warmed fractionally. 'You're further along than most initiates.'

'Am mucha talentia,' Aura replied, as if admitting to a secret.

'Where are you going?' Evandriel asked.

'I'll tell you when we get there.' Lenedha clapped her hands once and said, 'Eat, drink, catch your breath. Don't stray. I need to get this evacuation moving faster.'

With that, she strode back out into the courtyard, once again bellowing orders.

Jadyn squeezed Aura's shoulder, then faced Evandriel. 'So what now?'

The scholar was staring about him, drinking it all in. 'Vanith-era architecture, eighth century perhaps – look at those crenulations . . . I wonder if . . . What did you say, sorry?'

'Have you ever met my friend Elindhu?' Jadyn chuckled. 'You'd get along famously. I said, what are we going to do now?'

'We go with them, clearly,' the scholar said distractedly. 'Lenedha said we're "half in the Talam-Argith", which must be so: you'd never even know we were above a volcano. But this place isn't dead like the Shadowlands are now – incredible! And imagine, breathable water—'

Jadyn smiled at Aura, remembering the lake in Semmanath-Tuhr. *We don't have to imagine it*, he thought, sharing a wink. Then he indicated the young men and women scurrying about. 'So, these are Sanctor Wardens, then? Not dead, just hiding?'

'Indeed, but just trainees, Lenedha said,' Evandriel answered. 'But she cannot be the only master – which means the Wardens do still exist.' His eyes went to the gates, where the one she'd called Camryn was standing guard with five initiates. 'I pray she's right, that the Exemplar can't get in.'

'Elysia, make it so,' Jadyn agreed – because his premonitions were still all of disaster. 'The sooner they move on, the better.'

But Aura went still. 'Am not sure Goddess be listening,' she breathed. 'Is not good . . .'

*

Vazi Virago and Yoryn Borghart faced the closed archway, standing uneasily on the precarious stone pillar jutting out over the volcano's crater, gasping in the heat and struggling to breathe through their scarves. The foul smoke was making their eyes stream, tears cutting tracks through the ash coating their skin. Borghart felt like he was melting, and the yawning crater beyond was having a vertiginous effect.

It's calling to me – like the Devourer's Maw . . .

Their quarry had disappeared through the archway, locking it behind them – and now they couldn't get it open. Violence had no effect, nor did his glyma, and neither of them could work out how their enemies had got it open.

'The Nepari witch picked the lock,' Vazi realised. 'Look – you can see the marks she left.'

'Then do the same,' he replied.

'You think I'm a jagging sneak-thief?' the Exemplar shouted. Her dagger was already in the lock, but nothing she tried seemed to work.

'How do these bastards keep eluding us?' Borghart cast about him, but no inspiration came. Logic, premonitions and guesswork all failed. But clearly, there was a way. That Auranushka Perafi had done it just deepened his own sense of failure.

Then he noticed that the kneeling Vaziella was no longer even looking at the door, instead staring past him at the eastern skies, with an expression on her face like she'd seen her own death coming. The invincible Exemplar looked utterly petrified.

'No,' she whispered. '*No—*'

Following her eyes, he felt his brain freeze: there were shapes in the sky like distant birds, but they were moving faster than any bird could fly.

Not birds, he realised. *They're man-sized. Vazi's 'Serrafim'*. Irrationally, he spun and hammered on the door again, shouting, '*Let us in – please! We yield – just let us in!*'

Nothing answered except the volcano, which snarled like a hungry beast.

*

Vazi couldn't move, skewered by dread as if Genadius already had his hand around her heart. She could already see him: his skin charred and peeled away, flayed by fire, his immortal flesh weeping pus and blood, and with no lips his shark teeth were clear to see. His golden eyes were fixed on her from kylos away, but she knew he'd be here in minutes.

She hated herself for being scared witless – *Genadius was coming* and she *couldn't* react.

The Devourer's Maw will be a mercy compared to him, she knew. She stood then, and actually tried to throw herself into the crater – she actually foresaw that plunge – but *he* wouldn't let her move. She had no volition at all. Borghart stared at her in shock, realising what she'd just failed to do, then spun around himself, pirouetting helplessly as he sought escape. But he too was out of time: their lives were measurable in seconds now, before they were taken and died screaming – when their captors permitted them to. A dozen or more Serrafim, blurs of dark light, were streaking in, with Genadius himself foremost.

'I see you,' his voice hissed into her skull.

He was twelve seconds away . . .

Eleven . . . Ten . . .

With a moment of supreme effort, she tore her mind free of him, stared at the door and somehow realised: there was no key, not a physical one. She couldn't say how she knew but it came to her in a burst of clarity, perhaps triggered by the faintest smear of finger-prints on the door, which she traced while mouthing words she'd never heard and didn't know, hearing now what someone had said here, months ago . . .

The door clicked and opened.

Serrafim were blazing out of the sky like eagles swooping on rabbits, their fore- and after-images raging towards them. Paralysis gripped her again, but Borghart had grabbed her arm and now he pulled her through the doors into the courtyard of a keep.

They spun to slam the door again, but before they could, Vazi was battered to the ground by a young man, who went to place a dagger against her throat. Two others hurled themselves at Borghart. She caught the boy's dagger hand by the wrist, slammed her forehead into his face, then looked up at people in mail and green tunics, looming over them, saw too many blades to counter, and shrieked, '*SHUT THE JAGGING DOOR—*'

Too late.

The door crashed open again, torn from the hinges in a burst of splinters and flying metal that carved through the young men and women before it, then the Serrafim followed, mowing down any who remained standing.

The young man holding Vazi was scythed in two and torn away, but before she could rise, a burned and bloody skeletal foot crunched down on her chest, cracking ribs and all but emptying her lungs. As gauzy-winged angels swept by, cutting down other defenders in a bloody swathe, Genadius' hideously ruined visage loomed over her.

'*Vaziella,*' he rasped wetly. '*So good to see you.*'

27

Between Worlds

The End of the Wardens

Only one verified account of the last days of the Sanctor Wardens is known. In it, a Warden chronicler wrote of being trapped by forces beyond any man, of demons in angel guise: 'False angels with wings of light, possessing such speed and power that no blow could be parried.' This blasphemy proved that the Wardens had always been evil, and that Jovan Lux could summon Serrafim to his aid.

CHRONICLES OF THE NORTH, 1346

Isla Huntaru, Sea of Pelas
Autumn 1472

All of them – Jadyn, Aura, Evandriel, even the trainees and Master Wardens – sensed the danger too late. One moment they were all spinning round as the archway door flew open and Yoryn Borghart and Vazi Virago appeared – not attacking, but fleeing something far worse than themselves. For a moment the pair were helpless, unresisting as the guards grappled them.

An eye-blink later, six beings had exploded through the opened portal: one blackened and hideous, and five radiant creatures with wings of light.

Then the carnage began. The burned one planted a foot on Vazi Virago's chest, while another went for Borghart, but the other four swept onwards, moving in a blinding whirl to mow down the young trainees protecting the door.

'Shut the doors,' Jadyn cried, already halfway to the keep's entrance, with Evandriel at his heels – but Aura was transfixed. Through the opening he saw a glorious blonde Serra blurring towards him, blade extended. He went for the left door as Evandriel took the right, but he already knew they were too late . . .

In a vivid premonition he saw Aura spitted through the chest by the blonde Serra, a second before he and Evandriel were cut in half by those following her through . . .

The oncoming Serrafim were exactly as Aura had envisaged such beings: beautiful beyond cognition, and full of disgust for scum like her. She saw her final moments with utter clarity, the glinting blade punching through her breast and the blazing face which would be her last sight.

NO, she thought . . . and *willed* with all her soul. *NO*.

She raised a hand to ward off the blow and time *slowed* – and not just in her own perception.

Time slowed for the angel, too . . .

Jadyn could not quite believe what he was seeing. He and Evandriel had almost got the doors shut when the Serra flashed past like a ray of light, shooting towards Aura. The stunning, perfect woman in pearlescent robes had her golden-hilted sword presented in a precise lunge and he saw her spit Aura and kill her . . .

. . . except it didn't happen, because, unaccountably, the Serra all but *stopped* in mid-air, her blade's tip just an arm's-length from Aura's chest. Aura herself looked astounded, but she was already swaying aside, one palm held up to the Serra as if holding her in place, while her other hand blurred into action, producing a thin-bladed knife from somewhere about her body.

The Serra's sword lanced past Aura's shoulder.

Aura's stiletto punched into the angel's chest.

The winged woman gasped, shock rippling through her as her flesh was pierced and she flailed, tried to plant feet and staggered gracelessly, her wings flickering.

But then she planted her feet and whipped her blade around, blindingly fast, and Aura should have been falling in two halves.

Instead, she was ten paces away.

Even the angel looked amazed – but she ripped the stiletto from her chest and flung it at Aura, while glyma-light welled up in the wound. Again, Aura should surely have been slain – but she caught the stiletto effortlessly and flashed back another ten paces onto the trestle table, moving between the moments, exactly like the angel woman.

Jadyn rose, the images of what Aura had just done, as if time was hers to command, the way she'd forced the Serra to stop, pounding through his head. It took him back to catching coins flung at point-blank range – and to the Hejiffa Dhouma.

He *moved*, and so did Evandriel. The scholar raised a hand, making a gripping gesture.

You hold 'em, I'll hit 'em, Jadyn thought at Evandriel, hoping he'd understand, as Jadyn's blade leapt to his hand. Then he launched himself at the glowing woman, seeing neither beauty nor holiness, just a deadly being who had sacrificed humanity for power.

She sensed him coming, but her turn was at normal speed to him, because he was moving at her pace. He parried her blow, then Evandriel's attempt to slow her took effect, leaving her tearing at the air, trying to break free, still moving, but slower than he now, as he went on the attack. Quickly he realised that for all her formidable speed and preternatural resilience, she wasn't an expert duellist. Her glorious face filled with dread as she saw her personal End of Days coming, hurling all her strength into ripping free of Evandriel's magical grip, trying to flash upwards, out of reach . . .

He lunged, but she somehow blocked and leapt—

Until Aura's thrown dagger slammed into her back.

She gasped, sounding bewildered, but he had reached her; swinging his cutlass at her neck, he severed her head, which fell at his feet, jolting as the body toppled backwards.

'I'll still kill you,' she shrilled, as her body landed, twisted, then began to crawl towards her head. 'I am immortal!'

Holy Elysia!

On instinct, he pulled her gold-hilted longsword from her dead hand and buried it in her skull, the Miravian steel ringing as it cleaved through thick bone and brain. Only then did the Serra's body finally flop, motionless . . . lifeless.

Jadyn stared at Aura, mouthing, '*What the jagat—?*'

'Is dead now,' she answered prosaically. 'Must go.'

They looked about, saw the doors were still open and the few trainees there were staring aghast at the dead Serra. Outside, more Serrafim were pouring through the open archway. The only Wardens in sight were dead.

'Shut the jagging door,' he shouted, '*NOW!*'

As the Serrafim burst through the archway, there was a moment in which the attention of the young trainee warden holding Yoryn Borghart was distracted. A flood of perceptions struck him, all with death in them all. These beings were here to kill, and to them, he was just another dog to be put down.

Actions speak louder than words.

With his left hand he pulled out his dagger and punched it into the young man's throat, a bare second before a blurring blade plunged into the boy's heart. The body fell away.

A moment later a boot crunched into Borghart's chest, pinning him with the weight of mountains. A sword speared his left palm and the dagger spun from his grasp.

He went rigid as death closed in.

But the Serra holding him said, 'You're no Warden.'

Steel, tingling with glyma-energy, stroked his throat. More of these radiant beings had arrived and were fanning out, before tearing into the thin line of green-clad men and women backing towards the keep.

Vazi, a few feet away, was under the foot of the burned Serra. *Genadius*, he guessed. *Does he know she left him to die? Probably.*

'Mercy,' he croaked, looking up.

His captor, a black-haired, olive-skinned Aquini, asked his master, 'Milord, is this the one you told us to take alive?'

'That's the one, Zapheer,' Genadius replied. 'We'll deal with these Warden scum, then take our time with these two.' His ruined visage contorted into a ghastly grin.

The black-haired Serra licked his lips. 'To torture a torturer? How poetic.'

Even with his life in the balance, Borghart's logical brain recalled that the Hierophant Genadius' favourite poet – and supposedly his lover – had been an Aquini named Zapheer.

These really are people who ruled us, then supposedly died . . .

Zapheer saw that recognition in his eyes, smiled toothily and clasped his throat, then exerted himself enough to pull the glyma energy from Borghart's body, a dizzying and debilitating sensation that almost made him faint, leaving him magically helpless.

But the aegis flowed in, in its place, and Zapheer appeared oblivious to that, his attention snatched away by some internal trauma, for as one, the Serrafim had gone rigid, their eyes flying to the still-open doors of the keep.

Jadyn Kaen was there, just inside the doors, holding one of the angels' gold-hilted swords. At his feet was a Serra – or at least the body of one, beheaded. The torso was pumping liquid light from the neck-stump.

Then the doors slammed shut.

They can be killed, Borghart thought. *Akka be praised.*

He reached for the aegis, trying to find a way out of this.

Reina Lenedha was with most of her students in the courtyard when a dozen or more divinely beautiful killers entered, but she found her flow in seconds, her training enabling her to move in time like these deadly 'angels'. She blocked, parried, spun away from deadly glyma-bolts, even wounded a few with her own blinding ripostes.

But her students were still learning, and to her eyes, they were moving painfully slowly.

To Serrafim eyes, they moved like prey.

In seconds, most of those young men and women Lenedha had spent years teaching were cut down, and part of her died with them.

But Baldison, Leilla, Cora and Runaffi, four of her best, formed up around her, their speed almost matching the Serrafim as they backed towards a postern gate on the east side of the keep.

The Serrafim closed in again, four of them attacking in harrowing flashes of singing blades, perfectly coordinated despite fighting in silence. They lost Cora to a sword thrust through her right eye; Lenedha stepped in before their formation fell apart, blocking two blades at once, then slashing open a black Serra's face, so deeply that the angel screamed and gave ground.

They bleed glyma-light, she noted dispassionately. *What are they?*

Sensing wings behind them, she spun, ducked under a back-stabbing thrust and rammed her blade up into a male angel's belly. Driving forward, she lifted the creature off his feet, his wings of light flapping frantically, and slammed him bodily into the closed stable doors, pinning him there like a butterfly. The Serra, screaming hideously, dropped his gold-hilted elobyne blade – which Runaffi caught left-handed and split the angel's head in two.

Light streamed from the wound as the being collapsed.

The other attackers howled and recoiled, clearly not so immortal they couldn't feel fear.

'Move!' Lenedha roared, and her students reacted instantly, running in double-time for the postern door. Runaffi took the rearguard position, fighting to close the portal in the face of a shrieking, hate-filled female angel closing in. He slammed it in her face, his shoulder to the barrier as he threw the bolt—

Lenedha shrieked a warning, but too late: a glowing blade punched through the door and into Runaffi's chest. His body convulsed, the sword was withdrawn and he collapsed.

A low voice snarled, 'There will be no hiding, heretics.'

Baldison and Leilla were gaping at Runaffi, their best friend, as the reality of death hit them. 'They're monsters,' Baldison sobbed. 'How can angels be demons ... ?'

'Secure this door,' Lenedha bellowed, snapping them out of their paralysis. 'Then head for the chapel. Come on, this is for Ruffy and Cora!'

Her voice broke the spell of fear; both leapt into action, helping Lenedha to roll a heavy water barrel against the door. Waves of glyma-force were crashing into the barrier now. It was ironbound and sturdy, but wouldn't hold for long against such power.

Then they heard screams, and crashing sounds on the floor above. *They're coming in through the roof . . .*

'Move,' Lenedha snapped. 'Baldi, leave Ruffy – we'll come back for him.'

She shoved Leilla ahead of her, grabbed Baldison's arm and pulled him along. The young man was stumbling, blind with tears. 'Come on, lad,' she encouraged. 'Our friends need us.'

'But . . . Ruffy . . .' he sobbed.

'Shut *up*, Baldi,' Leilla snapped. 'We've got to get through this first.'

Good girl, Lenedha thought. Windows were shattering somewhere above them and there was a massive *boom!* as something smashed into the main doors.

Someone got them shut, Elysia be praised.

'The chapel, Leilla,' she repeated, as they reached the main corridor. 'Help Baldi.' She grasped the girl's shoulder. 'You're doing well. I'll catch up with you.' She ran for the entrance hall, praying she'd be in time to help get whoever was there to safety.

Yoryn Borghart looked at Vazi Virago, pinned and helpless beneath the foot of the burned angel. But as his eyes locked with hers, he was struck by a powerful premonition: *Vazi, dancing through a deadly combat, cutting down Jadyn Kaen and Aura Perafi and saving the empire.* How he knew that, he couldn't tell, but it was utterly certain. *She will save the empire.*

But with Zapheer's blade at his throat, he was dead the moment he moved.

Vazi must survive this, that much was clear. 'Please, you've got this wrong . . .' he tried. 'We're on your side—'

'Shut up, or I'll break your face,' Zapheer snapped, his eyes on the castle. The courtyard was littered with the dead and the fighting had moved inside. 'This won't take long,' he predicted. His gaze shifted back to Borghart. 'Can I make a start on this one, Master?'

Genadius held up a hand, cocking his head as if listening to unheard music. 'Wait. I sense something ... There's a danger here I don't understand ...'

The burned Serra's visage was unreadable, but Borghart heard something unexpected in his rasping voice: doubt.

28

The Ultimate Sacrifice

Building a Myth

Angels, known as Serrafim, are said to watch over us, protecting us from evil.
They are the Guardians of Humanity, created by Akka Himself. Sightings of them
are reported constantly by zealots trying to prove their own holiness. The Church
encourages such sightings, even if they are palpably untrue, because they add to
the myth. That's how religion layers lies upon half-truths, until it feels like truth
to the gullible. And if anyone questions that 'truth', they go after them like rabid
dogs: no one tortures, maims and murders like a religion.
THE CHURCH OF LIES (BANNED PAMPHLET), ANONYMOUS, 1440

Isla Huntaru, Sea of Pelas
Autumn 1472

With Jadyn, Aura and Evandriel were seven trainees and five servants
in the hall, none of whom looked older than twenty, all paralysed by
precognitions of death. Jadyn, seeing their glazed faces, took charge.

'Pile tables against the door,' he shouted. 'We need a barricade.'

Thankfully, they responded, four of the burliest racing to join
him in getting the huge dining table on its side and rammed up
against the double doors, just before a blaze of glyma-light gleamed
through the timbers. The doors rattled in their frame, the timbers
creaking but holding.

Another crash sounded as the Serrafim tried again, then a window
on the east wall disintegrated in a shower of glass. Its iron bars
held, though, keeping at bay the furious glowing face which had

appeared – but they couldn't stop the blaze of glyma-light that blasted into a serving girl, hurling her against a pillar, where she collapsed bonelessly.

Someone snatched a spear from a decorative suit of armour against a wall and threw it, but the Serra's shields shattered it in mid-air. 'Yield or die,' the angel called, his voice full of menace.

Everyone dived for cover, waiting for the next glyma-blast, flinching at the sounds of crashing above. The enemy was already inside.

'We've got to move,' Jadyn told Evandriel, huddled next to him beside the barricaded doors. The scholar had his hand on the wood, infusing it with slow-time to keep it intact a little longer. Aura was behind the next pillar, cowering as more glyma-bolts scorched the stonework.

The scholar looked at the side doors. 'That way,' he began.

Then Reina Lenedha burst in through that very door, a bloodied sword in hand. Taking in the scene instantly, she called, 'Staff and trainees to the chapel.' She saw Jadyn and dipped her head, one commander to another. 'Sier Jadyn, we have a portali gate in the chapel. We'll cover the retreat, you and I.'

'Aura be with Jadyn Knight,' Aura said swiftly, as Evandriel darted towards the trainees, evading another bolt from the angel lurking at the broken window.

Jadyn gestured at the ceiling. 'They're already inside upstairs,' he told Lenedha.

'I know.' The reina noted the headless Serra on the floor with an approving look. 'At least two are dead – they *are* mortal, people.' She plucked a shield from a wall display and threw it to Jadyn, took another for herself and shouted, 'Move, everyone – *go, go, go!*'

Trainees and servants dashed for the door while Jadyn and Lenedha stepped into the path of the glyma-bolts from the window, catching most on the metal-banded wooden shields, though a few got through, wounding two more servants and a trainee – then they were gone.

The blows on the main doors were getting heavier.

'Us now,' Lenedha said. Jadyn gestured to Aura and they bolted for the exit, as the Serra began hacking his way through. Even as they reached the side door, the main doors burst apart, sending wooden splinters and iron fragments spinning across the room. Beautiful beings with gleaming faces poured into the room, but Aura was already through, Jadyn followed, and Lenedha slammed it shut, threw the bolts and rolled aside as energy blasted it, then metal crashed into the barred timber.

'Keep moving,' she gasped, kneeling and strengthening the barrier with slow-time, while Aura and Jadyn ran down the corridor towards a T-junction and a passage.

Jadyn winced at the pain shooting through his hurt knee.

'You be fine?' Aura panted anxiously.

'Fine,' he lied, hobbling past another door off the main hall. Opposite was a corridor, which Aura took, shouting, 'This way for chapel,' presumably guided by premonition.

As Jadyn started to follow, the door behind him crashed open. He turned, too slowly – a Serra filled the door frame, face ablaze and glowing blade raised. It lunged—

—but Jadyn had awareness enough to blur aside, Aura raised a hand to *slow* the Serra, then Lenedha appeared from the side and swung, beheading the Serra the instant it became aware of her. The perfect face contorted in shock, the head spun and the neck stump spurted pale glowing ichor. The body crashed to the ground and they heard gasps of disbelief from behind it, but Lenedha had slammed the door, bolted it and slowed time around it, then they pelted on.

Neither immortal nor invulnerable, Jadyn thought again, *but there are too many of them.*

They caught up with the rest waiting at the narrow chapel entrance, and more people were scuttling in from a side corridor. Someone thrust one of the tuelawars at Aura, who brandished it awkwardly. Evandriel's robes were scorched and smouldering from glyma-blasts. They could all hear the sounds of fighting above them and behind.

'Into the chapel,' Reina Lenedha shouted, 'move, people: *move!*' She chivvied them through, leaving Jadyn and Aura to bolt and barricade the final door to the hall behind them before taking up position as rearguard.

Moments later it crashed and rattled. 'Yield or die,' a Serra called through it.

'*Ve a jagat tu mismo!*' Aura shrieked back. '*Chupa escoria!*'

Lenedha ran to pull them away. 'We're all inside – fall back,' she told them. Dropping her voice, she told Jadyn, 'Listen, in the vestry behind the chapel there's a portali gate, but more importantly, there's an artefact set in the floor that sustains this place; it's the anchor that suspends it between our world and the Talam-Argith. One of us has to reach it to break it – but at the last possible moment. Understand?'

CRASH! The door before them rattled as they backed into the chapel.

'What does that do?' Jadyn hissed back.

'It'll help us to escape.' She met his gaze. 'Whoever does it might not get out.'

Holy Elysia, Jadyn thought.

Aura, seeing them whispering, was making *What?* gestures, her expression suspicious. All the futures he'd seen with her melted away.

CRASH!

'It should be me,' he gulped. 'My knee . . . I'm slowing us down.'

'No, it's me,' Lenedha replied. 'I'm the captain of this ship. I'm only telling you, in case I don't make it.'

CRASH!

Lenedha shoved him. 'Let's go.' She shut and barred the chapel door as the door behind them began to splinter. They found the chapel emptying fast, as everyone scurried rapidly into the vestry. Evandriel had already gone, and Jadyn began to believe they might make it. He threw a reassuring look at Aura – as with a tremendous crash, a lone Serra burst through the chapel ceiling in a cloud of plaster dust, tiles and roof timbers crashing down around it. The angelic being landed, perfectly balanced, raising its glowing blade.

Even as Jadyn reacted, Aura *blurred* and she was suddenly in front of him, her tuelawar extended to take the first blow . . .

Aura glided into the Serra's path with no real plan, but her grip on time was solid. To normal sight she became a blur, but to her it was everything else that slowed. She planted her feet solidly, holding the hilt of the tuelawar with both hands. But she knew little of sword-fighting and the angel, a girlishly beautiful male with a mane of brown hair, quickly broke her guard and sent her weapon flying; for the next few seconds Aura frantically bent and contorted as he tried to skewer her, behead her or cut her in half, each time shifting herself aside from the foreseen blow by little more than a hair's-breadth.

Jadyn tried to intervene, but the Serra battered him away with glyma-force, so hard he hit the wall and slid to the ground, dazed. When Lenedha swung at the Serra, she too was smashed away, but that bought Aura a moment to cartwheel to her blade, then flash back, preventing the Serra from finishing the dazed reina.

She made sure to grip her weapon better this time. They traded lightning blows, then she darted round him, seeking to flank him as he spun to keep her in sight . . .

I'm faster than him, she realised exultantly, ripping her second stiletto from the small of her back and jamming it into the space the Serra was about to enter . . .

It buried in the winged being's left eye socket, up to the hilt in his brain, and the angel collapsed while Aura slowed herself and landed.

Everyone in the room was gaping at her.

She curtseyed, stunned at herself but feeling *glorious*. 'Am Magic Girl,' she reminded them. 'We go now?'

Lenedha, once again shouting at her people to *move it, NOW*, took the rear, shoving them onwards, but her mind was on the incredible thing she'd just seen. *Aura Perafi has been using the aegis for days, not months, yet she moves faster than these angels!*

She'd been a Warden for forty years and had only ever seen one other move like the Nepari girl: a master who'd been old then and was now long dead. *Every so often a prodigy comes*, the masters had always said, and clearly this girl was just such a one, someone who not only had the attributes that made the aegis usable, but an instinctive grasp of the art of moving faster or slower in time.

We have *to get her out*. 'Move, move,' she shouted again, crabbing backwards to join those still in the chapel. Danikos, a fellow master, had opened the portali gate behind the vestry. The staff were going through now, with the trainees, just three dozen now, a quarter of their original complement, lined up to follow. She felt crushed by the losses, but there was no time to grieve . . .

She grabbed Nilis Evandriel's arm, startling him, as he hadn't seen her arrive, and whispered, 'I've heard of you and what you've done. You started a rebellion we Wardens were too timid to join. Make that change: get everyone to the Trovian Keep in Qorium. Speak to our masters there.'

Before the scholar could reply, she shoved him towards the gate, then went from student to student, giving each a brief word, something to cling to: 'Baldison, believe in yourself. Leilla, let it flow. Jendra, more humility. Brezor, concentration!' Then she shouted, 'Follow Master Danikos; he knows what to do.'

The chapel doors were booming now, their unearthly foes closing in, but there were just two people to go through. Kaen and Perafi had paused, arguing over something – what she'd told Jadyn, she presumed. 'You two, take the portali gate,' she told them. 'I'll follow.'

'Why you no come now?' Aura asked her sharply.

'Because there's something I must do.' She went to move them on, when she was struck by a thought. 'Stay a moment, girl. I would speak with you.'

Aura looked at Jadyn anxiously; Lenedha could almost see the strings tying their hearts together, which warmed her, but it made her fear for them too.

'Hurry – we have a minute at most,' she told them.

The chapel door juddered at a massive blow, but it was the heaviest internal door in the keep and for now at least, it held. She looked at Jadyn and repeated, 'Go.'

Clearly reluctant, he went, but only as far as the vestry door.

She hurried to the rose carving set into the floor in front of the altar and pulled the handle, an iron ring, lifting a flagstone. Reaching into the hole beneath, she grabbed a large hourglass full of glowing dust, and fished it out.

'We only have moments, so listen hard: life is about *timing*: about being in the right place at the right moment. Then, and only then, can individuals make a difference – but they must have both the talent and the knowledge to seize that moment. You have the talent, Aura, more than anyone I've ever taught. Throw yourself into learning and living the aegis. We're all depending on you.'

Lenedha could see her eyes flickering to the hourglass and back, the premonitions hitting her, the realisation of what was happening here – and the denial, as she sought a better way. But there wasn't one, not in the few seconds they had, for glyma-force was now hammering into the chapel doors and they could hear the wood splintering.

'Go, Aura, Jadyn,' she ordered, '*go now . . .*'

Reluctantly, the girl rose, then she and Jadyn blurred away into the vestry and were gone. Lenedha waited for the change in air pressure that would tell her the portali gate had been closed, reflecting on a life never quite fulfilled – of training others while neglecting herself, counselling children about life and love and purpose, while never quite finding her own.

Regrets . . . yes, too many . . .

Then the Serrafim blasted in amid a burst of splinters, falling metal, glyma-bolts and desperate force, their glorious faces blazing with desperation, for they too perceived danger . . .

The hourglass contained the distilled matter that had created this pocket of time and space between worlds, both within the volcano's cone, hitherto a harmless place, and in the Talam-Argith, the Shadowlands, making it invisible and untouchable to either place. The hourglass shape was symbolic, but its function was vital: its contents, if released, would undo that separation of space and time and the two realities, the haven and the volcano, would collapse into one.

She felt tendrils of glyma-force as the angels closed in, trying to grip her, to freeze her so she couldn't do what she proposed, because their own premonitions were showing them the peril . . .

But she easily matched their speed and will, smashing the hourglass on the stone floor . . . Dust billowed out a moment before a glowing golden sword pierced her chest, the beautiful winged woman holding it shrieking in denial.

The dust then burst into flames, tiny red stars that began to rip through the air, tearing a rent in time and space. The angels wheeled, trying to escape, but they were already too late, for the volcano was rushing in.

Lenedha felt a moment of heat so intense that the air seemed to ignite within her body. Her last sight was the Serra woman who'd killed her, wearing the disbelief of one who'd thought herself truly immortal . . .

Then ravenous heat consumed everything, even her final thoughts.

Aura didn't quite understand what Lenedha had tried to tell her, but she knew one thing: that in a very few moments this space would be pure fire – and they had to get out.

She tore through the vestry, saw the stone door disguised in the fireplace. Jadyn, at her side, was roaring at her to *RUN RUN RUN*—

A booming blast heralded the angels' entrance into the chapel, and moments later she was struck by precognitive sounds and images: the sound of glass shattering pierced by screams of dread, a cacophony cut off mid-cry as all existence burst into flame and the vestry walls began to disintegrate. She launched herself at the fireplace, Jadyn beside her . . .

If it hadn't been a premonition but the actual event, they'd never have made it, but they struck the ground as a bearded man crashed a hammer down on something. They came to a halt, lying face-down in the dirt as the portali gate collapsed behind them and vanished into the flash of heat and flames erupting behind them.

Aura looked around the misty murk of the Shadowlands. Some were attempting to dispel the gloom with oil-lamps held in shaking hands. Jadyn crawled over to her and enveloped her in his arms, shaking with relief as much as she was. 'I thought you were dead,' he kept repeating, his voice breaking. 'I thought I'd lost you.'

'Never,' she managed. 'You have Aura for ever.'

Something *changed*.

Borghart felt it, and so did the two Serrafim, hideous Genadius and darkly beautiful Zapheer. Both froze, staring at the keep as if trying to see through stone, and Zapheer's blade wavered as a wave of premonitions struck, all-encompassing and unmistakable—

—the sights and sounds and physical impact of a volcanic eruption.

The two Serrafim had to be locked into some kind of shared consciousness, their minds so caught up in their comrades' shared experience as they burned and died, because both had taken their attention off him and the Exemplar.

Borghart had no such entanglements, and the need to preserve Vazi overruled all. One hand stole to the razor-sharp dagger Zapheer had been too arrogant or distracted to take from him and he slashed it across the back of Zapheer's right thigh, right through the tendons.

The angel's hamstring parted, he lurched – and his instinctive counterblow, a driving downwards thrust, plunged his gleaming blade not into Borghart's throat, but the ground.

Borghart jack-knifed and rose as the angel lurched towards him, thrusting the knife upwards into the space Zapheer's face was about to occupy – the blade went through the chin and straight into the brain. Borghart left it there, instead tearing the glowing angel-blade from the dying Serra's grip – even as Genadius turned, his burned skull-face snarling.

Beneath him, Vazi grasped his foot and jerked him off-balance – but that inadvertently took him away from Borghart's slash. He hit the ground, lunged for the archway behind them as Vazi rose, her face swelling with urgent dread, seeing the first beams of searing heat and glowing red shooting out of the windows and broken roof of the keep, which was fast disintegrating.

Borghart threw himself at the archway, inhaling glyma like air, Vazi beside him as the keep was engulfed from within by a vast eruption of livid, molten lava.

The next moments unfolded in a vivid burst of fore-images: of Genadius flashing past them as the searing heat and fire washed over them, turning him and Vazi to ash in a heartbeat . . .

So that she failed to save the empire . . .

His reaction was pure instinct. He gave up on his own survival, instead veering away to dive at Genadius, bringing him crashing to earth. Vazi flashed by them, reaching the archway and turning . . .

Her eyes locked with his . . . and she *knew* what he'd just done. That was his reward.

Then she was wrenching the door shut, as Genadius twisted in Borghart's grip, drove a blade through his chest and tried to scrabble free . . .

He felt his body go limp, like a puppet with no strings, but it was momentary, for the searing heat caught them—

He saw Genadius burst into flame, screeching, but he felt little pain himself, his dying body already numbed.

She made it, he thought, a moment before the world winked out.

Vazi backed from the archway as premonitions of fire engulfed it, hurling herself backwards and slamming into the gravel slope, rolling uncontrollably beneath a boiling blaze of swirling flame, even as the archway disintegrated and collapsed. Though red-hot lumps of stone rained down around her, she'd dropped beneath the erupting heat and flames. Her senses were still adjusting to being back in the real world, but survival instinct took over. Shielding herself, she rose and started stumbling away. The ground was shaking, the stones shifting and the air was wreathed with toxic gases.

She stopped.

Borghart had sacrificed himself to kill Genadius for her and allow her to escape. She had no idea why, but he'd given his life for her. But she didn't want that life. With Alephi ichor inside her, she was no longer herself, and she could feel others closing in, preparing to take and enslave her as Genadius intended.

That's not a life at all . . .

Damn them all, she thought, and then with resigned, grim purpose, she began trudging back up towards the crater, the one place where she could be sure the ichor in her blood couldn't keep her alive.

Death will be instant there, she thought. *And infinitely better than life.*

29

The Arena of Light and Dark

The Last Blood Trial

Before they were banned by Jovan Lux, Blood Trials were common. The last one occurred just before the law changed, a dispute between a nobleman and a neighbouring freeholder over boundaries. The nobleman hired a professional duellist, but the freeholder had only his teenage son. The bout lasted six seconds, the noble's case was 'proven' and the bereaved father hanged himself. Such was justice in that era.

CHRONICLES OF THE NORTH, 1452

Hyastar, Miravia
Autumn 1472

After the rush to get him away before the marshals collecting Romara saw him, Gram made his way to the exit, expecting to find Toad gone. To his surprise the man was still there, and he greeted Gram's advent with relief. 'Come,' he said, 'we've got people to see.'

The carriage left the bastion and drove southeast into the countryside. Hyastar was surrounded on three sides by flat and fertile farmland, but on this side were densely wooded hills that crept to within half a kylo of the walls. The road ended in a T-junction that ran east to the Osprey River and the Miravia-Talmoni border, or southwest towards Folkstein.

When the driver brought the carriage to a halt, Toad ordered everyone out.

The other four vorloks looked at him curiously, but did as they were bid. Gram felt a palpable sense of menace in the air, augmented by the silence – no birds sang, the woods were still and the countryside felt empty.

'What's going on?' he asked.

'You'll see.'

They looked around uncertainly. It was late afternoon and the shadows were long. The Qor-Massif, the greatest mountain range in Hytal, rose in the southeast, late sun glinting on the ever-white peaks, and the air was fast growing cold.

Then a horn sounded, low and dreary, the sound muffled and deadened by the trees, and figures began to appear from the trees and along both roads.

'Who are they?' Gram asked.

'Quyan refused to aid you, but the vyr don't just have a queen,' Toad replied. 'There is also a king, and Sadithil wishes to help you. He sent these vorloks to your aid, to ensure that the Oculus Tempus spell was cast. Now he sends draegar, vorloks and their covens.'

'To do what?' Gram asked, alarmed. 'Storm Hyastar?'

Toad snorted. 'An army of ten thousand could not do that. These are the imperial heartlands; the vyr presence is small and discreet. But King Sadithil has been calling in favours ever since this Blood Trial was announced. He's managed to muster enough men and women – a few dozen vorloks and draegar and their coven members – to fill the east stand. If your woman can stay alive long enough, we can storm the field and bring her out.'

Gram gaped, then raised eyes to the sky in thanks. 'Then King Sadithil has my deepest gratitude, and I am in his debt – and yours, my friend.' He went to offered Toad his hand, only then asking, 'What's his price?'

Toad chuckled darkly. 'We'll discuss that if and when we free your woman.'

More and more people were arriving, ordinary-looking men and women, rough-dressed country-folk with a touch of wildness about them to those who could see: coven members, the followers of vorloks. As they passed, they bowed heads, in deference to Toad, he realised.

'So where's the King?' he asked, although by then he'd guessed.

'You're looking at him,' Toad replied, a little apologetically.

They camped in the trees that night, emerging from the woods before dawn to be ready to enter the east stand as soon as the officials opened the gates. Gram stayed close to Toad – or King Sadithil, as he must now call him – as they found their seats. Everyone had been told to keep their vyr-nature secret, which was simple enough at first. They purchased food from stalls and sang old songs of the countryside, traditional ballads and lays. As the hours passed, they watched the other stands slowly filling. City folk shouted derisively at the yokels, who retorted in kind. But the hidden vorloks kept the peace, reining in their people.

With the appointed hour approaching, the tension rose palpably, especially when the entire upper hierarchy of the Vestal Order appeared in the opposite stand. They were all comfortably seated, some with their womenfolk and even children to see Romara put down, an education in how the world was. But there were guards aplenty to keep the riff-raff away.

'When do we move?' Gram asked.

'Not too soon, not too late,' Toad replied. 'There's another thing at stake here.'

Gram turned suspiciously. 'What?'

'By coming here, I've challenged Quyan. It'll either break me or break her. If we mess this up, I'm finished. But if we succeed, we'll likely be needing a new queen – not that I wish my former wife ill.'

'So when do we move?'

'At the last possible moment, and only if your Romara is failing.'

Gram thought about that. A sword fight could change in an eyeblink, and they'd have to see the end coming to act in time. And even if they reached her in time, the forest was half a kylo away, a long way to run with armoured knights chasing you on horseback. Toad was risking a lot of people for Romara. He was grateful, but it made him wonder just how indebted he now was to the vyr-king.

Then howls of derision from the city stands marked Romara's arrival in the arena, and all his thought turned to her.

Church bells tolled the time – fifteen minutes until noon – and outside the arena where the Blood Trial would be fought, those who'd been unable to gain entry were baying, pressing up against the cordon to try and shove their way in. But the stadium was already full. Word of a Blood Trial had got around swiftly and people had been pouring in from the countryside and the city alike.

When this had been a province of the Aquini Empire, this oval-shaped, high-walled arena had been a gladiatorial field, then used for chariot-racing, a place of spectacle and chaos. The Miravian kings used it for jousting, while the empire hosted tourneys for the Vestal knights; this was where Exemplars were crowned. Ten thousand spectators could be squeezed in, including the six hundred or so dignitaries of the Order seated in spacious comfort in the central section of the west stand. The north and south stands at the top and bottom of the oval were packed with city folk, while the country-dwellers had been shepherded into the giant east stand, where they were pressed in tight.

The cells beneath the stands were all but empty, but they hadn't changed much since the dark days of the slave-gladiators: they were dark, claustrophobic and reeking of damp, mould and piss. Two passages circled beneath the stands, with four corridors like spokes leading into the middle.

While he waited at the north entrance, Dranit Ritter watched the crowds and thought of the gladiators who'd once been shipped here from all over the empire by the Aquini slave-takers, to die as entertainment for the emperor's subjects.

We haven't come far, he thought bitterly. *In fact, we haven't changed an iota.*

Trumpets blared, boots tramped: Romara Challys was being led along the torch-lit passage, still wearing the Foylish torc that prevented her using her glyma. A knight walked with her, carrying the longsword she'd wield. Her colleague, Healer Burfitt, was trailing them, ready to step in and bind her hands to the weapon's hilt.

She must have been a fine commander, Dranit reflected, *to command such loyalty.*

As she passed she paused and said, 'Thank you, Dranit,' with grave finality. 'No one could have done more.'

'Elysia be with you,' he wished her. *May she be merciful, and make your death swift.*

As she stepped into the arena, Romara felt a sense of restoration. She knew this version of herself well: the woman she became in battle, when tactics and strategy had been exhausted and everything came down to kill or be killed. She always sought to avert that moment if she could, holding it off for her men's sake; but that was impossible here: rationality had to be set aside so fury and fire could be given leave to reign.

Soon, she told that simmering rage, *but not yet.*

She'd slept peacefully enough, soothed by Gram's visit, though troubled by what he'd said about ninneva and how it really worked. She still wasn't sure if she could reach the state he described, and that frightened her. She still meant to have her weapons strapped to her hands, because she couldn't envisage doing as Gram had done and healing herself. She was damaged goods. But she did intend to try, so at her request, her hands were still free.

But she'd been fed – decent food, for the first time – and outfitted in armour, the familiar weight of helm, of knee-length chainmail shirt, breastplate, pauldrons and greaves. She'd even found a side-weapon in the armoury that spoke to her: a short dagger-sized metal fork called a sword-catcher. She'd trained with one long ago and still recalled the movement required to trap the enemy blade between the tongs and twist, to lock up the foe's blade for a few crucial moments. Naturally, they wouldn't give her a flamberge, but they would let her fight without the magic-suppressing torc, and she didn't need elobyne to reach the glyma now.

What mattered most was control. *If I go berserk, I'll get cut to pieces – and I'll look like a monster.*

She had no idea who Enzo Karax was, other than the descendant of a famed Exemplar, but there was something in his demeanour as he appeared from the dark passage opposite that told her he felt absolutely no doubt or fear at facing a known draegar.

Single vorloks and draegars have been known to kill entire pentacles, she thought. *What makes him think he's so good?*

It could just be glyma-arrogance, for all Vestal knights tended to think themselves utterly invincible. This felt like something more. He was certainly handsome, like a bronze statue of some ancient hero come to life – but she'd been told he was retired, someone who ought to be worried about using the glyma.

So who the jagat is he?

Dranit didn't know, and nor did Augusta's people, who'd never heard of him.

Once Romara left the shadow of the tunnel mouth, the crowd saw her and rose, most shouting in derision, as she slipped into a state of hyper-awareness, seizing on every sound and sensation to take with her into the dark. She began to chaff for it to all begin – and end.

When the stony-faced magia escorting her finally removed the torc, glyma flooded in. She looked up at the banked rows of people, feeling their hatred and fear. Here, she was the personification not just of an enemy, but of Evil itself.

Corbus Ritter was sitting with his cronies, including the Moon-masked and Owl-masked Night Courtiers. Then her opponent, Enzo Karax, entered the arena, visor down and anonymous, and all her attention went to him. He seemed absolutely calm, looking around in a way that struck her as nostalgic, as if remembering this place in another time.

The next few minutes were filled with ritual: Dranit produced a summary of her accusations, the challenge from the Night Court on behalf of the Hierophant was read back, accusing her of base-less lies which threatened the Crown. Finally, her willingness to fight and die to defend her testimony was reiterated. If she lost, her words and the knowledge shown by the Oculus Tempus spell would be erased.

If she won, they would be attested as fact.

She barely heard, for she'd turned all her attention inwards, bending all her thought upon Gram, remembering his voice and face, the way he made her feel when he held her, his declarations of love which left her feeling both unworthy and elevated.

No burst of ninneva-inspired magic came – but she felt fear evaporating, giving way to a profound sense of freedom. She felt increasingly *whole*. No matter what befell her now, she had built within her an inner citadel. Even if Hromboli and Sister Faith crawled from the Maw itself to torture her again, she knew she wouldn't break.

Gram, I love you, she told the wind, knowing he'd hear.

I'm here, he sent back. *I love you too.*

She sensed his eyes on her and looked up, drawn instinctively to the east stand, which was packed with rough-clad country folk. She saw him instantly in the middle of the press, towering over those around him.

The love that filled her as she recognised him outweighed even the terror of him being seen and caught. *In the end we all die*, she thought. *What matters are the moments like this.* She tried to stretch those moments out towards forever.

'Seconds out!' the stentor blared.

Holding her mental of image of Gram before her inner eyes, she made her attempt. Taking the boiling glyma inside her, she imagined that instead of hatred, it was love. Instead of rage, it was passion. Instead of destruction, creation. Then she sought to use it, not to destroy but to repair . . .

Incredibly, it wasn't even hard: she had the key now, and turned it. Her fingers and toes broke and reformed in a blinding instant, making her convulse, while adrenalin flooded in, drowning out pain and fear. She raised her hand, now whole and strong, and flexed fingers she thought would never move again.

I did it, she thought, looking up at Gram, awestruck. *Just as you knew I would.*

Burfitt saw too, and blurted, '*Elysia be merciful!*'

She mouthed her thanks, then he was grabbed by the marshals and pulled back into the tunnel. The gates slammed shut.

Now there was just her and Karax out here.

She faced him, letting ninneva enfold her. It was akin, she thought, to swelling to giant size and gazing down on Creation. She was momentarily certain she could see mice on distant mountaintops, smell cooking-fires as far away as Petraxus and Solabas. She felt truly alive, for the first time since she was captured and tortured – perhaps for the first time in her life.

'Let Truth be revealed,' the stentor called sonorously, bringing her back to the here and now. The world, her whole existence, shrank to a circle of gravel and sand sixty paces across, and a man in old-fashioned black-lacquered armour.

The warning bell rang. Enzo Karax raised his visor to salute the archon's box, where the Night Courtiers lurked. His face was too per-fect, too youthful and elegant to even be human, Romara thought. Then he lowered the visor again, raised his flamberge and empow-ered it.

My love, a memory of Gram whispered in her ear, *be strong.*

Anger is not strength, Obanji added. *Strength is a strong stance and the knowledge that you serve truth.*

I love you, she whispered, addressing them both. *You too, Elindhu and Soren and Jadyn, and even you, Aura. And you, Dranit Ritter, for all your courage and kindness. I love you all.*

The bell tolled.

The fight began.

The first blows of the Blood Trial were routine, a feeling-out of defences. Enzo Karax attacked with cautious, easily read blows, but defended with alacrity. Romara attributed that to the surprise he must surely be feeling at her self-healing. Their blades hammered together in flurries, then they both backed off and circled. She con-centrated on his sword and his feet – and her new awareness of the fires of sorcery banked within him.

He's just playing.

That might explain the absolute certainty in his demeanour – and in truth, and for all the ninneva's work in restoring her, she couldn't get near him at first. He was smirking as he circled, his parries increasingly theatrical as he began to play to the crowd.

Romara's calm held, though the beast in her growled.

Instead, she channelled that anger into effort, upping her tempo, coming at him faster, hammering at him harder. *Crash, crash, crash* – the steel belled, she lunged at his throat, snarling, he read her intent perfectly and slashed open her right cheek – then spun easily away, while she staggered and backed up. He could possibly have taken her then, in the chest or the neck, ending this, but he was a cat, toying with a mouse.

Blood ran down her neck and her pores flooded with sweat. The urge to roar and charge filled her as Enzo made a contemptuous come-and-get-me gesture. The crowd roared its approval.

Calm, she told herself, darting in with new combinations to unlock his defences, using more of the savage strength of the vyr, unconcerned about the threat to her inner stability, confident in her newfound serenity.

But Enzo kept sliding aside, riposting with debilitating cuts and stabbing counterblows to her flanks and thighs. In a few minutes she was riddled with shallow wounds, bleeding slowly. He was whittling her down, all the while putting on a show.

This jagatai is good enough to be Exemplar like his damned ancestor, she realised. *He could have killed me thrice over already.* He was reading her every move, even when she went in hard and fast, as if he could see each blow coming. *I need to be stronger and faster.*

But that would mean sacrificing her humanity, becoming the beast the crowd so badly wanted to see slain.

Jag it, she thought. *They all know what I am.*

She backed up, giving herself enough distance to ensure he didn't take her unawares, then let the change hit her, hard and fast. The force flowed into her, a surge of energy that became strength, muscle and a glacial fury that filled her veins with rivers of ice. The mail encasing her burst at the side seams as she roared, then her single horn punched through her helm.

She heard screams of alarm, and a strange roaring sound from the east stand. When she stole a glance that way, she could see that half the people there had also changed, and wolf howls were ringing above the growling of beasts. Trumpets rang out and soldiers began pouring into the lower reaches of the west stand to protect the Order's leaders.

But Enzo Karax lifted his visor and grinning like a fiend, shouted, 'Let the real duel begin!'

Dranit Ritter was at the front of the south stand with Lubano, so he had a perfect view of the moment when Romara Challys lost her grip on sanity – or perhaps she'd just decided that appearances didn't matter any more. She stepped away and Enzo Karax – a swaggering prince of a fighter – let her go, clearly unconcerned. *Everyone* saw her change, the way she bulked up, splitting her mail – and most chillingly, the way her beautiful face mottled, the skin going transparent. He groaned, sure she'd ruined everything she was fighting for.

Then he became aware of a larger situation: the *entire east stand* was changing, as if she'd unleashed a virus they'd all caught. 'Holy Akka, that whole stand's a bloody vyr coven!' he gasped in Lubano's ear. This place was about to become a bloodbath.

Evidently that's what most of those around him thought, because many people were dashing for the exits, while soldiers poured in – although mostly to protect the dignitaries in the west stand, it turned out. Dranit clung to his perch, whether from stupidity or bloody-mindedness, waiting to see the vyr pour into the arena and hurl themselves at the west stand.

They didn't, though; instead they chanted, 'ROMARA! *ROMARA!*'

She howled back, a shrill keening that could have broken glass – then she charged at Karax, whom she now over-towered by at least two feet.

*

There was none of the madness she'd felt when this transformation had gripped her before; no blind rage, no desire to rampage and destroy, just the same calm Romara had taken from the ninneva, underpinned with love.

The transformation was just a tool, a way to take on a foe who was otherwise beyond her. Winning was now very much her intent – for herself, for her love, and for the people in the east stand currently screaming out her name.

She went at him in a bound, sword scything blindingly, forcing him to flash aside – and *damn*, he was fast, faster than before. But she stayed with him, making him give ground, riding out the sight-defying ripostes that carved furrows in her torso, down her thigh and one arm, taking hits that would have otherwise crippled her, howling in frustration because she still couldn't land a blow, because now it would only take one.

'Stand and fight, you jagging coward,' she snarled, shouting to make sure everyone heard, in case he couldn't take a little name-calling before a crowd.

It worked; he slowed his retreat, trading blows instead of running. Her longsword crashed into his flamberge, over and again, belling against glyma-reinforced steel and sustained by the same power, neither bowing nor breaking as she drove at him, steadily driving him back . . .

She had a plan, at last.

She'd been herding him, faster and faster, with wide, sweeping blows. Although some hung on in fascination, the common folks in the end stands had mostly fled, while the vyr in the east stand continued to snarl for her, and the Order commanders opposite shouted for Karax. She guessed that the moment this ended, there would be a pitched battle, one this storied arena could never have dreamt of.

Finally, she had Karax where she wanted him, in the north end, where the oval was narrower, his options for flight were fewer – then she unleashed a controlled burst of savagery, hacking and slashing through combinations in speeds at the edge of sight. But still he read them, waiting for her to over-reach . . . which she did.

Karax leaped aside, then used a glyma-leap to escape the north end, turned and tried to trap her instead – but she whirled and followed suit, jumping more than twenty paces to reach him, and slashed – while opening herself up to a riposte, her belly wide open.

Deliberately so.

He took the bait, ducking under her wild blow and lunging in with sight-defying speed – but her attack was a feint, and he hadn't read it. Her sword-catcher momentarily snared his flamberge and she counter-swung at his head, thinking she had him.

But he *moved*, catapulting away *without touching the ground*, his blade scouring her belly, making her yelp, terrified that her stomach had been opened up. Somehow, her newly thick hide turned the blow. He landed thirty paces down the arena, with something flashing behind his back, almost like wings of light that instantly vanished.

The way he'd moved wasn't just impressive; it was *impossible*.

'Holy Akka,' she heard someone exclaim. 'Did you see that?'

She saw a flash of gold in the man's eyes and realised, *The bastard isn't even human.*

They shared a moment of recognition of that fact – and that this fight had completely changed. He *needed* to kill her *now*, before more was revealed.

And I need to rip his mask off and show them all what he really is . . .

She roared, a full-throated beast's roar, and went for him with every shred of speed and strength she could muster, while he became a sight-defying flicker of movement that ignored time itself, and a heartbeat later, Enzo's flamberge plunged through her belly and out her back . . .

Enzo Karax could see her blow coming, Romara knew. He was already moving aside and launching his own killing blow . . . But he'd erred.

He'd thought the fight would be over when he rammed that long wavy blade into her, and though he had his eye on both her blade and sword-catcher, he'd forgotten in the rush to kill her that she was a weapon in herself. She gripped his sword-arm, holding him in place while his flamberge skewered her, the glyma-energy cauterising and burning – but she was close enough now to ram her horn into his chest . . .

As it plunged in, he screamed, shrill enough to burst eardrums – but it wasn't blood spurting from him but a pale, luminous fluid that curdled in the sunlight as her bulk and momentum carried him along. Then she slammed him bodily into the south wall.

As they struck, her horn punched through armour and ribcage, then she wrenched sideways, opening him up as if steel and sinew were cloth and butter. Karax convulsed, dropped his blade and grabbed her head with a strength that belied his human form, trying to pull himself from her horn, while her arms locked round him and she forced it in deeper and *tore*, ripping his ribcage open. His gleaming wings reappeared, flashing faster than sight as he lifted himself and her into the air, and the whole arena, human and vyr, recoiled in shock, gaping up at them.

As he tried to gouge Romara's eyes and blind her, she withdrew her horn – then she drove it in again, this time into his preternaturally beautiful face. He saw it coming, but somehow in her blurring vision she saw *exactly* where to strike.

The bloody horn plunged into his eye socket and out of the back of his head.

They fell together from a height of ten paces, crashing down into the middle of the arena. She hurled him from her, pulled the flamberge from her belly, though it felt like she was ripping out half her entrails with it, and staggering, brought it to guard. She still clung to ninneva, though she was at the edge of endurance now. Healing herself was beyond her, but all she had left was to make sure he was dead.

The false knight's body had hit the ground, rolled and sprawled. He wasn't moving at all.

For a moment, there was complete silence.

The two Night Courtiers behind Corbus Ritter rose, howling in anguish – then they erupted into the air, landing in the arena facing her. The Owl-woman conjured fire in her hands, while the Moon-masked man drew a blade from beneath his robes to finish Romara off.

But she was no longer alone, for spectators were pouring over the walls of the east stand. In seconds, people with horns and claws, with the visages or appendages of beasts, were closing around her, snarling at the masked Night Courtiers, who drew together fearfully, brandishing fire and sword to deter the attack.

The two Night Courtiers shrieked – and shot straight up into the sky. In seconds they were nothing more than dots streaking away. The clamour that ensued was deafening, but for Romara, sound and sight and even pain were receding fast.

I did what I could, she thought numbly. *I did all I could . . .*

She saw Gram striding towards her, but her legs were going and before he could reach her, she folded into the onrushing darkness.

30

Lost in the Light

Of Light and Darkness

We will always associate Light with life and goodness and Darkness with death and evil: such is the way of a day-dwelling species. But light is not 'good' and darkness is only light's absence. Good and evil are concepts that vary from soul to soul. One person's saviour can be another's enslaver: these are the complexities of human interactions. Simplifying deeds to merely good or evil is to rob them of the crucial nuances that permit true understanding. Ignore the temptation to simplify and you'll see things as they really are.

NILIS EVANDRIEL, RENEGADE SCHOLAR, 1470

Miravia
Autumn 1472

Soren woke naked, sprawled in a field of lush grass and bobbing wildflowers, the same hillside they had camped on. How he got there, he had no idea. His last memory was of Elindhu in her glorious erling form, naked and holding him as they fell towards a lake of white light that blasted through him and swept all awareness away.

Where's Fynarhea? I went looking for her . . . didn't I?

Whatever had happened, he felt good: the sunlight was warm, the air clear and clean in his lungs, the flowers' fragrance sweet and intoxicating. And despite all he'd gone through, he felt incredibly whole and hale – not in an over-stimulated, excited way, but natural and wholesome, like the first bite of a ripe apple, or the flush of success, or the radiance of a loved one's approval. He felt like he could run forever, leap houses and swim oceans.

His phallus was also absolutely rigid, which was a little disconcerting.

Then he heard a gentle sigh and caught the outline of a golden body through the long grass. He crawled towards it, emerging into a space of flattened grass to find Elindhu, still in her erling form, with her oddly proportioned but alluring face, gazing up at him with a dazed, disorientated expression. Her big amber eyes were glazed, then her eyelashes fluttered as she blinked away sleep and her mouth fell open as she took in his face. Her filigree hair writhed beneath her, spreading out like a peacock's tail.

'Soren, you're alive,' she exclaimed. 'Wonder of wonders.'

He just stared, drinking in her wise-woman allure and her bronzed body, her big black nipples and that silvery hair framing her angular, bird-like face as the aroma of feminine musk and desire enveloped him. He couldn't look away, his gaze trailing down her breasts and belly to her cleft that was weeping fluids. He was so hard it hurt.

'I thought we were dead,' she breathed, reaching up for what might have been intended as a familial hug, but as their faces pressed together he fell atop her and their mouths locked in a burst of salty sweetness, her thighs opened and she thrust herself up to meet him, swallowing his member entirely in a burning wetness that over-whelmed him. He came instantly, as did she, hips bucking as they pulled apart and stared in horror . . .

We just killed each other, he thought wildly.

But there was no bolt of agony, no surge of uncontrolled energy, just a moment of bliss – and such was the urgency in his body that his phallus stayed thick and hard. Elindhu pulled his mouth to hers again, and he resumed thrusting and couldn't stop, until he sensed another eruption coming and pushed as deep as he could and spent himself, all fear forgotten, clinging on to a glorious fulfilment that never ended.

Gradually, they came down to earth. The sun was higher and flies were buzzing about them, lapping at the salty sweat on their bodies.

Their ardour was receding, but not that sense of well-being. Elindhu found herself lying on her side, gazing into Soren's eyes, thinking, *By the Holy Twelve, where did that come from?*

In the rapture of her first climax she was certain she heard Obanji whisper in her ear, '*Bravo, girl,*' and whether that was real or just her subconscious exonerating herself didn't matter. She felt no guilt, just gratitude. She'd stepped outside reality into a dream where a woman of her age could be the lover of a young demigod who used her with such gentle vigour. A miracle, whatever happened next.

But what happens next is what we have to deal with now, she sighed inwardly.

Whatever had prompted that furious coupling, be it blueback reaper venom or some property of the lake of light beneath the Talam-Argith, or just thirty years of pent-up needs, she'd been swept along, but the sense of unreal perfection she'd felt was receding – not because it felt *wrong*, but how could it be *right*?

'Soren,' she murmured, stroking his cheek to soften the coming blow, 'are you well?'

Soren's gorgeous face lit up. 'Never better. It's like a fantasy come true . . . um, not that I was fantasising about you . . . or, er, maybe a little.' He nuzzled her face. 'Well, maybe a lot.'

'Stop it,' she mumbled, not because she wanted him to, but because her brain was now working again. 'Give me a . . .' Her eyes went to his loins and she groaned. He was ready again, and so was she. 'A minute.'

'A minute? One second, two seconds . . .'

'Idiot! Shush, I need to think.' Then she sat up and examined herself. Her wounds were gone; even the dark patch under the skin around the spider-bite had faded. She looked about, but her oak and elobyne staff hadn't reappeared – then she remembered it burning up, along with her clothes and a crowd of giant spiders. *And I saw Aryella Starbright*, she thought, amazed. *She took us into her, and immersed us in power.*

Then a really obvious thought struck her. Raising a hand, she breathed, '*Flamma.*'

Fire came, not with the usual rush of vindictive glyma force, but with a quiet exhalation: a flame an inch high that danced on her finger-tips, warming her but not burning the skin as it usually did. This was gentler, more controlled. Not as potent, but easier, with more clarity.

'We can still use magic,' she breathed in awe, 'but the energy is different.'

With a concentrated frown, Soren duplicated her spell. 'Akka on high. Me too.'

'We've just found a way to use sorcery without the glyma rage,' she exclaimed. 'This isn't glyma, nor what the vyr take from nature, and it's not aegis. It's new. . . or maybe *very old* . . . And love-making wasn't harmful – think of the consequences for the Order.'

We might be able to be properly human, finally.

Soren chuckled. 'So all we have to do is persuade everyone with the Gift to follow ghost voices into the Shadowlands, dive into a bottomless pit full of giant spiders, fall into the void and hope. I'm sure everyone will be rushing to do that.'

'Put like that, maybe not,' Elindhu chuckled. 'But it's still world-changing.'

For us, anyway.

Soren grinned, and reached for her. 'Your minute's up.'

'No, wait! she said, firmly enough to halt his advances. Tempting though it was to linger in this dream, it also felt dangerous. 'Good-ness' sake, boy, I already feel like you took a mallet to my nethers! I'll be aching for days.'

I actually forgot that this could kill us when we embraced – we were lucky. And there are other perils here. He's just a boy . . .

'Soren, this has been wonderful,' she said, in a voice designed to let him down easily. 'But I'm nearly fifty and an erling, and you're – what, seventeen? I like you . . . By the Twelve, I *adore* you, right now. But I'm not Fynarhea.'

'I don't want you to be,' he said, gently enough to disarm his words. 'And I'm not Obanji.'

'Fair point,' she conceded. 'But I'm still thirty years your senior, and mostly I'm *this*.'

With that, she melted from her erling shape back to her pseudo-human one, the Elindhu she had always felt more comfortable being, shrinking a foot, widening at the hip and waist, her breasts swelling, the nipples shrinking and going pink. Her skin paled and her hair knotted itself into its usual tower of grey braids. Once more she was the plump little moorhen she thought of as her true self: a guise designed to fend off unwanted attention, especially from randy men.

'This is the me I like to be,' she told him. '"Aunty Moorhen". Not so sexy, eh?'

'Aunty Eli,' the boy said, with a man's resolve, 'are you saying a different woman inhabits this body?'

He wasn't responding as she'd wanted . . . or feared . . . or maybe hoped . . . which woke certain fears she hadn't known she had: the scariness of being the centre of someone's attention, when she'd spent a lifetime trying to avoid just that. 'Uh . . . I'm saying I'm a different woman when I'm like this, and . . . uh . . .'

'I *know* who you are,' he interrupted. 'You have two natures and I admire both, regardless of age or appearance. Don't erlings live longer than humans anyway? So what does age matter? You're still you.'

'It's not so simple as that, Soren. I built this human body to hide and repel, and I don't feel sexual in it. It's for me to deal with the human world and it's mine alone. When I am "Aunty Moorhen" I don't want randy young men around me.' But as his face fell, she added, 'But when I'm in my erling body, I really am someone else. That woman never got the chance to grow up and have adult relationships, so in many ways she's as young as you, trapped in an older body.' With that, she flowed back into that body, lithe and alien to him, but she knew it had allure, and it felt so good just to be her real self. 'I'm both of them: I'm a lot to take on,' she told him. 'Thirty years older, and not just a different race, but a different species. You barely know me, Soren var'Dael.'

She watched him take that in, but he returned her gaze steadily. 'I know that . . . but I've been wanting you for weeks, I swear. I've lost everything but you.' He leaned in, nuzzling her face, and murmured, 'I need you, Aunty.'

'I'm not your jagging aunt, and being last one standing isn't any kind of excuse to throw away reason,' she retorted. But her own longings took over. 'I got a taste of love and lust as a young erling, and I chose to be a woman because I love to be with men. I never got to fulfil those desires.' She groaned, because he was so gloriously masculine and so very close and she was so tired of being sensible. 'Oh, go on then,' she sighed. 'Do what you will . . .' Then she had a wicked thought and said, 'No, *I'll* do as I will.'

It'll end in tears, she thought, as she rolled atop him. *But it's what we need.*

Hyastar, Miravia

The first moments were pure confusion, everyone gazing in stunned surprise at the sky, where the masked man and woman had vanished. But Enzo Karax still lay there, sprawled in the arena with pasty, glowing 'blood' welling from his death wounds. A being who'd flown, shown impossible strength and resilience, and whose body was now lying in a growing pool of luminous fluids that were decaying fast, turning putrid outside the body.

The arena stank of sulphur and burnt elobyne dust.

Gram was among the first to reach Romara. He was dimly conscious of the Night Courtiers fleeing straight into the sky as the wave of vyr men and women hurtled in to protect their champion, but his main focus was shielding Romara from the chaos, feeding her the energy of life as he fought to keep her here with him.

Trumpets were blaring, Order men were pouring in, officers shouting commands for the men to form a cordon facing the east stand. But vorloks and draegars were now openly showing themselves, towers of hide and horn, their coven-members likewise displaying their bestial sides, yammering and howling at the hated white tabards. This was about to get horribly bloody.

Gram cradled Romara, keeping everyone else from her while he fought to keep her alive, while his people surged past, hissing at the thin line of soldiers, eager to tear into them – but knights of the Order were converging from the stands too, men in service and some veterans still entrusted with elobyne.

'*Archon*,' Gram heard King Sadithil roar. 'Archon, a parley—'

Gram looked up at the throne, where Corbus Ritter was surrounded by a group of his diehard supporters. As he gathered his robes and rose, Dranit Ritter leapt atop a buttress on the arena wall and shouted, 'The archon has breached the Order's statutes. That was no veteran knight that *he chose* to champion the Order – that *thing* calling itself "Enzo Karax" was *not human*.'

Corbus' face turned ashen.

'Look at it,' Dranit shouted, pointing at the body of Karax, now decaying with weird speed, the flesh already desiccating, the pale 'blood' smouldering in the sunlight. 'Tell us who and what it really is!'

'And what of the Night Courtiers?' Augusta Martia broke in. 'We all saw masks and black robes – right before they *flew away*. No knight or mage can do such a thing! Who were they? *What* were they?'

Everyone looked at Corbus – who lost his nerve and scurried for the nearest stairs. A few of his closest allies went with him, but many more peeled off, lingering uncertainly. The whole arena was utter confusion, the Vestal fighting men and women hesitantly confronting a vyr horde, but unwilling to precipitate battle when they were in the frontline, and in the minority, for a commander who'd fled.

The vyr king stepped forward and called to Augusta Martia, 'Milady Augusta, we are age-old enemies, but I believe we have a mutual foe we should fear very much more.' He jabbed his finger skywards. 'What say you to a parley, Milady?'

Gram held his breath, because they were many kylos from safety. If Augusta – or anyone else with authority – ordered an attack, he doubted he could get Romara safely out.

Thankfully, Augusta Martia showed leadership when no one else was and put aside centuries of enmity. 'A parley,' she agreed. 'Let us talk, before further blood is shed.'

Gram exhaled a breath he didn't know he was holding . . . just as Romara opened her eyes.

Sea of Pelas
Autumn 1472

After escaping the Wardens' keep, Master Danikos led the survivors to another portali gate, just a brief tunnel to a large sea cave in the cliffs on the north shore, where the Wardens had kept their ships, safely moored out of harm's way. After retrieving Evandriel's felucca, Danikos took their little fleet westward on the prevailing southwesterly, with every sail billowing to get them as far from the erupting island as fast as possible, and before any further enemies came, and to get out of range of the rocks and boulders that the volcano was hurling skywards. Although all the ships were overloaded with trainees and baggage, they were ploughing through the waves at exhilarating speeds, and Huntaru was receding fast.

It's amazing to be among other aegis-users, Jadyn thought, *but we're overloaded*. He prayed the felucca could manage.

His knee was throbbing badly, so he'd once again taken the tiller, leaving Evandriel and Aura to work the ropes. But as the wind eased, the further they got from the eruption, the sea and air calmed.

Evandriel and Aura joined him, to survey the laden felucca and catch their breath. 'Well, my friends, we're entering the endgame now,' Evandriel mused. 'Our enemies have shown their true nature. Clearly these "Serrafim" stand behind the throne of the Hierophant – and whatever their plans are, they have begun to enact them. The fate of Coros is at stake.'

'This meant to cheer us up?' Aura asked.

'I was aiming for portentous but uplifting,' Evandriel said wryly, just as the wind parted the black smoky clouds and the sun streamed through, illuminating the water around them as brightly as if they were sailing on a sea of light.

'There, nature did the uplifting bit for you,' Jadyn noted.

'Dark clouds pass, but light is eternal,' Evandriel quoted. Then he frowned. 'What's that?'

A rainbow had appeared, apparently naturally, but Danikos was adjusting his course to sail towards it. Jadyn shifted the tiller to follow, watching the arch of fractured light shrinking as they drew closer. The air beneath it was unnaturally dark.

'It must be a kind of portali gate,' Evandriel marvelled. 'A gate at sea he's summoned, or perhaps made visible . . .'

One by one, each of the three vessels sailed beneath the rainbow, which was only just high enough to clear their mastheads – and emerged in a misty landscape under a night sky. As the rainbow faded behind them, darkness closed in.

Jadyn peered down and saw no water at all, just a thick mist boiling and churning beneath their hull. Cold winds propelled them under familiar stars: they were in the Talam-Argith.

We're sailing the Shadowlands, he thought in amazement. He'd never heard of such a thing. Even the Order, self-proclaimed masters of this realm, didn't do this.

'Where are we going?' he wondered.

Aura squeezed his hand. 'Not caring, so long as we be together.' She gazed backwards and added, 'Am thinking, did Exemplar and lictor survive?' She frowned, then added, 'No . . . No, not thinking they live.' She sighed in relief. 'Thank Akka, I think we be free of them, at last.'

Vazi Virago stood at the edge of the crater lake, staring down at the molten lava. The heat was baking her skin, drying the sweat as it formed, sapping the moisture from her eyes, the spit from her mouth, the very marrow from her bones.

Her golden destiny had vanished: her premonitions no longer showed her ascendant in glory. Instead, all her potential choices led to torture and death. The Serrafim were coming for her – she could hear their voices, snarling hatred for what she'd done to their beloved Genadius.

Sorry, Borghart . . . you should have let me die, and saved yourself.

She'd always despised suicides, but she was already dead: her flesh was turning to stone, and if she had a mirror she'd see gold in her irises. If she opened a vein, her blood would be pale and sluggish. *If I killed myself in any other way, would I even die?* she wondered. A blade, even to the brain if she could bring herself to do it, felt untrustworthy, but this crater offered instant, unforgiving oblivion: surety.

Better that than to be taken alive by the killer angels.

So she spread her arms, cast aside her dreams and flew . . .

. . . until an angel caught her and bore her into the sky.

Book Three of the Talmont Trilogy,

THE FALLING SKY

will be published in 2026

ACKNOWLEDGEMENTS

Book Two in a trilogy generally gets a bad rap: middle book, starts in motion and ends with not a lot resolved, right? But I enjoy them, because it's often the section of the overall narrative arc where we get to spend the most time with the characters and explore this new imaginary world. Often, intriguing things can happen, planned and unplanned. So I hope you've enjoyed this one, and thank you very much for reading.

Once more, I'd like to thank Quercus UK, especially Jo Fletcher and Anne Perry (still not that one) for commissioning it. Also my agent Jon Wood, for his continued guidance and support. Thanks again to Rory Kee and Patrick Carpenter for another great cover, and Nicola Howell Hawley for her map.

Thanks also once more to my trusty test-reader team of Jon, Heather Adams, Paul Linton and Kerry Greig – you each have your own perspectives and unique insights and feedback that make you truly a team. I'm very lucky to have your help and support.

Hello to Jason Isaacs, tinkety-tonk and down with the Nazis, authoritarian tyrants and religious fanatics of this damaged but still wonderful world.

Marching on together.

David Hair
Hastings, 2024